finding samson

By the same author.

The Bishop, the Mullah, and the Smartphone: The Journey of Two Religions into the Digital Age (2015)

fɪndɪnɢ samson

Iron Age Superhero

Bryan Winters

RESOURCE *Publications* • Eugene, Oregon

FINDING SAMSON
Iron Age Superhero

Resource Publications
An Imprint of Wipf and Stock Publishers
199 W. 8th Ave., Suite 3
Eugene, OR 97401

www.wipfandstock.com

PAPERBACK ISBN: 978-1-5326-7919-3
HARDCOVER ISBN: 978-1-5326-7920-9
EBOOK ISBN: 978-1-5326-7921-6

Manufactured in the U.S.A.   05/23/19

Psalm 83

With cunning (*guile, imagination, ploys, stratagem*)
they conspire (*plot, scheme, collude, intrigue*) against your people

contents

insight

Thirty two hundred years ago

One could almost say old Abdon started the rot himself. He was so prolific. If a survey had been taken, without doubt he would have had more sons than anyone in the nation. Forty. And thirty grandsons to boot. Well, you don't get numbers like that through a life of abstinence, which only exaggerated the gossip. What easier form of underground comedy to spread than that of the nocturnal pursuits of the Judge of Israel.

Most people smiled good naturedly about it. Some even argued virile rulers were good for the country. Proof of their energy. Trouble was this gave rise to a further set of jokes about the man's strategy for populating the thinly settled regions. They spoke of the thirteenth tribe, and how it would eventually unbalance the confederation. All in all, the situation generated so much humor that it settled everyone. Made them complacent.

Then Abdon gave each and every one of his male descendants a donkey. It was too much. Seventy one similar looking men riding solemnly around the nation.

At least it sped up the legal process. Only had to enter a town, divide up the grievances, and by lunchtime every verdict in the district had been handed down. Apparently in some of the smaller villages, this contingent would outnumber the inhabitants. And later that night, the obligatory evening repast must have set the poorer communities back a shekel or two.

Anyway, Abdon's evident appetite must have aroused many of the young. Inevitable. And so when talk of the ancient underground fertility rites arose, and stirred the loins of said youth, they began to think, why not? Look at Abdon. Not that it took off just like that. But it all got mixed up in

1

the general chatter and conversation of a nation at ease with itself, thinking about the greener grass over the fence.

More than fifty years of peace had passed. And now? A new generation never exposed to the sword, to war, or political repression. An intelligent, questioning population all too concerned with working on their nonexistent problems and broadening their minds. The comedy of Abdon just added spice to the talk of improving their lifestyles.

Foreign travel didn't help matters either. Overflowing coffers were spent on holidays at the coast. The shopping was 'just so exquisite' down there. Prices were cheaper than ever in Philistia with their falling exchange rate. Exotic fabrics were shipped directly into their ports, and at the street markets, you could browse for hours. Cool beers were served in the seaside taverns, along with delightful cuisine from the harborside restaurants.

And the night life. Oh, the night life. At first the visits were made surreptitiously. But once the nation was alive with Abdon jokes, stories of coastal evenings started to surface.

It was all so deliciously daring. Especially considering they had also endured fifty years of authority, of tough rulers and judges. Five decades of old priests and militia who could remember the conflicts from Jephthah's days. Well meaning men who drummed every detail they could remember into the brains of their offspring.

There wasn't a child among the tribes who didn't know the hero's names, and how they brought the nation to its current prosperity. But now, those who had lived through it were all sixty plus. Old men, lecturing to smiling teenagers. Wrinkled brows, knowing they weren't getting through, reading the body language of scorn.

The Mayor of Gaza

On the afternoon of the Mayor of Gaza's great breakthrough, he was trialing a prisoner experiment. The chariot pulled to a stop, and a guard was waiting.

"Ashmil, isn't it?"

"Yes, my lord, good afternoon."

The Mayor's hands were synchronized already with his speech, fingers spreading inquiringly.

"Has the training made sense, Ashmil?"

He was referring to the 'good soldier bad soldier' pilot for eliciting information from reluctant captives.

"Yes, my lord."

"Good. This will be an interesting real-life practice. Are you sure you know what to do?"

Not that it mattered since this incident was rather trivial. Or so the Mayor had been informed, although he didn't yet know the details.

"Yes, my Lord, very sure."

"Refresh me on what the fellow did."

"He is a captain my lord, and was on duty in the district when the skirmish took place." It had become commonplace to omit the words 'red light' lest they offend. "Apparently he struck an Israelite emerging from a bordello. The aggrieved lodged a complaint with the military unit at the entrance to the city center. The accused was taken in but has denied the assault."

"I see. Let's go then," the Mayor's hands widened slightly, and his brow rose, to indicate action.

They walked into the adjacent building and down the gloomy stairwell into a jail known as 'grinders haven'. The name described the inner moneymaking part of the enterprise, where prisoners endlessly pushed a great flat wheel around. Two floors above them, a grain milling venture prospered. The staircase ended, and to the right was a passage with a single torch on the wall. Three doors, all barred and locked. The stay of visitors down here was frequently short lived. As he strode along, the Mayor grimaced at the little pun. Short lived.

There was a pause, a rattle of keys and some scrabbling with the lock as the guard opened a door with his left hand. His right firmly grasped his stubby sword. Such blades were designed with narrow corridors in mind. Easy to swing and stab where a longer blade would find difficulty maneuvering in the confined space.

The prisoner sat on the floor at the rear of the cell, his arms bruised, and legs scarred.

"Your worship," he uttered, unsteadily rising to his feet.

"Quiet," barked the guard. "Who asked you to speak?"

Reasonable start, thought the Mayor.

"Ashmil, bring that torch over here, let me see how the captain is." The light illuminated the man's injuries. "Good grief, what have these people been doing to you?" Without waiting for an answer, he berated the guard. "Who permitted this? What do they think we are running here, some sort of interrogation center? Thank goodness I came."

Ashmil stood stolidly, shuffling his feet slightly.

"Fetch me some water and a fresh garment. I had an inkling mischief was afoot." He glared, before the guard retreated. Turning back, he addressed the prisoner. "And it's just as well I came down myself. Tell me how you are treated from now on. You must."

The captive peered up.

"Have you eaten today, captain? Have they brought you anything?" He inquired although he knew the answer. As the prisoner shook his head, he rolled his eyes, with a slight backward glance as if to check the guard had not yet returned. "Terrible. Have you any idea how hard it is dragging this city into the modern era?" He fished around in his bag and brought out a package containing bread and two figs. "I know it's not much, but I was halfway through lunch when I began to worry about this."

The inmate fell on the morsel. "Thank you, my lord."

The guard came back, bearing a bowl of water and a clean tunic.

"Leave us alone," the Mayor muttered in disgust.

"My lord, military procedure forbids us leaving civilians unattended with inmates."

The Mayor stood before the sentence was complete.

"Just get the hell out of here and give this poor man some peace!" he yelled, his face only inches from the guard.

For a full three seconds, Ashmil stood his ground, staring back, before replying. "As you will my lord, I shall be down the passage."

Snatching the torch from him, the Mayor set it in the sconce on the wall. Sitting on one of the low stools, he indicated the prisoner should occupy the second. After washing himself, the captain picked up the new tunic hesitantly.

"I am sorry," apologized the Mayor, standing and turning out the door while the soldier changed.

Returning, he reseated himself, as did the prisoner. Time to prod. He began judiciously. "He sounds a churlish fellow, this Israelite."

Again, the captive hesitated. But warmed by the empathy, he opened up a little. "Churlish," he repeated. "Two faced. Hypocritical."

"Oh?" murmured his new friend.

"All this religion of theirs, and their proclamations about pure living— rubbish. He was down in the district too."

"No," breathed the Mayor.

"He came out of the place almost on top of me. It was all so quick, him tumbling out the door, the bruises on the girl's face, him yelling at me. She didn't want to say anything, but eventually told me. Games with ropes." He paused. "My lord, I will admit to you, as a reasonable and understanding ruler, that I did hit him. But it was neither hard, nor injurious, and I felt he deserved it."

This is simple, mused the Mayor. Human nature is straightforward. "Tell me some more. Where is he from? Which tribe?"

"Benjamin."

"What's his line of work?"

"I believe he is a trader, your worship. In antiquities."

"Antiquities?"

"That's what the girl told me, my lord."

A trader in antiquities.

And then he saw it. It was amazing how fast.

Corrupting a nation. Corrupting an entire nation. It was perfect timing, the precise season. His mind soared as it harvested the field of opportunity.

"Yes, my lord, antiquities," repeated the prisoner, concerned about the lull in the conversation.

The Mayor awoke from his reverie. "Yes. Antiquities. In Benjamin."

He tried to think of something to say but his mind was still flying. He stood, bringing the listening guard to the door. "See the captain is fed more regularly," he murmured before walking out to his waiting chariot.

Ishiel

Ishiel was such a naive person that he made an excellent spy. He travelled about happily and enthusiastically, always asking questions. He was genuinely interested in others, and he had a wonderful gift. People confided in him. The Mayor categorized him as a confidee. He wasn't sure there was such a word, but it described Ishiel.

"How would you like a trip to Benjamin, Ishiel?" asked the Mayor.

"Benjamin, your worship?" His eyes seemed about to pop out, and he visibly trembled. "A lovely place I understand. Had an uncle who went there once. Apparently, the hills are quite pretty this time of year. Oh, Benjamin. Yes, yes, Benjamin!"

The Mayor laughed, liking Ishiel and his mannerisms all over again. "You really are a talent. We should have you speaking in one of those tavern contests."

"Oh no, your worship, don't frighten me like that. No Egyptian beer, please. No Egyptian beer." Leaning forward, eyes raised, his forehead wrinkling with intimate certainty, he nudged the Mayor knowingly. "They use water from the Nile."

Again, the Mayor guffawed. "I want you to find out how a certain man is getting on over there. A trader in antiquities."

Benhad

Benhad's family were not well known around Gaza, but the Mayor was acquainted with their services. Troublesome issues could be handled quickly and silently by Benhad and his tall sons. Their network of contacts was that referred to throughout time as the underworld. Despite their anonymity, the Mayor arranged a clandestine meeting. At a neutral house that could be relied upon to spread no gossip.

From an upper window Benhad watched him walk down the street. He didn't look up, but occasionally glanced behind, though not in an uncomfortable manner. His gait was different today. More purposeful, felt Benhad.

As the door opened, the Mayor flicked a requisite nod across at the man of shadows, and with a final peek out the upstairs window, he sat down.

"I need to remove someone."

Benhad did not bother with any camouflage questions like, 'am I the correct person to be talking to?' He knew the Mayor too well. "Who?"

"An Israelite, a leading Israelite."

"Which leading Israelite?"

"Abdon."

"Abdon. You must be joking."

The Mayor knew he would get this reaction. Benhad had never pulled off a job like this. To do away with the very leader of Israel. A treasonable and war threatening act. He remained silent, and let the man pour invective on the idea.

"You must either be mad, or tired of living. Philistia lives quietly next to Israel, relying on their trade for numerous articles and services, and you want their Judge killed."

More silence.

"In any case, I wouldn't do it. How would one get away? The man is surrounded by his huge family, and he never comes to Philistia. He travels around Israel with his donkey train. What do you think I am going to do, plunge a knife into his breast, walk calmly past the gauntlet of his sons, get on my ass, and return safely through fifty miles of Israelite territory?"

"How much will it cost?"

"Didn't you hear me man, it can't be done! Nobody, but nobody kills Israelite Judges!"

"Incorrect. Nobody has killed an Israelite Judge—yet. Do I need to tell you how to do it? I thought a man of your trade was a lateral thinker!" exploded the Mayor, although he was not angry.

Benhad sat back. *Good grief, he is for real.*

"Something else," the Mayor added. "No suspicion of foul play."

"Oh, this is too much. A cut throat is very hard to write off as an accident."

"You think too directly, my good man." The Mayor's tone sweetened. "Always using swords or knives or ropes. Have you ever thought of poison?

A secretive, quiet approach. Even better, makes the death look like natural causes."

"Come on, how do I get that into him? Walk into his tent and ask him to swallow something for me?"

"A cook does that for him every night."

Joram

"My, what a marvelous shop!" The stranger shrieked as he flew in the door. "I heard about you down south, and simply had to visit. Had to. The half was not told me!"

Good grief, what have we here, thought a startled Joram.

"Oh, I simply must have one of these." His visitor pounced on a pottery jug. "That will look absolutely splendid in my living room. Splendid!"

He bounced around the store, chattering excitedly. Abruptly he wheeled as if remembering his manners. "Oh, I am so sorry," he laughed hugely. "What a sight I must appear, and I haven't given you a chance to speak. I was just so happy to arrive. Now, tell me how you got started, you must!"

Joram began to smile, though unsure whether it was over his guest's antics, or his contagious enthusiasm.

"Alright," he began, "we deal in antiquities."

"There you go! You have not told the half!"

And this time Joram laughed. He led his eager guest around the shelves, describing where the various products came from, and their heritage. "And these ones," he declared, "we import from Gaza."

The stranger leapt on that. "Oooh, Gaza," he tittered, nudging his host and winking broadly. "Tell me about Gaza! Tell me about Gaza!"

"Really, what is there to tell?" queried the happier Joram.

"What is there to tell!" chortled the charming one. "What is there to tell!" Suddenly he put a finger to his lips, glancing quickly about, and hunching his shoulders in mock secrecy. "Oh, I've been much too loud, far too noisy," he barely whispered in between stifled gasps of mirth. "But I have heard, I have heard about, about . . .," he leaned up to Jorams ear, ". . . the pleasures of the night there. Oh, are they true, are they true?"

Again, Joram chuckled at his infectious manner, watching the man's eyes bulge with anticipation.

"Well," he ventured. "There are one or two places down there."

"One or two places, one or two . . . places!" the visitor broke out again at his own emphasis on the word, waggling his ample hips.

It was too much. Joram could no longer hold himself back. He glanced out at the empty street. The fellow seemed like someone you could confide in.

And an hour later, Ishiel was back on the road out of Benjamin.

Benhad

Setting up a new cook for Abdon was easier than Benhad thought. He imagined there would be all manner of security restrictions, but surprisingly there weren't. Besides his family, Abdon only had a few retainers, and staffing was a casual affair. Due to the sheer size of his household, the task of preparing sustenance for the Judge of Israel was not a straightforward task. A team of half a dozen was required. And, fortunately for Benhad in these prosperous times, there was a regular turnover of personnel.

The Mayor gave Benhad two months only. The first three weeks were taken up merely getting into Israel and close to Abdon's home town in a manner unlikely to raise suspicion. Imbibing in the taverns opened up local chatter. One week after settling in, they got a lucky break. One of his sons started work as a junior cook.

After getting his boy in, there were four weeks left. Within a further fortnight, the materials he had ordered arrived from Egypt. No discernable effects, read the guarantee. Just slip it in, and two hours later, the victim keels over. Evidently the deaths appeared like heart attacks. No odor would linger. Apparently, several Egyptian princes had been dispatched with it recently, but the stuff was still quite new, even to the markets Benhad was familiar with.

He hefted the bottle with its green viscous liquid carefully. "Make sure only Abdon gets it," he warned. "Don't want a whole bunch of them going down. That'll make them smell a rat."

The meal

The pseudo cook prepared a special dish to be served on individual plates. He got the idea of crafting each helping into an edifice resembling an Israelite flat cake. It provided the excuse for delivering each plate individually to each diner. The chief cook loved the idea.

That evening was pleasantly warm, and the son of Benhad swooped in and out, joking with everyone, both in the kitchen and out. He took particular care over his preparation of the flat cakes out the back. Seventy one dishes in rows on the rear table. Flamboyantly, he began pouring a green sauce on each dish. After ten plates were done, the others' attention went back to their own tasks. When he came to Abdon's, he glanced around. No one was watching. He pulled out a small leather pouch. Squirting some extra green thick fluid onto Abdon's dessert, he speedily secreted it again in his clothing.

When he had finished all seventy one, he walked past the roaring fire of the kitchen and surreptitiously tossed the pouch into the flames. Nobody noticed anything.

Helpers arrived on schedule to serve up the plates. Benhad's boy scurried in and out with many of the dishes, taking care no one took Abdon's. Soon he picked up four plates at once and carried them to the center of the gathering. Placing them in front of the judge and his three eldest sons, he stood back with a cheeky smirk. When he didn't move, they glanced up. He quipped it was difficult to get all seventy one correct first time round. Rapidly scooping up all four dishes he redistributed them in a different order. Again, a third time, with a faster movement, deceiving the eyes. And apologized with a grin. They laughed good naturedly. With that, he retired to the kitchen.

After supper, the old man complained of pains, and was put to bed. One hour later, someone checked on him, and discovered his worsening condition. Panic started to set in, and the eldest boys rushed off to find a physician.

Fortunately, a northerner happened to be staying in the nearby village. While fraternizing in the local tavern, patrons found out he dealt in emergency medical cases. He was summoned and brought into Abdon's tent. Casting a professional eye on proceedings, he acted decisively, immediately issuing orders. He had servants heating water, providing blankets, quietening the donkeys, and other occupations designed to give the old man the best environment possible.

But it was all to no good. Despite the best efforts of the energetic doctor, Abdon expired two hours later. The medic shook his head knowingly. Rendering condolences to the family, he mentioned the difficulties in resuscitating such victims, and what a delicate organ the heart was. He had seen this sort of thing before.

The community was in shock. The Judge of all Israel was dead. Impotently his family sat there. Either weeping or staring stonily into the distance. A few of them tried to question the physician. But they didn't know what to ask.

Of course, the doctor was above suspicion. But one of Abdon's younger boys did start to raise a few queries. About the evening repast.

'What on earth are you talking about! Are you accusing me?!" Benhad's son recoiled in disbelief.

"You brought him the meal and did the swap around act."

He stood straight up from his washing chores, throwing down his cloth and drawing his face close to his accuser. "I can't believe it! This is ridiculous!"

The Israelite backed away, disconcerted by his vehemence.

"Do you think I would be so stupid as to poison the Judge of all Israel? Do you think I would be that thick as to draw attention to myself by playing with the meals like I did?" He stood back, raising his voice so the others could hear. "I mean, give me a break! If I wanted to poison your father, don't you think I would have been a bit more secretive?!"

He turned on his heel and stamped out of the tent, turning to shout from the entrance. "You ought to be ashamed of yourself!" Marching back, he pointed his finger, nearly weeping with rage. "Go on then! Search my belongings! Have a look! I'll be out with the donkeys; I need some intelligent company!"

He spun around again and stormed out. The accusing son stood open mouthed before stammering, "I was just trying to help. You never know . . ."

Nothing was found.

An older brother fetched him back from the asses where he was stroking them softly. "He didn't mean to annoy you. This is upsetting for all of us. Come on back with me."

Two days later, still offended, the son of Benhad left the encampment. He could not stay under such a cloud. It would be better for all if he moved on. Twenty miles back toward the coast, at the prearranged spot, he met up with his older brother, who, having a different mother, bore no resemblance to him. Looked more like a northerner. "Great show," he said.

The Mayor

As the Mayor entered his factory, he could see several men bent over forming clay figurines. Beautiful statuettes. Female shapes of gorgeous proportions and enticing stances. The foreman broke into a grin. "Your worship, good to see you."

"How are the men, how is life," bustled the Mayor, hurrying in, smiling around at everyone in a jolly mood. "What I really mean is, how is production?"

The gathered group laughed because he always got promptly to the sales figures. The Asherah figurines seemed to be in ever increasing demand. Recently the Mayor had started a new line of miniatures which were gaining in popularity among the Israelite tourists as 'Mementos of Philistia.'

"How many are we knocking out each week?" the Mayor inquired.

"Mmm, if you count the Mementos, nearly thirty last week. But the week before we hit thirty three."

"Can you raise that to seventy five?"

Joram

In a short space of time, the news of Abdon's demise permeated all corners of Israel. A family funeral was held, with various dignitaries attending, both local and international. After the vigil, everyone returned to their everyday life.

Weeks trickled by. No replacement judge emerged. Everyday topics of conversation surfaced again.

About this time Joram received an invitation. It was hand delivered and beautifully bound in a leather scroll. The invitation mentioned Joram's trading enterprise in antiquities had been heard of, his reputation was growing, and certain people were eager to make his acquaintance, with the possibility of developing mutually agreeable business ties. It was from the Mayor of Gaza himself.

The prisoner

One week later as he entered Gaza, Joram felt good about life. That unfortunate incident with the girl was now distant. In fact, he regretted reporting the event, as his furtive adventures might have come back at him. But he hadn't heard more, and it was now months ago.

Next morning after a light breakfast he walked through the busy streets to his appointment. The Mayor rose. "Ah, my good man, a pleasure to meet you after all this time. I have heard so much about your endeavor in Benjamin." he began. "Come in, come in please, to my humble abode."

He gestured for refreshments to be brought as they sat around the Mayor's low table. Small talk ensued for a while. Suddenly, almost in mid-sentence, as though he had recalled something, the Mayor jumped up and said, "let's go for a ride around the city, and show you a few sights."

"Why not," replied the relaxed Joram. Once in the chariot, the Mayor instructed the driver where to turn while prattling on. They seemed to travel haphazardly around, looking at this and that before stopping at the Mayor's factory.

They climbed down and went in, with the Mayor his usual bright self, cracking jokes with his workers, and introducing them one by one to Joram. It was plain to see what the factory manufactured. The clay goddesses were everywhere, at all stages of production. Finished erotic ones stood near the door. Without appearing to, the Mayor was watching Joram's body language. It was what he expected. Slight discomfort, but definitely not outright rejection. After all, this Israelite was standing in a building manufacturing foreign gods.

They stayed no longer than ten minutes. Then back into the chariot and on around town again. After some time they stopped and had a pleasant lunch. The view from the restaurant was pleasant and the wine superb. After the slight embarrassment he had felt at the goddess factory, Joram had recovered. The man's divines were his own affair, he told himself. He attempted to move the discussion onto potential business opportunities.

But before he got a chance, the Mayor was up, and after paying the bill, they were back in the chariot. They drove straight across town, with the Mayor pointing out various buildings, before turning down a quiet narrow street. A street very familiar to Joram.

Still in a loquacious mood, the Mayor gesticulated around with his waving hands, telling him all about his marvelous city. Seemingly at random, he abruptly ordered the chariot to stop.

They were exactly opposite the house of ill repute so familiar to Joram. The Mayor did not halt for a second in his banter. He simply pointed out what tremendous old architecture it possessed and laughed briefly about the rumors surrounding the place. Abruptly, his eyes flicked at Joram, disconcerting him with their curious directness.

Joram felt queasy, but he managed a brief grin. There was a second's pause, but the chariot quickened its pace away again.

Through the dusty streets they continued to move. Without a command from the Mayor, the vehicle stopped, and they all got down. For the first time, Joram noticed the driver wore a sword. Into a large, apparently empty building they all went. After passing through a couple of heavy doors, they began descending the stairs.

"I must show you something," murmured the Mayor.

Two flights down, the stairway ended in a narrow passage. A single torchlight hung along the wall. What the devil, thought Joram. They paused.

"Joram, dear friend," the Mayor intervened gently. "Please stand back and let us open this cell. There is a slight risk of danger from the occupant. My driver will ensure all is safe."

In growing apprehension, Joram saw the driver draw his sword and proceed to open the locked door with his left hand before disappearing inside. Smiling at Joram, the Mayor gave a shrug of apology at the delay. After a few seconds the driver reappeared, beckoning them. In astonishment and mounting curiosity, Joram followed the Mayor in.

Seated on the floor was a wretched figure who appeared as if he hadn't bathed in weeks. There was something familiar about him, thought Joram. "What's going on here?" he managed to blurt out. "Why have you brought me down here?"

"Relax, Joram," the Mayor said firmly. "This is one of the few quiet places left in the city. We can talk man to man down here. About business."

Hearing Joram's voice, the man on the floor jumped up. Blinking away, he drew closer. Unaccustomed to the light, Joram thought briefly as he backed off.

"Your worship, this is the man!" exclaimed the unkempt creature.

Joram recovered and peered into his face. Recognition flashed. Oh, good grief, you fool, you great fool. Turning he found the driver blocking the door. He almost panicked until the commanding voice of the Mayor broke through. "Captain, sit down, this man is my guest." As if ordered to, the driver threw the unwashed one back into the corner. "Be silent, captain," cautioned the Mayor again, as the captive started to open his lips again.

Two warnings were enough. He subsided onto the floor. The Mayor turned to his guest.

He delivered his message slowly, as an instruction, pausing deliberately between each sentence. "Joram, I have a business proposition to put to you. A very lucrative one. Let me get straight to the point. I want you to become a distributor of Asherah goddesses in Israel for me."

"Asherah goddesses?"

"Yes, Asherah goddesses. As simple as that. Your wholesale price from me will be very reasonable, and we estimate you will be able to retail them at forty percent profit."

A silence descended for perhaps ten seconds. Taking Joram by the arm with his large, but surprisingly gentle hand, the Mayor steered him out of the cell. "Let us talk through some details," he told the shopkeeper quietly.

The strategy

So Joram added Asherah goddesses to his stocks in Benjamin. And the Mayor was correct. People thought Joram had made a daring move. He was displaying the true freedom of art by challenging the old mores. The Asherahs were examples of the finer parts of a neighboring culture. Those who purchased them were enlightened. In fact, owning one soon became evidence one was not constrained by old ideals, and this was indeed a new age of less restricted thought.

The Mayor stepped up the campaign and introduced a further five Asherah distributorships in Israel. At that point, the first of several enterprising

Israelites contacted the Mayor directly, requesting supply. Factory production soared.

Six months later, he moved again. Flush with cash, he funded construction of an Asherah grove. Its motto was, 'Where the bold venture.'

Predictably, lusty adventurous types were the first to go, and enjoyment they found. Several delicious Philistine girls were stationed there, and crowded evenings of delight followed as Israelite youth sated themselves with these creatures.

Within another four months, he had introduced fertility groves and cult prostitutes in three other tribes. When he heard some Israelites were building their own elsewhere, and charging more fees than he did, he laughed with delight.

Still no judge had yet arisen to rule Israel.

It was a very good start.

Learning history

Philistia lay between the two most powerful nations on earth. To the northeast, over that great arc known as the fertile crescent, stood Assyria. To Philistia's southwest lay Egypt. Originally settled by nomadic Amorite bands with their herds, the region was soon identified for its strategic importance by both of these superstates. They were awoken to this fact by the invasion of Egypt by the Hyksos.

Sweeping down from the north, the Hyksos moved right through the flat coastal plain that was to become known as Philistia, finally gaining mastery over Egypt itself. From then on everyone recognized the significance of this route, and how it avoided the difficulties of conquest by sea.

The Hyksos were neither of Egyptian nor Assyrian origin, but in their time were very successful. They brought fearsome new weapons and military know-how. They had perfected the horse drawn chariot and the composite bow, which gave them speed and firepower.

Furthermore, they were skilled in developing defensible cities with huge walls capable of resisting battering rams. And build them they did. All along the narrow coastal plain. Each of these settlements became somewhat self-ruling, like a series of city states. This method of government remained in place even after they were conquered and reconquered from either the north or south over the following centuries.

Prior to the time of the Mayor of Gaza, the Egyptian empire under the famous family of Ramses had dominated the region. Egyptian settlers moved in to mingle with the existing inhabitants and added some of their own culture to the already advanced literary skills there.

But the Ramses dynasty was itself under threat. Enemies known as the Sea Peoples from Caphtor, the ancient name encompassing Crete, Cyprus and the Asia Minor coast, launched massive marine assaults against Egypt. One of these was fought back at the very mouth of the Nile. Egypt was forced to concentrate on defense in order to survive, and her influence waned in Philistia. She was exhausted by these incessant struggles.

The same Sea Peoples added some of their number to the hybrid residents of the coastal plain, and as Egypt withdrew, the city states took affairs into their own hands. By then, their center consisted of five metropolitan areas, Gaza, Ashkelon, Ashdod, Ekron and Gath. Each was ruled independently, but where useful, each would cooperate with other members of the pentapolis.

Israel

At the same time the Sea Peoples were establishing themselves on the coast and forming Philistia, the nation of Israel arrived from the other side of the Jordan river. Under circumstances the whole world knew about.

Originally, they had been led out of Egypt by a magician called Moses. Employing various tricks, he persuaded the Egyptian Pharaoh he was no man to trifle with. He could turn the Nile river to blood, and raise plagues of frogs, or clouds of dust that blocked the sun. Pharaoh stood firm however until Moses' final horrific deed. He brought down the angel of death to slay the first born son of every Egyptian family. That was enough. The Israelites were freed from Egypt where they had been slaves for four hundred years.

Characteristically, Pharaoh changed his mind shortly after, and sent his army out to retrieve them. However, Moses, in his supreme drama, parted the waters of the Red Sea so his own people could escape. Thinking they could catch up, the pride of Egypt's armed forces followed. As the last Israelite exited the dry path, Moses commanded the waters to return over the chariots pursuing them.

After many trials and tribulations in the desert, they eventually arrived at the Jordan river, armed with several powerful assets. Firstly, they had a recent history of miracles which had given them both their freedom, and food and water in the desert. But most importantly, they had a deal with their God. He had supplied a powerful moral code, known as the ten commandments, and purportedly delivered it to Moses on tablets of stone in a fiery, desert, mountain top scene. And their God had given them a vision. A land of their own.

Moses' successor, Joshua, became one of the most successful military commanders ever. Anyone who had seen him start out would have realized this immediately. They didn't have any problems crossing the Jordan river. The waters parted once more to let them through.

Following this display, Israel brought the formidable city of Jericho down without a battle. After marching around the metropolis for seven days, their priests all blew trumpets together, and the high protective walls of Jericho simply fell over.

Joshua didn't stop there. He took on anyone who challenged him and thrashed most who did. At one stage, five Amorite kings banded together to try the overwhelming force theory. Joshua simply marched overnight and surprised them before they were ready. In disarray, the Amorite mob fell to pieces. Legend had it Israel's God assisted by arranging a serious hailstorm. It was said more perished from hailstones than by the sword.

But Philistia was not conquered. Neither Joshua, nor his followers, succeeded in dislodging the five cities. So, it was the two nations arrived together, one from the sea, and the other from the river. And for hundreds of years they skirmished and fought each other, alternately gaining and losing ground.

Enjoying all the technological advances each succeeding wave of invaders or settlers had brought with them, Philistia appeared to lack only size and cohesion. That was until the Mayor of Gaza established himself.

He concluded Philistia only lacked imagination and creativity.

The five mayors

Naturally, the other four mayors of Philistia heard about the successes of their colleague in Gaza. It was a common saying in the Pentapolis that there were only two degree of separation for news to travel. Eventually he was questioned point blank at their monthly gathering. In the middle of a tedious list of regional items, Edred, the Mayor of Ekron, pushed his papers to one side.

"Enough of this," he stated. "Somehow the Judge of Israel died mysteriously, and we hear your Asherah trade is doubling each month. We conclude you're making money hand over fist. We are curious. Somewhat curious."

Gaza's leader looked up slowly, knowing Edred would not have asked the others, yet that they too were of the same mind. His direct gaze took in each in turn, and they felt he was searching them, to see their readiness. A slight smile appeared as he breathed quietly, "I have absolutely no idea what you are talking about."

For a couple of seconds they were silent. The Mayor of Ashdod, normally a quiet individual, but an intuitive one, spoke up. "I think you could lie more convincingly; I know a camel salesman who could give you some tips."

They all joined heartily in the ensuing laughter.

"Alright, alright," the one from Gaza agreed as they quietened down. "Incidentally, we sent a full letter of condolence to Abdon's family, which I am sure you all did as well," slowing down at the end of his sentence, and looking quizzically around. "It's a pity another judge hasn't arisen, but there you are. They do have niche political processes."

He sat back. "What would you like to know?"

Knotted brows lined the foreheads of the other four as if the answer was obvious. The Mayor of Ekron explained for them all. "You could drop some hints about the money you are making, that might be a start."

In mock astonishment, the Mayor of Gaza queried straight back, "I get the feeling you think you are missing out on something?"

"Come on, come on," pushed Ekron. "Don't drag it out."

"No, I'm serious," said the Mayor of Gaza in a firmer tone. "I really am."

They sat up.

"I could tell you what is emerging, but what do I gain? Competitors? Detractors?"

"What are you going on about?" blustered Ekron, his annoyance mounting.

"What am I on about?" The Mayor of Gaza did not hesitate. "Quite simply, I am on about the biggest move any of us could make in our lives. I am on about the chance, here and now, to influence history. Now, do you think I am going to treat that as a diversion from our boring agenda, no, I am not."

Their attention was now complete.

After a stunned silence, the Mayor of Ashdod beamed broadly, and gestured openly, "speak."

The four looked across, then back to the one from Gaza, and nodded assent.

"Good," he began. "I am glad the topic has come up, and to tell the truth, I was prepared. Before we proceed any further, and you will appreciate the gravity of this once I start, I have brought non-disclosure agreements. This cannot escape into the public arena."

With raised eyebrows, the magnitude growing at the man from Gaza's pace, they silently read over the documents. Beginning with the Mayor of Ashdod, they all applied their signatures, passing the papers to each other to witness. The Mayor of Gaza sat in silence, gathering back the completed agreements.

After checking the documents he declared. "Gentlemen, I think Israel needs us back as rulers."

They stared at him in amazement. It was right on cue.

Understanding history

The Mayor of Gaza, alone among the group, read his history books. It was no secret. He was an avid observer of the past. He had pored over Egyptian texts, scripts from the Euphrates region, and, significantly, Israelite law as enshrined in the books of Moses. He felt Israel's own written history contained the key to dealing with them effectively.

Before reading all he could on the topic, he had wondered why, in Philistia's past, they had sometimes beaten Israel, only to have the tables turned on them a generation later. Some Philistine historians had tried to blame it on Israel's God. They theorized this God of theirs was two faced. During some eras he cared for them. But when they annoyed him, he would desert them, and whoever wanted to could conquer them with ease.

The historians pointed to the most recent of their conflicts, starting nearly seventy years ago. The Israelites had been quite strong up to then, but again their God got angry with them. With very little bother at all, the Ammonites from Edom and Moab, inland of Israel, marched in and took them over. The pickings were excellent. For eighteen years, those Ammonites milked Israel for every penny the nation was worth. All in all, a highly profitable undertaking.

Until Jephthah came along. Interestingly Jephthah was a brigand, born out of wedlock. His own Israelite family cast him out as a youth because of his questionable birth. He was a surprising choice. Matter of fact, he too was equally taken aback that his countrymen approached him in their hour of need. Unsurprisingly he demanded all kinds of conditions from the elders of Israel before he accepted the liberator role.

Coincidently, just at this stage, the Israelites started to make things up with their God and get him back on their side. Eighteen years of oppression had sickened them. Anything was better than the servitude and taxation regime they lived under. However, their masters inland got wind of this attempt to stack the cards with a religious ace, and sent in the troops. They were not going to have their goldmine upset by a few fanatics.

Israel's elders were thrown into a panic. Promising all kinds of things to Jephthah, they finally talked him into accepting the task. Having secured his position amongst his own people, he switched his attention to defeating the oppressive foe.

Being a successful outlaw must have taught him a few things about the law and he began his campaign like a diplomat. He sent a letter to the inland kings asking them why they were invading Israel. It was one thing to demand the exacting tribute they did every year, and station a few garrisons inside Israel. It was quite another to march in a full-scale battle force.

Now in those days, such ambassadorial approaches were rare. If kings wanted to invade somebody, they just went ahead and did it. The Mayor chuckled when he read about this move by Jephthah. He would have enjoyed meeting such an intellectual robber baron.

Predictably, the inland monarchs were rocked by this missive when it arrived, all neatly printed out, and signed by Israel's new leader. Somehow they managed to get a reply together after rummaging through whatever history books they kept. Having been introduced to those sons of the desert further inland, the Mayor could appreciate they would have been no match for an articulate negotiator of Jephthah's ilk. Their answer went way back to the original Israelite invasion several hundred years earlier. They maintained they were only after the land Israel had taken off them at that time.

In turn, Jephthah responded with a second letter. This was one piece of literature the Mayor actually had. Jephthah's rejoinder to the inland kings had eventually found its way into the Mayor's hands. Jephthah pointed out that Edom and Moab had been bypassed by Joshua. Joshua had expressly requested permission from both the King of Edom and the King of Moab to move through their territory. Both had refused, so Israel complied and went around the long way. Indeed, Jephthah refuted every argument the inland monarchs made, concluding with the obvious; Israel had occupied this territory for three hundred years—why had the inland kings waited so long to assert this claim?

In the Mayor's estimation, it really was a brilliant piece of work. Had Jephthah not been an Israelite, he could have found work anywhere in the then known world as a foreign affairs consultant. The inland monarchs couldn't match him. They made no reply. But there was no intent of withdrawing simply because they lost some debating points.

Jephthah summoned together the makings of an army. Undoubtedly all desperate men fighting for freedom. Then he marched. To the east.

Very fortunately for Philistia on this occasion, they decided not to join the war against Israel. If the inland kings won, life in the region would be back to normal; if Israel succeeded, it wouldn't have been smart to also be fighting them. And Jephthah did win. In a complete reversal of events, he drove the kings of the east so far back, they had to sue for peace on very disadvantageous terms. They lost several cities and hadn't emerged as a threat to anyone since.

That was over fifty years ago. Jephthah's victory ushered in the current golden era of Israelite prosperity. Through a series of five strong judges, Israel had forged ahead economically. Politically, they were at ease. Only the old could fully remember the times of horror under the inland kings. Thankfully, thought the Mayor, they treated their smaller neighbor, Philistia, with simple curiosity. Somehow it never occurred to them to try and take over the five coastal city states, just to enjoy good times there.

At first it was a puzzle. Israel could clearly become a cash cow to another nation, but what was the secret to ruling them? And the Mayor found it in their own history books. It was related to their faith after all. But not how the historians imagined. The Mayor had a more enlightened interpretation.

He decided you could take their God out of the equation, and it would make no difference. The important facets were their beliefs. Once he started reading from that premise, it all made sense to him. The books of Moses were very strong about predicting failure and oppression if they deviated from their religion.

It finally dawned on him as he sat in the cell questioning the captain on the striking of the Israelite tourist. Their ideology was a self-fulfilling prophecy. When they were faithful to it, they believed they were invincible. And when they were unfaithful, their guilt betrayed them. It was all in their minds.

They were programmed for success or failure.

Continued . . . the five mayors

"Yes, gentlemen, I am perfectly serious," he repeated to the open mouthed four, "Israel has never been in a more precarious position."

Finally, the Mayor of Ashkelon cleared his throat. "Okay, I think we can skip the monthly agenda now."

Couldn't have thought of a better start, conceded the Mayor of Gaza to himself as he joined in the ensuing mirth.

So they listened. Just look at the facts, he said. And sure enough, there was logic in his words. He was correct about Abdon. The judge was out of the way, no replacement had arisen, and Philistia was making money from the Asherah trade.

The Mayor talked for thirty minutes without a pause. He strolled around the room, using his hands as always, to draw the past and shape the future. As he slowed down, he alluded to possible riches and power beyond imagination, if they could rule their neighbor. "This is our best moment in life to alter history. Think on that."

They sat there. Looking at each other, gauging reactions. He followed up. "I suggest we consider this opportunity seriously, and meet again a week from Wednesday."

On cue, the refreshments were borne in by the waiting servants. The Mayor knew how important it was to keep them here for a while. True feelings surface during relaxed small talk. Jovially, he started pouring wine.

Asaph

Rowing as a slave in a Mediterranean galley had two outcomes. Firstly, it was such hard work, the rowers became immensely fit with powerful arms. Secondly, it was so torturously hot under the decks, that they suffered burnout. Sold out of the ancient Egyptian village with their lilting talk where his parents owed debts they could not repay, Asaph had reached the first phase, and he knew the second was approaching.

But he had two assets, one inborn, and the other learnt from a childhood village elder. He was naturally curious, and he had been taught to focus. He loved watching people. He examined his fellow rowers. He studied the guards. He pondered the actions of the captain. And he thought long at the oars, making sense of them all.

From one of the strongest of his rowing companions he was taught the nature of the slave rower mind. This large, but simple man, had identified his wellbeing with that of the ship, which was true in a way. If a naval galley was pursued and stood in risk of being taken by a rival, the commander was under orders to scuttle the vessel with all rowers chained to their places. This incentive bred a strong desire to pull the oars harder when escape was hanging in the balance. The large slave, two down from Asaph, had exhorted the others with his very heart and soul, in the narrowest of retreats from two Libyan craft. In an eight hour rowing marathon, he personally had pulled the oars at a rate hardly credible while singing, yelling, screaming and cajoling his fellows to follow his example.

Even the captain came below deck to lend moral and psychological support. Not a single stroke of the whip touched that rower's shoulders. For eight hours he had been a hero. Even a galley slave has his day, Asaph had thought as he pulled during the unending duel. He could see the man row harder because he had the support of the crew. It was not just the threat of drowning which caused him to do it. Asaph could see it was the effect of being accepted by his overlords as an ally, the raising of his stature in this contest from that of mere slave to be dispatched at will, to almost a human being, striving for goals common with his superiors.

When darkness fell they slipped away from the larger Libyan craft. The rowing rate was kept constant for another hour until the sentries were sure they were alone on the vast ocean. Then they slackened their pace but kept pulling for another two hours before quitting and sleeping at their places like dead men.

The large man never recovered from this superhuman exertion. Something had broken inside him. He could still row, but his performance was only mediocre. In another civilization, he would have been richly rewarded and hospitalized until his recovery was complete. But not in a slave galley. Asaph saw him taken up to the deck two weeks later by the burly guards. No words floated back down the stairs, but those near the front later swore they heard the sickening slick of the knife, and the guttural helpless striving for breath and choking sound of the blood being sucked back down into the lungs during those last few seconds when a living being suddenly, in disbelief, finds its own throat has been cut, and rebels futilely against the inevitable.

Never give yourself fully to anyone, Asaph promised himself.

Sometimes the rowers would sense they were tied up alongside another slave driven vessel. The bumping of the boats together would invariably tempt one of the chained to try a rhythmic knocking on the wooden hull. If this was returned, there was a good chance it was a fellow galley. But spoken communication was impossible. They would have to shout to be heard through two ships sides of the thick planking, and that would bring the guards running.

True, replacements came in occasionally. But these were usually from villages like Asaph's. Unwitting fodder for the naval machinery of Egypt. Even, rarely, when a rower from another galley was transferred to their ship, they learnt little. He too, came from a similar locked in world.

Self taught

When he first arrived, he was rudely introduced to boat chatter. It was of the gutter, and the relating of bygone stories of sexual conquest. Coarse erotic humor flowed as continuously between the members as did the verbal abuse they rained on each other. But Asaph was listening, carefully, and soon heard contradictions emerge, finally realizing, in his teenage naivety, that the tales were fabricated.

Without a teacher, it took him a long time to grasp why men would act this way. But he got there, finally seeing this banter functioned as a meaningless rejection of their circumstances. Everyone knew they were going to die after a short period of this living hell, so their minds consciously, or unconsciously, gravitated to fantasy.

As part of this voyage of discovery, Asaph eventually concluded escape was possible. It was an immense realization. Nobody told him you could rise above your circumstances by altering your thinking. He arrived there tediously, the long way, by himself.

Freedom beckoned.

None of his companions had heard of a galley slave getting away. Only occasionally did they have any encounter at all with other galley slaves. So how would they know? They simply believed escape wasn't possible, a message sarcastically drummed in continuously by the guards.

It was a euphoric breakthrough, giving him hope. He held onto it tightly, because the only other options were despair or fantasy. Once he had convinced himself of this, he began to focus on the method.

For several months he toyed with the idea of working with a group to launch a joint takeover of the ship. But he decided mentally their spirit was broken. Maintaining secrecy would be impossible because one of the slaves would tell the masters, numbly grasping for a crumb of recognition from above. Even though it would earn that one nothing but disgust from his fellows, Asaph was convinced such a venture would end that way. And it wasn't the slaves' fault. It was just what happened when you brutalised men into this nightmare.

Whatever he tried, he knew he would only have one chance; a single escape attempt with no assurance of what would happen, indeed where he would even be, when he got above decks. It might be in the middle of the trackless Mediterranean, which would probably condemn him to a watery grave if he jumped. In truth, the idea was most likely not to succeed. But if he remained as a rower, he was dead in a few years. So, at worst, the escape gamble would only shorten his brief existence.

Maybe at best.

Less than half a chance

In his nineteenth year, a replacement rower was put beside him. The man was older, but they got along comfortably together. They spoke of their backgrounds, and their villages, and families. He was a latecomer to the galley slave trade. He had left behind a wife and children. Debts again, had brought him to this end. He related one day how it was either himself or his two young daughters who had to be sold. He personally was given this choice. Despite his toughness, Asaph almost had to fight back the anger such a story raised. What manner of man could sleep after extracting such human payment for a sum no doubt trivial?

Two months later, they knew each other so well Asaph decided he could tell his friend he wanted to escape before the year was out. He felt he was at the peak of his muscular powers. But he still didn't know how. His friend then made him an amazing offer.

He said he would help him, even if it killed him. Asaph wondered what he meant. The older man went on. He too, had been thinking of such a possibility, and had concocted a plan. However, it required two of them to execute it, and, at best, only one would survive. The accomplice would almost certainly suffer a terrible death. Asaph was breathless as his fellow related his thinking.

After hearing it, he tried to persuade him the plan just required a little modification for both to make it. In a language of hints and side chatter to keep their topic free from other ears, they continued this strange debate. True, his confidant conceded, they could both go for it, but it would lessen the chances of either making it. As it was, they might only get part way through the plan before discovering one of their conjectures was wrong. In that case, both would likely die. As it stood, even with luck, Asaph would have less than half a chance. This discussion rose and fell between them, as circumstance would allow, for about a week.

His argument was logical, Asaph knew that. But at what a price. Both knew his friend would meet his end at the hands of the crew if Asaph escaped. And he was in awe. Someone was willing to give their life so he had the chance of a better one. His older friend argued the guards would be doing him a favor anyway. Who wanted this for a life? Asaph took it more personally: he was important to someone.

The move

Five weeks later the conditions were perfect so far as they could ascertain from below. The men had been rowing hard all day and were exhausted. Chained into their places, they were sleeping deeply. All but two. Outside, a good breeze was blowing, and they could hear the furled sails slapping. A gentle ocean swell was rocking the boat. Amidst this movement, and the clanking chains, as the men shifted in their sleep, these two bided their time. Eventually the moment came.

A single senior, burly, guard came down into the hold to check the status. He hung his swaying lamp on the nail driven into one of the center posts, as he had done a hundred times, and peered around at the filthy bodies sweating and snoring on their planks. Walking along the aisle between them, he casually examined each row. Two one side, and two the other. As he reached Asaph's seat, he paused. A stiff body with open eyes stared ahead.

It was not the first time the guard had come across a dead rower. Grimacing though, he glanced past Asaph. His mate is dead, and he is dreaming of young girls, he thought.

He stooped to touch the body to ascertain whether the death was recent or not. With unbelievable swiftness, an incredibly strong pair of hands materialized around his throat, cutting off breath and voice. In the same instant the dead body flung its arms around him pinning his arms to his sides.

The guard couldn't believe it. It took him a couple of seconds to grasp what was going on, before striving to free himself. But the fingers were locked deep into his throat and he couldn't breathe, let alone shout for help. He started struggling, desperately trying to bring his hands up to free himself from the awful grip. However, the arms holding him were so strong from years of rowing, it was in vain.

With sudden horror, the guard knew he was trapped. His head pounded with blood, as his stricken eyes stared at his tormentors. He was not conscious of dying, not even of blacking out. The two slaves hung onto him tightly for several minutes. All too aware of being tricked by a feint, they were determined to kill him twice over if need be. His thrashing body had not awakened any other slaves, due to their exhaustion, the constant moving of the boat, and continual clanking of chains. So far, the plan had gone perfectly.

Carefully they released their respective grips. With bated breath, Asaph's friend reached inside the guard's tunic for the article they were not completely sure about. And luck was on their side. Yes, this senior did keep his key on a string that hung around his neck. Their eyes locked in silent jubilation.

Their following deduction was likely to be true. Asaph inserted the key into the manacle fastening his ankle to the floor. And they were correct. One key fitted all. They had speculated it was too complicated for a slave ship to operate any other way. Asaph crawled out into the center aisle. Quickly scanning the snoring rowers, he assured himself all was well. Stripping the guard of his uniform, he swapped them for his own stained, rotting loincloth. After dressing himself in the outfit, foot wear and all, they carefully levered the corpse into the place Asaph had so recently been in.

Attaching the manacle, the lock was fastened again. As much as they were able, they folded the still supple body into a sitting posture. In the dark it would pass for a rower, sleeping at his place.

Finally, Asaph gazed deeply at his friend. Not a word had passed between them during this entire episode. Asaph felt his tears rising. His companion gently pushed him away, nodding towards the ladder. Asaph wheeled, and without looking back, strode along the aisle.

Up on deck, the warm wind hit him and reinvigorated him to the next phase. Along the deck of the vessel he could see a few others dimly. As one of them swiveled briefly in his direction he waved back, using a hand gesture he had noted the dead guard using occasionally below decks.

It seemed to satisfy the sentry who turned back to the group. Hoping he would not appear unusual, Asaph walked along the deck away from the small cluster. He did not know what to expect, but he knew what he was looking for. Two items would be perfect, one would be enough, but he would go without either if he had to.

Primarily he was looking for something that floated and was easy to get into the water with. Unfortunately, the deck of the galley was sparsely fitted with loose equipment. The best he could manage was a wooden pole fastened to the side of the boat. He imagined it was used to push the craft from the harbor side. It was not the best floatation aid, but it was better than nothing. However, he could not find any fresh water. The two of them had guessed chances were against finding a receptacle containing the elixir of life, but he had tried anyway.

The ocean was dark all around him. In their planning, they had identified this chancy aspect too. He might have come up on deck to find the boat was moored near a wharf, which would have caused him to believe in a deity. But they were not. So, he chose the next most practical maneuver. He would merely go with the direction of the current. They had thought through this step down below as well. The plan was not going astray in his mind. It was being executed perfectly. Each decision was prompted by the circumstance.

Masked by the night, and the strong breeze, and the water slapping against the hull, Asaph went over the side of the boat. He was at the opposite end of the galley from the group above deck when he went. As he lowered himself over the side, he checked them again. They were all engrossed in their chatter.

He entered the water holding his pole and submerged briefly. Pushing himself out from the boat, he kicked silently until he was about one hundred yards from the craft. Looking back, he could still see the animated group on the deck, with the swinging lantern above them lighting their faces. He relaxed and let the wind and the swell move him along, watching the glow gradually recede. After less than an hour, he could see them no more. He was alone.

He was not afraid. The act of moving freely in water again, as he used to in the river near his village when he was a child, enchanted him. Simply moving through any medium without chains was reward enough in itself.

In the middle of the deserted expanse, he lay back, observing the stars. A blend of victory, bonding, and sacrifice, flooded through him. If it ended now, he would be content, and, scanning the trackless waters, he laughed for the first time in years. What an act of folly, he thought. Who would cast themselves into the deep like this?

Liberty

He gradually grew aware of bright sunlight. And voices talking as if from far away but getting closer. Rolling slightly, he felt the hard surface he was lying on. Suddenly he grasped he was alive, and that he was on the deck of a ship. For one awful second, he thought no, it can't be.

But as his eyes opened, he saw unfamiliar faces bending over him. Breathing a sigh of relief, he relaxed into a smile. This led a gnarled old timer peering down at him to straighten up cheerfully. "You'll be alright lad. When you've had something to drink, you can tell us what happened."

Asaph's mind worked rapidly. Obviously the man didn't think he was a slave. As he drew himself up, he understood why. He was dressed in the garb of a guard. As the water was being brought, he knew he could change the course of his life. He was on board an Egyptian slaver similar to the one he had just escaped from. "A curse on those Libyans. Those rats. Those sons of whores," he began. Once he started speaking, it just flowed out. He even amazed himself.

After several hours he was back to full strength. Two days and nights on the open ocean were nothing for his superbly conditioned body. He was assigned to help the other guards driving the rowers. Even the captain was forced to marvel at his skill in detecting tricks of recalcitrant performers.

They say a poacher makes the best gamekeeper.

The Mayor of Gaza

Following the four cities commitment, the project began in earnest. Runners were dispatched daily to coordinate plans and activities. Sword and spear production were organized. Men streamed in to sign up. Every second day, the Mayor went out to the training barracks where the shock troops were stationed. He read every military manual he could lay his hands on and had some good theoretical concepts to work with. Besides, he was convinced the whole affair would succeed. Even if he only had untrained troops. History indicated it.

On his way around the city he called in on his various enterprises. The Asherahs were still going strongly, with sales spreading throughout Israel. Often, he laughed to himself over the irony of the situation. The Israelites were funding their own takeover. It was too much.

He was musing away in the back of his chariot, when he noticed someone, and stopped the driver. Walking up the street from the port was a powerful young man dressed in military garb. His arms bulged with muscle, and his chest was as broad as a barrel.

Asaph watched the chariot halt, as the occupant caught sight of him. He was older, perhaps by ten or so years, and conveyed authority. Asaph tensed as he swung down from his vehicle and came over. But although his eyes were on Asaph, they did not contain danger signs, rather curiosity. "Excuse me, young man, may I introduce myself?"

"My name is Asaph," he said simply.

The Mayor beamed. "Have you been long in our fair town, Asaph? Seen its attractions?"

His indirectness relaxed Asaph. "I have spent much time on the ocean," he confided. "To see your land would be good."

A wider grin emanated from the Mayor, charmed with the lilt of his language. "Couldn't agree more my boy, couldn't agree more." He led the escaped galley slave into a nearby tavern. They sat down, the Mayor indicating, "let me get some refreshments. Wait here." Striding up to the bar, he stood where he could order drinks from, yet look across in a friendly manner at the seated youth.

The newcomer was slightly taller than the Mayor's above average height. It did not make him a clumsy giant who would have to duck under doorways however. Rather he conveyed balance and strength. His face was serious. It seemed to shift between reluctance and centeredness. As the wines were being poured, the Mayor shrugged back at him, waving his hands in a manner indicating these barmen were always so slow, please forgive me.

Walking back to the table carrying the drinks, he nodded to acquaintances on the way, maintaining his connection with the citizenry. Asaph noticed all this, knowing he had also been assessed.

Half an hour later the Mayor had hired himself a platoon leader, on condition he received a favorable report from the commander of the galley anchored in the harbor. A mere formality. Asaph was more than accommodating, and even accompanied the Mayor back, introducing him to his recent overseer.

He waited outside in the chariot, intoxicated with freedom.

The five mayors

"The military move in three days."

The monthly meeting between the five mayors of Philistia was brief. Perhaps the shortest in living memory. After their leader from Gaza had spoken, the other four were silent. They all nodded, packed up their papers, wished each other success with firm handshakes, and departed to their own towns.

Battle

With no particular fanfare, the troops started walking into Israel. They each had a simple message to deliver to their various destinations. It was a solution to a problem which did not yet exist. But by the time the soldiers had penetrated far enough, the Mayor knew the crisis would have been created.

Of course, he wasn't invading. No, he was sending in a peace keeping force. Philistia had heard about lawless bands upsetting Israel and was acting to protect them. And he was correct. Isolated villages heard about Philistia's platoons, and local would be heroes aroused bands of men to retaliate. Local youths were easily persuaded to join, and local mothers fretted.

Asaph's guerrilla unit marched around Israel for six days before they were attacked. They were walking alongside a wooded area when forty men burst from the trees, running down a gentle slope to the road. Asaph's scout spotted them first. "Rebels on the right!"

Within seconds his band of thirty spun to face the onslaught. Iron tipped spears were held upright until the yelling mob was less than ten yards from them and closing fast.

Asaph shouted, "down!"

As one man the entire force dropped their lances to their waists, gleaming points toward the foe. What had been a motionless, silent, line of soldiers was now a loud wall of sharp steel. Shouting, "for Philistia!" the troop rushed at the oncoming Israelites.

The attackers had become the attacked, some attempting to reverse direction. But it was too late. Asaph's timing was perfect. His men hit their yielding foe with their lances held firm, seeing twelve impaled. Those soldiers who missed sped by, and within several seconds pierced a further five, mostly in the backs of those now fleeing.

Asaph was exultant. He had run through one of the first dozen himself. With the roar of battle and blood pounding in his ears, he swerved past the screaming Israelite clutching the shaft buried in his stomach.

Virtually one third of the Israelite fighting force had fallen and the remainder were in disarray. It was every man for himself as they fled back into the forest with Asaph's band in hot pursuit. Chopping and hacking with their blades at the retreating opposition, they brought down others easily.

Asaph lost none of his momentum, surging through as his adrenalin leant him energy, and bringing his sword crashing down on the head of a second fleeing Israelite. The force of his blow split the man's skull, and he crumpled without a sound.

Speeding past, he focused on an individual some four yards in front. Knowing the day was his already, and there was no fear of reprisal from this motley crowd, he picked him as his live captive. Springing across the last two yards, he tackled him from behind, crashing to the ground. His knife was out as the winded victim arose begging for mercy.

Adventure and success, Asaph thrilled to himself as he frog-marched his captive back to the road. Sheer excitement and relief caught hold now it was over, and he started to laugh.

The village

"Good people," Asaph said loudly to the gathered Israelite crowd. "We came to deliver a message of peace from your brothers in Philistia when this wickedness was attempted on us."

Beside him stood his band of thirty soldiers, now blooded and with no more than a few bruises and scratches between them, although one had somehow contrived to break his nose to the amusement of his fellows. They guarded three bound prisoners while Asaph spoke to the town elders. Gathered behind them stood the rest of the silent menfolk. He guessed the women and children were hiding in the houses or fields.

"All we desire is to bring protection from lawless bands. As does Philistia. But even as we made our way here, we were molested by brigands. Thankfully we were able to overcome them before they plundered the homes of your fathers."

From the gasps and hands flying to mouths as he entered the town, he had guessed his three prisoners were all locally known. Probably lived in this community. Maybe some of those who escaped were standing among the crowd.

"Surely this is unjust," the former galley slave continued. "And those who walk in such ways cannot be tolerated. To demonstrate our peaceable rule, let us show these ruffians that villages like yours can no longer be terrorized, and families will be able to sleep in the calm of night. Come, witness their fate."

So saying, he ordered his men to tie the captives up against three trees on the edge of the village. Commanding the crowd to follow was unnecessary. When the unfortunates were lashed securely to the trunks, he faced the silent throng.

"Even in dispensing justice, our arm is not cruel. Our delivery is swift."

Asaph signaled to his troop leader, who walked over as if he were strolling to the well for a drink. When he reached the first prisoner, he drew his sword free in one rapid movement, and plunged it directly into the young man's chest.

The Israelites stepped back a pace. Even though expected, the killing still shocked. One began choking in horror, and fell to his knees, his eyes almost popping out. "Easy there, Eliphaz," murmured a couple stooping to hold him in his grief. As they lifted him up and led him away, Asaph could hear the sobs turning to shrieks, and he knew it was the father.

From one of the houses came a high-pitched screaming. A woman ran out. Surely it comes, he told himself, diverting his attention from the receding group. She flung herself at his feet and begged for mercy. Several of the older Israelites came forward to take her away, but Asaph's men waved them back.

"Why ask for mercy? You have done no wrong. It is these ones," signaled Asaph ominously with his sword at the remaining two live prisoners.

"No, my lord, no, no!" she sobbed. "I ask not for myself."

"Then for who?"

"My only son, my lord. Only eighteen years old, a mere youth, he was led astray by his peers. Oh, surely you can understand, you look so young yourself!"

Asaph looked around at the pair bound to the trees. Yes, there was the family likeness. Turning back, his resolution weakened. Had his own mother wept as he was led away to the galleys?

Even so, to your task.

"But he attacked us. Behold, is he not as guilty as the others? How can he be spared?"

"Oh, my lord, no, please no . . ." Her pleas tapered off as she sank to the ground wracked with tears.

Asaph raised his eyes to the level of the crowd, scanning them as they waited for his next move. Slowly he walked back to the wide-eyed youths tied to the trees. He hefted his blade more firmly, as if to emphasize a point. His voice had an edge of softness now.

"Philistia comes not to create strife. Rather she brings peace, security and happiness. Must a woman teach us here today? All men are young once, and all who walk under the sun commit folly. But is a mistake worth a life?

Far be it from us this should always be so. The voice of a mother can be heard by the merciful ear of Philistia."

As he heard the watcher's breaths draw in, he flashed his weapon at the trunks of both trees. The severed ropes fell.

"These two shall be bonded as slaves to Philistia for five years. A ransom of one hundred pieces of silver each year is placed on their lives. After, they shall return as free, and wiser men, may it be so."

In disbelief the woman sprang up, her face shining. "Oh, my lord, thank you, a thousand blessings upon you." She flung herself at his feet again. Asaph glanced back at his men, anticipating the ribbing he would receive later.

The crowd, expecting more bloodletting, palpably relaxed. A murmur wound through their ranks. Five hundred pieces of silver? Of course, it was a fortune. But the foolish boys were saved, weren't they?

The business seminar

Two days behind Asaph, and his compatriots elsewhere in Israel, came the second wave of platoons. All were armed, but expected, and mostly received, less resistance. It was integral to the Mayor's plan. Never leave them alone to come a decision, he emphasized to his generals. We will organize the outcomes.

Sitting under the trees outside the village, the scene appeared like a picnic, not a takeover. A mouthwatering repast was spread on the table in front of the village elders and the diplomats from Philistia, supplemented by some of the finest wines from the coast. Apprehensive to start with, the Israelites began to relax. It didn't seem at all like an occupying force.

A plump cheery merchant from the coast chatted away amiably, interspersing jokes with discussions of mutually beneficial business arrangements.

"You must all come down to Ashkelon as soon as you can," he gushed. "I am in touch with markets in Crete that would pay generously for grain from your region. Our freight companies are updated monthly on Mediterranean prices and can set up all the arrangements. Naturally, there are certain fees and commissions, but I can virtually guarantee a four percent improvement in revenue."

Elihu nudged Joseph over their dry reds. Four percent higher! For grain!

On and on went the merchant, wandering through various export schemes, and commodity trends. He spoke for at least sixty minutes, to an audience increasingly riveted by what he had to say. By the close of his session, not a few of them were already getting used to the idea of Philistia running affairs.

Eventually the leading dignitary from Philistia rose and summarized.

"In order to develop economic opportunities such as my colleague has been kind enough to open up before us all here, there are obvious prerequisites of law and order. No doubt many of you are aware of the attacks made on several of the advance parties from Philistia. This can only indicate one thing—lawless elements afoot, standing in the way of progress."

He paused, indicating a change of topic. "Philistia proposes the following. Firstly, we intend to expand trade and investment for all. Secondly it is necessary to establish small local units to maintain harmony. Regrettably police forces must eat, and that is a tax burden we must all bear.

"However, we are confident an overall economic expansion plan will more than cover the cost of keeping the peace. The objective of Philistia and Israel must be betterment for all, and a rising standard of living. Are there any questions gentlemen?"

He stood for a moment studying the astonished faces. They all knew they had just been taken over. Not a man there couldn't recite the history of previous subjugations. But none knew how to take this one. They had expected terms of a harsh regime to be meted out.

Instead they had received a financial plan.

Angry old Jacob

The village elder knew he was losing the argument, but he persevered despite his seventy years.

"The Philistines have always been our enemies. From the time of Moses until now, they have fought against us, oppressed us, and ruled us when we disobeyed the Lord our God. We have brought this upon ourselves with our willful disobedience, and we shall suffer for it."

It was all too quick, and too different to explain, and he had lost his clarity as he strutted about waving his finger. Deep down he knew it too, but his fire was up. "Did Jephthah rise against the kings of the east for this? Did he remove those wicked rulers so we could let ourselves be overrun by the coastal monarchs? No! He believed God would help Israel in their hour of need, and he overcame them. We need to repent and remove the evil influence of Philistia from our midst!"

Ten minutes later he was emotionally exhausted. He slumped into his chair, holding his head. The younger men in their thirtysomethings exchanged glances. Nobody wanted to be the first to speak. There was a tinge of embarrassment in the air. The tales were too much in their blood to reject completely. But the world was moving on. Modernization was here. Philistia was offering financial growth, military security, delightful trades on the coast.

This was no oppression. It was bounty for all.

Sure, there were the foreign idols and the discos. But Philistia had not forced these on Israel. It was simply market forces at work. If people wanted to worship the Lord God of Israel, they were free to do that. There were no restrictions. But who could tell the old man in his dotage these things?

After some silent gesticulating, Elihu knew he had been selected to handle the aged one and retain harmony in the village council. He stood up.

"Of course we all appreciate the guidance of Jacob these many years. He has been a strength to us over a long time. I'm sure each of us remember instances of his personal advice. Why, it's not too long ago he caught Joseph and me, when we were twelve years old, eating plums out of his orchard. That was a woodshed day for us two, I tell you."

The council roared with the laughter of relief. Elihu was a master at sliding past difficult situations. They sat back to enjoy a round of humorous village tales.

Jacob also knew Elihu, and that his own moment was gone. He would end his days under the yoke of Philistia. It stretched out before him. For the first time in the history of his nation, the blow had fallen pleasantly. All his learning had taught him the takeover would be oppressive. But it wasn't. And he didn't know what to say. Couldn't deliver an effective explanation to the very ones his God had entrusted him with. Accepting his inadequacy, he sat back to listen to Elihu's stories.

Elihu

"You devious blighter. As I recall, it was you who talked me into scaling Jacob's fence. I didn't want to go. 'He's not there, he'll never know,' I can still hear you."

Elihu's eyes lit up. "You are such a dreamer, Joseph. And what a vivid imagination you have. If you had simply been quiet, and not stepped on that branch, he wouldn't have heard a thing."

"Branch? He clears his orchard religiously, you know that."

"Okay, whatever it was you trod on. Tell you what, he knew how to use that cane. If my father had seen the results on my backside, he would have repeated the dose. They wondered why I washed down at the stream for the next week."

Their chatter died down as they walked on, until Elihu spoke again. "You know, that wasn't really like the old man. I think he got carried away there a mite."

"Mmm."

"Mind you, from his perspective, it's a huge shock. It's a biggie from ours too, let's get real."

"I know."

"They walk in here, and we are all steeling ourselves. Then they unveil a monetary incentive package. What do you think?"

Joseph didn't answer as they walked back in the late afternoon warmth. He knew Elihu would come up with something himself. Presently he did.

"We wait."

"What do you mean, we wait?"

"Our ancestors told us our nation would be taken care of. Blessed, if you must have the religious word. I'm not a man of war. I don't know how to hide in the hills and organize bandits like Jephthah. I'm a businessman. But I do know a better income when I see one. I'll wait to see two things."

Elihu stopped on the path, as though he were making an announcement to his friend. "Firstly, whether it occurs, and secondly if it's a blessing."

Jackpot

And indeed, within the year economic improvements did start to filter down. Trade was rationalized; the Cretan markets lived up to their promise; the coastal warehouses were built; and everyone in the commercial chain benefited.

The Mayor of Gaza insisted some of the money trickle down into Israel itself. It was part of the strategy. He had spent a long time examining the downfall of empires. It was necessary, he said repeatedly, not to extract money from them, but to put some in their pockets. The former always led to discontent, the latter to placid servants.

Asaph

Asaph waited outside the palace marshalling his troops.

"Behold, you there, Gilpaz, have I not asked you to take more care of your belt. And your helmet. From where does that dent come? Can a soldier of Philistia wear a village basin when he walks with his lord?"

"The dent fits one the same size in my head. A stone meant for you hit me. You should be grateful."

"It cannot be true. Surely it would have knocked sense into you, but it is lacking as before."

Suddenly the Mayor was outside, and the line transformed itself into a wall of muscle and iron. He smiled. "Let's go!"

The Mayor climbed into his chariot, and the platoon split into four, walking along both sides with contingents at front and rear. Their eyes ranged across the crowd, this their turn at protecting the chief man of the city. Trundling along the cobblestones of the town's streets, the Mayor felt good about the prospects for his little nation. He even found himself enjoying these parades. Then again he was simultaneously aware of that fact. Pride comes before a fall, he reminded himself. Learn from the past. You claim to read it.

Turning into the stretch leading into the city center, the crowd's numbers grew. Asaph saw it was more difficult to scan everyone. He glanced around with a look blending empathy and warning. His men understood it clearly. Concentrate. In truth it is not simple. Do it anyway.

Asaph moved between the four groups constantly, encouraging here and there, not joking now. It would not do for a tragedy to occur during a moment of humor. He was in the front contingent when he noticed a different type of cloak in the first row of the throng ahead. More foreigners than ever visited Gaza these days.

It happened quickly, as he imagined it might, the rapid movement drawing his first reflex. The arm from the strange cloak coming out from the sleeve it was folded into as Eliphaz judged his distance was at its briefest, his target looming large above him across the heads of only two soldiers.

And Asaph was also throwing, even as Eliphaz was with the swing he had practiced long hours for in the forest. The helmet winged its way up and over the soldier's heads, intersecting with the trajectory of the spinning blade, as the Mayor was turning, seeing the final follow through of the flinging arm, and the knife commencing its journey towards him, only to strike the flying helmet and clatter uselessly to the ground.

As the blade hit the pavement the soldiers on that side of the chariot wheeled, grabbing the unbelieving Israelite with the popping eyes who could not grasp the fact his God had not kept his side of the deal. Asaph restrained the short stabbing sword of the second private.

"Not here," he whispered, stuffing the would-be assassin's own cloak into his mouth to stifle any untoward noise. But the crowd saw it, or the small part there was to see, and they pressed forward, murmuring with the shock of such an attempt in their own town. Asaph stood tall and shouted, "all is well, let us pass on!"

Five soldiers split from the group carrying the bound and wriggling figure down a narrow, shaded, side street. Asaph swung up into the chariot beside the blanching Mayor. "Be not afraid, it would not do us good with these your people," he said to his face, with a fixed grin, fully aware the sound of the crowd muffled his words to all but the Mayor.

The Mayor took this in too, along with the speed of the saving of his life, the accuracy of a flying helmet, and the lack of public commotion.

"Were you lucky?" he asked Asaph.

The one-time galley slave stood still awhile. His face shifted from its dedicated focus now the job was done, to a relaxed gaze as the words came to him. "It was as you say, my lord. Who would teach us the throwing of helmets?"

The Mayor grinned widely, feeling very alive, the adrenalin beginning its surge as his brain processed his narrow escape. "I thought so. But it doesn't matter, does it? We're still here aren't we?"

And he laughed hugely at this, but mostly from the relief following his trauma. "You should be a poet. I love that rhythm of the sea in your voice," the Mayor added in his euphoria, attempting to connect more closely with Asaph as his emotions assigned meaning to the event.

Two days later, Asaph was appointed personal protector of the Mayor of Gaza. It was done without fanfare because the Mayor did not want publicity about foiled murder attempts to spread. It might give the idea to others. Henceforth however, all those who mattered knew Asaph was always near the Mayor.

The village

Five Philistine soldiers delivered the message to the elders. No punishment would fall on the village, their leader told the Israelites. Philistia concluded the man Eliphaz was deranged due to the death of his son. Apparently the boy was a disturber of the peace, and lost his life for his own misdeeds. This would not assuage the grief of a parent. However, it was the man's own doing. He alone had received the death penalty for such an outrage. No-one else would be held culpable. Philistia was sure this would meet with approval in Israel.

The captain stopped. With gaping mouths, the villagers stared at him, at last seeing he had finished and there would be no reprisal. Looking around in embarrassment, Elihu finally stood.

"Yes, yes, we understand completely," he stammered.

He even thanked the troop for coming, and wished the Mayor of Gaza good health.

Thoughtful old Jacob

Elihu and Jacob had sat talking now for some time outside the old man's home. Jacob wanted Elihu to relax, as this was an infrequent visit. Time had given him the chance to regret his final oration at the village council, knowing he had let his religion get away with him, and that any move like that today would likewise divert the younger man into community gossip.

They had discussed the Eliphaz incident, and the handling of it by Philistia. However, Jacob felt there was more, but that Elihu didn't know how to express it.

So he brought out his best vintage, an aged red with a wistful aroma. Elihu was appreciating his second goblet before he made an opening gambit. "You know Jacob, I wasn't there in Jephthah's days."

The stooped old man immediately divined his intent. Experiences, emotions, history and belief all welled up. But he knew better this time. He would not permit them to hold sway. This would be an important conversation, and he was not privileged to hold many these days. The younger man also knew his meaning had been picked up and held his peace. Presently the words came.

"That is true. It was in another time, an olden time perhaps. We had real enemies then," Jacob almost spoke nostalgically. "We paid horrendous taxes, and we starved. Beaten, raped, and pounded into submission. In one way it was more straightforward. More understandable."

"They must have been exciting times. The threat of overwhelming numbers, the risks, the night time briefing around camp fires."

"Oh, don't romanticize it, young man. We were scared for our very lives, and only did it because we were pushed to the wall."

Elihu could see his mind roll back the years, so he remained silent.

"But our community was united, all the petty quarrels forgotten. During the times of trouble we were poorer, but we worked together, we prayed together, we ate and drank together."

Jacob fell silent, recalling rising in the dark at another's rough tap on the shoulder, sending him off for his watch over the hills, his favorite assignment, seeing the glorious dawn over the patched grass and white rock hillsides, knowing the day of reckoning was drawing nigh, alive with the beauty and the thrill of the impending fight for freedom.

Every day was a gift. Yes, they were wonderful times. But they were my times, not this young man's.

Elihu watched him return from his reverie, with a sense of envy he could not explain.

Jacob smiled, a bestowing smile Elihu felt. Conferring the future, a very different future onto him.

They were both quiet for some time, each with their own thoughts, until Jacob opened a seemingly different conversation.

"You have nothing to worry about, do you?"

"No, I do not. We do not. The nation does not," Elihu responded, wondering where Jacob was heading. "We all work hard at our businesses and are rewarded for that. Philistia is our master, but life is pleasant, and I make more money than ever."

"Why are you not content then?"

"I didn't say I wasn't content." The younger man's answer was wary, but lacked conviction.

Jacob hesitated, weighing up the risks of being direct before deciding he had nothing to lose. Either Elihu could answer, or perhaps he was not the leader Jacob hoped him to be. "Elihu, I am an old man now. Who knows, our opportunities to talk like this may be numbered. My dry red stock certainly is. So, I am asking that we speak directly to each other, man to man. From our hearts." Jacob paused again to give the thought space. "Why did you come here today, Elihu?"

Ah, he's cornered me. The relaxing, the wine, the disclaimer, the empowering question. I must visit more often. With a laugh, Elihu quipped, "you've got me, Jacob, that was very good."

He contemplated the fading windless day; hearing village sounds carry through the early evening air.

"You are right, I am not content. I have no reason not to be content. But I am not. I would like to think it is simply part of me, of my personality. But it is not. I feel a connection with this land of our fathers, and with our heritage. I am not saying everyone does, but I do."

He stopped.

"Go on," motioned Jacob.

"Everything is fine, we have peace and prosperity. We are not oppressed. But it is not fine. We are not free. We have not kept to the legacy of our ancestors. We have been overrun before, as you have personally been through. But not like this. Not a pleasant unfreedom."

"Are you about to raise the battle standard and summon the tribes to rebel?"

"No, I am not. Nobody would come."

incite

The wife of Manoah

The wife of Manoah was cleaning pots in front of her farmhouse. Their dwelling was a comfortable walk up a gentle slope from a village named Zorah, the path leading through a wooded section at one point. A pleasant view across the front yard to a copse of trees added to the setting's charm. If one ventured through these woods, a more expansive vista of a valley with a stream awaited.

Inside, like virtually all such rural homes, there was no division of rooms. It was an open area, complete with bedding, utensils, foodstuffs, clothing, and chairs arranged neatly. It was not unusual to find favorite animals, such as a cow, or a milk yielding goat, wandering in and out at will, and especially so here, as the childless woman befriended creatures.

Her husband, Manoah, was working out the back of the house on this ordinary day; this day that would suddenly turn into their most important day.

As she glanced up at the trees, the visitor was standing there. Later she could not recall whether he had suddenly appeared, or whether he had been there for a while. It was as if he somehow materialized. He was just present, in an unsurprising manner.

She gazed at him. Without feeling afraid, yet also wondering why she was not. He was strange, but not foreign. He appeared normal, but not ordinary. He was a man, but more than a man.

Then he spoke. He said, "you are sterile and childless, but you are going to conceive and have a son. Now see to it that you drink no wine or other fermented drink and that you do not eat anything unclean, because you will conceive and give birth to a son. No razor may be used on his head, because

40

the boy is to be a Nazirite, set apart to God from birth, and he will begin the deliverance of Israel from the hands of the Philistines."

He had spoken very clearly. The woman was astounded. She had never seen him before. If he had ever passed through the village markets, she was sure she would have remembered him, so striking was his appearance. Even so, he had delivered his lines as if he was merely an envoy. But she knew he was greater than a messenger. Without thinking she turned around to see if her husband was watching also, from behind, perhaps from the door of the house. But he was not, so her gaze flew to the front again.

He had gone.

She stood up. There might have been time for him to disappear into the trees, she supposed. And yet there would not have been. But she did not actually see him depart, just as she did not see him arrive. After several minutes, she realized she was still standing there. Unmoving. Quickly, she ran for her husband. He was still at the rear of the house. In fact, he was so close to the dwelling, fixing the plough, she wondered how he could not have heard the visitor speak, and come running.

But as he sat there, she knew he had not heard anything. Not a single word. So she told him everything. In a rush. As the words tumbled out, they seemed to take their own course. "A man of God came to me. He looked like an angel of God, very awesome."

As soon as she spoke, she wondered why she had described him like that. But she hurried on. "I didn't ask him where he came from, and he didn't tell me his name. But he said to me, 'You will conceive and give birth to a son. Now then, drink no wine or other fermented drink and do not eat anything unclean, because the boy will be a Nazirite of God from birth until the day of his death.'"

Her husband was startled, and jumped to his feet. He believed in angels and had often told his wife he wanted to see one. But this was not the reason he leapt up. Rather it was because she was so level headed, so practical, so possessed of common sense, that she was the last person he expected to claim to have seen an angel. If he had tried to persuade her he had seen one, she would have ignored him and told him dinner was on the table.

"You? Are you serious? An angel? What are you talking about?"

He had already discarded the message, as his attention was on the messenger.

"An angel," she said again. "An angel." As though she needed time to get used to the word.

"What did he look like? How . . . how tall was he? Was he big?"

He stopped and grabbed her by the shoulders. "What did his wings look like?"

Looking into the impetuous eyes she knew intimately, she began to chuckle.

"Wings," she giggled. "Wings!"

Breaking free, she circled the yard, arms outstretched, mimicking a bird in flight, shrieking each time she wheeled past him.

Presently she petered out, the laughter died down, and she drew to a halt in front of Manoah. After some time, she smiled lovingly, and gently told him, "no wings."

Later, over their meal, she went over every word she could recall. They discussed the message back and forward. She felt it was straightforward. He didn't. There's something else, he kept telling her. But what, she would ask. And again they would go through the message. We get a son, she would tell him, and these are the instructions for raising him. What else needs to be told?

After breakfast the next morning, he started again. She told him, "Manoah, you're jealous, aren't you? You wanted to see him, but he came to me."

Surprisingly, he didn't answer back. He stood staring at her for a moment before closing his eyes and praying. Out loud. "O Lord, I beg you, let the man of God you sent to us come again to teach us how to bring up the boy who is to be born."

After a while she went outside to start the chores. She was smiling. Without knowing why, she felt very good, on the edge of an adventure, and with a future. But she never expected to see an angel again.

The Phoenician

The Mayor of Gaza reclined gratefully into the sumptuous chair as the smiling Phoenician ruler lowered himself into his.

"You have certainly done well recently. The whole Mediterranean admires you."

"Thank you for that observation," the Mayor replied. "I hope our prosperity is also yours. I hear Phoenician finance has found its way into some of our export schemes."

The older man laughed at the disclosure. "I should have known you would have your finger on the pulse."

He reached over to the cheese board again. "I must say these are highly palatable. I will inform my chef to get supply details from your people if I may."

The Mayor of Gaza's hand swept out. "It will be my pleasure to send you a case with my compliments."

The Phoenician settled back, a sign to talk over the real business. "She is an intelligent girl, you know."

"And a very attractive one, too," the Mayor replied, bringing a proud smile to her father's face.

"It must come from her mother," he rejoined happily, before summoning a more serious look. "In earlier times, I may have been more reluctant."

"As a man in your position should always be. It is not a trivial affair."

"Matters of state never are. I am sure your countrymen are the same as ours, not appreciating the connections we foster personally for the wellbeing of all."

"I agree completely but let us not speak of that. I have spent many hours in your daughter's company, and find her a wonderful, charming, woman. Were you a lowly woodsman, I would feel the same."

The older man grinned at the polite untruth, but nevertheless relaxed in this predictable, astute, exchange. He enjoyed men of renown who conversed intelligently. As both a political ally and potential son in law, he was comfortable with this rising star of the region.

"And, one must think of the future. None of us will last forever," added the Mayor, the assassination attempt never forgotten.

"Children are a blessing from the gods," his host replied. "I look forward to sitting in the fire's corner with my grandson."

"We both look forward to cementing our heritage together," the Mayor came back, as they raised and clinked their wine goblets together.

"I understand you have a wedding date in mind," enquired the Phoenician.

"One that fits an empty slot in your busy calendar, my lord."

The Phoenician could not help chuckling again at the thorough planning of this meeting. And, as if arranged for this moment, she moved confidently into the room. Her entrance was graceful, expressing purpose and delight.

Both men beamed and rose, still holding their goblets.

"Father, don't tell me you've been boasting to our guest about Phoenicia's dry reds," she said mischievously, holding him gently on the arm, while kissing his cheek.

They both laughed, the parent enchanted as always, and the Mayor enjoying her self-assurance.

"Oh no my dear, we haven't had time for that yet. But it was most certainly next in line."

Eyes twinkling, she then engaged the Mayor. "My lord, I confess I managed to sneak one of your delicious cheeses when your man wasn't looking. They are quite tasty, and I was hoping another case would find its way to our monthly ladies meeting." Her teasing eyes met his, and she briefly touched his arm now.

He met the glance of the older man, before they laughed a second time.

"Make that two cases, my lord. Your daughter's timing is impeccable."

"Ah, she has a sixth sense for these things you know, let me give you some advice for when she takes you to the markets in Tyre . . ."

Realizing what he had let slip, but also that she already knew, he joined in their mirth at his disclosure.

"The loose tongue of an old man has betrayed me, alas." He took his daughter's hand, almost formally, and gazing into her eyes with a father's love and respect, said, "yes, with my blessing."

Her eyebrows lifted and the Mayor's hand rose to meet hers as she stepped towards him. With eyes glistening, she waited graciously as the men toasted each other.

The wife of Manoah

Exactly one week later, to the hour almost, the wife of Manoah found herself out the front of the house again on her own. Weeding. Discussions with her husband had gone on every night on the same topic, although over the last few evenings, they had shortened. She had managed to get him into bed relatively early, being determined not to miss a single night in the month if she could help it. If an angel promised a baby, she was going to keep up her side of the deal.

Then, without sound, or warning, yet without surprise, he was there again. He didn't speak however. He simply gazed at her, the piercing warmth of his eyes seeming to share some future pain of hers. But she knew why he was there. She hurried back inside the house, breathlessly telling Manoah.

"What?" he shouted, almost dropping the cup he was drinking from.

They both ran out again, and the visitor was still there. Waiting. Manoah stopped, not knowing what to say. Embarrassing seconds passed while it became obvious he had merely wanted to see the angel. Quickly he gathered himself together.

"Are you the one who talked to my wife?" he enquired, immediately cursing inwardly for such a self-evident query.

"I am," said the one in front of him.

Struggling for words, Manoah managed another question. "When your words are fulfilled, what is to be the rule for the boy's life and work?"

His wife nearly scolded Manoah for simply asking what she had told him twenty times already, but as she started to open her mouth, she caught the visitor's eye.

His compassion silenced her.

In that single glance, she sensed he knew both her nature and her husband's. That their relationship was one of his impetuosity and her practicality, and it didn't matter. Didn't matter at all her life partner was asking questions which had already been answered. Didn't matter at all the two of them were so different.

"Your wife must do all I have told her. She must not eat anything that comes from the grapevine, nor drink any wine or other fermented drink nor eat anything unclean. She must do everything I have commanded her."

Manoah kept his eyes on the visitor, knowing what his wife was thinking. Idiot, he told himself. Finally, he remembered his manners.

"We would like you to stay until we prepare a young goat for you."

However, the visitor replied, "even though you detain me, I will not eat any of your food. But if you prepare a burnt offering, offer it to the Lord."

Manoah had not yet moved to prepare the meat. He was mesmerized.

"What is your name, so that we may honor you when your word comes true?" he eventually asked.

There was a pause of some seconds. They both felt the visitor knew what he would reply, and yet hesitated to give the impression he was thinking how to communicate something significant.

At last it came out.

"Why do you ask my name? It is beyond understanding."

Beyond understanding.

The rural pair looked at each other on their small plot of land. Each with their private thoughts of what this might mean.

They went back to the house to fetch the young goat. While they wordlessly killed it and dressed the meat, they peeked outside from time to time. The visitor had walked over to their wooded copse, and sat down, back against a shady tree. They worked on, gathering up some dried grain to cook with the meat. In silence.

When all was ready, Manoah scooped up the board on which the meat lay and walked out. Stacking up the wood for the fire, he worked quickly. His wife came out with the grain on a platter, and in her left hand, a branch off the fire inside. The dry wood caught. They stood back from the growing blaze.

The visitor stood and began walking over to them. As he moved across the intervening ten yard distance the flame seemed to grow larger, the closer he got. But they were not fully aware of this until he was only two or three paces from the fire.

To their horror, they saw he was not stopping. He was going to step into the blaze. But this only struck them one brief second before he got there, so they did not have time to react. When he reached the fire, the scene changed utterly.

He walked into the flame and ascended with it, de-materializing as he went. By the time he had gone up ten feet, the visitor had disappeared. The entire process from stepping into the blaze to his vanishing took three seconds.

It was so vivid and shocking the couple fell over. They were not aware of being pushed but they found themselves face down. Instantly, Manoah jumped up.

He was ashen. "We are doomed to die! We have seen God!"

Cautiously, his wife got to her feet, taking her time, smoothing her dress. She stared up in the air, following the smoke's trail. Eventually she said to him, "if the Lord had meant to kill us, he would not have accepted a burnt offering and grain offering from our hands, nor shown us all these things or now told us this."

Idiot, he told himself again.

The metropolitan birth

Her shrieks of pain had grown louder but began tapering off. Now they ceased completely.

The Mayor glanced at the doctor. He was smiling.

"Relax. It's always like this."

Just then the cry of a baby echoed forth from the adjoining room.

"See," confirmed the medical man.

But there were no other noises, no congratulating of the mother, no pleasurable murmurings, as one would expect when they placed the infant in her arms.

The doctor sensed this too, and also that the Mayor had. In the same moment, the midwife came to the door and beckoned him.

He stood quickly, but still calmly. "Wait here, I'll go see."

Quiet voices muttered, words masked by the wailing of the newborn.

He has good lungs, the Mayor surmised. Or she.

The medic was ominously long in the room, so he set his mind to other matters. Eventually the doctor emerged, not in a hurry, not issuing orders, not calling for action. And the Mayor knew it was bad news.

"I am so sorry," he said, sitting beside the Mayor, with genuine remorse. He had known this family for decades.

It was not an uncommon thing in these times, the Mayor knew that, but it was still a shock when it was so personal. Presently without speaking, he enquired silently with his eyes. The baby was still crying in the background, but less now, as though someone was comforting it.

"Loss of blood. The child was big. It caused a tear," the doctor answered straightly.

"It?" He could not help himself, even faced with this news.

"He."

"The boy is fine," the medic added, indicating with his hand back towards the diminishing noise. "Very sound in fact."

The Mayor wasn't sure how to act. His new wife dead, and his son, his only child, alive and eager for life.

Yes, I know it was a political marriage. Although I thought I loved her. But I never said.

His mind gravitated to national affairs, to how he would explain to the old Phoenician ruler, and whether it would affect their growing links. And he cursed himself as he did, that he would think about that now, when he should be mourning. But he knew himself. It is the way of strong men.

"May I see the lad?"

"Yes, indeed."

He held him. In his arms, gazing into his yet sightless eyes, bonding with him, feeling the future with all its potential. The child seemed quick witted, even there at birth.

A sheet covered her, a shape now, still, on the bed.

The blood. The women were mopping up the redness, but there was so much. It mingled with the aroma of the cleaning.

Passions of life and death overcame him as he held the one and gazed at the other. The women went for more water, and the baby fell silent. Plans and ideas and strategies vanished in the quiet.

Is she merely a casualty?

Get a grip on yourself.

He told the midwife to fetch Asaph from outside, and went back to the waiting room, trying to leave behind what could not be undone, to return to the world. The real world, he affirmed to himself.

Asaph came running, and his eyes lit up when he saw the Mayor standing, holding the child, wrapped in blue.

"A boy?" He could not help himself, for he knew the man's desires.

The father laughed, then fell silent.

Asaph caught it, divining trauma, but remained quiet.

The Mayor spoke. "She died delivering him."

Asaph fell back a step, his face grey. After a few seconds he uttered, "my lord, my sorrow is great, as must be yours."

From anyone else it would have sounded like a prepared eulogy, but not from this man with the lilting tongue.

"We must move ahead," the Mayor uttered simply, meaning exactly what he said. We have succession, he told himself, that is the bottom line. "I want the best, the utmost for this child. This is a new beginning for us all."

He felt his voice start to come back, his commanding self returning, the emotive room receding. "You, my protector, will have a part to play. I have long thought about this. You will train this boy in the physical arts. You will ensure he is as good as he can be. The best there is. Our nation will need such a one to lead them into the future."

The escaped galley slave fell to one knee, even though the Mayor didn't request that sort of thing. But it was mostly to cover a rising tear, an emotion that caught him by surprise, the nearest thing to being appreciated since his escape at sea.

The rustic birth

In the small house looking out on the copse of trees up the path from the Israelite village of Zorah, another birthing took place. This baby seemed to force his way to get to grips with the world. It had been like that all through the pregnancy. The unborn child had kicked and rolled around inside his mother, awakening her repeatedly at night. Even though it was her first child, she knew from rural gossip that babes did not normally strive in the womb like this one.

So out he came, bawling in defiance. When they cleaned off the after-birth, and washed him down, they marveled at his physique. It was not that he was chubby and fat. He just looked powerful.

Manoah picked him up and cuddled him for a while before returning him to his mother. Unexpectedly, the sun broke through the clouds, illuminating the interior of their house through the open door.

"Samson," she murmured.

"Do you think so?" Manoah inquired, squinting in the brighter lit room, sensing the moment. "Yes, the sun. Samson."

"The power of the sun," she said.

The rustic child

On the way down to Zorah, the wife of Manoah had trouble keeping her son close to her. Market day drew in stall displays, hawkers, farming families, and the occasional musician. The six year old scampered ahead, rounding a corner in the path, and there they were. Half a dozen nine year old boys, trying to grow up fast. They swiveled at the sound of Samson's running feet, and their precocious leader started jeering immediately.

"Long hair, long hair, brown bear, brown bear!"

The youngster heard the taunt, and halted. As he hesitated, the other boys joined the cat call. Without a word Samson ran at them. The move startled the band, who were expecting him to flee. Uncertainty held them as the gap closed.

He simply ran into the lead jeerer, knocking him over. Even as he struck him to the ground, the young assailant wheeled and grabbed another lad by the arm. He swung him around, leaning back as he circled, the nine year old shrieking with fright. Suddenly he was freed in mid circle, cartwheeling into another two boys, the impetus tumbling all three into a thorn bush.

"Samson! Samson! Stop it!" called his mother as she appeared around the bend, seeing everything in a glance, and his now turning on the remaining pair who were still rooted to their spots in astonishment.

He drew up at her command. The older boys scrambled out of the bushes and scuttled down the path, fighting back tears of shame.

The wife of Manoah rushed up, eyes blazing in a mixture of reproof, surprise and pride. "What do you think you were doing?"

He stood silent for a while. "They called me names."

She softened, as her nature was to listen, and understand quickly. She stooped to his level. "I know they did. And sometimes people will do that to us. But we must learn to ignore smart words."

She paused. "My mother once taught me a little poem," she said.

"What is a poem?"

Gazing into his eyes, she explained, "it's a saying to remember when things aren't going right. Listen to my mother's one."

"Out of a fool comes words of heat,
  But out of the strong comes only sweet."

He stood there stolidly, eyes wide, trying to take it in.

She felt the surge of affection and hugged him and laughed.

A week later, Samson scurried into the family home holding a live wildcat by the scruff of its neck.

"You can't bring that in here!" Manoah cried.

His wife braced herself, her years filled with these outbursts. As the bewildered boy stared blankly at him, she intervened.

"How did you catch it, Samson?" she inquired.

"Chased it up a tree."

"Chased it up a tree?!" Manoah again, unable to hold back his amazement.

She laid a hand on the boy's arm, bending down. "These creatures like to live in the wild, Samson. They prefer the forest and the woods. We might have to let him go."

As she stood upright, she added, "of course if he wants to stay after you put him down, then your wildcat friend is more than welcome. Let's set him free and see what he does."

Unsure for a moment, Samson held the dangling creature before dropping it to the floor. The cat hit the ground running and shot out of the house. Manoah drew his breath in. How could a six year old catch such an animal?

Manoah's wife walked out to the fields to ponder without interruption. He had not inherited his father's impulsive tongue. Rather his impetuosity came out in his actions. She wondered how such an adventurous, silent type, would lead a nation.

However, she was grateful the angel had delivered more than he promised. Two other boys had followed Samson. Getting three seemed proof it was all divine. A good God would give more than he stated.

In turn, she should do more than the angel asked. She must see to his training as best she could. Considering what was available, she laughed to herself. Why on earth would an angel pick an impoverished farming couple? Without even asking, she knew their only option occurred once a week, around early evening, in a village some distance from Zorah. Old Lamech told the historical tales of Israel to the youngsters.

The storyteller

On the appointed evening, together with Samson, she trudged for a couple of hours through the gathering dusk, and joined the small band around the fire outside the elder's home.

As they arrived, a woman called out in delight. Her son flinched when he saw Samson, his psyche still sore after his tumble into the thorn bush. Engrossed in their reacquainting after some time apart, neither mother noticed the older child poke his tongue out at the six year old. Samson glanced vaguely at him.

When they were all seated, Lamech threw another log on the fire, and sat on his outdoor chair. "Tonight, I am going to tell you the story of Gideon. He lived a long time ago. But he listened to God. And Gideon saved Israel."

Three mothers silenced the pair still chattering, the thorn bush lad, and a friend from his own village. Their eyes flashed at Samson.

Lamech hardly noticed, as he was underway. "Our story starts after Israel had been overrun by another nation. The Arabs. They lived in Midian. Midian had four kings, Oreb, Zeeb, Zebah and Zalmunna. Every year they traveled to Israel to steal our crops."

His long arm unfolded and pointed away. "Do you know where Midian is? Far to the east of here. Which means the Arabs had a long way to come. They managed because they rode camels. Some say the Arabs invented camels, but I don't think so. However, they were the first to create a camel army. They could go anywhere. And unfortunately for our forebears, they came here. Thousands of them. Over the Jordan river and into Israel."

Samson's mother made a note to explain the number thousand to her son.

"They pitched their tents on the flatlands, and held huge feasts. And they would race around the countryside stealing anything they could lay their hands on, and killing anyone who got in their way. Now, after a few months they got bored, and returned home. But by then, they had eaten or destroyed most of Israel's food.

"Our ancestors had little to eat after they left. Many starved. But others left the flatlands and went to live in the hills. Camels don't like climbing, so it was safer up there. However, there was a problem. It's harder growing food in the hills.

"Life was terrible, but slowly they understood what had happened. Many years before, our fathers worshipped the Lord our God faithfully. But they had grown tired of it. Soon after they stopped worshipping God, the Arabs invaded. People realized this, and they called on God to forgive them. They asked God to stop the Arabs stealing everything they owned."

He straightened up, as if to emphasize his next point.

"About this time, Gideon and his family were trying to hide food from the Arabs. They had learned some farming tricks. Gideon was threshing his grain in the winepress so he would not be found."

Lamech halted suddenly, wondering whether he needed to explain the difference between winepresses and threshing floors, even to these rural children.

The teacher in him decided. "Who has been to a threshing floor? I'm sure some of you have," he asked, raising his own hand.

The mothers jostled their uncertain offspring. Samson lifted his hand, along with five others. Thorn bush nudged his mate, and they both sniggered with intent at their nemesis. Samson's mother caught the interchange, finally recalling the boy whom she had not noticed in the joy of her friendship renewal, her mind now alive about repercussions with his mother.

"I thought so," exclaimed the old man. "Vineyard owners keep their winepress clean, because the grapes are all put into it when they are ripe. The grape growers wash their feet, and tread all over the grapes. All the juice comes out. And the juice is clean, because the winepress is clean. Imagine threshing grain in the winepress. You'd have dust and straw everywhere. It would be a real mess.

"So, Gideon probably thought, I'll thresh grain in the winepress because that is the last place thieves will look. Robbers normally expect the winepress to be all tidy and clean, so they won't seek grain there."

He sat up proudly at his reasoning, but the children gazed at him uncomprehendingly. Two of the mothers felt for the old man and whispered admiring comments down to their offspring.

Somewhat mollified, he got back onto the tale. "There he was, down in the winepress, wondering why life was so hard. Suddenly, without warning, an angel appeared to him. Now this hadn't happened for a long time. So long in fact, I don't think Gideon even thought he was an angel."

It caught her by surprise, and the wife of Manoah visibly shifted. Her movement caught the attention of the two nine year old boys—and Lamech. His gaze flickered to her, the boys, and her son. Oblivious to everything, Samson sat open mouthed, waiting for the story to continue.

Lamech started up again. "Gideon looked up, and there was the angel sitting under the oak tree."

This is too much, Samson's mother thought.

"The angel said, 'the Lord is with you, mighty warrior.'"

Lamech paused for effect. "Now if an angel appeared to you or me, what might we say?"

You're kidding.

"I'm not sure what I would say," confessed the old storyteller, "but I know what Gideon did. He started questioning the angel."

She stifled a giggle. Oh, would that Manoah was here.

Lamech didn't falter. "Gideon straightaway asked the angel, 'But sir, if the Lord is with us, why has all this happened to us? Where are all his wonders that our fathers told us about when they said, 'Did not the Lord bring us up out of Egypt?' But now the Lord has abandoned us and put us into the hand of Midian.'

"You can tell he had been thinking. And he asked a good question. However, God does not always answer in the way we expect."

You can say that again, the wife of Manoah told herself.

"The angel just ignored his questions and complaints," continued Lamech. "Instead he said, 'Go in the strength you have and save Israel out of Midian's hand. Am I not sending you?'"

Lamech peered up, imitating the hero talking up from the winepress to the angel. "He asked him, 'but Lord, how can I save Israel? My clan is the weakest in Manasseh, and I am the least in my family.' Down came the reply, 'I will be with you, and you will strike down all the Midianites together.'"

His face took on a quizzical look. "Now at this point I imagine Gideon stood there pondering. And I also think the angel waited silently too. Angels are not in the habit of repeating instructions needlessly."

The wife of Manoah burst out in a brief laugh. Lamech glared at her, curiosity piqued now, but annoyed by her interruption. Other mothers shuffled uneasily as thorn bush and friend silently mimicked her. Feeling all eyes on her, Samson's mother rapidly composed herself.

The story resumed. "Gideon finally replied, 'If now I have found favor in your eyes, give me a sign that it is really you talking to me. Please do not go away until I come back and bring my offering and set it before you.'

"He wanted proof, you see. He wanted to believe Israel could rid itself of the Arab menace, but he wasn't sure he personally could do it. And he wasn't completely sure this was actually a message from God. But the Lord is patient with us, and the angel said, 'I will wait until you return.'

"Off scurried Gideon to get a young goat, one of the few the Arabs had not yet stolen, and he killed it to prepare a meal for the visitor out there under the oak. He also made some bread without yeast, just like your mothers do sometimes.

"Making bread without yeast is an important symbol to us in Israel. It's quicker making bread that way, even if the bread doesn't rise. It was first baked this way long ago when Moses brought Israel out of Egypt. Gideon knew about this story too. So maybe he thought he'd better prepare the bread quickly because something urgent was about to happen.

"He brought everything out and offered it to him under the oak. The angel said, 'Take the meat and the unleavened bread, place them on this rock, and pour out the broth.' Then the angel did something amazing. He touched the meat and the bread with the tip of his staff. Immediately fire flared up out of the rock, and burnt up the meal. And in the middle of all this the angel disappeared. Completely out of sight. If Gideon needed proof, there it was, right in front of him. But he was shocked and feared he might die. After all, Moses taught our ancestors nobody could see God and live.

"However, the Lord said to him, 'Peace! Do not be afraid. You are not going to die.' Which was logical really. An angel would not have told Gideon all these things, only to kill him."

At least our angel didn't need to tell us that, the wife of Manoah mused. Perhaps angels learn too. Or they appear to women nowadays.

Unselfconsciously she smiled broadly, and again the old man caught it, wary now. She too, saw his expression, and warned herself about her own God given task, and secrets she must keep. Her mind wandered briefly at this personal reminder, before glancing over at the nine year olds making quiet asides to each other. She flicked back to Samson. He had not moved.

Why, he hasn't noticed anything, she perceived. He doesn't even re-member those boys. Doesn't feel anything about that fight at the thorn bush. He brings wildcats into the house as though that is normal behavior. He drinks in battle stories.

Lamech's commanding voice cut across her thoughts. "That very same night the Lord said to Gideon, 'Take the second bull from your father's herd, the one seven years old. Tear down your father's altar to Baal and cut down the Asherah pole beside it. Then build a proper kind of altar to the Lord your God on the top of this height. Using the wood of the Asherah pole you cut down, offer the second bull as a burnt offering.'

"Now this was a dangerous thing to do. Not so much against the Arabs, but against the local Israelites who still worshipped those gods.

"Anyway, Gideon did it all right. But he did it at night. Next morning when the villagers woke up, they discovered their Baal idol was destroyed. Everyone asked around, and because it was a small village, they soon found out it was Gideon.

"Down tramped the men to his house. They wanted to put him to death. But Gideon's father stood at the door to protect his son. He said if Baal wanted to slay Gideon, why did he need the help of these men? Let Baal do it himself. And Gideon survived.

"The time drew near for the Arabs to arrive. Once again, great numbers came, and camped down on the flatlands. About the same time however, word went through Israel about Gideon, and how the angel had appeared to him. When Gideon called for helpers to fight the Arabs, he got a lot of support. Many men came.

"But Gideon was a worrier. He still feared the visit by the angel was all in his imagination. Again, he asked God for some proof. 'If you will save Israel by my hand as you have promised—look, I will place a wool fleece on the threshing floor. If there is dew only on the fleece and all the ground is dry, I will know you will save Israel by my hand, as you said.'

"When Gideon woke up the next morning, the fleece was wringing wet and the ground was dry. He squeezed out a whole bowlful of water. But he still wasn't completely convinced. He asked God for a second test. 'Do not be angry with me. Let me make just one more request. Allow me one more test with the fleece. This time make the fleece dry and the ground covered with dew.'

"Now I am sure you can guess what happened. When Gideon arose at dawn, the ground was heavy with dew, but the fleece was bone dry."

Triumphantly, Lamech gazed around the circle of faces lit by the flickering fire, confident the group were absorbed in his tale.

"Gideon stopped asking for proof after that. But I can understand why he did have those questions. After all, Israel didn't have an army. God was asking a lot of Gideon, and Gideon had no idea how he would defeat the foe.

"Gideon went and camped near the Arab forces. By this time thirty two thousand men had joined him. At this point, another message arrived from the Lord. God said, 'you have too many men for me to deliver Midian into their hands. In order that Israel may not boast against me that her own strength has saved her, announce now to the people, `Anyone who trembles with fear may turn back and leave Mount Gilead." When Gideon did this, twenty two thousand of his men packed up their tents and left."

Enchanted with the fire and the cadence of his words, the children listened intently.

"That left ten thousand. And God spoke to him again. He said 'there are still too many men. Take them down to the water, and I will sift them for you there. If I say, `This one shall go with you,' he shall go; but if I say, `This one shall not go with you,' he shall not go.' Gideon led them all down to the river's edge to drink. The Lord told him, 'separate those who lap the water with their tongues like a dog from those who kneel down to drink.'

"Now this might seem a curious way to separate out the people from one another. But one thing was for sure. Only three hundred men lapped the water from their hands. Most kneeled down to drink. God told Gideon to send the rest home. Perhaps God chose those three hundred because they were vigilant, and didn't kneel."

He mimicked scooping up water and lapping it while peering around, and the children shrieked with laughter. Samson's mother waved across at the parent of thorn bush, receiving a friendly grin back. Having failed to arouse Samson during the evening, the two boys had lost interest, and were laughing with the others at the old man.

Lamech plunged on. "Gideon had only three hundred men left to defeat those thousands of Arabs. He was scared by this stage. But he had come too far to turn back. That very night the Lord gave him an interesting instruction. He told Gideon, 'get up, go down against the camp, because I am going to give it into your hands. If you are afraid to attack, go down to the camp with your servant Purah and listen to what they are saying. Afterward, you will be encouraged to attack the camp.'

"No sooner was he down there, when he heard one of the Arabs talking. 'I had a dream,' he told his friend. 'A round loaf of barley bread came tumbling into the Midianite camp. It struck the tent with such force that the tent overturned and collapsed.'

"The Arab's friend responded, 'this can be nothing other than the sword of Gideon son of Joash, the Israelite. God has given the Midianites and the whole camp into his hands.'"

Lamech's hands swept out towards the children, emphasizing his point. "Can you imagine that? The Arabs themselves were expecting defeat!

"Gideon raced back up the mountain and called his three hundred men. 'Get up! The Lord has given the Midianite camp into your hands.' He explained what each man should do. Everyone had to carry a trumpet and an empty pot with a lighted fire torch inside, and head down to the Arab camp.

"When they were in position, at midnight, they all broke their pots, which suddenly exposed the hidden firebrands. Holding the torches up, they blew their trumpets with their other hand as loud as they could. And in between, they shouted 'a sword for the Lord and for Gideon!'

"Out streamed the Arabs in a terrible fright. They ran into each other in the darkness, and into their camels. Now a camel is not a friendly animal, and I suspect the worst thing you can do is run into one at night. It would probably kick you. The Arabs got into such a fluster they even pulled out their swords and attacked each other.

"Gideon urged his small army onto them, and they fled back to Midian. It was a great victory for Israel, and the Arabs were driven away. Israel was free from oppression once more. The Lord had saved the tribes with only three hundred men. Gideon was a true hero, but he only won because he listened to God."

Lamech wound down. "And I can see some of you are tired, and it is probably way past your bedtime. I think it is time we all went home."

As the women gathered up their children, Samson's mother reassured her old acquaintance they must get together soon, pointedly engaging her son in a friendly manner. The old man remained in his chair, noticing how powerful the lad with the intriguing mother was.

She led her boy out of the village and back over the gentle hills in the coolness of the clear, moonlit, night.

"Did you enjoy that story?" she ventured presently.

They walked on a way before Samson asked, "are there other people we can fight like Gideon did, mother?"

The metropolitan boy

The son of the Mayor of Gaza was late for his lesson, and he knew it. Running along the corridors of his father's huge house, he calculated his short cut. Taking a left turn, he swung into a side room. Seeing the shutters were drawn wide he sprang towards the open window, grasping the bottom frame with both hands. His legs came up neatly behind him, folding in as he used his weight to handspring through. Arcing through the air, he released his grip, hitting the ground and flashing past the astonished gardener.

Pulling himself up to a halt in front of a door, he casually opened it and walked in. "Good morning sir," he said politely to his Greek teacher of history. The white haired old man, notorious for reprimanding the slightest tardiness of his bright young pupil, replied, "good morning. Achish. How are you this morning?"

"Very good, thank you sir. And how are you also?"

"I am fine, thank you. Now, do you remember what we studied last week?"

"We learned about iron sir, and I liked that."

At that moment, the door opened a second time, and the Mayor of Gaza strode in. Smiling widely at this endearing, not infrequent habit of the Mayor's, the elderly teacher beckoned him in. "Please, come in, sit down, my lord."

"May I? I know you are studying recent iron age technology, and it has always fascinated me."

"Our forebears made iron swords, father," the young boy said animatedly, before his teacher had a chance to respond. "Did you know other nations can't make swords like we can?"

The Mayor's eyes lifted, connecting with the old man before returning to the lad.

"Why don't you tell your father more, Achish?" the tutor requested proudly.

"Certainly, thank you sir. Father, Philistia brought the science of smelting iron from across the sea. Iron is much stronger than brass, so this is a good skill for Philistia to have."

"Oh, why is that?" inquired his parent.

"You see father, when armies fight each other, the side with iron swords is better because an iron sword can break a brass one. Father, I think Philistia should be careful not to let other nations learn how to make iron swords. Why should we teach their army how to beat ours?"

He went on. "I had an idea too father. Would you like to know what I thought of?"

"What is that, Achish?" queried the Mayor, winking surreptitiously at the Greek master.

"I think we could make iron ploughs for farmers. They would be stronger than wooden ones. Farmers would be able to plough more ground."

"Good thought, Achish. Did you talk about this last week too?"

"Actually, no. I thought about it myself."

"Should we teach other nations how to make iron ploughs?"

The six year old pondered this for a moment. "No. But we could make ploughs and sell them. Philistia could earn money doing that."

The Mayor could not suppress himself. "Achish, that is a very good idea. I should have thought of it myself."

He rose in unison with the beaming tutor. "I had better leave before I get shown up any further. And I believe I might run your idea past some merchants I know, young man."

The friend maker

"Achish!"

"Hey, Jethro!"

"What are you eating?"

"Melon, from our garden. I love melon. Here, have some."

The boy peered past Achish, then pulled him aside.

"Here comes Jashup. I don't want to play with him, let's hide."

Half looking back, a bewildered Achish followed him into the narrow alley, his young brow furrowing. They scurried into a bazaar selling vegetables, and ducked under a table when the merchant wasn't looking, squatting on the ground behind the draped cover.

"Jethro."

"What," his little companion squelched between mouthfuls of melon.

"Why don't you like Jashup?"

"Just don't."

They munched on as Achish thought. "Jashup has a cool brother," he added.

More melon eating.

One more try. "I went to his place, and his brother had a bow and arrows. Sharp ones."

Still more melon eating.

"Let's go now! Let's go and look at the arrows! Jashup knows where he hides them!"

He was out from under the table before Jethro could say anything. Quickly leaning back under the cloth, he beckoned urgently. "Come on, come on, that fat man is coming!"

Shooting out of the alley, they almost collided with the passing Jashup, who drew back upon seeing Jethro.

"Hello, Jashup!" Achish shouted gleefully. "Jethro and I want to see your brother's arrows! They were neat!"

The eyes of both boys flicked back and forth from each other to the exuberant Achish.

"Didn't you, Jethro?!" Achish shrilled. His small voice rose above the hubbub of the noisy Gazan street. "Jethro thinks your brother is cool!" he exclaimed, whirling as he spoke.

"He does?" Jashup couldn't help letting the words escape.

"Come on, let's go!" their young leader said, pulling at their arms.

Jethro peered sheepishly across at Jashup. Both flicked a glance at the vibrant son of the Mayor of Gaza, and back to each other one more time. Jethro broke the impasse, smiling almost involuntarily.

Jashup laughed jubilantly. "Race you there, Jethro!"

Three little figures sprinted away.

The five mayors

The Mayor of Ashdod had already started his story. "Anyway, I am down at the ironmongers checking on this sword, when an Israelite walks in. He's sweating like a tavern keeper on tax collection day, breathing heavily, and audibly cursing. It's an entertaining diversion, so we all fall silent.

"He says, 'hell of a way to come with a plough just to get it sharpened.' We look at each other, then Jobaal, the ironmonger. He's the friendliest guy in the world, you couldn't upset him if you let a snake loose in his factory. He grins, 'let's go see your implement, my friend.'

"We troop outside, and there is this hired bullock wagon, I don't know what the fees are from Israel, probably five shekels or more. On it is the plough. Not just the iron tip. The whole plough, arms, handles, the works, all still in one piece."

The rest of the mayors were drawn in, especially Ekron, who loved tales of incompetence. An interesting contradiction, it occurred to the Mayor of Gaza.

"Clown!" Edred from Ekron chortled.

Still, it's intriguing how the others like him, the senior man mused.

Ashdod continued. "Jobaal peers at it, glances back at me while suppressing his smirk, and turns to the chap again. 'I was just wondering,' he says in his chummy tone, 'that next time you might think about taking the iron blade off, and bringing only that across.'

"This Israelite stops in his tracks. I swear you could see what little there was in his brain move. At last he says, 'actually, that's not the point. The thing is, you guys have a captive market with this iron trade. We have to come all the way over the border to buy these ploughs, at great expense. You don't know how tough farming is, all the profit goes out the gate.'

"Jobaal is good, he really is. You need to come across and hear him one day. He pauses a little, as though he is listening to this oaf, then he says, 'I understand how you feel.' He points back at the top of the door of his establishment. In the wall above it are four iron nails. It's his logo, everyone in Ashdod knows that. It's a play on words. For iron. But this dimwit won't know that. He says to him, 'iron working is dangerous. We would love to expand into Israel, but there are safety considerations we have to take into account.'

"'You see those four nails?' he tells the guy. 'Four hard working men died last month making ploughs. The furnace blew up.'

"By then, the rest of us are barely holding ourselves together, but we manage to look stern. The Israelite turns ashen. 'Are you serious?' he lets out. Jobaal nods back without comment.

"Then the visitor regains some bluster, and has one more go. 'Anyway, that's not the point. You could station an outlet in Israel where we could get the ploughs sharpened.'

"Jobaal doesn't hesitate. Not for a second. He says to him again, 'I understand how you feel. But there is no sea air further inland. You can only sharpen ploughs near the ocean. You know Philistia descended from the Sea Peoples. Our ancestors discovered this feature about iron generations ago.'"

Laughter burst out, but Ashdod wasn't done.

"Jobaal can't resist one more go. His voice drops, he looks around, steps closer to the guy, and says, confidentially, 'few people know this, but there are health problems for inland peoples if they stay too long near the sea air. Us Philistines, we've had hundreds of years of it, so we are immune. But you guys, you should only visit occasionally, and not remain long.'

"That said, he steps back and waits. So help me, this Israelite stands there, stunned for a few seconds, then he asks, 'can you do it this morning?'"

The gathered mayors collapsed, none more so than Ekron.

They're in a good mood now, the Mayor of Gaza felt. Time to start the agenda.

"Developmental strategies! That's a good one!" Edred broke out in glee as he scanned it.

The man from Gaza waited. Then again a funny story fires him up, he realized.

"What does it mean?" continued Ekron.

Perhaps it wasn't a good idea holding the meeting up here after all, the leading Mayor thought, gazing through the open windows, across his city and out to the blue Mediterranean. Incorporating the enticing horizon as a metaphor for far-sighted thinking had seemed a good plan, but he now doubted the Mayor of Ekron would grasp it.

Push on nevertheless.

"Yes, strategies for future development, Edred. That's the topic. We can't just sit still, otherwise the future will pass us by, and hand the baton of success to others."

But Ekron wasn't finished. "Nicely chosen words my good colleague, but out our way the country people have another saying—'if it ain't broke, don't fix it.'"

The Mayor of Gaza laughed genuinely. Not too bad a comeback. "Well spoken, my good friend. You are absolutely correct. However, I am not proposing to change or fix anything. Rather to enhance. I think we can learn how from Israel."

"Israel? Since when they did enhance anything beyond our lifestyles?" Edred was on a roll. "Or provide us with jokes to tell our children?"

"Perfect analogy. We had to enhance our thinking to get them to enhance our lifestyles. Wasn't that so?"

Edred sat back to untangle the logic.

Believing he had fended him off, the man from Gaza began. "To get to the point, we need to recall when Israel was strong. Before our time. During Jephthah's days. How do you think he got them to overthrow the inland kingdoms? Israel was the underdog, with a ragtag army of rural volunteers. Yet they whipped their adversary."

His hands drew maps in the air, widening and narrowing, depicting the varying sizes of the warring armies. Graphically mesmerized, even Edred remained silent.

"How did they do that?" the Mayor of Gaza continued. "Because they had a strong belief in their destiny and their God. An unbelievably strong

belief that made them unbelievably strong. We defeated them by undermin-
ing that belief. That turned them into weaklings, and we marched in and
took over. Sorry," he added with a wry grin. "We were invited in to restore
law and order."

At last some muted chuckles. He got to the point. "Now we in Philistia
don't have such a belief system."

Ekron awoke. "Don't tell me you are getting religion. That you too have
seen the light. You're the last person I would have expected."

The others roared with the light relief.

The visionary knew he had to change tack. "Look, take the example of
our Asherah goddesses. They are cute, attractive money-spinners. Our fore-
fathers brought them from Egypt. The Asherahs fulfill a purpose of course.
Nobody is denying that. They helped us defeat Israel. They also keep our
people satiated with sex. They were designed for the flesh, if I may use that
term."

His cynical take on their own society silenced them. He moved ahead,
exploiting the fresh attention. "However, who among us goes home inspired
to expand their horizons because of the Asherahs?"

That set them thinking.

"Our people need to be motivated. We are now a ruling nation. We
must provide a strong belief system to rouse the masses to greater heights.
We need to sway hearts and minds."

They began nodding in agreement, enjoying phrases like 'ruling nation,' and 'greater heights.'

The Mayor raised his tempo. "We can do this through a new religious
strategy. A new concept of god. If we want to maintain our present position,
we need a deity aligned with economic growth and military expansion."

He was hitting his stride now, hands graphically synchronized. "Such
a being should reward bravery, and honor those who do marvelous things
for Philistia. He would be possessed of immense powers. Victorious exploits
would be attributed to him. He would be inspirational, drawing the best out
of our people."

However, noticing Edred growing agitated once more, he knew it was
time to get a discussion going. "My dear colleague, I think you have another
question, unless my grasp of body language has deserted me."

Ekron burst out, "but this is a complete change of direction! At first
you persuaded us Israel's God did not exist. And your take over strategy
worked. Their God didn't rescue them. It seemed like you were right. Now
you are suggesting we develop a god of our own. It doesn't make sense!"

"Ah, my good friend," the one from Gaza chuckled. "Thank you for
raising this apparent contradiction. But think about it. There is a world of

difference between developing a strategic religion, and personally believing in a god."

He locked eyes with his colleague. "In other words, although no such beings actually exist, inventing some heavenly power is useful for keeping society going. It gives ordinary folk meaning in their daily lives."

Ekron persisted, "but I could never follow a god we invented."

"Oh, yes you could," claimed the man of strategy. "Particularly if your political power depended on it. I can very much imagine all of us falling into line."

At that, he burst out laughing. The others started to snicker with him as the nature of the game dawned on them.

"Yes, for ten thousand, I could get religious," chipped in the Mayor of Ashkelon.

The Mayor of Gaza pointed at him, beaming widely again. "What matters here are the minds of the populace, and what they believe. And what they can be called on to do. That gentlemen, is the major purpose of religion. Let's not fool ourselves. We will have to rely on our people to do greater things in the future. To keep ahead in today's world, you can't relax."

He knew he had said enough for this occasion. So he wound it up. "I have a solution I will unveil in one month's time. The next step."

His hands swept up to the horizon. "Meanwhile, I hope you've enjoyed the view. You can see forever from up here."

Dagon

A month later they stood around the table looking at two models. The first was a statue of a magnificently muscled male in his prime. At least the torso was. The lower part of the body was the tail of a fish.

"Gentlemen, meet Dagon. He is our past and our future. We all know where our ancestors came from. We are peoples of the sea. Our blood lines developed through generations of battling with, and mastering the waters. Even today we fish from it and make a good part of our living from trading across the ocean. Hence Dagon has the tail of a fish."

The Mayor of Gaza pointed to the upper part of the body. "But we are also people of the land now, a powerful nation in our own right. Our agriculture is important, as is our military might. Dagon bears the upper body of a man of strength. His bearded face speaks of far seeing knowledge."

The hands were now flung wider to encompass the future. "You may not know it, but we have borrowed the concept from Babylon. They have experimented much longer with religion than we have. Given our small size and recent history, I believe we can make faster ground if we adopt proven strategies."

Next to Dagon was another model. It was a building with columns and staircases throughout.

"And this is his temple." The Mayor moved over to it. "Dagon will reside in his own sanctuary. One in each of our cities. We will organize inspirational rallies throughout the year. Special priests will be trained in the art of mass persuasion. Dagon will become the central figure of our positive belief system."

The Mayor of Ekron spoke up, unable to contain himself. "This is all very impressive, but do you really think you can tamper with the future?"

The senior mayor stared briefly at him.

Is this man impervious to history?

Be graceful anyway.

"Actually, men continually create the future, Edred. Our forebears did when they arrived from the sea. They established cities and formed a culture. We live here thanks to their vision. Unless we move forward, and provide fresh dreams and goals for our people, they will stagnate. We have started Philistia on a path to greatness. Advancement and change are expected now. We have to move with the times we ourselves have begun."

But knowing the man from Ekron responded to lesser urges, the Mayor of Gaza lifted the top of the model building away. "Take a look inside," he said. "We will use Dagon's temples for public gatherings, for celebrations, even for drama. Can you imagine sitting in here Edred, with your family, fingers curled around a goblet of dry white wine, watching a play? Or listening to music, along with thousands of others?"

It was enough. A smile escaped from Ekron before he was aware. Recovering quickly however, he peered into the model, looking for something to grumble about. "What about these pillars holding this thing up? Not sure that will work."

"We have taken advice from the finest architects in Babylon over this design. Those columns will hold three times the weight of the capacity crowd. God himself could not move them."

State religion

Philistia responded as the Mayor had predicted. Ready for a transition emulating the superpowers, and a success focused worldview, they took to the new religion hook, line, and sinker.

At first, priests were imported from Babylon. They were costly, but got the belief going. These immigrant clerics brought a torrent of stories about

Dagon. People listened avidly to the tales, narrated with passion each week in the city squares. And it wasn't as if any locals were going to travel all the way to Babylon to verify them.

Building a religious training school was early on the agenda, so Philistia could begin educating its own clergy. Drawing on lessons learnt from Egypt and Babylon, a seminary was constructed in Gaza itself.

"Location is important," stated the Mayor. "If you let religious schools grow in the countryside, you lose the influence of the urban polity," he told them.

Seeing their nonplussed expressions, he elaborated, "keep them in town, visit them often, and they will follow the beliefs of the city. Stick them in the country, and you lose contact with them. Besides, who knows what effect scenes of rural tranquility will have on their ideals?"

Statues of Dagon also found their way into the military schools and gymnasiums of Philistia. This was deliberate, as the Mayor wanted connections between the religious and armed sectors. In fact, each battalion had its own priest stationed with it. These devout, bearded young men, eyes often glazed over, were trained to bless the troops each day.

The Mayor also integrated the Asherah figurines into the new cult. He upgraded them from mere baubles and fertility grove statuettes to a new level of temple prostitution. Utilizing sexual desire had never been a sticking point with him. Dagon's ritual services became a mixture of incantations, scantily clad young girls, exultation of youthful strength, and exhortation of the peoples for their future.

Philistia's young needed no encouragement. To have their urges blessed by their rulers was an easy bait to swallow. Even the Mayor of Ekron was forced to admit it was another successful move.

It felt gratifying to be right. To analyse society and the human race correctly. The Mayor of Gaza didn't just believe he was a man of destiny. He knew it.

Security concerns

"Some of their old men tell stories about the history of Israel."

The Foreign Security Chief was submitting his monthly report to the Mayor of Gaza. Alongside the Mayor sat Asaph, and two generals. They glanced at each other but said nothing.

The Chief continued. "For example, near the border, there is a small town where a village elder tells youngsters tales about the battles Israel fought against her enemies in bygone eras. It could be dangerous."

As his eyes flicked around the table, picking up early warning signs, the Mayor realized he had better say something. He stood to gain attention.

"Michach, you are doing a wonderful job. You are our eyes and ears out there. I want you and your men to keep up this great work. Information is one of the greatest assets we have."

With a slight blush, the Chief eased back in his chair. Asaph watched, trying to anticipate the Mayor's direction.

"We have a number of alternatives here gentlemen," their leader declared. "Firstly, we could send a few strong fellows to deliver a message to these story tellers. Imprison one, beat another up, something like that."

His alert eyes moved from man to man. "What effect do you think that might have on them? I mean put yourself in their shoes. If we acted strongly, how might they respond?"

Silence.

"Go on, please, some opinions gentlemen."

"Do we give a damn how they would react?" queried one general.

Asaph ventured, "like it they would not."

"You are both correct," said the Mayor. "Both absolutely on the money. That's why we have a team here. Let me explain."

The team's intrigue was obvious, so he walked behind them around the table, hands framing their thinking as they followed his path. "Point number one. Do we really care for them because they are nice people, and we love them? I mean why should we worry whether they like it or not? We rule Israel for our own reasons, not to increase their happiness.

"Point number two. If we bully these old-timers telling tales to children in the villages, everyone will notice. It will be talked about, and we will look like an oppressive regime. I can hear their version now, 'Soldiers beat up old man over fireside chats.' Feelings will fester, antagonism will rise, and late night discussions will take place.

"To prevent this we will have to station even more militia in Israel. The troops will drain our cash reserves, while being at the same time a visible reminder of their subservient status. Productivity within Israel will drop because they will no longer work willingly. It will become a vicious circle. We will have to raise taxes to cover the extra military costs, but face a decline in revenues.

"This happened once before in the history of our region. Many generations ago, one Jabin, ruler of an inland kingdom, took over Israel. To keep the peace he hired a professional general, Sisera by name.

"Sisera built up a veritable arsenal of firepower. He had nine hundred iron chariots. Now you would think with those at his disposal, he could keep Israel under his thumb. But Sisera's problem was he had to feed and house all the horses that drove those nine hundred chariots, and the army of men that sat in them. To do so, he was compelled to tax the living daylights out of the Israelites. And did they love him for that? No, they did not. It got them complaining to their God. They started to wind up their religious fervor."

He hesitated, knowing he was lecturing on history again. No, continue, they need to understand.

"A woman freed them actually. Name of Deborah. She used to sit under this tree she named after herself. Sound pathetic? It probably was. But one day she sent a message to an Israelite leader called Barak and told him to take on Sisera. He listened to her and decided to have a go, and enticed Sisera into attacking him up a hill. Not a good move with chariots. The Israelite ragtag army came running down on top of them.

"Sisera escaped when he saw his offensive going astray. But he got enticed twice in one day—and again by a female. On the run from Israel, a woman named Jael offered him a place to rest, and when he was asleep, she placed a tent peg through his brain with a mallet."

They winced as the Mayor rendered the incident graphically with his theatrical hands.

"We never want things to get worked up to such a state. Not over old men telling bedtime stories," he concluded, bringing his fingers together, chopping a point home.

"To sum up, I maintain we want the Israelites happy, growing more grain, pumping it through our warehousing system, earning more money for themselves. Which they can spend on holidays down at the coast. And increase our own wealth to boot."

Then came the clincher. "Michach, I have a question for you, and I am sure you can answer it."

All ears pricked up.

"I am sure your people note who else attends these story tales besides children. Who accompanies them there?"

The Chief could not see where he was heading. Guardedly, he replied, "my lord, their mothers go with them. To oversee their return home, one assumes."

"Yes, that is probably correct. To your men's knowledge, do any fathers attend?"

Michach, still not perceiving his intent, slowly responded. "No, my lord, I believe not."

"Exactly. That is what I expected. Not a single father in the economically productive ages between twenty and fifty attends, I would hazard if we knew the exact statistics. Do you know why?"

He hesitated once more, lending the question magnitude before answering it himself. "They are too busy making money. They look forward to getting the kids out of their hair so they can do their bookwork. Do we want to change that?"

Asaph could now feel the swing back to unity emerging. The Mayor gestured at the same moment, palm upraised, fingers gratuitously outspread. "We are fortunate to have a security system such as the Chief has developed over the years. Without his information, we would not have the opportunity to discuss incidents like this and make intelligent decisions. I applaud the Chief's work and think a round of appreciation is due him."

Amidst the hand clapping, Asaph could not but marvel at the man's talents for directing men.

The Greek

The boy had gone with Asaph to the gymnasium, and in the pleasant late afternoon, the Mayor sat conversing with the history teacher, one of his favorite relaxations. "Look," he said, attempting to prove a point, "take that legend about Gideon that the Israelites like to relate. To this day, in fact. It's full of holes."

"Holes? You almost said, 'any intelligent person can see it's full of holes.'"

"I could have, but there was no need in the present company."

They both laughed.

"Seriously though, let's start at the beginning. This Gideon is threshing grain in a winepress, and I understand one of their theories is because he thought the Arabs wouldn't look there. Come on. Those Arabs would be after every drop of drink they could get, and they'd head straight for the winepress.

"But that's a minor point compared to Gideon's tale about the angel. Firstly, he doesn't even think it's an angel, and there I agree with him. Nobody argues with divine beings; it's simply proof they weren't divine beings."

"Perhaps that illustrates how clever the divine beings are," the Greek interjected. "Perhaps they want to hear a man speak his inner thoughts. Therefore, they do not appear as an awe inspiring God, which would hush everyone up. Instead they come looking like ordinary men."

"Fair enough," came the reply. "Good point. But why should you believe him? If an angel disguises himself as a man, then you think he is a man. Not sent from God, but merely the next tribe over. What authority does he have?

"Anyway, let me continue while I have my train of thought, and before these goblets of dry red confuse us."

They both chuckled, replenished their receptacles, and sat back.

The Mayor went on. "The whole episode can be explained by two factors; firstly the weirdness of everything Gideon did, and secondly the Midianite penchant for magic."

"Are you suggesting their minds are inferior?" the old Greek prodded. "To yours and mine?"

The Mayor peeked around, mimicking a check of the room for inappropriate listeners. They both roared, and he exclaimed, "Right here and now, you are absolutely correct. This vintage gives us a definite advantage."

"Which is a good metaphor to employ. Israel is a natural grapevine. Any news about angels pours out like an upturned vat. And Gideon's tricks raised plenty to talk about. His angel disappearing into the sky. The frolics with the fleece."

He jolted forward, nearly spilling his wine. "Yes, the wet fleece. A herdsman was telling me once, he had heard about a desert tribe laying fleeces out on dry, cold evenings. Some property of wool attracts moisture from the night air. In the morning you have dry ground, and a dripping fleece."

"A herdsman you say? A superstitious herdsman tells you some gossip? Indeed, that's obvious proof."

"Now, now. I'll try it myself one day. You wait. There's more. These rumors don't only spook the Arabs, they also impress the Israelites themselves. Thirty two thousand arrive. Proof to the Midianites that Gideon is a magic man. It's all a self-fulfilling prophecy.

"Almost ludicrously, after sending most of them home, he picks three hundred who lap water like dogs. It's right there in their literature. Which reminds me. This wine is clearly stimulating my thinking. If I was their historian, I would have cleaned up the story. No need to include trivia like that. They should write their heroes up like heroes. Not flawed human beings. But I digress.

"By this stage, all the buzz about great numbers of people swarming through the hills has the Arabs on edge. They start spreading their own anecdotes and dreams, one of which Gideon himself heard. At this point, it all came together for the man. He is down in their camp, listening to their wild imaginations, when he realizes all his own weirdness has in turn affected them.

"And that, I maintain, is his genius. He seizes the moment and performs his midnight act with the hidden torches. And the wretched trumpets. Three hundred Israelite trumpet players would certainly enrage a camel herd, let alone terrify a Midianite throng."

The Greek chimed in. "No doubt you have a theory worth investigating here, but before discrediting the deities too much, let's look at it from their viewpoint. However you may paint the picture, all this weirdness, as you put it, did rile their enemy. It sounds like a clever, meticulously thought out strategy to me. Too clever for a mere mortal to think up."

"I felt you might come back like that. Because what you are saying is, this God is actually very smart. He, or it, gets entangled deep into the foibles of human nature. As an argument, I can follow that. But only to a point."

His eyes gleamed, and his companion knew he was talking from the heart now. "And that point is, none of it can be proved. We are now in the realm of what we choose to believe. And that is the mystery of these people. They demonstrate the power of deep choice. And yes, it appears as if miracles happen. But they turn out to be explicable miracles, such as the Arabs getting spooked by rumors of magic in the hills.

"Having said all that, they are hardly going to change, nor do I want them too. I do know they fall easily when they have a guilt complex. And it is that, my good friend, which ultimately places these jugs of fine wine and cheese on our table here."

The soldiers

"Eli, you are one dumb idiot," fumed the oldest soldier, battling his way up the trail on this hot afternoon. "Bringing us this way."

"You're just too old for this sort of jaunt," replied Eli, sweating away behind him.

"Don't give me that rubbish. Always the same pathetic excuse, age. Can't you clowns think of something original? I don't know, the quality of the intake goes down every year. They land me a bunch of nincompoops and expect me to drum army discipline into their unyielding skulls."

Swearing as he stumbled over another root, he paused to stretch and look ahead. "Wait," he cautioned. "Someone up there."

Drawing themselves up, hands shielding their eyes from the sun, the younger two peered upward.

He was alone. About one hundred yards away. A big boy. Standing there staring down at them.

"What's his problem?" inquired the third man named Jerram.

"What's your problem?" retorted his senior. "Standing there gawking at some yokel. I thought you were a soldier. Get a move on."

Reluctantly the three resumed their climb, occasionally looking up at the interloper on the skyline. He didn't move.

"Starting to annoy me, your little yokel is. If he doesn't move, he'll learn the word kick when I get up there," muttered Eli.

"You wouldn't know how to kick a stone down a path," snapped back the leader. Then glancing up himself, he decided the figure ahead was impertinent as well. "Won't get the chance anyway. I might stuff his feet into his ears."

As they proceeded up in the heat, the riling presence of this unmoving youth drew them together momentarily. When they came nearer, they saw him grin.

"He's mine Eli, if you touch him, I'll break your face. After I break his," muttered Jerram.

"He won't have a face left to break. You'll mistake it for his arse."

The trick

As he watched, an angry wave surged through him. Their presence was jarring, out of place. In turn, he could tell he annoyed them. One threw a rude comment back to his companions. They all laughed. He deliberately said it loud enough for the youth to hear. In ordinary circumstances it should have sent anyone scurrying off the trail. But he stayed there, working out what to say.

Breathing heavily, they arrived at the top. He looks bigger up here, thought the oldest soldier, stealing a glance at the others. But he knew if he didn't challenge the boy, he would be roasted later. Swinging back abruptly, he opened the gambit with the military's oldest question. "What are you doing here?"

For a few seconds the lad didn't answer, merely gazing around at the vista, his nonchalance adding to the aggravation. Finally he replied pleasantly, "it's a nice day. Great view."

Even now the soldiers could have scolded him and walked on without losing face. But the youth spoke again. "Pity there's some Philistines blocking it."

The eyes of the three locked in disbelief. Anticipating the coming outburst, the young man was prepared. Quickly he held up his hand in warning, and shaking his head said, "uh, uh."

Before they could say anything he bent and picked up a small rock. Cracking it against a boulder to show its hardness, he extended his arm toward them as if to say, 'watch this.' Curiosity stilled them.

Clenching his fist around the rock, he ground it to powder. The fragments spilled out the bottom of his fist onto the earth. After several seconds he released his grip and slapped his hands together to dispel the remaining dust. His grin broadened.

The wide-eyed soldiers stepped back a pace.

"The path goes that way," said the youth. Still grinning.

They jumped at his voice, and hurried past. Glancing back occasionally, they scuttled down the trail until they were lost from sight.

With a short laugh, Samson turned on his heel and strode down towards a village where smoke lazily drifted up from the fireplaces. He crossed through the woods, oblivious to any danger lurking there.

Striding into the hamlet he saw housewives gossiping outside their homes, watching their children play. Not a few noticed as he walked through, the conversation hushed, eyes diverted.

Hurried whispering commenced once he was past, some admiring his receding form, a young man in as prime a condition as they had seen, long hair cascading down his thick neck and curling loosely over his shoulders.

Outside the village the path led into the next copse of trees. Breaking through, he saw a brook, seven yards wide, meandering across a clearing.

That will take fifteen running paces from here. My right foot, toes pushing, will hit the edge. I will land beside that shrub on the far side.

And he was in the air, even as he visualized it, alighting without a care.

Soon he was out on the flat lands walking alongside the fields with the young grain peeking up. He knew he was entering Philistia, and his exuberance still lingered after sending the soldiers on their way, something he had never done before.

But as he followed the bend in the road his life changed.

Forever.

She was carrying a water pot. He approached her from behind, intending to pass her by, nearly restrained by his shyness, but stealing a glance anyway. Her eyes met his.

She was beautiful.

He tried to look away, confused for the first time that day. But he saw something else.

She will trip on that stone. She might drop the water jar, or even fall.

As she stumbled, her gaze was diverted, and he was there. Grasping her arm, catching the jar with his other hand.

"Wow," she exclaimed delightfully. "That was fast!"

His face reddened, as the realisation he was holding her caught up with him. "I'm sorry," he stammered, releasing her. "I thought you were falling."

She laughed. A lovely laugh. "It was just as well you here to catch me." Her eyes were twinkling.

His strength was gone now, and his confidence with it, tongue tied after her self-assured reply. She sensed it. "Would you like a drink of water?"

"Yes, that would be nice," he finally got out.

They sat on a fallen tree trunk and shared some water out of the jar. She started the talking, guessing his words would not flow easily. As she spoke, she began to appreciate his stature. She had noticed his intense eyes, and his uncertainty. But now his body and shape were there.

"Where do you come from?" she asked.

As she spoke, he noticed the Philistine earring she was wearing. If he mentioned his village, she would know he was an Israelite. But in the same instant, he knew she could tell already. "Oh, over the hill some way back," he tried to remark carelessly, but his tone was wrong.

She stepped in. He was such a boy. "Isn't that an Israelite village?" she queried mischievously.

He was taken aback. When she saw his dismay, she made a hasty recovery. "My father does a lot of business with Israelites."

It was all she could think of. "He likes them. He thinks they are more honest than many Philistines."

Samson gazed over at the range he had come across, remembering the stories of his birth, the fire flickering as Lamech talked, and the tales of angels. A brief nostalgia arose. But the hormones were stronger, and he came back to her.

Slowly their chatter resumed. They talked about life in their respective villages, the farm disputes, the landscape, and the councils.

"Don't upset our constable," she laughed. "I've never even talked with him. They say he's fearsome."

It prompted him to mention meeting the Philistine soldiers and sending them scurrying. He halted, knowing he had to explain.

But he had aroused her curiosity. "Why did the soldiers run off?" she asked. "What did you do?"

"Oh, it was just a trick I learned once."

"What sort of trick?" Her face was closer, a hint of her feminine aroma reaching him.

Caution gave way to bravado. He picked up a small stone. "Like this," he said, squeezing it tightly in his hand. Releasing the ground up dust, he slapped his hands together.

She blinked, thinking her eyes had deceived her.

"It's just a trick," he added. "Anyone can do it if they're shown how."

Staring down at the fragments in disbelief, she wondered, not for the last time, who he really was.

"May I walk with you?" he asked, aware of the long pause while he had thought about how to change the topic.

"Yes, of course."

She stood with him, as he scooped up the water jar. They strolled along leisurely, until she pointed out her house to him, an ordinary dwelling some distance from an ordinary village.

"I had better get back home," he said appropriately.

She stopped, thrilling for his halting conclusion.

"My name is Samson."

"I am Keziah."

"I would like to see you again. If that is alright," he added quickly.

She warmed to his tentativeness, giving her wide smile which went past his strength, to the boy he was. "Yes, that would be lovely."

It seemed only minutes before he was at his parent's house again, running up through the woods he had emptied of rabbits, seeing his mother and brothers on the stoop mending garments.

Her face lit up, still marveling after all these years, wondering when the great adventure would begin.

"I've met a girl." The words rushed out, surprising them both.

"Oh, that's nice," his mother replied, breaking her daydream. "Where does she live?" She was already weighing up tribal preferences.

"Timnah."

"Timnah? That's a Philistine town."

"She is so beautiful. I think I love her."

She stood up, shocked, then suggested to her younger offspring, "boys, why don't you go down to the stream and see if there are any fish for our supper?"

Happy to be released from their clothing chore, they sprang up and scampered away. With her arms folded tightly against her, she uncharacteristically glared at Samson. "But she is a Philistine!"

"Look I know that. But she is wonderful. You will like her."

"But Samson, the message from the angel. Surely . . ."

"This girl is different mother. She is nice, really nice. I want her, mother. I want her." He spun round and strode off to the fields.

Engagement

"A Philistine girl? He wants a Philistine girl? You must be joking."

His wife had calmed down, regretting her earlier exchange with her son. "I wish I was. But that is the fact of the matter."

"The angel was wrong, wrong from the beginning, I knew he was." Already Manoah was pacing up and down the room. "From the start, the very start. What did the angel think? Did he imagine one tongue tied boy was going to free Israel? Don't those angels know what is going on here?"

She waited. Always she waited.

He went on. "Now the lad is very strong, no doubt about that. But he doesn't seem to be a leader."

She remained silent, knowing the final comment was close.

"Anyway, I don't care what you say, angels have wings."

She sat there gazing at him, wondering again why God had chosen this man to father this all important child in Israel. Now here they were, facing a challenge of their son's manhood, and inadequately prepared.

"Do you want to tell him he can't go any further with this girl?"

"Me!" Manoah burst out. "You're his mother!"

"And you are his father," she replied quietly but firmly.

She slowly stood, not in an attitude of resignation, and careful not to convey contempt. Peering around her as if she remembered she needed to finish some job, she walked out of the house. Following the familiar trail through the copse of trees which once shaded an angel, she came up the slight rise where she knew her son would be.

He was sitting on his favorite rock, staring out over the far side of the valley. A young man, with his life before him, brought up on tales of angels and heroes and rebellion. And with strength and power and hormones coursing through him.

She sat beside him for a while before asking, "is she pretty?"

And thus Samson began to frequent the paths to Timnah trying new routes, and finding short cuts. These new discoveries added to the whole adventure that was love. On one occasion he took a side path from the easier road. This trail led up a steep incline but gave a beautiful view from the top. It was followed by an equally steep drop. As he came out of the descent, the path took a sharp turn to the right and led into a valley he had not entered before.

He knew it would lead back to the main trails, so he continued through until the woods thinned, and he came to the edge of a vineyard. Seeing nobody working there, he tried some of the juicy grapes. It was a treat after the hill climb, and he resolved to use this path more often.

"Would you marry me?" He was sweating, and not from the walk.

Her wide-eyed face was ready.

"Yes, oh yes."

"Mother, she said yes!"

He danced around the room, picking up three plates, spontaneously juggling them in front of her. "She said yes!"

"That is wonderful, Samson." She knew to respond positively. "I am so happy."

Manoah was in the fields, ploughing. His wife had warned him the lad would probably come home with a wedding arranged, and he had the good sense to be out working.

The woman walked purposefully towards him, carefully treading across the clods of earth the oxen-drawn implement had cast up.

He knew what she had to say so he did not stop the beasts until she was close. She saw the resignation in his eyes, and knew they needed strength from each other now. There was no need for words, and the stillness somehow bound the two of them closer.

Achish

Philistia's annual games were being held in Ashkelon. Gaza's team had trained for several months at their chosen sports. Achish had focused on sprinting. Asaph had retained an Ethiopian, after learning of their abilities on the track. This tall black man had taught Achish breathing techniques, and the dimensions of his own stride. It enabled the youth to cover more ground with each pace, decreasing his finishing time over fixed distances.

Asaph himself, even in middle age, could not resist entering the games. He was in weight lifting, having never lost the arm power from his rowing years.

The team traveled up easily in one day, the wagons moving smoothly along the new coastal highway. On its sandstone hillock, Ashkelon could be seen from miles away. Its founders had chosen the most sensible location, a higher plateau of land abutting the sea. Over the centuries a wall had been constructed around the edge of the rise to encompass the town.

The result was a huge castle with imposing fortifications standing straight up from the edge of the escarpment. About one hundred and fifty acres in extent, it towered above a merry little harbor and the blue ocean.

On this day the city walls were decorated with palm fronds, and gaily painted fabrics hung from parapets and windows. The foremost city gate, famed for its brick arch, was scrubbed and festooned with posies.

Local history explained how the arch came to be there. An earlier mayor had visited Egypt. There he saw the wonder of gravity-held wedged bricks that men could walk over. On his return to Ashkelon he had one built at the main gate. For some reason the fashion never caught on, but the arch was famed throughout Philistia anyway.

The caravan from Gaza wound its way into the bustling port where Phoenician, Cyprian and Egyptian craft were moored. Not even the team arrivals could halt the endless bartering of the merchants dispatching loads of Israelite grain into the vessels and arguing over delivery terms. A clamor of financial disputes mingled with the joyful cries of young women high on the walls, jostling each other for a better view of the young men on the wagons.

Pointing fingers and shouting welcomes, the local citizens called and laughed, tossing small fruits and flowers into the air, and the fragrance of eastern oils wafted through the tumult. Gaza's team stood up in the moving wagons, the boys blowing kisses at the wide-eyed girls on the walls. As they clattered through the gate, some of the lads could not resist reaching up from their wagon and trying to brush the underside of the arch, nearly twelve feet above the ground.

Dense crowds lined the main street as the carts trundled by. As they broke into the square, the visitors from Gaza spotted local athletes milling round with those from Ekron, Gath, and Ashdod.

They leapt from the wagons, moving in a dream through the welcome speeches, intoxicated with their youth and their strength and the success of their nation. Asaph watched from a distance, warmed by the constant mob at the side of the son of the Mayor of Gaza.

The future is his.

Weight lifting was early in the games. Achish swapped roles temporarily, and was now mentor and motivator.

"You know you can do this old man; your arms are like no other in all of Philistia. Who here can even hold a finger to you? So you vie not against these churlish villagers, but you compete so we can both stand on the podium. It is us that we strive for, each other."

The younger man grasped him in his arms momentarily, Asaph feeling a surge of adrenalin bonding him with this youth.

His name was called first, and he strode up to the weights. With a fluid motion he picked them up, back straight, arms flicking the bar to his shoulders, using his thighs and calves to stand. Then the push up over his head, holding, holding, until the shout from the judge, and the drop of the iron to the floor again. Cheers from the crowd, loudest from the handsome youth in the front row.

Achish's turn followed an hour later. After the preliminaries, the nine fastest sprinters would go through to the final. Achish was in the second heat, running down the main street of Ashkelon, about one hundred and twenty yards. All the entrants were loosening up, their bare feet padding back and forwards as the crowd's excitement grew.

They were called up. One minute to go. Achish started greeting his competitors, moving among them and shaking hands. His action prompted others to follow suit. As he chatted briefly, wishing them good luck, he found himself in front of a striking young man. The fellow was about his own age, with a finely shaped athletic body. His muscles would have graced the statue of a god, and his tanned skin glowed.

However, it was his tone that caught Achish's attention. He was classically good looking, with chiseled features. But as he spoke, his voice carried disdain. Achish felt his very eyes were sneering. He spoke a few clipped sentences, before glancing away at someone's call. Achish automatically swiveled to the voice. In the second row of spectators he spotted her.

Her beauty leapt out at him. She waved, and Achish's heart raced until he saw she was greeting the athlete beside him. Her eyes flicked to him, staying for a couple of seconds.

Her hair was long, curling into ringlets that she brushed aside occasionally, away from her widely spaced eyes. The loose, long dress she wore lent grace to her stunning figure.

The runners were called to their places. He was rocked by the encounter, the arrogance of the youth, and the drawing beauty of the girl. As they hunkered down, he could not concentrate.

"Come on boy," he muttered to himself, at exactly the moment the starting shout rang out.

All the athletes sprang up from their crouch in unison—except for the son of the Mayor of Gaza. Then he too, realizing he was late, was up and away. But again, in a fluke of fate, with his body rising, he caught the eyes of the young woman again. She was looking directly at him. In a slow motion like scene, he dragged his gaze away, his body starting to respond to the run he knew he could make, seeing every runner ahead of him.

Suddenly his training came to him in a rush, and he was in the race. His stride lengthened to the pace the African had taught him. With thighs and calves working like oiled springs he gathered the rearmost pair of sprinters about twenty five yards out. His body now pounding, he knew he had the best of a further three in front of those and overtook them at the halfway mark.

Now, just five runners were in front, and only brief seconds remained. At full stretch, he reigned in two more at eighty yards. Three more, led by the bronzed one, hung tantalizingly out of reach. Somehow, tapping into a reserve of fury for his late start, he crept up on the third man, and with a mere five yards to the tape, passed him.

Third place.

The runners slowed, breathing in gouts of air, not speaking as their minds and bodies returned to normal. Achish loped around by the barrier, aware of the cheers of the spectators. In the front row were the kindest eyes in all of Ashkelon, Asaph, appropriately silent.

Achish turned again at a further uproar. There was the victorious tanned youth, on the shoulders of two others, saluting the crowd. Despite himself, Achish scanned the multitude, but could not see the girl. Abruptly he wheeled. "Let's go," he said tersely to his companion.

The encounter

"It's not a big deal, old man," he said, after a long silence in the back street tavern. "I'm in the finals, that's all that counts."

Asaph was quiet. He had hoped the lad would talk the situation out. Stationed near the finish tape, he was unaware of the exchange of glances between Achish and the girl. But he had seen his uncharacteristically slow take off.

They finished their drinks, and moved on to other things: where they would eat tonight, what entertainment was in town, the chances of picking up some of these pretty Ashkelon girls. The subject of the weight-lifting finalists came up.

"Amongst them is a blacksmith from Ekron who is truly built like a city wall. It is said he can lift an unwilling horse," mused Asaph.

"Only a horse? Why, old man, I've seen you pick up a chariot to change a wheel. With the horses still attached!"

Their humor restored, they stood to make their way out of the tavern. Still joking, Achish stiffened as he nearly collided in the doorway with the race winner and his stunning companion. He stepped back, motioning them inside. They paused, recognizing him, then entered.

Achish put out his hand immediately. "Congratulations. A good run."

The athlete shook it briefly but said nothing. An uncomfortable silence ensued until the girl stepped forward.

"Michael thought you ran very fast."

At her strained tone, Asaph glanced at Achish.

Michael shifted awkwardly, his eyes cold.

"Yes, a good run," he nodded at Achish.

Again, the quiet hung for several seconds.

"Get us some drinks," Michael ordered the young woman.

She was stung, and the men from Gaza saw it. As she moved towards the bar, Achish called after her. "I didn't catch your name, sorry."

She wheeled, her curling hair swinging with her.

"Delilah," she beamed back at him.

A lift for freedom

The blacksmith was huge. Bigger than Achish had imagined. Not sculpted like Asaph, but still solid, with thick arms hanging beside his ample, taut, waist. The finalists were down to three by now: Asaph, the smithy, and a hanger on from Ashdod. Onlookers sensed the real battle was between the former two.

The blacksmith stepped up, heavily bearded, with years of hard toil obvious in his honest lined face. The weights had been added to as never before. This was the heaviest ever attempted in any games on the coast. His pudgy hands gripped the bar, and he squatted, blowing in and out through his mouth as he prepared himself.

His body swayed as he caught the full pull of the dumbbells. The massive thighs trembled as he paused for the thrust upward. He swung into it, bringing the bar up to shoulder level. He hesitated again, breathing heavily. Then the final push. Up, up, up, the weights went, and they were there. A three second count, the approval from the judge, the crash down of the bar.

The smithy clapped his hands together, affecting not to hear the applause.

Asaph stood as silence resumed. Later Achish would retell this scene many times. In fact the blacksmith had caught the crowd's heart, with his hardworking, country looks, and unrefined figure. Few clapped as Asaph took to the stage.

With barely a pause, he moved straight into the routine. The bars rose to his waist, his breathing still relaxed. It seemed effortless. A pause came, followed by the lift to shoulder level. With only a breath intervening, the bar was up, the crowd silenced by the apparent ease. He held them for a further two seconds after the official shout. A controlled crash of the weights to the floor was followed by Asaph's exit.

An eerie silence descended, breached only by Achish who stood clapping. The noise broke the spell, and the crowd hurriedly joined in, with many heads turning, and the rising hum of conversation.

The third man could not even get the weights off the floor.

Fifteen minutes later the two finalists came back. The blacksmith emerged to cheers, but Achish could see he had already lost his confidence. Several more irons had been added to the bar. He stepped forward, grasping the bar. But it was to no avail. His will had been snapped.

The ex-galley slave came up, his face a blank. Asaph faced the crowd, stooped to the bar, held it as before, and stood. Again the weights climbed, appearing as if they were false, such was the ease of the lift. Pausing at his shoulders he saw beyond the crowd, past the city walls, out to the open sea, where another was bidding him to leave, to go quickly.

And the bar rose high above his head, held aloft like a flag of freedom.

The gathering saw only the magnificence of the act and rose cheering as the weights were brought to the floor. Asaph stood there, returning to the scene, a self-conscious smile emerging.

"How did you do that old man!?" Achish leapt forward, pounding his mentor's arm repeatedly. "I mean, I knew you could, but wow, I didn't know you could do it like that!"

The blacksmith came over, his face open and generous. "I could never have done that. Your lift was unbelievable. If you ever need a job lifting horses, come see me."

Joyfully, they clapped each other on the back. In the midst of the jollity, Achish glimpsed someone further back in the crowd. He saw her curling ringlets swaying as she left.

Debrief

They sat in the same tavern again, sharing a celebratory jug of wine, the older man relaxed now. Achish fell oddly silent. Asaph took a guess. "You think about the girl, do you not?"

The younger one stirred slightly, gazing dreamlike out the window, over the colored lights of evening in the festive city.

"What hindered your run, Achish?" He hardly ever used his companion's name without some meaning.

The younger man turned slowly back from his reverie, but still did not speak.

"Was it she?"

Achish picked up his goblet, took a sip, then placed it firmly on the table. "She is a stunner, isn't she?" he grinned. "I mean, she is an absolute beauty."

Asaph's face lit up as he pieced the backstory together. "Did you see her in the crowd? At your race?"

"Ah, my old friend, my watcher, what would I do without you? Always keeping an eye out for me. Come on, admit it, she really is something else. Weren't you smitten yourself?"

He couldn't help chuckling at the lad's manner, even as he stammered, "Yes, . . . in truth, no . . . she is youthful, and I am aged . . ."

Achish roared with laughter, clapping him on the arm. Seeing patrons turn at the noise, he hunched himself comically, finger to his lips. "Don't embarrass yourself, old man. Your secret's safe with me, you know that."

But abruptly he swung away before muttering, "pity she's got that jerk Michael for a boyfriend. Don't know how he beat me."

Asaph's ears pricked up.

"Yes, okay, actually I do, if I'm honest," Achish confessed. "You're right, old man, I got distracted at the start. Unforgivable."

Two other patron's voices rose from the far end of the tavern, reminding Achish where they were. He laughed out, "good grief, here I am spilling the beans to you like you're some counselor, old man. It's just a girl."

Bull dancing

The young athletes could not resist attending the bull dancing next morning. Although the Mayor of Gaza disapproved of the sport, in this instance, he was overridden. Ekron relished the spectacle and had united the three remaining mayors behind him.

Arriving in good time, Achish was welcomed to a choice seat by his fellow Gazans. He scanned the arena until he sensed someone was standing beside him.

"Can you see her?" Jesher asked.

"Who?"

"The girl."

"What girl?"

"Don't give me that line, you dark horse. We all saw it."

"Why, you cunning little warthogs, you guys. Talk about dress up a story. Alright, I did see some girl in the stands. Are you telling me you haven't scored in Ashkelon yet? Come on, the infamous Jesher. You have a reputation to uphold."

"Ah, Achish, you're the clever one, who can divert a topic like you, my son? Tell the boys the truth, that's all we're asking."

A smirking group of six surrounded him.

"Uh oh," said Achish, peering down at the gates. "Looks like the first competitor is ready."

Laughing back at Jesher, he boxed his companion lightly on the arm. "Now don't tell me I arranged that timing. But I fear the officials will call for silence."

A large, muscular bull was released to an eruption from the stands. All attention was on it. Pacing about, it snorted up into the crowd, its long horns menacing.

"Those guys are madmen," Jashup exclaimed. "Who in their right mind would do this?"

At the end of the arena the gate opened, to more cheers from the throng. Out stepped the first athlete, clad only in a tight fitting loincloth.

"I've heard of this guy," Achish informed them excitedly. "He's from Gath. He's done this fifty times. They always put him on first."

The contestant from Gath sauntered down the middle of the rectangular enclosure, waving to the crowd as the bull watched him. Officials trumpeted for silence.

Stamping the ground, the bovine snorted again.

Gath's hero didn't falter. Walked steadily towards the animal. The crowd was transfixed.

Again, the bull stomped, then trotted off in a circle, eyes locked on the human.

Suddenly stopping, he sat down on the ground, as if in contempt of the creature.

The bull continued circling, pawing the ground, until its protagonist jumped up and walked towards it again. Confused, but sensing it would be hemmed in at the end of the arena, the bull backed off a last few paces. Everyone could see it was gathering itself.

Finally, it charged. Galloping straight at its nemesis, it lowered its head. The crowd were on their feet, but still silent.

When the animal was but two yards away, the dancer launched himself at it. In midair, grabbing both horns, he arched into a handspring high over the bull's head. Landing with both feet on its back, his arms shot up in a victory salute, before he leapt off, and ran a further ten yards away.

A cacophony of applause and whistling filled the arena, confusing the bovine, whose target had seemingly disappeared. Achish and his friends were on their feet, shrieking with relief and admiration.

Shaking his head in disbelief, Jashup declared, "now that gentlemen, is bull dancing at its best." He slowly sat again. "But they are still lunatics."

The final

The running finalists were loosening up. Michael was trim and stood detached from the group. Others milled around, waiting for the call. With barely two minutes to go, Achish appeared. As he laughed and chattered with the sprinters he moved casually alongside Michael.

"May the best man win," he said.

Then he walked to his starting place, without looking at the crowd. His eyes were fixed on the finishing tape. The call to get ready came, and they all went down. The bodies stiffened, waiting for the shout.

"Go!"

To the untrained eye, nine superb sprinters rose as one. Yet from where he stood, Asaph could see the minute difference separating a champion from the field. Achish exploded out of the block fractionally ahead, yet without fouling. He was up and away, not seeing anyone, running down his own tunnel, eyes glued to the finish.

Michael sprang up at the takeoff, aware something was different. Glancing sideways he saw Achish slightly ahead within the first ten yards. Michael's acceleration was still increasing so he gave himself over to that. But forty yards later, his opponent was still there.

Achish saw only the tape, his mind clear of everything but the race. At the fifty yard mark he felt he was flying, yet still had a reserve.

Michael knew he had to draw on something extra if he were to beat him. His rate picked up further.

At the same point, Achish's legs hit another level, pumping him down past the throng. He knew he was gaining speed, even faster than he had ever run before.

Michael stole a further sideways glance at eighty yards. Achish was now pulling away from him, but his own body could give no more.

As Achish breached the tape, he felt the push of its breaking. Slowing to a jog, he saw the last of the runners come through. As yet he was unaware of the other placings. Some of the competitors came across and shook his hand.

In the melee Achish caught a fleeting glimpse of Delilah. As she approached Michael, she laid a hand on his arm, but he shrugged her off and moved away.

At the victory presentation, Michael moved forward coldly to receive his second place wreath. Achish stepped up eagerly to the podium.

Following the presentation, he climbed down, jostling with his teammates, who slapped him playfully while they traded repartee.

"Delilah!"

She whirled to his voice, beaming. "Oh, you ran so well Achish, you ran beautifully."

"Michael, is he about?" he asked cautiously.

She stiffened. "No, he had to . . . he had to meet someone. Business."

"Oh. I wanted to tell him it was a tough race. He is an excellent runner."

"I will let him know you said that."

"Thank you. We leave tomorrow."

"I know."

Their eyes held for some seconds.

"Goodbye Delilah."

"Good fortune Achish."

Success

Back in Gaza the reception was tumultuous. Having won the most prizes overall, the townspeople were in a rapture. The Mayor himself came out to meet the returning athletes, shaking hands with, and bestowing a garland on, every single participant, regardless of their performance.

Dagon's temple was packed that evening. Huge torches lit up the auditorium. Every seat was taken, and the overflow was directed onto the roof. Singers and dancers entertained the waiting crowd, and a troupe of actors sprang onto central stage, weaving in and out of the two stout columns, dramatizing the power of their god.

Finally the athletes themselves were paraded onto the stage, to music from a band set up near the idol itself. As the melody reached its crescendo, the Mayor strode in to the cheers of thousands. Here was the man who had transformed their nation.

He motioned for silence, before gesturing for the athletes and officers to be seated behind him. When the place was completely still he spoke.

"I am proud of you."

He let the sentence float around the vast room.

"I am very proud of you."

Again, silence, the smaller sounds of people moving in their seats dropping away as curiosity mounted.

"I am extremely proud of you. All of you. Of those who competed in the games, of those families who raised the competitors, and of those who tried but were not chosen to represent Gaza. I am proud of you."

The gathering was connecting into his speech, and he knew it. Everyone craves recognition. Give it to them.

"I am proud of those who have taken this city, and our nation, to new heights. I also ask you to be proud of yourselves, and of your achievements. For without them we would be as we used to be. And we are not as we used to be. No more. Philistia stands proud today, Gaza alongside her sister cities."

Applause and cheering burst from the masses. The Mayor laughed, directing the praise back onto the athletes with a sweep of a theatrical hand.

"These games bond us with our brothers and sisters up and down the coast. As we move forward, we know, with a surety, this tie is unbreakable. We have learnt the power of unity. Indeed, what other way is there to move ahead? So, I am proud of you."

He swung round again to encompass the athletes once more. Time for some humor.

"We are even in the presence of a long honored member of our community, one who is out there showing our youth there is life after forty. His weight lifting is the talk of the coast. You see," and he chuckled as he glanced pointedly at Asaph, "I warned him I might turn up next year and compete against him."

Again the crowd erupted.

Now serious, he leaned forward at the podium in the pose all knew, his other hand acknowledging the stone idol, the move stilling his audience. "The gods do not smile on us randomly. Never forget that. Dagon supports us when we support ourselves."

His voice deepened. "Our success is earned the hard way. We do not rely on Dagon to win for us. No, we succeed through our own endeavors, and our nation continues to rise, our benefits increase, because we understand self sufficiency. Yet Dagon is part of us, standing for all that we have become, and all we shall yet be."

One with the assembly, Achish was enthralled. Youth, success and adventure. It was intoxicating, yet he knew he mustn't let it go to his head. Stay open, learn with confidence, listen to others. The words of his upbringing.

The lion

Summer heat burned the hillsides. The last rains were a memory. Songbirds departed, flying over to the inland mountains where there were still small lakes and springs. Little by little their tiny brains warned them this was the answer to their plight, and their numbers dropped.

It became tougher for the small carnivores, the rats and foxes and wild cats, to find game. Competition heated up with the weather. The wild cats had to hunt rats, even though they didn't like digging for their living. Pressure on the food chain changed the frequency of mealtimes for all creatures.

It finally impacted the top of the pyramid, the large cats. Although there were only a few in the district, none wanted to be a statistic. They altered two things; they ventured beyond their usual hunting territory; and they broadened their diet.

The wife of Manoah woke earlier than the rest of her family, as she knew she would. But she didn't arise in case it awakened her husband. She lay there, listening to the sounds of her world, conscious of the aroma of her house, mingling with those of the emerging summer's day.

Today she was a mother, she reminded herself, in the changing seasons of life. The past had passed. She often wondered if the main project of her life was over, and she had failed. What could she have done differently? He was to deliver Israel from the Philistines, not marry one.

It had kept her awake many nights in turmoil, resenting the deep sleep of her husband. But she smiled to herself at their different responses too. How typically feminine. And how very male.

With that thought, she got up, unconcerned now whether she roused the family or not. It would be a long walk, particularly under this sun.

She looked across to see her oldest son sleeping, one last time. But he wasn't there, and she laughed to herself about the unique elements of her existence. Of a son who could wake and leave the house so silently that she of all people, for she knew herself, would not hear.

Outside, she picked her way carefully down the path, stealing through the familiar copse of trees that would never be cut down, not so long as she lived and remembered anyway. Adept in her own place, she could not even hear herself as she glided around woods and shrubs.

Perhaps this time, arose the youngster in her, as she stealthily came up behind him sitting on his rock again, looking across the valley. Then her hand was reaching, the little girl in her thrilling she had finally managed to surprise him. But inches before the touch, he spoke quietly, without turning.

"Mother, be careful, I saw an asp here yesterday."

A rush of disappointment, pride, and love swelled in her all at once.

They sat there awhile, she with her arm around his broad shoulders, something she had never stopped doing, and he never spoke of it. Looking over an ordinary vale they both knew so intimately, she wondered what his thoughts would be, but did not ask either.

Her euphoria lingered all morning, and she teased her kin over their kit bags.

"I've told you before, I will need at least three garments besides my wedding outfit. When will you men realize? And you will be washing them in between times, yes, you four," she said pointedly to the males in her life. "And I had better check all your bags too, you hopeless creatures. It's a long walk back here to fetch soap."

She prattled on, turning to Manoah. "I trust you informed Simeon we would be away at least a fortnight."

"Of course I did, he knows it's a wedding. Give me strength."

"Young Simeon will need all the strength he can get if that cow decides to give birth," she giggled at him, he fully aware she knew every detail of their rural economy. "I'll wager she delivers a bullock," she laughed.

On the road, unusually, Samson chattered away.

We are moving, his mother thought. We are doing something. He loves action.

"You know what," Samson exclaimed mid-sentence, as they neared the hill section. "I know the road goes on round here, but there's a path up this hill and over the top. It's a great view."

The already weary family gazed up at the forested steepness, and the beginnings of a trail that resembled a bush entangled ladder. Slowly, she began to chuckle, silent mirth to begin with, then as they caught on, a contagious laughter set in.

"What?" asked the bewildered Samson.

Eventually they calmed down and she came over and leaned on his arm. "Oh Samson, my dear and lovely son who doesn't understand the rest of the world is plainly normal. You are a darling. I've got a better idea. Why don't you enjoy that mountain goat track yourself? You've got days of people and socializing ahead of you. Some time alone now might be a good thing."

He gazed at her, grasping parts of it. He loved her too, feeling a rush of affection. "Will you be all right?"

"We will be just fine."

"The path comes out and meets the road again."

"I am sure you will get there before us."

With that, he sprang on to the trail, disappearing uphill rapidly and noisily to the resigned wonderment of his kin.

The young lion came alert at the sound. Something was close, and he could hear the direction it was moving. The noise was not like that of a deer, but it was large. His hunger, combined with his feline inquisitiveness, had him pacing silently through the woods. Taking him to the edge of the vineyard, his path was now angled to where his prey was sauntering through the tended grapes.

It only took a second for the lion to recognize the vineyard was made by man, and the creature walking through it was also human. But his eagerness had taken him too far. He slipped into the plot, loping down one of the cleared tracks between the plants.

Seeing him now, he picked up his pace parallel to the man, just three paths across. He knew he had all the time he needed, that he would speedily crash through the two intervening rows of grapes. His excitement mounted over the anticipated kill.

Samson heard the sudden breaking through the grapevines, and as he spun quickly he could see the creature only five yards away. Giving away all pretense at stealth, the cat charged, grunting heavily before gathering itself for the jump. It would leap up at him, to knock him over, to bring him to earth, to gain some part of his upper body in its maw.

But as Samson swung toward the noise, it was clear he was the one with all the time in the world. The lion seemed sluggish, threading between the vines. Samson knew immediately how he would deal with this encounter, counting the beast's steps, noting the distance between each one, calculating when it would leave the ground, and commence travelling through the air to him.

As it did so, Samson's stance altered, putting his weight into meeting the creature as it sprang. He knew the cat would be dislodged from its flight path by his forearm blow but would slowly flip to land feet first again. During that time he would raise his right leg over the beast's back. Life was pouring through him, his mind devoid of fear, only on the mechanics of the next action, nothing else intervening.

Astride the lion his arms reached out long before the creature could turn to seize his thigh, and he held both jaws, the right hand grasping the upper, and the left finding the lower, aware of slotting his fingers between the teeth, avoiding the pointed, sharp, canine pairs.

His hands jerked apart, forcing the lower jaw of the beast down, ripping the cartilage and muscles, tearing the mouth asunder. His right arm wrenched the upper head back, and he heard the neck bones pop, feeling a sudden lack of connection with the rest of the body.

It was over.

In four seconds.

From when the beast left the ground, to when it was still.

For a moment he stood holding both jaw pieces as though they were two sides of a sack. Although the body was still in one piece, the lower jaw was now attached by only a strip of flesh and hung slackly in his left hand. His right still held the top of the creature's head. It was motionless, there being no nerve linkage left to the dying brain.

Dropping the carcase, he stood back. It fell softly, like a relaxed body might fold itself prone.

That was a lion.

He looked at his hands, covered not in blood, but in lion saliva. Wiping himself clean on the grass, he sat beside the animal.

It took four bounds to reach me. They're not as fast as people say.
It wasn't that hard slaying the creature. They make plenty of noise, so you hear them coming. If it had come down that nearer grapevine row, I might not have heard it so early. Lions should think of that sort of thing.

I guess it had to angle across somehow, and they don't know how to count steps.

I thought their neck muscles would be tougher. And the bones weren't too strong. I heard three pops when the neck broke.

Kind of like rabbits. That's how come it went limp so soon.

Breaking necks is a quick way to kill. If a group of lions ever attacked me, that's the way to handle it. Shake, rip, drop.

After some time, he realized he may have been day dreaming and didn't know how long he had been sitting there. Springing up, thinking his parents would be far ahead, he bounded through the vineyard.

He didn't stop until he came out at the main junction between his trail and the road. Scanning across the shimmering, treeless, fields of grain, he saw his family. He had beaten them after all, and they slowly strolled towards him in the heat of the afternoon.

"How was that trail, dear?" his mother asked.

But the world was not the same. Her question was so ordinary, so normal, so out of a new context.

"Fine, mother, fine," he stammered out.

She knew something was different, but he avoided her eyes, and pointed out sights on the road ahead. They began walking again.

It wasn't long until they reached a familiar bend in the road and the house appeared.

She was waiting for them.

"Mother, father, this is Keziah."

That night and the next, the socializing and the new people swamped over him, submerging the sinewy form of the cat as it approached. But as he retired it surfaced again, the feel of its jaws, the crack of flesh and bones breaking, the sudden slack body. In the second night he awoke in the silent dark of the slumbering house, with the blackness and the late hour and the strangeness.

The beast was slow, breaking groggily through a row of grapes while he waited for it, arms crossed.

Sure.

Lions aren't that slow.

Waking again early in the morning he quietly dressed, slipped outside, and ran through the wheat fields. When he reached the valley, the sun had risen, revealing the landscape. Entering the vineyard, his jog slackened to a walk as he made his way up between the rows.

There it was. The putrefying corpse of a dead lion. Torn apart. He drew closer and was surprised by a sudden buzzing sound. A swarm of bees had made their home in the carcass and he could see the hexagonal combs. His fingers dipped down irresistibly. Honey. It was beautifully sweet.

Standing back, he walked around for a while and returned to the same spot. Still all the same.

The final realization dawned. Yes, the lion seemed slow. But it was not. Something had happened in that moment that enabled him to speed up. Faster than a springing lion. And stronger too.

Again he paced around, swinging his arms, flexing his fingers, conscious of his physical frame. He felt very, very, good. Powerful, young and invincible.

It was time to head back.

He walked up the path, hearing new charismatic voices filled with laughter. His confidence vanished. Glancing down at his rural sandals, he knew he was bracing himself.

Their backs were turned to him. Two newcomers. Expensively dressed, skins glistening with oil, wearing exquisitely crafted footwear. As the youthful one held court, everyone laughed with him, and at his whim.

Keziah sensed her betrothed at the door, her smile widening. Following her movement, the golden youth twirled too, somehow quicker than a lion. He began to thread through the rows of youths.

He will reach me in eight steps.

"So, you're the groom!" Achish laughed. "Haven't seen you down at the gym, but looks like you can do a day's work!" He thrust his hand out. His stance unaltered, Samson understood he should grasp it.

"The name's Achish. Great to meet you! And congratulations!"

He spun to wink at Keziah in front of everyone while still holding Samson. "What's your secret?!" He laughed quickly back at him. A chorus of cheers rose with his enthusiasm.

Not waiting for a response, Achish swung round again as Samson remained rooted to the spot. "And this is Asaph."

Dropping Samson's hand, he dragged the senior man forward, clapping him on the back. "We would've arrived earlier if this old man hadn't had me running about the hills. Him and his training regime."

He reached out quickly once more and held Samson's upper arm, eyes sparkling, and voice rising above the mirth. "Talking of fitness, Samson, these clowns here, these sterling young men raised alongside me, they could benefit from a lesson or three in weight training!"

Jesher: "Great idea! Let's use that tavern near the gate! Asaph could show us how to lift vats of wine!"

Achish: "The only whine you could raise would be a whimper, Jesher!"

Jesher: "Haven't heard of that winery."

Achish: "You have mixed motives, you guys, so help me, I know you're all on heat over that tavern keeper's stout daughter. I've seen eyes flicker; you can't fool me."

Samson: *bewilderment.*

Jashup: "What do you mean? She's made for you, Achish! Didn't you see her biceps?"

Achish: "Jashup, I forgot to tell the boys your mountain name—Dancing with Bull. I mean Dancing with Bulls."

Jashup: "Actually, I have been practicing my handsprings. Could you kneel down here for a moment so I can show the lads? Won't hurt a bit."

Achish: "Jethro, he's talking to you I believe. We've decided to field a dancer at the next games, and you were shortlisted. Didn't Jesher tell you?"

Othed: "Talking of wine, my goblet seems not to have any. Has Achish hidden it somewhere?"

Achish: "Absolutely. I was thinking of your health, and your snoring, and your keeping everyone awake. Why, I understand you sleepwalk if you've had too much! I meant to warn the lads."

Keziah: "Come with me, you silly boys, I will find some," giggled the entranced bride to be.

A bubble of chatter moved away as Achish led his following out the back door into the yard.

Samson: *envy.*

By midafternoon, the summer heat had reduced the youths to lethargy. Samson's parents had walked further out into the grain growing district with Keziah's family to explore some farms. Only the younger Philistines and Samson remained at the house.

Do it now. Show him.

Samson spoke as he stood. "I have a poem for you."

Achish: "A poem? "You want to tell us a poem?"

Samson: "I want to add spice to this one, so I am suggesting a wager."

Achish: "A bet on a poem? Like, whether the poem will make it big?"

Jesher: "My cousin does poems, Samson. In taverns. Great business. Come on down to Gaza, and we will set you up in a gig."

Jashup: "Your cousin, my arse! That guy started in Tyre, before moving down our way."

Jesher: "Hold on, I think he knows my cousin, maybe it's something like that."

Achish: "Hey, hey, Samson has a poem for us. This is his idea. Give the man some space. Tell us your poem, Samson. We will score you on it."

Samson: "No, no, it's not a poem like that. It's to see if you can work out what it means."

Achish: "Oh, you mean a riddle. A trick poem with a hidden meaning. He means a riddle, guys. Like that fellow, what's his name, you know, down in the district. He has these quiz nights."

Othed: "Meriah! I won one night. Took home a chicken."

Phicol: "Took home a chicken! Do you run a home for chickens?"

Jashup: "Is that what we ate for dinner last week? Your pet chicken?"

Phicol: "That is so inhumane. We should report you to the bird protection society."

Achish: "Guys, guys! Come on, the host has a riddle. It'll be good for us. Make us think."

Achish: "Samson. Please."

Samson: *Keep going. Don't let them rattle you.*

"Yes. A riddle," the Israelite forged on. "A riddle like a poem for you to work out. A wager on a riddle."

Achish cocked his head sideways. "Sure. Great idea. These boys love to throw away their money." He waved his hand down to quiet the group.

"Here is the wager. I will give you seven days to answer. If you do, I will give each of you a change of clothes and a linen wrap."

"Not bad, not bad, Samson," replied Achish. He leaned back in his chair, leading the clapping.

Come on. You're nearly there.

"However, if you fail to answer, you must each give me a change of clothes and a linen wrap."

A few low whistles emanated as the Philistine youth counted their number. Thirty. Again the eyes flicked to Achish. His smile had not dimmed. He stood, anticipating the descending hush.

"Do it."

The lads erupted.

Samson shook the hand, oblivious to the cacophony.

Achish sat again. "So, what is this riddle like a poem that will take thirty of us all week to solve?"

Say it.

"Out of the eater came something to eat, and out of the strong came something sweet."

Done.

They had expected humor, but now sat there uncomprehendingly. Achish peered up at him. "Yo there boyo, that's different. Rhymes too. Like a poem."

Samson grinned. "It is a poem, Achish," naming him as one would a foe. "A riddle in a poem. Someone like you should be able to work it out."

I can use words too.

"Seven days." Still grinning, he walked out.

Achish slowly swiveled his chair around, smiling widely.

"What's so funny?" Phicol asked.

"Gee, this Israelite boy has come out of his corner and stymied you all, that's what. And not a bad riddle for a country lad. Any ideas?"

They gazed at each other, hoping someone would start the ball rolling.

"Did he say a suit of clothes?" Othed asked.

Achish laughed again. "No, he said a chariot wheel and a pair of sandals. I do wonder sometimes."

A day passed, and the group was out the back of the house again, with Samson in their midst once more. Torpor had descended in the afternoon heat, and several had drowsed off.

"Sweet eater, Samson, it's something to do with a sweet eater isn't it?" inquired Achish.

"Do you have a solution, Achish?"

"No, no, just trying to clarify. No big deal. Don't worry about it."

Days two and three yielded nothing either. A conversation began.

"Hey, it's not my fault," Achish exclaimed. "The fellow gave us such a tough riddle."

"You accepted the wager," came a voice from the rear.

His fingers spread out like his father. "We all accepted the bet guys. Did I not hear cheers when I took it on? What's got into you?"

"A suit of clothes apiece, Achish," explained Othed. "I mean, that's fine for some of us."

It was only a minor barb, but he knew better than to pounce.

"Hey, this is Uncle Achish here, does he ever let the team down? When a party needs finding, who lets you know? If you are short of a girl, who comes up with one? Yo, buddies of mine," he exclaimed, leaping up and parading around the room, tousling the hair of a couple and kicking life into Jesher, supine on the floor.

"Get away," Jesher came back with. "That last woman you set me up with cost a fortune."

"Why, was it my idea you bought her that expensive dress?" Achish asked gravely. "I honestly thought you could read price labels."

He scrutinized the warming group, "Did I get that wrong too? I don't know, this Achish, my word, he is a hopeless case."

Dodging playfully as a soft blow missed his arm, he bounced on his toes like a boxer. "Okay, guys. You want me to unravel this riddle, I'll do it. One more time I will ride on my white horse and rescue you all. One more time." His eyes rolled hugely as his upraised palms waved about.

"White horse! Whose white horse? I have a donkey I could paint for you though." Jesher was back.

"I'll take three," rejoined Achish, still bouncing.

Asaph watched from the far side of the room.

All about honey

"Keziah, want to take a walk?"

She looked up from her sewing at Achish. Samson had gone into the village with his parents for a couple of hours. Enjoying the attention from the son of her nation's leader, she readily agreed. "Yes, of course."

They sauntered down the lanes between the shimmering wheat fields, the hot blue sky above them, watching the larks circling in their endless quest.

"He's quite a guy, this fiancé of yours, Keziah."

"I'm glad you like him."

"How'd you meet?"

"We bumped into each other on the road," she said, giggling out the story of a tongue tied youth.

Achish listened avidly before commenting, "he's a bit of a poet though, isn't he?"

"A poet?"

"For sure. He posed the boys quite a question. Didn't you realise?"

Gee. She doesn't know.

She hesitated. "What do you mean?"

"He put this riddle to us."

"What riddle?"

Why hasn't Samson told me? I'm going to be his wife.

Achish pushed ahead. "Okay, goes like this,

"Out of the eater came something to eat,
  And out of the strong came something sweet."

She stopped on the path. "What are you talking about Achish? What's going on? Why are you telling me this?"

He capitulated and told her the details.

"Thirty suits," she breathed. "Why did you accept?"

"Don't really know. Just seemed to be the thing to do at the time."

Mastering herself, she swung in behind her man. "I don't know why you are telling me, Achish. Seems like you will end up buying Samson lots of clothes. Maybe it will be a lesson not to gamble so readily."

He laughed. "Oh, you're right, you are so right about that, Keziah."

Moving closer, he added, "only thing is, I'm in trouble over this. It was me who accepted the bet, and the rest of the guys are a bit put out about it."

Stopping, he gazed across the fields before remarking, "if someone could help me find the answer, it would get me out of jail."

Keziah

"Samson," she spoke quietly, as they walked hand in hand along the moonlit path on the fourth night.

He was looking up at the stars, seemingly trying to make contact with something, she thought. Returning her gaze, he replied, "mmm?"

"I hear you tested the guests with a riddle."

He laughed.

She halted on the road, withdrawing her hand.

He stopped. Puzzled.

Silence.

"Why, what's wrong?"

More silence.

"It was just a bet with those guys," he said.

"It's not the wager, Samson."

"Then, what?"

It rushed out. "Why didn't you let me know? I am about to become your wife, and you didn't even tell me."

Oh.

"Really, I was going to, I was. If I win the bet, we get lots of clothes. We could sell them in the markets, and earn good money," he added eagerly.

"That's not the point. You didn't tell me."

He stood still, clogged, apprehensive, unable to anticipate the steps in this encounter.

"Do you really love me Samson?"

There was a silence of some seconds before he stumbled out a reply. "Of course I do. You know I love you."

She started walking back, knowing he would catch up.

The ploy

"Let me help you with those water bags, Keziah," Achish called out as she left the house the next morning. "It'll get me away from Jesher's banter. Gee, can that lad spin a yarn."

He warmed to his theme as they walked along the beaten path to one of the district's wells. "Jesher was a javelin thrower at the Ashkelon games, and to be fair, he is pretty good at it. But they matched him up against a beanpole from Gath. This guy was built like a rake, with fingers that would reach the well if he pointed at it. Perfect for throwing spears.

"So, our Jesher sees all this at a glance. We are sitting behind the throwers, and Jesher manages one of his imitations back to us. He rolls his eyes, spreading his hands and fingers down like his arms reached his toes. It was only a second, but so obvious. We burst out laughing, and the tall guy spins round, then back to Jesher."

Keziah was already enthralled, laughing the story along.

Achish continued. "The tall guy asks Jesher, 'What's wrong?'

"'No, nothing,' replies Jesher innocently. He sidles up to the lanky one. 'Tell you what, I've seen those guys before,' he says to him. 'They come to events to put people off. I wouldn't listen to them if I was you. Just go through your routine, and ignore them. Trust me.'

"Jesher picks up his javelin, and starts smoothing it down with his cloth, then thinks of something else to tell him. 'One word of warning,' he says quietly. 'They will number your steps silently as you do your run up for the throw, and if you cross the throwing plate, they will leap up and yell for a foul.'

"The thin one is all eyes and ears now. 'They will?' he asks. Jesher nods. 'Just ignore them,' he says."

"When it comes to his turn, the beanpole starts his run, and we can all see he is counting his own steps. About five steps before the end of the lanky ones run up, Jesher gets this quizzical expression on his face, with both palms out, as if to say, 'what's he doing?'

"So help me, it was funny, it really was, we could not control ourselves, and all burst out laughing. The skinny guy hears us just as he throws, and off goes his javelin out to the side. Jesher has his turn next, and does the throw of the games. Walks away with first prize. We had him on later at the tavern, but he was all denial, meanwhile chortling along with the rest of us. One naughty boy."

"Oh, you tell that so comically, Achish, you amusing boy yourself," Keziah chattered back amidst her laughter, liking him so much, wondering what might have happened if it was he who had shown the interest in her instead of Samson.

"Hey, ah . . ., did you manage to find out anything?" Achish suddenly broke in as they drew the water up.

"Achish, why are doing this to me?" Her mood changed immediately, tears apparent. "I love Samson, and he loves me."

"Of course you do. It's just like, you know where I'm coming from Keziah. Yo, this is Achish. Have I ever done anything to upset you?" He spread his hands wide, palms up, imitating an innocent Jesher now.

Despite her trauma, his antics brought another laugh. She briefly wiped her cheeks. "I know that. Only I wish this pressure wasn't on me. My parents are at me as well."

"Hey, you're in a tricky spot here Keziah. Honestly, I didn't want to drag you into this, but we all need it to end happily."

He gazed at her for a while before murmuring, "seems a bit unusual Samson didn't tell you first."

Achish doesn't think Samson loves me.

Her face betrayed her feelings, and he saw it.

"Look, he's a great guy. Don't go questioning yourself too much. Men think differently. Sometimes they don't open up."

But you do, Achish, you do.

Suddenly his mood changed too.

"Hey, girl, here's an idea. Put the old thinking cap on, you know," he said, tapping his head with his finger. "Thirty suits of clothing are going to cost Samson a pretty penny. And here I am trying to talk his bride into going broke. Real scholar at times, this boy Achish."

She giggled.

"I'll pay for the clothes myself. My winnings from the games at Ashkelon will cover it. Hey, I haven't had time to spend them yet. Maybe this will teach me fiscal maturity!"

Laughing with her now, he went on. "But we can't tell Samson. He might tell the other guys. I will look a real clown. The whole thing will come unstuck. I can't let Samson know until after we tell him the answer."

She started to comprehend.

"Okay, here's the plan," he rushed out, excited over his little intrigue. "We proceed as normal, we find out the answer to the riddle. Immediately afterwards, you and I will see Samson in private, and explain the whole thing to him. He gets the suit money, and I get out of trouble with the boys."

His ego could not be suppressed. "Actually, it's not too bad a plan, if I say so myself."

She smacked him on the arm.

Day six

"If you loved me, you would have told me about the whole thing earlier Samson. You know you should have."

"Look, I told you I'm sorry."

"If you really love me, you know what you should do."

His eyes were on his feet, shifting uncomfortably on the roadside.

"Why don't you open up to me Samson? What is it, that you hold things back? You could take a lesson from Achish about how to share your feelings!"

Achish.

"You should tell me everything, that's what you should do," and without waiting for an answer she stormed away, back towards the house.

Samson

That smooth talking slime-ball.

Why would Keziah listen to him, of all people?

Share your feelings? What is she talking about?

Achish

"How much does a new suit set us back, boyo? You know I can't read price labels."

"Jesher. Mate. Would I let the lads down?"

"Only in the middle of that practice tug of war, before we went to Ashkelon."

"What are you talking about? That was to keep you all on your toes for the actual event. Letting the rope go suddenly like that helped build the team resolve."

"Just coincidence there were cow droppings behind me when I fell?"

"Time and chance happen to all men. Anyway. It's under control. Keziah is on to it."

"Keziah? Really? Getting the girl to pimp on her man? Come on, guy. If we have to shell out for the clothing, so be it."

"No, it's not like that, honest. And I promised. Remember?"

"Sure. But I mean . . ."

"Trust me."

Day seven, morning

She came into the room early, tip toeing past the sleeping young men, slumbering deeply after their feasting the previous evening.

Keziah stooped over the young Israelite, touching him, bringing him to wakefulness. She was clothed in a light blue wraparound, her curves accentuated. With her finger to her lips, he rose quickly, eager to restore himself to her. Achish watched from beneath his almost closed eyelids.

The couple tiptoed out of the house to the road, where the early morning mist and the coolness covered the land. Her pace quickened, and she took his hand, leading him to a secret place of hers since childhood. They walked across several fields, off the path, down a valley, where a stream could be seen leading into a wooded area. The trees were pleasant to walk under, and they proceeded down past fallen branches towards the water.

Breaking out of the woods, they came to a little clearing with soft grass underfoot, near the brook. She moved into his arms without speaking, her upturned lips seeking his. He bent towards her, feeling her softness. Her arms were around him, his manhood rising, his whole being urgently wanting her.

She did not hold back, as his hands slid under the garments. What did it matter in the proper timing she said to herself. We will be doing this on the morrow, after the wedding itself. They lay down, he spreading the blue cloth on the ground. "No, no," she cautioned, aware of the blood from her first encounter. "On the grass."

As her body was unveiled, she reached into his clothing, also wanting him. In their inexperience, he could not wait. She lay back on the grass, he kneeling beside her. She pulled him towards her, and he could feel the glorious sensation as he pushed into her.

Quickly, it was over. His powerful body shuddered as he spent himself. She felt it, squeezing him and straining up against him.

He slowly relaxed.

They had talked little during the entire time. She broke the silence. "I love you Samson."

They lay in each other's arms.

"Tell me, Samson, tell me."

Everything appeared beautiful. "It was a lion, Keziah. I killed a lion with my bare hands."

He could see her confusion. "You remember when I first met you, how I ground that rock to dust?"

"Yes, yes, I do," although still bewildered.

"It is not a trick, it is my strength." He walked over to a tree, grasping a branch some three inches thick, growing from a trunk beside the stream. "Look," he told her, snapping it without effort, as if it were a twig.

She was stunned.

"I killed a lion, Keziah. And when I went back, some bees had made honey in it."

The walk back was almost silent.

"How come you are so strong, Samson?"

He took time to work out his reply. "I will tell you one day."

Time for lunch. The group gathered as normal, chattering happily, admiring the repast. They swung round as Samson walked in. He braced himself, immediately sensing bad news. Achish smiled condescendingly, clapping him on the shoulder with apparent affection. His words were brief.

"What is sweeter than honey?
And what is stronger than a lion?"

He had tried to say it in a friendly manner.

In later years, the wife of Manoah would wonder how the significance of this moment slipped her by on the day it occurred. In her very presence, her son had been found wanting by a confident, charismatic, young Philistine. Thirty laughing voices informed him he was no match for them.

Decades later she would summarize it in very few words; prior to Achish outfoxing him, Samson wanted to marry a Philistine: then everything changed.

On that day, in that ordinary room, in that typical house, not far from an average village, utterly predictably, his rage ballooned, paralleling the rising mirth.

"You found out." he croaked, oblivious to how obvious his statement was. "You worked on my woman."

As he marched out, he called, "I'll be back."

Achish whirled to his friends, hands high and waving, eyes gleaming. They all clapped while Jesher refilled his goblet. "Yo there, good one brother!"

After a while, as the laughter subsided, Achish quipped, "better see our groom again, tell him all's good, it's only a bet. Such is life."

Sympathetic, now their pockets were safe, they called after him. "Yes, for sure, tell Samson we are saving a drink for him."

Keziah was in the kitchen, tears welling. She pointed with her chin towards the door. Achish walked outside. Only Samson's parents were there, their backs to him, facing down the road to the coast. He followed their line of sight, but the road was empty.

Hearing him, they turned.

ignite

Thirty

It felt better, his feet pounding the earth. When Samson left the house, he had run towards Philistia. A half-baked plan formed as he ran. And now he was close. He could see Ashkelon, even though it was miles away. In all his rural life he had never seen a town so large.

But as Samson drew near, he saw the ramparts extended up from the edge of the plateau, making the town appear higher. It was perched on top. An illusion of power, designed to intimidate.

The road wound past the walls down to the harbor. As he slowed and jogged past the trading ships he heard merchants arguing and cursing over deals.

Evidence of wealth lay everywhere, in the fancy pottery, the yarns, the bulging sacks of grain, and the scurrying traders. He was reminded of his mother's tale that 'shekel', the very word for money, was a derivative of the town's name, Ashkelon, this den of bargaining, of buying and selling and taking wealth and power from others.

An epiphany shed its sudden light, linking events together. It was clear now, the cunning takeover of Israel, the comfortable ruling terms, the money enriching this seaside port. They had usurped his homeland smoothly and pleasantly. A clever, manipulative, patronizing superiority.

Exactly the same as that smart talking Achish.

Leaving the bobbing boats with their booty, he sprinted up the cobbles, and through the arch. His sudden appearance startled some folk, and eyes flashed. In front of him now, crossing the street just inside the gate, was a well dressed man.

Instant decision. He ran straight to him, knowing his number of paces, and when the victim would slowly turn, not understanding, and only display terror at the last. As Samson's hand stretched out, it was not towards a father or brother or citizen; it was towards a number he must reach. Seizing and shaking his neck, he felt it snap, and the body fell like a loose bag. Or it would have, had he not grabbed and removed the suit and wrap from it.

Several people saw the killing and stopped in their tracks. His speed was confusing, and nobody spoke. It was too unbelievable that anyone could do such a thing, so fast, in the middle of an ordinary day on the street.

He wheeled and ran towards the watching group. They took a few seconds to realize this butcher was heading for them before they split and ran in different directions, finally giving voice. Coming up behind the first man, using his arm like a battering ram, he struck him between the shoulder blades, knocking him flat, and breaking his back.

Turning fluidly, even before that body hit the cobblestones, he covered the ground to the second. Finding himself in an alley with no escape route, this one faced Samson, trying to defend himself. The fist smashed through his defenses, breaking away his lower jaw, part of his face actually spinning away through the air.

Samson stooped, pulled the garments off the pair, and threw them into the corner of the street. Everything was so quick, so terribly rapid.

Finally, a screaming broke, from the throats of a pair of women who had watched in silent horror the first ten seconds of Samson's killings. Their shrieks alerted the neighborhood, and heads popped out of doors and around corners.

Already he was running down another street to where a group of men had been talking. Uncertainly, they stared as he loomed up, confused over his appearance and the yelling. Then he was too close, and they grasped he was the threat and he was not stopping, his physical impact shocking all. As his fist swung it connected with the face of the first victim, breaking his neck again along with sundry cheekbones.

Again, it was beyond their comprehension for any single person to race up and begin slaughtering them. They outnumbered him twelve to one, and this disparity glued them to their places. Before any others moved, Samson mowed through four more, breaking necks or hitting them so hard over the heart that, in the case of one poor unfortunate, his ribs cracked inward and his heart was mashed.

He could feel every move he was making, aware of his wonderful speed and power. Like the lion, it seemed they were all moving slowly, that this was a game amongst handicapped children with measured movements, who could be stopped by a solitary blow.

And he was still counting.

Ten. Twenty to go.

As he threw a further man in the group to the ground, hearing his skull break when it hit the cobblestones, the remaining three started to move, beginning their escape.

He was now almost laughing, but not at the trail of carnage. He was simply completely enthralled in the mechanics of this task he must complete, his brain utterly focused on calculating his moves, the pace of their retreat, and the time it would take to slay each one in sequence. Before the last one reached the corner, Samson was onto him. His hands were out, grabbing his victim's hair and shaking it like a dog shakes a rat, hearing the popping of the neck bones again.

Momentarily he retreated to the pile of bodies and stripped them of their clothing. It gave Ashkelon a respite, sixty seconds in which few constructive moves were taken by the townspeople apart from shouting to each other, which brought yet more people out onto the streets.

Finally, the minute was over, and Samson was up and away. Racing towards the noise, eagerly anticipating his power again, he rounded the narrow corner into a square. As soon as he ran in, two other women, alerted by the shrieking from behind him, opened their own lungs. And this time a new cluster of men started towards him, in the strength of their numbers.

If anything, this approach caused him to speed up, and he flew into them like a whirling bunch of boulders held together by strong rope. His fists and feet were spinning around him as he launched into the air, kicking a man down, striking one with the right fist, and another with the left as he revolved.

From afar, one of the women said later, it resembled a scythe moving through a wheat field. Nothing could stand in front of him. Every few seconds his tally rose higher, while he coolly counted off the rising total.

For several seconds the men of the town threw themselves at him, not comprehending a human being could act like this, convinced numbers must bring him down. The realization was not long in the coming. He was unstoppable.

They started to flee, but not before the tally had soared. "Five more," Samson stated audibly, chasing several towards a corner of the plaza. Two were down before they reached it, then a further pair, a hand around each neck, banging them together with such force that their bodies immediately went limp in nerveless death.

As he dropped the corpses he heard movement behind him. He whirled, seeing the man running at him. In a flash he took in his size, knowing his physique was the same as Achish's. The fellow was well built, rippling muscles flowing as he covered the ground.

Samson stopped, waiting for the impact. His opponents arm went up, so slowly to the Israelite, although not to those watching from the rooftops as they related the tale later. He ducked under the outreached hands. Both fists crashed into his ribcage, breaking the bones, pushing them into his lungs, feeling the puncture of air and blood. A female voice floated over the square.

"Michael!"

Thirty.

He stopped, stripped the bodies, threading his way back into the square, retrieving his gamble. Meanwhile the town fled, not realizing he had finished his gruesome task. He picked out one large cape and began throwing everything into it, running back and forth from the bodies.

Scooping up the bag and tying it together at one end, he ran down the main street, seeing the arched gate draw near. Seized by the thrill of his strength, he could not resist. As he ran towards the exit, he shifted the bag to his left hand. Leaving the ground three paces in front of it, he jumped, his right arm swinging high, hitting and pushing the top of the arch up. The bricks were wedged against each other to leverage gravity. Their builder had never considered such sudden power might be exerted from beneath.

Still in midair, he pushed a segment up, and flicked it down to one side. As he started his descent, so did the clump of blocks and mortar, falling heavily onto the cobbled path, smashing into fragments which rolled for several yards. The entire move had taken two seconds.

Some locals, alerted from the harbor side by the shrieking inside the city, were running up towards the gate when they saw this performance. Later they swore it appeared like a flying giant from below. He must have had wings to leap so high, and the strength of a god to break the ancient arch.

Voices of alarm died, as the sounds of grief spread. Word came from soldiers who were still at their posts on the city walls. A large man had been spotted running towards Israel with a bag on his shoulder. Townspeople began timidly walking on the streets again. Naked bodies lay broken, scattered about.

Flies were already landing.

Paying the debt

He walked into the house, hearing subdued voices devoid of mirth. Without glancing at his sandals, he strode through the group as it parted for him.

Threading amongst the rows of youths while numbering his steps, Samson stopped in front of the silent, once golden, son of the Mayor of Gaza, seeing this encounter clearly.

Out came the suits, one by one, thrown to each recipient. Everyone quietly caught theirs until Jashup broke the awkward lull. "Love the colors, Samson."

Nervous laughter seeped out as they pretended to admire each other's booty. Holding the last tunic, Samson ceased moving until the chatter died. "Looks like your size, Achish," he said.

"Yes, it does Samson," was all he could manage, flicking his gaze to Keziah, with immediate regret.

Samson followed the glance, locking eyes with the girl, then back to Achish. Without a further word, the Israelite strode out. By the time Keziah reached the road, all she could see was his rapidly receding form.

Back inside, Achish held his suit, wondering where it came from.

It seemed familiar.

Achish

The guests quietly made their farewell the next morning. Achish had explained to his friends privately that a dignified, unquestioning exit, would be appropriate. Not to upset Keziah further, each one packed away their new suit of clothing rather than wear it. With embarrassed goodbyes, they all went, eager to leave in fact.

When they were some distance from the house, Achish suggested he might take a side trip to Ashkelon. Asaph said nothing as the younger man refused offers of company, promising they would all meet up again soon in Gaza. But he separated himself temporarily from the group for a quiet word with the youth.

He wanted to speak about his role in ruining the wedding, but Achish already seemed to have a poorly timed Delilah agenda. So, his words were simple.

"Walk with care. Remember your birth, who you are. It will do you ill to be found in compromising situations." He paused. "If I did not speak so, I would answer to your father."

Achish knew he meant more, but his mind was cluttered with fears.

"Thank you, old man. I know what you're thinking, but there's more to it than that." Stepping back sprightly, he lifted his voice. "And don't let those shirkers lead you into some passing tavern. Lucky if they can find their way home!"

Waving briefly, he walked on alone.

Achish went straight to Ashkelon, arriving late afternoon, still carrying his overnight bag on his shoulder. The harborside was ominously quiet as he strode through. Striding up the incline he saw the shattered arched gate. Guards were chatting amidst the brick rubble. One of the captains recognized the son of the Mayor of Gaza.

"What's going on?" queried Achish.

The soldier considered the question. "No, I don't suppose news travels that fast does it?"

"What do you mean?"

"We had a madman in the city yesterday. A mass murderer. Came running through the gate and started slaughtering people."

"What!"

"It was unbelievable. Only one man."

This is ridiculous! It cannot be!

Steeling himself, Achish asked, "how many did he kill?"

"Thirty. All men. Just picked on men," the captain replied. "He must have been insane. After he killed them, he stripped their clothing, bundled it up and ran off with it."

Remain calm.

Keep the conversation going. And think as you talk.

"Did anyone identify him? Was he recognized?"

"No. Nobody had seen him before. Young man. Powerfully built. And fast. So fast you wouldn't credit it. At one point twelve men tried to stop him. He took out the whole group without slowing down."

Twelve!

Can't be true. One man takes out twelve.

Wait. Keziah's story. He claimed he killed a lion. I thought, oh sure, he found a dead one.

Keep talking.

"And what about the arch here? How did it break?"

"He smashed that too."

"You've got to be joking!"

"No, quite a few people saw it. When he left, he jumped and pushed the top of the arch out—from below. Doesn't seem possible does it?"

Think Achish, think, boy.

"Actually, I came here to see Michael, your running hero. Do you know where he lives?"

"I am sorry. Michael was among the thirty."

His hands closed tighter on his kit bag.

"But you could see Delilah, his girlfriend, if you like. She is taking the loss alright, I understand."

He found her fifteen minutes later, after asking directions. She opened the door to his knocking, teary eyed. Then wide eyed.

"Achish!"

They stared at each other.

Achish broke the spell. "I have heard. I am so sorry."

"Please come in, do come in," she reached out her hand.

He stood there. She collapsed onto him, weeping. Aware of the street scene, he awkwardly held her and moved her through the front door, kicking it shut. Her lips came up and met his, her arms snaking around his neck.

It was a surprise to them both, feeling their gorge rise so fast. He gave way, feeling the soft contours, her body pushing against him. It was so sudden, yet so wonderful, melding grief and fear and longing and youth together in an intimate frenzy. Her dress came up, as she was reaching under his flowing robes and falling back onto the bed.

Afterwards, lying together, her tears continued for some time. Tears for Michael, tears for herself, tears for the world. And for this wonderful youth who came back.

Later, over the dinner table, she told what she saw. How this strong man was killing people all over the place. She caught a glimpse of the slaughter from her rooftop. As soon as she saw it, Michael appeared. He obviously thought he could overpower one unarmed man, and ran at him. Normally, he should have been able to, coming from behind. But at the last second the butcher swung round. Almost without effort, he slew him barehanded.

Achish listened without comment or explanation. Questions coursed through him. What if he had not made the bet? Samson might never have come to Ashkelon and killed Michael. In that case he may not have lain in Delilah's arms.

His agile mind switched to the prosecuting view even as she talked. 'Young man's foolish behavior leads to death of former lover.' He was implicated. Nothing that a court of law could put him away for. But there was a link. And it would threaten his future, the golden birthright. Damn this Samson.

"I need to return to Gaza tomorrow."

Her disappointment was obvious.

"I'll come back soon, don't worry. But there are a few things I have to do."

"Please hurry back Achish, please."

Two days later he was standing around a bonfire in the woods outside Gaza. All thirty young men were there. And Asaph.

"You must be kidding!" recoiled Jesher after Achish delivered his brief update. "Thirty men? He gave us dead men's clothing?"

Silently Achish took his gift from Samson out of his bag and threw it onto the flames. Without a word, all the rest did the same. For a long time after, they remained quiet, staring into the blaze.

"Just seems unbelievable," Jashup finally muttered. "For a while there, he seemed a nice enough guy. Then he goes berserk over losing a gamble. I mean . . . I don't know what to say."

"I know. We were partying with a mass killer," Achish said. "Come to think of it, he didn't talk that much. Maybe it was all bottled up."

Silence descended again as the fire consumed the evidence.

"It's not as though we're guilty of anything. However, we don't need to be implicated here. Let Ashkelon start its own investigations. We were a long way away. I think we should keep this to ourselves."

They all murmured assent.

Asaph glanced around at the somber faces. It was the first time he had seen the group in this mood.

The wife of Manoah

"He never used to work this hard."

Manoah and his wife gazed out the farmhouse door to the fields where Samson was weeding. Following a confrontation with Achish, Manoah had impulsively ordered the remainder of his family back to Zorah, missing the return of Samson with the thirty suits.

After Samson arrived home, he poured himself into the property, laboring from dawn to dusk. She asked him where he had gone after the wedding collapsed, but he just looked at her blankly.

Who would tell a mother about a mind's workings? If he pondered the slaughter, he could not repeat it. From the age of six, she would recall, he moved on, discarding gory details.

Although concerned, they were secretly content the marriage had not gone ahead, so they did not press him any further. She had reminded Manoah it had been prudent to go along with it because the thing had come to naught in the end.

"And, we can do with the cash from those crops," she quipped, trying to bring humor back into the house.

He laughed, breaking into a cough. "You're right there."

Her mind switched men. *We might have soup tonight. Manoah doesn't sound healthy.*

Samson

"I think I will go and visit Keziah, mother."

She glanced up curiously as they ate the fruit she had brought down to the cornfield. "Keziah?"

He paused, wondering why she found this strange. "Yes, Keziah."

She sat quietly, instructing herself to learn the patience she had attempted to teach her husband.

And her son sat there, puzzled over her silence.

He walked up the path and knocked on the door of the house just outside Timnah.

Presently it was opened and the girl's father blanched with surprise. "Samson?"

"Hello. How are you?" responded the Israelite.

"I am fine."

Recovering from his shock, the parent motioned outside by nodding his head. "We . . ., we didn't know what to do Samson. We thought you had gone." He halted, bracing himself. "Keziah has married another."

"Another?"

"Yes."

The young man retreated a few steps, turned his back and gazed up at the sky. "Achish?"

"No, no, not Achish, he didn't want her," the older man replied, instantly regretting how the words came out.

"But there is her sister. She is not yet betrothed," he bumbled on, digging himself deeper.

Do they think I am that stupid? That I can't I tell one girl from another?

Slowly, still facing away, Samson uttered, "do not blame me for what will happen next."

Without looking back, he walked briskly down the road, turning into a shady spot under a tree beside one of the wheat fields. The warm wind blew over the standing grain creating wavy patterns. Grain stooks were stacked drying in some fields, but the harvest was only starting. Above him, birds sang in the trees. He paced around, unable to sit.

Suddenly he heard a slight movement behind the tree. Before he himself knew it, he was around the trunk grabbing towards the sound.

A fox is a quick creature, and a silent one. This particular fellow had the misfortune to be near one faster, and keener of hearing. With no warning at all, a human held him firmly by the scruff of the neck while he kicked and growled his displeasure.

A fox.

Foxes! Outfoxes!

He laughed at the pun, his mind working on it. Still holding the writhing animal, he stood up.

Village smoke.

Angling with the wind.

And then he saw it. It was amazing how fast.

Looking around, he spied a copse of trees. Running across, he found the vines he was seeking. The fox was tied around its feet, and mouth, to stop it biting through its bonds. Within five minutes he was back with another fox. Again, it was trussed up, followed by another, and another, and more. His single mindedness lent speed to his quest. The number rose. After two days and nights, three hundred foxes lay bound in five wooded zones around Timnah.

Snatching up two pieces of dried wood, he began creating fire by rubbing them together. A spluttering flame came into being within two minutes. Heaping together enough sticks to create a steady blaze, he focused his attention on the foxes, lying helpless in rows watching him.

Picking up a pair of the squirming creatures, he selected another strand of strong vine, and tied one end around the small of their bodies before their back legs. The vine allowed about four feet of space between the two animals. Picking up a dried piece of wood, he thrust one end into the fire. When it was alight, he retrieved the brand and tied it into the vine between the foxes.

The two creatures were beside themselves, thrashing inside their bonds away from the flame. Samson carried them to the edge of the woods, and quickly removed the vines binding their legs. They sprang up, still tied around their waists to each other, and to the burning wood. Frantically attempting to avoid the blaze, they shot away, spilling fire as the brand clattered along behind them.

Seeking refuge, the maddened pair headed straight into the nearest wheat field. Retreating back into the grove, he performed the same task over and over, releasing crazed braces of foxes with firebrands.

Finishing the first group, he ran out of the trees to the next one about a mile away. It only took a few hours to loose all three hundred.

As the last two leapt away, he stood observing the scene. Severe conflagrations had broken out, and smoke billowed up from numerous fields.

Virtually the entire grain crop of the district was ablaze. Disorganized shouting could be heard from different quarters, and he could tell it was every man trying to protect his own produce. To little avail in the summer heat.

It was time to head back.

The Mayor of Gaza

"A giant! With pet foxes! Running around setting fire to the whole country! Indeed, this is a new one," exclaimed the Mayor to the general who brought him the news.

Achish flicked a quick glance at Asaph.

"Perhaps not a giant, my lord," replied the uncomfortable soldier.

"Just how big then? Is he larger than Asaph here?" laughed the leader of Gaza.

"Your worship, some say he is, but these are superstitious villagers."

"What about the foxes? I want to know about the criminal foxes," broke in the gleeful Mayor. "Are they still at large?"

The military man grimaced. "My lord, the creatures were observed by many villagers. As for the perpetrator, he was seen returning to Israel."

"And nobody tried to stop him?"

"They were too busy fighting the fires, my lord."

Achish met Asaph's eyes again.

Think, boy.

Enjoying his banter, the Mayor missed the exchange. "Let me see, one man starts some fires, an ordinary sized man. One who trains foxes. Local villagers see him, but instead of stopping him, they run around putting the fires out. Meanwhile he, or his foxes, light some more, until the entire populace is engaged in putting down the inferno."

The soldier's reprieve came from an unexpected quarter. "Father, we were down there recently. We heard of a very strong Israelite. The general could be onto something."

It took the Mayor by surprise. "What? Are you for real?"

"Yes, I am."

He straightened up, looking his son in the eye. "You mean there is such a man burning the countryside down around Timnah? That this is not a cock and bull story from the locals trying to cover up an accident?"

"Sounds incredible, but that's what I'm saying."

What's going on here?

The Mayor's piercing eyes flew from person to person, holding each in turn for the second or two that tells a man he is under scrutiny. "Why didn't you tell me? You've been back a while now."

Asaph held his breath.

Achish's eyes rose and fell. "To be honest father, I hate to bring it up here, but something happened, and it caused me to . . . to ah. . . lose attention."

"Do go on.' The older man was all ears.

"I met a girl."

Oh, wily youth, thought Asaph. Speak a truth and avoid a snare.

"A girl," the Mayor repeated.

My own son.

The years rolled back. He had not remarried. Mistresses were readily available to one in his position. It was simpler. He smiled at the young man. But he was not to be sidetracked so easily. Glancing toward Asaph, he queried, "and I trust you know all the details, my protector."

"My lord," he replied, eyes twinkling and hands spreading in the manner of his master. "I am undone. It seemed fitting the lad should tell you himself. Perhaps I erred. Does the boy's heart rule his head?"

Bouncing back to his son with a wide grin, the Mayor wanted more. "Go on, tell me, what does she look like? How old is she?"

"Look, she's not too harsh on the eye, if you must know. But we are in an emergency meeting here."

The military leader began to breathe again as the Mayor laughed. "Yes, of course Achish. The fires. And the strong man. And the foxes."

The younger man went on. "Let me go down and investigate this one father. I got to know some people there, and a personal appearance might help."

"Absolutely, why not," the Mayor declared expansively, winking at Asaph. "Good idea. Do that. I tell you what. Spend a day or two extra down there. Take your time. These investigations need indepth local study."

Asaph

"How delightful is an apt answer," commented the older man when the pair were clear of the city gates.

Achish was silent for a while, as though he had not heard. But when he began speaking, it came in a logical rush, as from one trained to reason.

"This is ridiculous. We go down to a wedding and are challenged to a bet by an Israelite. He murders thirty innocents, and burns down the grain district. Meantime, we keep silent because it was really nothing to do with us. Only thing is, the longer we stay quiet, the guiltier we appear in our own eyes, let alone anyone else's. I could hardly own up to knowing about the Ashkelon murders in front of the general could I?"

He prattled on. "It's like events are out of our control now. And Samson. Who is going to stop this damned Samson? He has the strength of ten men, a hundred men."

He faced the older man, with a hardness Asaph had not seen before. "We need to get analytical here, old man. We need to look after ourselves. This Israelite is not going to ruin my life. Are you with me?"

His coldness shook the older man. This was a different youth, not bouncing on his toes now. Asaph was at a loss, and walked quietly alongside for some time before replying.

"Gifted I was not, with the mind of your father, nor indeed his son. It has been mine to serve. To serve I shall continue."

Achish glanced up presently with a happier face, charmed again by his companions lilting speech. "That's good. I keep telling you there is poetry in there."

They tramped on a while longer before he added, this time with the toughness back, "you just stick alongside me. We need to tie some loose ends up."

Achish

Seated in legal chambers as the representative of the Mayor of Gaza, Achish faced the Timnah village council. With relief he noted the parents of Keziah were not present.

A portly, red faced, constable began. "Relay our appreciation to your father," he said. "But we haven't been sitting on our arses. We've already uncovered facts pertinent to this case."

Asaph gazed around the group from the rear of the room, wondering how the son of the Mayor of Gaza would handle rustic personalities.

"That's great progress, constable," Achish complimented. "Tell me more."

"These fires were not accidental. We believe this to be the work of an arsonist. He torched the entire summer crops of this region, which sets our folk back immensely. Many of them will go into winter ill prepared now. We can expect food shortages, and an increase in theft."

"Do you know the identity of this arsonist?"

"I was getting to that," the round officer glared. "We believe his name is Samson, an Israelite who has visited our community several times. He was seen walking away from the conflagration, which is hardly the response of a concerned citizen."

"Good observation, constable. Our own intelligence network backs up what you say. Neither have we in Gaza been idle." Achish eyed the constable. "We take your plight seriously. Why else are we here?"

Without waiting for a reply, he leaned forward on his elbows, clasping his hands together on the table top, stilling the room. "This Samson will be brought to justice, have no doubt about that. Indeed, I know what you're all thinking. Look at all the peace and prosperity we've brought to Israel. It's like biting the hand that feeds them."

A murmur of assent rippled around. Yes, Philistia provided valuable trade linkages for the Israelites. And protection from brigands. Yes, this young man is right. Look what we have done for them.

"We in Gaza can understand how you feel about righting this wrong. But you're better leaving that to us. I understand he is one very capable individual. How does an ordinary man capture so many foxes and turn them into an army of fire-starters? I think his capture is best left to the authorities. I wouldn't want to see any of your people wounded or killed should they confront him. He sounds dangerous."

Hmm, true, shuffled the room. No sense risking ourselves here.

Achish stood, and walked to the window as if mystified. Asaph saw his father's pose in him then. The young man spoke as though in thought to himself, but loud enough for everyone to hear. "We need to dig a little deeper here to find out what really went on. I mean, why did Samson burn the crops? Why pick on Timnah?"

The village councilors eyed each other. Yes, why did he pick on us.

Achish faced them from the window, his eyebrows knitted. "Did he have some bone to pick with anyone over here? Is there some grievance he had?"

A council member started to recall events. "Good question. Now I think about it, maybe it was tied up with that wedding that went bad. What actually transpired there?"

Another chimed in. "From what I heard, Samson was going to marry the girl. What's her name?"

"Keziah," added a third. "They live on the northern road."

"Yes, Keziah. He was going to marry her."

"And?" asked Achish.

What, thought Asaph. This he knows already.

"The girl didn't marry Samson," the constable declared. "That much I do know."

"Why not?"

"I believe she was given to another," the second councilor murmured, an audible dawning in his tone.

"She was given to another!" repeated Achish, straightening up. "I bet Samson was annoyed."

The constable was the first to bite.

"Yes, such an act would infuriate anyone." He stood and faced his fellow villagers in as commanding a manner as he could muster. "Why did that family reject Samson? Does anyone know?" He marched to the front, seeing his opportunity to seize control of the meeting again.

"What the hell went on that some family in our midst sets up something like that? Arranges a wedding with an Israelite only to turn him away on the very day. Did they think he would shrug it off and go home?"

A villager called out from the back, "that's right. What a stupid thing to do."

He was joined by a stout housewife sitting in the middle. "Now every family in the district has been thrust into poverty!"

In the midst of the rising clamor, Asaph understood where Achish had led them. The young man remained silent as tempers erupted. Without interrupting the raised voices, he touched a councilor on the shoulder, indicating he had other business to get on with. Nodding at Asaph, they quietly moved out, retiring to a nearby tavern. Achish could see his friend's disquiet.

"Don't look at me like that, old man. I just facilitated a dialogue in there. These are local people coming to their own conclusions. It's not our right to tell them how to live."

Two minutes later, an angry group emerged from the building opposite the tavern. Asaph and Achish sat tight at their outdoor table. The mob moved off up the northern road, heading out of town.

After their noisy departure, Achish remained quiet. He peered into his goblet from time to time, restlessly rising and walking back and forth out into the street for a clearer view, before returning to fidget in his seat. Asaph waited for him to speak, but he would not.

Presently they saw a pall of smoke rising from the north. Asaph's heart quickened. Surely not, he told himself. Surely not. Let it be only the house. He stood up, gazing at the billowing evidence. His feelings nearly overcame him before he realized the breadth of his grief. It was more than the girl.

It was this boy.

Some time later the mollified gang returned. The constable spotted the pair and veered over to them. "An eye for an eye, is that not the ancient law? Fire for fire. Those people have joined the crops."

Achish stared at the dwindling smoke as the officer moved quickly off to rejoin his townsfolk.

At last he spoke. "I know what you're thinking. And it's not true. I didn't tell them to burn the place down over her."

The son of the Mayor of Gaza wheeled around, eyes defiant. "That was their move. It wasn't me who went into Ashkelon and killed thirty men. For crying out loud, Asaph, thirty men slaughtered!"

Achish stared across again at the remnants of the smoke, then down at his feet. Asaph could hear him sighing as he breathed out.

"We need to report back to Gaza," he finally said.

The measured reply came back presently. "Let it be so."

The joint project

"You're back early. How was the girl?" queried the Mayor of Gaza.

Oh, Delilah. The last person on my mind.

"I wanted to update you father," Achish said, cutting to the issue. "There is a lone outlaw out there. His name is Samson."

"And is he responsible for these fires around Timnah?

"Yes, he is."

"An interesting episode came to light in your absence. Did you hear about the massacre in Ashkelon?"

"I did. And I think Samson was mixed up with that too."

The Mayor went on. "Just came into the city and started killing people. Thirty in fact before leaving abruptly. No rationale, no cause. Very mysterious."

Achish stepped in to lead his father down the correct path. "We may also have some light to throw on that."

"Oh?' queried the Mayor.

"Samson was jilted by a Timnite girl. He was due to marry her, but the family dismissed him on the day before the wedding. It would seem he got very mad about that. He set about his slaughtering spree in Ashkelon, returning later to Timnah to raze their crops."

"Dumb thing for a family to do," mused the Mayor.

"That's what the locals thought too. They burnt their house down over them."

"Ugh," flinched the Mayor. "Not very nice." He thought for a while. "Mmm, I don't suppose we can blame the villagers, what with the loss of their harvest. An eye for an eye."

He gave himself another thinking spell, before concluding. "However, Samson still remains at large. He needs to be brought to justice. We don't want a rebellion now."

His mind wandered around all he knew of Israel, and the timing of these events, and he began to plan. His son was of age, and they may well be facing a crisis. It was an excellent chance to work together.

"I am going to take a personal interest in this episode, Achish. Israel is our economic engine. Her exports go through our ports, she buys our manufactured products, and we earn taxes from her. But I am always worried, let me repeat that, always worried about the element of her religion. Just one man can ignite unrest there."

The young man sat impassively. His father continued. "I don't know whether we are onto something big here or not. However, I do know a couple of things. Firstly, the time is right for you to be involved in a trying issue. Leading this nation is not a straightforward task. Good rulers have always been tested by fire, if you can ignore that pun in the current circumstances.

"Secondly, there's something sinister here. I'm just not sure what it is. I haven't got a feel for this problem yet."

Achish's own mind was already running. Clarity of thinking, that's exactly what I need now. And tough decision making. I've just had a crash course.

The Mayor resumed his lecture. "Let me tell you a story that might cast some light on my concerns." He ordered his personal assistant to bring a jug of wine in with goblets, and led his son into a more congenial room where they lowered themselves onto sumptuous couches.

The Mayor started out. "A couple of hundred years ago, another outlaw single handedly turned the tables for Israel. Name of Ehud. Left handed he was. Anyway, to go back a little prior to Ehud's emergence, Israel was ruled by one of the inland kingdoms at that stage. A king named Eglon. Eglon was clever. In fact he was the first king to organize a systematic rule over the Israelites. Had them paying tribute year after year. It was so well run that Eglon only had to watch from afar. He even got bored, it was that easy. Took to brewing beer.

"And beer led to his downfall. It gets hot in the inland regions, and if one enjoys cold ales, one tends to imbibe frequently. To cut a long story short, Eglon ballooned out, and became the fattest king in the region. He ended up building a second story on his modest palace for reasons related to drinking and his immense size.

"Firstly, it caught a little more breeze. Secondly, and yes, I guess there is an element of humor in the story, he built himself a private toilet up there. Don't climb into any jokes about wind," the Mayor smiled. "Eglon even had the Israelites bring the taxes to him themselves, they were that much under his great fat thumb. And it so happened this outlaw called Ehud got the job at one stage."

The Mayors tone changed, so Achish straightened up a little. "The Israelites tell us an important thing in their writings. They claim Israel cried to the Lord their God for a deliverer. And that God raised up Ehud."

He was on his topic now. "Our current prosperity is based on an understanding of these factors in Israel. History tells us whenever Israel was in a corner, and calling to this 'Lord their God' for help, something happened. It had a psychological effect on the whole nation, and they could whip anyone in a fight. Unarmed, without chariots, with less men, you name it. Didn't matter.

"Unless we grasp this element of their psyche, we are always in danger of losing Israel. I want you to see this."

The young man didn't know how to answer but spoke anyway to keep his father in concert. "Keep going, I don't follow all of it, but I can see your overall direction. At least I think I can."

Good, the older man thought. Knows what he knows, and knows what he doesn't. He continued. "Ehud made himself a short stabbing sword in secret before departing on his fateful errand. It wasn't the first time he had delivered the money to Eglon. In fact he had won the fat man's confidence by slipping in a word here and there about affairs in Israel.

"On this particular trip, he tied his sword on to his right thigh, under his garments. As you know, swords are normally sheathed on the left thigh. A group of his countrymen accompanied him. They arrived, and were received politely by Eglon's security. Soldiers escorted them upstairs, and the money was handed over with due diplomacy. And accepted with courtesy, no doubt. Downstairs they all went and left.

"The soldiers were still watching apparently, and when the group was a few hundred yards away, Ehud stopped, and made signs like he was parting company. He sent his companions on, and headed back. This raised the soldiers' curiosity, but not their wariness. The main event was over, and it seemed like he was returning because he forgot something.

"Ehud came back into the palace, joked around a bit, even lifting his garment from his left thigh, to show there was no sword. No-one knew he was left handed. He told the soldiers he had a message for Eglon, and two accompanied him back up the stairs. Again there was a bit of chatter, until Ehud said, 'I have a word for your ears only,' to Eglon.

"The fat man waved his minders out, and invited Ehud into his large bathroom. He needed to relieve himself fairly often, as you might imagine.

So he sat on his toilet seat. At that point Ehud uttered his infamous words. 'I have a message from God for you.'

"Legend has it Eglon rose to meet the blade. Ehud pulled out the weapon and plunged it so deep into him his belly closed over it. The historians couldn't resist noting his guts and crap came squirming forth. Probably the blow was so shocking, Eglon was unable to cry out.

"Cool as a cucumber, Ehud removed himself quietly from the bathroom, shutting it behind him, and went down the stairs. The servants came back up immediately, but saw the doors locked. Assuming he was relieving himself, they could not hold Ehud back. And so he walked out, and calmly sauntered down the street. For twenty vital minutes those servants waited until their anxiety overcame them. They broke in after repeated knocking, and there was their very dead boss on the floor.

"Ehud got clean away, and shouted the news to all the Israelites he could muster. Even took one of their wretched trumpets, and summoned a ragtag army with it. Eglon had not trained up a successor on the grounds that such men often prove their worth by doing away with their master. So his own state was headless. Israel swarmed in, killed ten thousand, and overthrew their oppressors. Ehud's move ushered in eighty years of self rule for Israel."

The tale done, the Mayor slowed for his summary. "I don't want that to happen. Neither do you, nor anyone in Philistia. I have attempted to learn from the past in order to secure the future. One lesson of Ehud is the surprise factor, a fanatic getting close to the king. And the king trusting him. Risky."

Achish tightened at the oblique reference to underlings.

The Mayor continued. "However, the prime lesson is how dangerous a single man can be. It only took one to galvanize them and overthrow Eglon. As you know, the major difference with us, is we don't treat them harshly. I have to put a lot of effort into keeping the rest of the mayors from doing this, let alone the generals.

"We can't rest easy. Unexpected things have popped out of Israel before. We need to be vigilant. Let's not treat the Samson question lightly. It hasn't gone away yet, I am sure of that."

Tell me, Achish thought gloomily.

The wife of Manoah

It was a pleasant walk down to Zorah with his mother, to ask about herbs for Manoah's rapidly deteriorating condition. Moving at her pace, Samson somehow appreciated her more than normal. Despite his father's illness, home seemed more attractive.

An animated group diverted them once they reached the hamlet, avidly listening to a traveler who had just passed through Philistia. Fires over the border had destroyed a grain growing region. At the behest of their council some villagers had burnt the family responsible to death, including two beautiful daughters, one of whom had spurned her betrothed at the very altar. The stranger's tale caused several eyes to flicker at Samson and his mother, disconcerting her. But the young Israelite didn't notice.

Knowing he had not spoken to his mother about anything, and could not now, he rapidly walked away, clear of the village,

Yet she knew enough, from the first words about the girls, and the stiffening beside her. And now he was gone. His impulsive leaving was his father's, but perhaps his lack of explanation was her fault after all, as she also sensed things and was sparing with words.

She went back alone to their quiet home in the hills. Her own life, once so full of promise because of a promise, seemed to be unraveling.

On her way she repeated the angel's words as a comforting prayer. 'He will begin to deliver Israel from the Philistines.' Speaking out loud to herself as she walked along, something she had done occasionally on her own, seemed to help. This time she dwelt on each word separately. Until she reached 'begin.'

Surprised, she stopped. Never before had she thought about the phrase 'begin to deliver.' Was that his role? Would he begin a task? Not finish one. Just start it. It was a small insight, but it was new. It gave her more to ponder, to make meaning of these rushed and violent events in what she often considered had become an ordinary life. Perhaps she was still involved in history.

Samson took the hill trail, up through the forest and down via the hidden vineyard, half hoping another lion would have the temerity to attack. A skirmish would feel good. But by the time he swung down onto the road into Philistia, he knew what he would do. Loping into Timnah, the council building was obvious amidst the cluster of homes.

As he neared the door, he jumped, kicking with his right foot. His impact carried him through the splintered frame, and he landed clear on his feet inside. At the noise, a group of gossiping men wheeled, their eyes widening. They leapt up, divining this was the lunatic who burnt their district down.

One immediately yelled at him angrily and Samson briefly recalled Keziah's comment about the constable. Grinning at them, he picked up a chair and threw it across the room. His action was so fast, his target was still rising.

Spinning through the air, one blunt leg reached its cycle as it struck this middle aged villager. Caving into his chest, it crushed the sternum, and stopped his heart instantly. Such was the power of the throw, the chair's momentum was not halted by the impact. The dead man was flung back, practically impaled, and together man and chair hit the wall, then slid to the floor.

The others saw it, unable to comprehend such strength and speed. Another pair of whirling chairs flew across, meeting the heads of two more councilors. One fell poleaxed with a broken neck, while the second flipped around the floor as his mangled brain attempted to signal his body. As the rest were scrabbling for the rear door he was upon them, cracking heads together once more, recalling Ashkelon.

The shrieking constable did manage to get out the back. Samson followed, picking up a heavy urn stationed near the door. Out in the yard, he had a clear line of sight and threw it. It spun through the air, hitting the official heavily in the back, breaking the spine in several places, and knocking him flat with the impact. Incredibly the urn landed on his supine body, and sat there.

His yelling had alerted the township however. Folk ran out, again without thinking, Samson surmised. Two men emerged from doors on opposite sides of the street at the same moment. Thrilled with his momentum, Samson flung one fist sized stone, stooped, picked up, and threw another almost before the first one struck. A woman watching later swore both men were hit simultaneously, and each propelled backwards into their dwellings again.

Further along, several people had run out and mingled as a group, excitedly shouting and trying to understand what was happening. Samson loomed up before they had the thought or space to split and run. Cart wheeling through, he kicked at throats and limbs, breaking necks, bones, and blood vessels.

Three fortunate ones only suffered shattered legs, but all the casualties flew out from him in a circular pattern, such was the power of his blows. Landing out of his last cycle, he used his momentum to punch up under the last one's jaw, ripping cartilage, flesh and bone apart. It took but a single clout from foot or fist to incapacitate or slay.

Running along the street, he observed yet more denizens slowly moving out of their dwellings, peering around, faces gradually taking on a look of disbelief and horror. He realized he could observe those in front, remembering their location, while swiveling to check the sides of the street, and simultaneously behind him.

It occurred to him he could watch approach from any quarter, even in the middle of a battle. He had time to calculate, and select his targets, knowing in sequence whom he would dispatch next.

Finally the carnage got through to the community. Their yelling transitioned to the theme of escape, backed up by the screams of the badly wounded. Instead of running out and milling around, the townsfolk started to flee. He was scything through another cluster of five, when he noticed villagers scattering further up the street.

This proved a life saving move for them, as he was still only one man, and could not follow every individual. It was also a lesson in crowd behavior. When he saw them exit, he picked up one more rock, pitched it into the departing back of a fat middle aged male, immediately broke off and ran out the opposite end of the disemboweled hamlet. He had been present for less than a minute.

Running again, he arrived at Eltekeh, less than five miles away. Slowing down as he strode into the main street, he saw the bustle of normal life. Except here a market had drawn in numerous rural dwellers as well. It would be a bazaar again, wouldn't it, the symbol of their power. His anger re-ignited as he seized a pole supporting a shade over one of the stands.

The edifice collapsed, causing people to whirl. Several women screamed when, using the pole as a staff, he knocked a fully grown male into the air. His body sailed up into another stall, tearing the shade cloth away before he landed on the trestle, breaking it in half. He had struck a second man meanwhile, this one also leaving the ground, and careening into two bystanders behind him. All three were propelled back into a third market stall, knocking its table over, scattering its contents, and again ripping the shade fabric asunder.

Racing through the market, he killed eight more before anyone thought of escape. Unlike Ashkelon, where a group had banded together to try and stop him, the nature of the market meant individuals were unfamiliar with each other. Therefore it was merely panic that ensued. Panic, and indecision.

Even as he ventured down another row of stalls, he wondered once more why it took them so long to think about leaving. It was amazing in a way, the element of surprise, and the advantage it gave, he mused briefly as he loomed up on a cluster, taking out three people in one swipe.

Further up the row, he saw two younger men scooping up their takings for the day before turning to flee. Samson's rage rose again—the money, always the money.

Dropping his weapon, he pulled out every pole holding up stalls and shade, as he strode down the center, concentrating briefly on destroying inanimate totems of privilege, rather than living beings.

Angered by a table of finely textured garments, he picked it up, complete with the stock, and whirled it down the market alley like an ordinary man might throw a dinner plate. It spun through three trestles and uprights bringing them crashing around each other, the noise pulsating through the village. With streams of fabric draped over splintered posts, and smashed furniture lying at odd angles, the scene resembled one of comic destruction.

Ultimately, after a half minute of mayhem, the crowd realized they should be elsewhere. Very fast. And the scattering began again. In all directions. Chasing after one group, he knew more out to the side would find safety as they fled.

Cornering this last half dozen fortuitously in a walled area, their terror was obvious, scrabbling at the bricks, shrieking for mercy. But he also saw a burning house, and a young woman weeping to a jeering mob. The dispatching was mercifully quick, using a stall pole swiftly with both hands, chopping down, across and behind, hearing the breaking of backs and necks. It only took five seconds to obtain silence.

In the background he could still hear warning yells mixed with the moaning of victims lucky enough only to be wounded. Still marveling at his powers, it occurred to him he had been slaughtering civilians, not trained fighters. He was immediately taken with the idea of challenging warriors, representatives of those ruling Israel.

Ekron. One of Philistia's five cities. Lamech said this road leads to Ekron. There are troops there. Soundlessly he departed.

Residents of Eltekeh later could not recall seeing him leave. It was as though he disappeared in the middle of his massacre. In fact it took a couple of hours before the remaining populace truly believed he had gone. But he had, and the short jog to Ekron gave him time to think of a strategy for once. This was no clothing retrieval exercise. No, it was time to leave a message.

Four soldiers guarded the gates, one with a spear and breastplate. He figured him to be their troop leader. They stared at his muscular figure, with a mixture of arrogance and envy. Samson couldn't resist, slowing his pace as he drew close. Nervously one of the four asked, "what are you about, boyo?"

Samson's hands came up in a flash grabbing him and a second guard by the throats, bodily lifting and throwing them into the small gatekeeper's house, feeling their necks break as they left the ground. The armored one out to the side was already swiveling his spear. Samson was ahead of him. As the first pair were yet in midair, he snapped back grabbing the upper shaft of the lance. The captain felt the spear stop as though it was embedded in rock.

It heaved upwards, torn from his grip, he watching it spin end to end. To his astonishment, before registering the searing pain, he saw it had penetrated both his body armor and belly.

The last soldier, the youngest, was still glued to his spot, in disbelief over his superior's demise. And now his assailant turned on him. Samson dived down, grabbing his two feet in one smooth action. He rose, swinging him as soldiers in antiquity had swung babies before braining them on rocks, the onlookers standing transfixed. As the young man yelled in fright, Samson let him go on an upward cycle. He flew through the air striking the chimney of a dwelling with his head, careened upwards past it, and sprawled unmoving on the roof.

For the first time that day, Samson halted. Nobody else was moving. Civilian life had frozen. It made intuitive sense, given the penchant to assume authority will look after itself. And if one's protectors cannot protect themselves, it pays to keep one's head down.

"Where are the troops?" he barked out. But they were not expecting dialogue. He strode up to three men beside the city gates, repeating himself slowly, his face close. "Where . . . are . . . the . . . troops?"

They snapped back to life, pointing down the street to the right, tongues still tied. One managed to splutter, "on the corner, on the next corner."

He stepped back, smiling. "Thank you," he nodded.

Onlookers later claimed he was only in Ekron for one minute. Those spared by the gate, having no experience of Samson's previous butchery, concluded they were safe. He must be after the military. In this instance they were correct. A curious few drew into the street to view the impending action at the barracks.

He used surprise again, running and rising at the entrance. As he neared it, his feet shot out, kicking the door off its hinges and into the room. Eight soldiers were lounging around, their swords and spears stacked in a corner. Plucking up a blade in each hand, he sprang across and plunged them into the chests of the first two militia.

Although the troopers could not credit his speed, they were faster than the gatekeepers, rising, even as Samson let go of the weapons and leapt at them. From the street townspeople heard shouting and screaming. A guard was flung out the door, catching his chin on the lintel as he left. The body spun up in a counter motion, looped in the air, and fell to the ground.

More crashes emerged from the room, as of the sound of furniture being broken, and a few last cries. A final sickening crunch of flesh and bone against solid wood brought a brief silence. Samson sprang back out the door he had entered only a few seconds before, causing the spectators to draw away.

He flicked them a grin, before spying a water well further along the street. Running down to it, he changed direction to the nearest house and kicked in its front door. It smashed backwards into the dwelling, but this time he didn't go in. Reaching around both sides of the exposed front wall, he tore out a thick block of masonry. Although made from the sturdy plaster and rock of the region, this chunk of wall broke off in his hands, like a man might break a piece of mud set by the sun. He pitched it accurately into the well where it tumbled down coming to rest only when the shaft narrowed. Immediately it got pounded into its new location by a second and third lump of debris.

Bystanders stood agog as he transferred most of the front wall to the well. The exercise took less than twenty seconds. Dust billowed from both the wreckage of the house, and out of the well as the rocks rained down it. In the midst of this cloud, Samson saw it had filled and left without a word. For several curious seconds, silence reigned as dust continued to swirl.

After an appropriate interval, a brave townsperson entered the military house. Scattered about the room were four groaning bodies in their death throes with either swords or lances piercing them. In the corner under the remains of a heavy wooden table were the corpses of another three. It appeared the table had been picked up, an awesome feat in itself, and thrown at the soldiers. Not only had it slain them outright, but it had broken against the solid wall behind it.

Others ventured over to the well, now so jammed with rocks and plaster that the last piece jutted above the surface.

Samson was out of sight by the time someone thought to go and look out the gates again.

Edred of Ekron

Most who saw the attack were dazed by it. It was so quick, and so destructive. Naturally, there were tears, but mainly there was wonderment. Questions flew about why someone would attack the guards, followed by amazement over the assailants might and speed. Look at that dead soldier on the roof. What about the broken table? How can a man pull apart the wall of a house?

Quite soon the Mayor of Ekron bustled down, raised from his afternoon nap. When he saw the damage, recriminations flooded in. An Israelite must have done this. Listening to the townsfolk, he started to take in the extent of the damage. They pointed out the guard on the rooftop, and the soldier with the broken neck three yards outside the room he was tossed from.

It was a living bad dream. Edred had to draw his senior into this problem.

"Leave the bodies where they are. This is a military matter, and we need assistance here. Don't move anything, don't shift the broken table. Others need to see it exactly like it is." He summoned his chariot and driver, mounted up and was on the road to Gaza.

Reaching the city at dusk, Edred drove straight to the palace of the Mayor. He was shown through to his senior colleague who was about to sit for dinner with his son. With no preamble he blurted out, "Ekron was attacked today. A massacre took place."

"Who attacked you?"

"That is the thing. That is why I personally came here. Otherwise you may not have believed another messenger." The Mayor of Ekron had learned to pause for effect too. "It was only one man."

The Mayor and his son glanced at each other, and that was all.

"Edred, did you see the man yourself?" the Mayor of Gaza inquired.

"No, I didn't. But there were plenty of eyewitnesses. In fact we left everything as it is. I wanted you to see it yourself."

"Good, good."

"You know something, don't you?"

The pair from Gaza's eyes met each other again, and the Mayor nodded to his son to speak.

"Yes, we know about this man. He is an Israelite. He is a murderer. This is not his first atrocity. We need your assistance in bringing him to justice."

"An Israelite. That doesn't surprise me. This is the nation we presumably had under our control. Meanwhile he has ripped the heart out of my city. Single handedly. I thought they were subservient!" Ekron's voice rose higher. "Exactly what do you propose?"

For several seconds the strongest man in Philistia held his gaze. "Don't lose your nerve on this," he said calmly. "Challenges rise up. It goes with the territory of rulership."

His controlled voice lifted slightly too. "You are nearly blaming me for something that happened in your city, not mine. It so happens we know a little about the cause already. Would you prefer we were less vigilant?"

His counterpart stared straight back but didn't reply. In the brief silence, Achish shifted his feet awkwardly. Without the slightest flinch, the leader of Gaza reached forward, touching his fellow mayor on his upper arm.

His voice was softer. "Edred, you have had a tiring experience. You did exactly the right thing coming to us. You will dine with us tonight, and stay here. This has been a very distressing day. Tomorrow all of us will go back and see it firsthand."

The challenge revealed

Four chariots pulled out of Gaza early the next morning. Separate vehicles for both mayors, and a hand picked group of archers in the other two.

Since they were alone together for the trip down the coast, Achish's father got straight to the point. "It would seem we have an extraordinary situation here, something that has never occurred before in the history of Israel. We are not fighting an army here. Only one man. It is almost unbelievable he can do such things, and yes, I am very glad Edred commanded the bodies to be left. We will see with our own eyes just what this Samson can do."

He doesn't seem worried though, thought Achish.

The Mayor gazed around the passing landscape for a while, before turning back to his son. "We got this far by thinking. We will get through the same way." Almost as an afterthought, he added, "and don't look concerned today. Just watch and learn. We need to act as a team."

Achish was relieved at the advice.

Even as they pulled in through Ekron's gates, the pair spied onlookers pointing at the body on the roof. They dismounted as the small group saw who had arrived, and quietly drew back. The Mayor of Gaza had long ago ceased to think about the effect of his presence on others. His mind was on the scene.

He had tried to imagine what it might look like, but the reality was more impressive. The rooftop was five yards in the air. It was incredible that any individual could have thrown a grown man up there.

He fixed his attention on the troop leader, in tight rigor mortis now, with flies already decaying his body. The spear had drilled through the armor but it was not as though the corpse had merely been pierced. No, the lance went right through both the body-plate and the man.

He had not yet spoken, nor had his son. They followed Edred down the street to the barracks, a growing train of townsfolk at a respectful distance behind them. A stink of decay emanated out through a heavy broken wooden door, and the one from Ekron offered them some cloths to filter their breathing. They went inside.

At first sight it appeared as if the band had been overpowered by superior numbers in a shock attack. Dead faces still had surprise apparent on them. Blood and gore were smeared over the walls and floor as if bleeding bodies had been wiped across them. They examined the smashed table. It had beams two inches thick. Broken like twigs.

Neither Achish nor his father could imagine an ordinary human being even lifting the table on his own. Seeing the enormity of the assailant's work, the Mayor's first thought was to rebuke himself for not clarifying more specifically how Achish should act. But as they left the barracks, he managed an approving nod out of sight of their hosts. Now, in the presence of these easily unnerved commoners, was no time to wonder out loud at the uncommon strength of this outlaw.

If only he really knew why I was silent, Achish briefly contemplated.

They were taken to the well. Peering in, they could only see a little way down. It was blocked with debris. When they observed the gaping hole in the residence nearby it was obvious what had happened. Achish followed his father as he completed his inspection. The Mayor had seen enough. They walked back up the street silently.

For the first time in the entire episode, the leader of Gaza was aware of men waiting on his next move, because they had no idea what to do themselves. He felt the thrill of the unknown challenge. He had built a small empire outfoxing this nation of Israel, convincing both himself and his subjects they had nothing to fear.

Yet here was something foreign to his thinking. He fought himself back to the matter. He needed confidence in front of them now, even before his own son, let alone the fickle Mayor of Ekron. He continued up the street, silently and deliberately, knowing the officials were behind him. And following them in turn were the residents of Ekron, open to his words, and to explanations and hope.

The procession passed by the shattered entrance to the military house. Keeping his eyes straight ahead as they walked past the supine soldier on the street, the Mayor of Gaza took another street leading to the city square. Expectantly the expanding assembly trailed them.

At a certain juncture he glanced back, and with a single look summoned a captain of Ekron he knew could be relied upon.

"It would be a good time to clear the streets of the deceased while the city folk are here with me. We need to think of the dignity of their relatives," he whispered solemnly, gently holding his arm as he spoke. The soldier nodded, backed unobtrusively into the crowd, and disappeared.

When the Mayor reached the square, he walked into the middle, slowly turned around and, smiling confidently but with compassion, waited for the gathering to assemble. He would not speak near the sights and smells of defeat.

"Edred, we need to start more history lessons." He said it loud enough for others to hear, and to know his familiar strong tone was still in place. The statement was incomplete, and he knew it. "Israel has never followed a game plan, they always go for the outside chance. Bandits lead them, then a judge with seventy sons. There was even a farmer who spoke with angels at one stage. Now we get a strong man. Always something different. Always trying something new. Quite pathetic really, quite pathetic."

Immediately he spoke up as if to formally address them all, knowing his words would spread like a grass fire through the community. "We have nothing to fear here, good people of Ekron. Nothing at all. We have brought prosperity to Israel. Think on this one thing. Do you think they themselves would threaten their own wellbeing by acting like this?"

He paused, letting the words sink in. Yes, why would Israel forgo all these trading connections we have set up for them? The murmur spread, easing their fears.

"I guarantee this murderous outrage is not the work of the nation of Israel. It is not part of an organized attack. No, it is only the effort of one man. If the leaders of Israel knew what he was doing, they would be horrified. Let me say that again. Horrified that one of their own number was trying to undo all the goodwill between our countries."

Achish felt himself relax under the oratory. He glanced at Edred, and their eyes met. Achish could see a flicker of respect.

The leader from Gaza drew to a conclusion. He was not about to make a tiresome speech. "We will be speaking with Israelite elders over this matter within the next few days. I know they will work with us to eliminate this problem. I know this with a surety."

It was time to introduce empathy. "However, that does not bring anyone back to life. That does not turn the clock back. If there are those among you who have lost loved ones, the heart of Philistia goes out to you. I know the loss you have to face. We will not minimize that. We are all deeply upset about this, and I want you to know our heart is with you."

He stood still for several seconds, letting his face soften deliberately, thinking about grief in order to present it in his voice and appearance. Finally the Mayor of Gaza spoke, huskily. "I am sorry, I am truly sorry this happened. But it will pass, and all our lives will return to normal. This I promise."

He stayed still a few more seconds before nodding at his offspring. They climbed into the chariot after a few words with Edred, and drove out the gates.

Two miles out of Ekron a small procession waved them down, and they pulled over. It was a contingent from Eltekeh and Timnah. A half hour later, the grim faced duo climbed back on board, now fully cognizant of the disasters that had struck the district, and silently went home to Gaza.

The generals

"No, we will not punish Israel for this attack. That would be an even greater catastrophe than what has occurred so far."

None of the generals commented.

The Mayor elaborated further. "Look what happened when some fools in Timnah decided to wreak vengeance on a family mixed up in the fire incident. They killed one household, and the resulting strike back from this Samson destroyed two villages. Do you really believe a mindless hit on a few Israelite hamlets will stop him?"

He could see he wasn't making ground, so he tried another angle. "What if Samson works alone? What if the Israelites don't know what he is up to? In fact, have no idea of his very existence?"

The generals shuffled slightly. "And what if we burn down a village or two without warning? Communities who have never heard of the thug? Do you think that will encourage them to help us capture him? Oh, come on."

He stood up quickly, swinging away to show his disgust.

"Philistia is a civilized nation, with numerous financial links throughout the Mediterranean world. How do you think bankers in Egypt would react to the news that we burnt down several cities in Israel, a nation presumably under our own control?"

Just as quickly, he swung back. "Let me tell you in no uncertain terms. They would get nervous, extremely nervous about their own money which currently keeps many of our prosperous ventures going. Interest rates would rise with their fear. The cost would affect all of us. Everyone in this room."

In full cry now, he rapidly added, "and do not, I repeat do not, go about calling this incident terrorism. Do you know what that emotive word will cause them to think? They will interpret it as saying there are repressed groups in Israel, struggling for freedom. Freedom fighters is not a term we want bandied about. There is no dissent within Israel. They are extremely satisfied with their rising standard of living."

Sitting in front of these economic and political realities, the generals glanced at each other, then back to the Mayor. Eventually one asked a question, the first of the day. "What do you suggest, my lord?"

Finally. A sensible inquiry.

"Simple." The Mayor began walking around again. "We get Israel to help us find him. We turn them against him. The world will see Israel and Philistia cooperate in halting this problem. In point of fact, he has not fired up the whole nation like some of their previous leaders did. Do you re-member Gideon and Jephthah, running around the country, whipping up the masses? This Samson doesn't do that. He wouldn't be able to, they have nothing to complain about. He's a loner."

In mid-sentence his own logic hit him. It only took a split second for the thought to flash through. No, a charismatic leader in Israel trying to work them up against injustice wouldn't work because we have brought them wealth, not slavery. The mastermind ploy would start a rebellion that didn't need public support.

His entire brain process was so brief, nobody noticed. His control was flawless, the aberrant thought banished as he voiced his orders. "We will send emissaries tomorrow to summon the elders. I will personally head the delegation for face to face talks. They will hear us. And they will assist us."

Politics

The procession into Israel was formally military. Generals, captains, and several armed platoons accompanied the Mayor, his protector, and his son. Just enough troops to make an impression; not enough to be considered hostile. They dressed in their battle garb, and even the horses wore trap-pings. All except the Mayor and his son. They wore tidy suits, the garments of politicians.

And the Mayor was correct. Seated in front of the Israelite elders, with Achish and Asaph behind him, he spoke with eloquence once again. All could plainly see the Israelites had no idea about Samson's escapades. Vivid portrayals of agonizing deaths, incapacitation, and whirlwind attacks upon unsuspecting civilians were portrayed in front of them. As the Mayor graphically described the slaying and carnage, their distress level rose. Surely a reprisal was in the wind.

But the Mayor remained placatory throughout. Eventually he ques-tioned them. "How did they feel about the atrocities perpetrated by one of their own?"

The Israelites sat silently digesting the information. Nobody knew what to say. It gradually became apparent from the group body language that they were waiting on Elihu. Grasping his election once more, he rose. "My lord Mayor, we need to say a couple of things to begin with."

Observe them, watch them, the Mayor told himself, taking in Elihu. He was below average height, with a kind but shrewd face. Stout, but not overweight. You wouldn't notice him in a crowd. But they look to him to voice their thoughts.

"Firstly, and most importantly, we extend our deep commiserations to the families in Philistia who have suffered losses. I trust you can deliver our sorrow to these grieving ones."

Elihu hesitated, allowing an interval of decency to pass between sentences, and an approving nod from the Mayor.

"Secondly, we had absolutely no idea about this act, or even about the existence of this young man Samson. He sounds like a lone killer."

The Mayor remained unmoved.

Elihu went on. "I believe I can speak for all of us by saying the friendship which exists between our nations is too strong to allow this sort of unfortunate event to upset it. Before we go any further, we need to reaffirm that with each other. Indeed, I am confident you wish this yourselves. Otherwise you would not have come here today as you have."

Nice stroke, thought the Mayor. Maybe there is more to him than appears.

"Of course, you are right," he agreed. "We continue to grieve, as we will for some time. But it is pleasing to note your hearts are with us at this time. I will relay your kind thoughts to the families involved."

Deliberately he had kept his reply brief. Let the Israelites talk some more. Let them come to their own conclusion.

In the short silence, it fell to Elihu to speak again. "Thank you my lord Mayor. This must be terribly stressful for those families, terribly stressful."

With no further comment from the Mayor, Elihu continued. "We need to make sure this cannot happen again." He turned to his fellows. "We cannot let the work of one man destroy peaceful communities. This must stop."

The Israelites murmured assent, conspicuously so in front of the Philistine contingent. Another of the elders stood, to Elihu's relief. "Samson must be captured. He must atone for his deeds. Elihu is right. We need to move immediately on this young man."

After this confirmation, Elihu spoke more confidently. "My lord, we would also be grateful if you could inform your people, and the aggrieved ones especially, that Israel will spare no effort in apprehending Samson and bringing him to justice."

The Mayor responded. "Thank you. All of you. Your support brings us comfort." He halted, to indicate he had another point. "There is a further angle which I am sure you will understand. Samson has committed these crimes against citizens of Philistia. While we are very grateful for your commitment to solving this problem, it does involve us. This is a joint effort, is it not? We need to act as partners."

He engaged Elihu directly, aware the eyes of both nations were on them. "This is an international incident, and requires an appropriate response. A

joint peace keeping force will restore the credibility of our special relationship to our trading partners. We also believe Samson should be brought
before an international court of justice."

Elihu's mind raced. Up until now the discussion had been about families and deaths; now it was political. It struck him that the phrase 'credibility
of our special relationship' was sanctioned, as it were by a 'joint peace keeping force.' His mind flew back to old Jacob.

The moment passed but the thought was saved. Instead, Elihu asked
politely, "what do you have in mind, my lord?"

"I am prepared to send a battalion to assist."

"A battalion! He is only one man!"

"Yes, that is correct. But he is extremely formidable. By himself he
caused all these disasters. You yourself classified him as a lone murderer.
We only want to help you apprehend him. We are not underestimating your
task."

The Mayor went on. "Our troops will be under strict control. Nobody
is being sought here except this young man. All discretion will be used. We
will work together in establishing justice."

It was now apparent the Israelite elders felt uneasy as their eyes flicked
around their group. Conflicting thoughts ran through their heads. Was this
an invasion? What could they do about it anyway? Who was this Samson?
Why did he have to try and upset a prosperous apple cart?

Eventually Elihu spoke out for them all. "This is a joint venture my
Lord. Israel will also muster a contingent. We have the ability to solve our
own problems."

It was not a point to argue about. The Mayor knew that. Let them have
their pride.

"An excellent idea Elihu, an excellent proposal."

Samson

To no-one's surprise, the battalion was well disciplined. They were under the
strictest orders not to molest anyone. Underlying their presence of course,
was the Mayor's agenda to make sure the Israelites worked on the case.

Samson was not long in the finding.

Walking home from the ravaged Ekron, he skirted the villages he had
decimated. Nearing Zorah, he felt he might be a threat to his family if the
Philistines arrived there. So he by passed his home town, hoping his father
was improving.

Not many miles later, he came to the cleft in the rock at Etam. He was
noticed moving through the small settlement, as was any new visitor in such

a place. He walked along the beaten path, turning into the crevice. In need of water after his long hike, he went on down into the earth through the rocky passage. It led deep underneath the village, eventually arriving at the spring. There he drank gratefully, in the quiet and cool of the underground.

Later he emerged back up the path to keep going, higher up the precipices to the south of the town. Few people visited these rocky wastes, and he knew he would find space there.

Living up there was no problem to a man who could catch three hundred foxes. Game was not plentiful, but his speed gave him all he wanted. At night, when the sky was clear, he watched the heavens.

I wonder if anyone ever counted the stars. You would have to start at one side, then remember exactly where you were. You couldn't look away, or you would lose your place. You would have to finish counting all in one go.

I had to count those men in Ashkelon.

And I counted their steps. And how long it took them to reach me.

I don't think animals can count. But that lion calculated how to reach me. Lions couldn't count time though. Or maybe they can but they don't know they are.

Counting time.

If I fight faster than others, that means their time is slower. That's interesting. When they're slower, I can see what they will do next.

That's why you can't trust people like Achish. He talked instead of doing things. Lions are straightforward compared to people. Unless they are fighting you. Then they're easier to work out.

I wonder why God made mankind like that.

Elihu

Elihu managed to put together three thousand men. Part of him wanted to impress Samson with the disapproval he had raised. But another wanted to show this Mayor of Gaza they could raise an army if need be. Yes, things were okay between Israel and Philistia. Yes, we all grew rich from this relationship. But we are still a nation.

A group of hand picked elders also came along. Elihu hoped he might be able to work through to a conclusion that didn't shed Israelite blood. There were three options. Find him, and simply tell Philistia where he was. Bring him in themselves. Or kill him. But Samson was a countryman.

Samson

From up in his aerie, he saw them.

My message got delivered.

An army.

Not in uniform.

It's not Philistine.

An Israelite army?

They don't have an army.

I haven't done anything to Israel.

Are they coming to thank me?

They don't know what I've done.

Unless the Philistines told them.

People talking again.

Philistia sent Israel, to get me.

My mother says I am meant to deliver Israel from the Philistines, and here they come, to kill me.

I've been at the top of hills before, watching men come at me.

He stood out, boldly silhouetted on top of the range. The multitude stopped. There was much talking while they settled down. Twelve split off and began the climb.

It took a further thirty minutes to reach him. He didn't move for the entire time. It unnerved them. As they got closer, they could see his magnificent physique.

Elihu was first to arrive.

He doesn't look warlike, thought Samson, as his stout figure parted from the group.

He stuck out his hand. "I am Elihu," he said simply. Samson hesitated before silently grasping it. "Great view you have. My first time up here, you know. I didn't realize it was so wonderful."

Be careful.

Words again.

"Do you mind if the others come over and join us?" Elihu gesticulated back towards the eleven.

"Three more," cautioned Samson presently.

Elihu summoned three, two of whom were carrying bags. Samson stood woodenly as they opened them. Out came bread, dried meats, and cheeses. His eyes widened. Elihu saw it. "A marvelous day for a picnic," he laughed, indicating to sit.

They reclined on the blanket and partook. After a diet of wild mountain goat supplemented by berries, the repast was welcome. Even relaxing. Samson gave vent to a loud burp, which caused good natured mirth to break out. The young strong man smiled.

Their eyes met, and it was a start. Elihu began. "You probably know why we are here."

Although he was unsure, Samson said what he thought was safe. "Yes, I do."

Elihu went on. "That was quite a ruckus you raised at Ekron. I am told you threw a soldier high up on a roof. Apparently it took three days for some Philistine to figure out how to get him down again."

He chuckled loudly, as if at the very Philistines themselves. "How exactly did you do that?" he queried in a friendly manner.

Samson didn't know how to handle this banter. Lifting his hand silently, he twirled it, suddenly springing it up in the air. The intended similarity was obvious, and the whole group, including those watching from afar, burst out into more laughter. "It wasn't too hard," Samson added. "He didn't have armor on."

To his surprise, this brought the house down again, and Elihu happily misconstrued the young man had some humor. Drinks were handed around and the conversation veered back to the view for a while.

Elihu was content with this, even somewhat liking Samson. He seemed a nice enough young man despite all he had done. However, time to move on. He swung around as if to call for silence and lowered his voice. "We have been asked to do something. By Philistia."

"I see," answered Samson after some time.

"We have been asked to, to . . . solve this problem."

He was so out of place, and jolly, that Samson could not believe he was serious. "With your little band?"

Elihu laughed. "Good one, Samson, I like that. You're right. We might have trouble subduing you. One point to you."

Unexpectedly the younger man burst out. "Did those Philistines tell you what they did to me? How they tricked me out of my wedding, how they killed my bride by burning her to death?"

"Yes, they told us most of it. They did," lied Elihu, wondering what caused the outburst.

Having started, Samson was now almost loquacious. "I'll bet they did. I bet they told you everything, the whole truth. They're really good at that. They're even better at wagers."

The voicing of it calmed him, so he sat back for a response.

Elihu knew he had to get honest. "Samson, you are right, they didn't mention that. But they are our bosses, you know. They rule the country. You have upset them somewhat."

"Have I?"

That felt good.

Elihu saw it, but couldn't read it. He in turn sat back to let the strong man speak again.

Presently he inquired, "why are you here then?"

The Israelite elder had no choice. "We have been asked to deliver you to the Philistines," he said, awaiting a curt dismissal.

"How many of them?" Samson asked carelessly, emphasizing the last word.

"About a thousand."

"A thousand?"

"More or less. A full battalion."

A thousand soldiers.

And then he saw it. It was amazing how fast.

He jumped up, to the groups surprise, suddenly active, walking back and forth excitedly, across the rocky tops. They could see he was thinking. He spun round. "I know, I know, here's the deal. I'll come with you. On one condition."

What's going on, thought Elihu, still coming to terms with the reticence and the outbursts.

"Depends what that condition is. I might not be able to do it. What is it?"

"You must swear not to put me to death. Just deliver me to the Philistines."

I must be dreaming, thought Elihu. But he had the sense to hesitate before agreeing.

"Of course, Samson. There is no way we want to kill you. You are an Israelite. Like us. Would it be alright if we bound your hands though? So you were our prisoner? I know this sounds pathetic, but we are under a lot of pressure over this. It would look good if we were able to deliver you tied up. I hope you understand. We bear you no ill will at all."

Samson thought awhile before answering. "Just before we get to the Philistine camp, you can do that. But you will send the army down there back home now."

What's going on, thought Elihu. It shouldn't be going like this. He seems eager to be placed in their hands.

"That sounds fine," he confirmed. "Only our small team will go with you." He immediately sent two of the younger men down to disband the horde below.

The General

The Philistine battalion was camped out at Lehi. Limestone walls rose either side from a dry landscape. Behind them, the region divided into a series of ravines and valleys, each leading up a dry watercourse to its end. General Sitterash could see it was a good place to hold a military exercise. He hoped it would only be just that.

Having seen the aftermath of Ekron himself, he was not looking forward to this encounter. True, he had over a thousand armed militia. But it was all too strange, this lone strong man who was faster than lightning. He envisaged getting a cry for assistance, rousing the troops, and marching off into the wilderness after this maniac.

It was impossible to calculate how many soldiers might be picked off at random in that rough terrain before they saw him. Even so, would close combat bring him down? He didn't know. His only consolation was Samson had never been attacked before. It was always he who had launched the offensive.

Gossip about the man was rife amongst the soldiers. Sitterash heard snippets around the campfires during his evening rounds. He was twelve feet high; he could fly, he could pull out trees.

Presently, an orderly reported a small group approaching. The general stood and walked out a few paces for a clearer view. The troops began to stir.

"Wonder what happened to their patchwork army?" he said in an aside to the orderly.

They drew closer. Tell you what, he told himself, they are not exactly in a hurry. And they don't look too beaten up either. Then a glimpse. Couldn't be, he breathed. By Dagon, it couldn't be.

Even at a distance he could see his stature. Not twelve feet, but distinctive nevertheless. Murmurs spread through the gathered soldiers. The band drew closer, giving the entire battalion time to come alert and wait expectantly. Yes, it certainly looked like they had him. Those near the front jostled for a view.

By the time the Israelites drew up, the camp was buzzing. Gesturing for silence, General Sitterash stepped forward to receive the bound outlaw.

"We have brought Samson to you," Elihu informed him formally. "We now leave him in your hands. Our job is complete."

The general answered, "thank you, kind sirs. We all appreciate the good work you have done this day. It goes a long way to restoring all the good will existing between Philistia and Israel. May we offer you refreshments before you depart?"

Elihu was keen to leave before any of the expected beatings began. "General, we thank you for the kind thought, but the day is far gone, and we would all prefer to journey on before dark."

"May your return trip be pleasant," offered the military man. The Israelites started to move out of the valley. Sitterash and his aide stood gazing at their departing backs.

When they were two hundred yards away, the military leader slowly swiveled to look at his troops. He was smiling broadly. It was all the army needed. An impulsive cheer broke out and started to ripple through, like a wave of jubilation.

The jawbone

The bound man saw something else at that very moment, and it triggered his own move. Lying on the ground was the jawbone of an ass. Samson's next step was fast, so quick those near him died without knowing.

His arms flexed and the ropes broke immediately. Such was the power of their breaking, they literally leapt away from him. Even as they were still falling, he sprang over and snatched up the jawbone by the natural handle of its smooth bone end.

Instantly he was slashing. Mentally rested after ten days in remoteness, but fit from chasing down mountain goats, his body was tuned to perfection. The first arc of the jawbone smashed through the heads of two nearby guards. He was onto a third, fourth, and fifth before a cry emerged from those nearby. The general was so close he became a statistic within seconds.

They were leaderless.

Unusual crowd dynamics took control, immensely favoring the lone fighter. The roar of the cheering was still waving back through the bunched battalion, most of whom had not seen him yet. The rumor mill had done its purpose in the previous twenty minutes though, so they were all relishing the outcome.

When those cheers at the front changed to yelling, those at the back simply heard mob noise. They thought it was the cries of their comrades enjoying themselves with the villain. So the rearguard nudged forward, cramming for a view. To Samson they were a cumbersome mass, slowly approaching him. He noted the change in expression as they drew near. Glee was slowly replaced by blankness, then horror. The closer they got, the more

aware they became, and the less able to retreat. Lines of unwilling, scrabbling, militia appeared, and he was transformed into a whirling, threshing
machine. Swinging round, scything through bodies, necks and heads, he
laid them down like harvested wheat.

Elihu

Elihu's band heard the cheering of course, one even coming to a halt, but
Elihu chided him. They continued on for a further half minute by which
time it was embarrassingly obvious something unexpected was happening.
Elihu glanced at a couple of his companions, and they all silently turned
around.

From a distance the desperate shouting and shrieking was confusing.
All they could see were milling soldiers. But, as a line of men blocking him
from view was leveled, they glimpsed Samson. He was free! And fighting for
his life! Elihu held up his hand to stop any thought of hurrying back to the
camp. If the Philistines had bungled it, he was not going to be found close
by.

Samson

Surprise. Speed. He exulted in his two advantages, marveling at how long
they lasted, and learning, learning, learning, with every slashing round. He
could see why more troops came to him, lining up to be slaughtered, as
fluidly as he welcomed it. In fact, he reveled in it, slaying them at the rate of
two each second, his body responding like it was created for this moment.
Without strategy, his lone assault adapted to the flow of mob behavior as if
it were the most natural thing in the world. There was no fear. Just seeing,
and anticipating, and doing, much earlier than these enemies who were like
decrepit old men in uniform.

The jawbone held good, killing every time, sweeping through a chest,
abdomen, neck or head. Often a soldier would raise an arm for self protection only to see that severed as well, sometimes in the same swing that
would bash through his throat. Samson was splattered with gore and blood,
matting his hair, changing him from a human being into a creature from
Hades, his eyes staring out from a wet red visage. This very appearance assisted and yelling transitioned to screaming as lines of men were pushed
toward this harbinger of death.

Eventually the surprise phase ended. The remainder of the battalion understood terror had struck, and their shoving stopped. Confusion
replaced it. At least a minute of indecision, while the inward movement

ceased. He sprang forward. An orgy of two or three deaths per second continued, as the awful figure slashed and carved his way on. Same technique. Speed and power.

Only now he was slicing through their ranks like a knife. His progress was a line, with bodies spilling away either side, his focus on the soldier ahead, and the two either side. He was actually running towards those before him, batting aside bodies as if they were dried reeds. The men flung left and right in their death throes, crashed into companions, leaving a terrible gash through the middle of the regiment. Such was his rate again, that the crowd could not answer. Too many individual decisions amidst confusion and terror eliminated any team advantage they might have had.

After his golden minute of rampage, the third dynamic unfolded. As he sped forward, those three or four away on either side were bypassed. Seeing his back as he roared onward, decapitating their fellows, was maddening. A fresh surge swelled from his rear now, rage re-energizing them.

Whirling as he went, Samson saw them regroup, realizing the most fruitful part of his assignment was approaching. He would now be surrounded by alert attacking men, from all sides. Recollecting the lessons of Timnah and Eltekeh, his adrenalin soared, anticipating once again exactly how he would deal with this encounter, thrilling at the prospect of his highest kill rate.

Abandoning his straight line forward, he switched to a sharp cornered zigzag pattern. Kicking out and around through the throat of one to his right, his second foot stove in the chest of the one before him. Leveraging off that dying soldier's body, he bounced upright, swinging the jawbone around through the arm of an unfortunate to his left. He was now facing the men behind, who believed they possessed surprise. In the briefest of exchanges, two of them understood they were the surprised ones, seeing the blood jet from their shattered chests fractionally before oblivion.

Two more in their cluster knew nothing as the jawbone clove their heads, but the last, due to the oddest of angles, felt the weapon crash through his rear thigh, severing the main artery. Samson flicked to the right, dealing with a further five before making another surprise shift backwards. His rapid changes of direction denied even the quickest from establishing a pattern to his progress.

Those outraged soldiers surrounding him were convinced their numbers must prevail. But he was too swift. As Samson spun around he could see two on his left starting to draw swords, but he knew he would be full circle again before they were a threat. The trio behind were closer, with weapons raised, so he swung lower, underneath the blades in their slow arc, using the jawbone above him, cutting through all three arms, seeing the beginning of their owner's looks of astonishment. Before he moved on, he registered the next two privates behind the dismembered ones, noting their weapons and position for when he faced them again.

His move carried him to his right where a burly soldier had a spear. It appeared as if he were tentatively pushing it towards him. Samson grabbed the shaft in his spare hand, jamming the blunt end back into his exposed neck, feeling it break through before he released it.

Now, facing the two on their left who had their swords out, recalling how he would handle them, he smashed the jawbone down on one head, and up again to the next. Knowing his next move even before finishing this one, he sprang backwards to the surprise of those on his right and left.

Turning as he jumped, to meet the two privates who had hesitated when their compatriots lost their right arms, he laughed as the new assailant to his left flung his spear, which sailed under Samson, impaling the soldier to his right. He was clear of the falling bodies, confronting the privates, who were reeling with shock at events, before being surprisingly, suddenly, slain themselves.

It takes a long time to get a common thought through to a leaderless, maddened, mob. Nevertheless, after the pushing inward, then confusion of something going wrong, followed by the aggressive flinging of numbers at him in anger, reality eventually struck, ushering in the fourth and final period of the battle. Most of the battalion was down by now though, and the clamor dimmed audibly from vast numbers shouting, to a lesser moaning of the dying. A paradigm shift occurred; formerly convinced one man could not do this, the remnant now had no doubt at all. They were finally of one mind. Leave! Quickly!

He experienced the dispersal immediately as they shrank from him, and knew it was now merely a clean up job. Chasing groups down would lower his rate, as he had learnt before. He followed thirty men in such a band, and was on them in less than five seconds. They were bunched, confused, half with weapons out, some looking behind, and others simply heading away as fast as they could. As his method shifted from the defensive whirling machine to the hunter, he veered around the ground, thighs and calves pumping, chopping his way through seven or eight, with up and down swings across his body as he ran. Dispatching them in as many seconds, he chased after another section. And he was still fast. His ground coverage made them appear ambling. That group was destroyed, and the pursuit of yet another began.

The final dozen of the thirty scrambled over a stony ridge, only to find themselves walled off in a depression. Samson reached the rim, grasping their plight immediately. Dropping the jawbone, he used the fist sized rocks piled on the ridgeline.

For a moment the soldiers thought they had a reprieve. He was only going to throw stones. In what seemed like a fraction of a second to the soldiers, three were down, almost as one, with none actually seeing the projectiles. To Samson they stood there, not comprehending anything apart from their companions being violently struck backwards, crumpling without a sound as each piece of granite connected solidly and squarely with the middle of their faces. Only five seconds passed before the pit was silent, and he wheeled, scooping up the jawbone again.

Inevitably the flight in all directions did impact his hit ratio. For perhaps another fifteen minutes the nature of the valley, with its restricted exits aided him by channeling escape. Some did manage however, even going up the valley sides. He saw individuals climbing and knew it was not worth pursuing while numbers remained on the flat.

So it petered out. He decided to chase one bunch of fifty up the valley, hoping they would trap themselves. He reached the tail enders as he raced around a corner, crashing the jawbone down on heads as he sped by. First the right side, then swapping hands, onto eight on the left, another nine on the right, back and forth like a baton held by an athlete. It took a further two hundred yards to lope up past most of them. Rounding a corner, the head of the pack encountered a sheer rock wall.

Five left. Samson slowed to a walk. The quintet glanced at each other, realizing they were done for, and as one drew their swords. They would fight like men. It brought a sneer of respect to their adversary, sauntering towards them like a haughty apparition, dripping with the life fluids of their comrades.

They were not fools however, and knew to attack from all sides. He gave them all the time in the world, grinning all the while. Circling him, their hopes rose at his apparent indecision. At a sign from the eldest, they lunged in together. It would have taken out any normal man.

When they sprang, Samson bounced up, cartwheeling through the air. As he sailed over the man in front of him he was actually upside down in the sky above. He crashed the jawbone neatly through his head, splitting it like a melon. At the same instant he twisted his own body, landing on his feet outside the circle, but facing them.

It was so fast, the soldiers barely had time to appreciate the leap, bewildered at the acrobatics. As the body slowly sagged to the ground, the eyes of the remainder were drawn to the horror of what was previously his head.

Samson, still smiling broadly, beckoned them on. Two of them, enraged with hate, charged with flailing swords, not caring anymore.

To Samson it was still slow motion. He stood slightly crouched, waiting as their arms inexorably moved up, exposing their torsos for an eternity, then swooping under the blades, swinging the bone in one deadly arc. Two chests smashed.

He glanced at the remaining pair. Both became gibbering idiots, dropping their weapons and pleading for their lives. They were basket cases.

Suddenly he slowed.

It was over.

Gazing around, he felt a great tiredness descend.

The soldiers knelt, arms outstretched, blubbering unashamedly.

"Go," he told them. It was the first word he uttered since Elihu bade farewell.

They jumped at his command and scuttled down the wadi.

Dropping the jawbone, he walked quietly after them.

Returning through his carnage he saw bodies, and blood, everywhere. Copious blood, from the blunt savaging nature of his weapon.

There were uniforms, the garb of Philistine soldiers. But there were not husbands, or sons, or fathers, or brothers, having kissed and promised their families a safe return.

There were just steps to recollect, numbers crowding his mind, and still red mounds. With neither sorrow nor regret, nor jubilation now the task was complete, there was merely a tired, thirsty, silent, individual, wending his way down.

Elihu

Silence descended on the desert landscape. A handful of survivors fled past Elihu, who saw them coming and motioned his band to one side.

Presently a blood caked figure walked out. As he came, he noticed the Israelite group but made no effort to communicate. He was terribly tired. Almost staggering, but still holding himself together.

As Samson wended his way down the valley and disappeared from sight, Elihu emerged from what might have been a trance. He jumped out from where he was standing, to break from his shock, and called for the rest. They followed him up, encountering the heaped bodies everywhere.

Eventually he spoke. "I think . . ." But his voice was stuck, so he cleared his throat to speak as one in command. "I think we need to look around here. We will have to report on this. We will tell what we saw."

Another of the Israelites shook his head. "It's a dream, an unbelievable nightmare."

Elihu could not detect whether the speaker meant magnificent or terrible, or perhaps didn't even know which.

"Something significant happened here today," Elihu declared, trying to capture a moment, but knowing it was an understatement. He forced himself to think. "We will make a count of the bodies, at the very least we should do that."

They nodded. Elihu assigned them into different areas. It only took an hour due to the close nature of the killing field.

One thousand and eleven corpses were found.

Samson

That was tough.
Lots of bodies.
I might come back and count them.

I need water
Oh, water from our stream
What I would give

Just sit here a while
Can't get up
Hell of a place to die

I know I don't pray
But I think this was an important fight
I'm sure it's what that angel wanted
And I'm about to die of thirst here.

Just then he noticed a shaded place at the foot of a cliff. He staggered over to find it was a hollow in a rock. Stooping, he crawled in to sit out of the sun.

The floor of the small cave was wet.

Water.

Feeling around to one side he felt a small stream trickling down. Cupping his hands, he was able to fill them and drink. After several mouthfuls, he recalled old Lamech's tale about Gideon's men lapping water. It brought a smile to his lips, the first for some time.

The awful truth

The days passed peacefully in Gaza. Business was picking up again after the nervous jolt, and the Mayor took pains to assure his people a combined hunt for the Israelite thug was underway. Thousands from both Israel and

Philistia were scouring the countryside for him. He was known, the official statements said, equally reviled by citizens from both nations, and would be apprehended.

Then, on an otherwise peaceful afternoon, a pair of feverish privates, footsore and weary from a slog through desert wastes, dragged themselves back through the gates of Gaza. They reported to their captain, but they were near hysteria. Immediately, he dispatched a runner to the Mayor's palace. Could he urgently come down to the barracks please.

The Mayor was holding a future strategies seminar for Achish and other promising young men. It was relaxing, getting back to being the mentor, passing on what he had learnt.

The messenger surprised him with his urgency. He even questioned the man in the classroom. It was to do with some soldiers returning from Israel, he was informed.

As soon as he heard the reply, he regretted asking in front of the gathered youths, and pulled himself together abruptly. But despite the humor he summoned, they had all seen him flinch. He called his driver, mounted the chariot and drove back to the base with the runner. Without Achish. It would have appeared too much like favoritism in front of that particular group.

Jumping off his vehicle, he went straight inside. As soon as he caught sight of the pair, he knew. He knew deeply and sickeningly in his gut. They were still covered in dried, matted blood, and their eyes were near delirium.

Not many questions were needed. The general was dead, and most of the battalion. The Mayor nearly asked how many attacked them, but held it back. In fact, as soon as he realized he had withheld it, he stopped probing. In his confusion, he didn't know what to do, even briefly flirting with trying to keep the whole thing a secret.

He needed time to think. To come up with answers. "Ensure these men are rested thoroughly," he instructed the captain. "They will remain in barracks until further notice from me. No-one is to see them. This matter will not be discussed by anyone. Am I understood?"

He had lowered his voice for the last order and it sent a shudder through the military man. "Understood my lord. Absolutely."

The journey home was silent. As they rode, the breeze brushed past him, and his logic began to return. He knew he had to confirm the event. Immediately he sent the driver off to pick up Achish, and Asaph from the gymnasium where he was working out. They were back within half an hour. He relayed the news to them, holding himself strongly.

Not now. Don't break now.

But they could already see the stress.

"We have to verify this slaughter personally," he told them. "Personally and privately. Asaph, go down to the barracks and ensure no further word escapes regarding this. I have asked once. Twice will not do us any harm. Bring the best of the two stragglers back with you. We need a guide to find the battleground." He thought some more. "I do not think we will take anyone else. You two arm yourselves. I am not taking a force over there. This is undercover."

Two hours later they were underway with provisions and light arms. They drove inland, wheeling north, avoiding villages where they could. If they had to drive through one, the Mayor put on a cape.

It was too far to reach that same day. Camped out under the clear sky, the three strong men of Gaza sat at their own fire, distanced from the drivers and the soldier. The Mayor didn't know whether he could share his fears. Even with these two. On the other side of the flames, they both remained silent as well, for fear of awakening questions.

So they examined the stars, brilliant and close in the deserted hills.

Asaph wondered why he felt detached. He, too, was in the center of these circumstances. But he was calm about it, and, conscious of his serenity, started to examine himself. It didn't take long. Life was already a gift in whatever form it came. Seven years in a slave galley made every day of freedom wonderful. But there was more. He enjoyed observing and guiding, but that events were not his to control. He shortened it all down to a simple phrase.

He was in the grip of events, but he would not let them grip him.

Achish obsessed about his future. Gone were the golden days of running athletic races, and boisterous youthful fun. Instead there was murder and intrigue, trickery and maneuvers. It kept him awake most nights. There was only one solution, and he was united with his father on this: we must silence Samson.

We are gripped by this, and we must free ourselves.

The Mayor knew he was facing the greatest challenge of his life. Nothing fitted his theories. All he knew for a certainty was that if he wasn't careful, he could lose his power and his very life over it.

It was tightening his grip on him, but he could not get a grip on it.

They were up and away early next morning. Veering around the home district of Samson, they went north again, heading for the battle site. It only took a few more hours.

"This is the valley, my lord," remarked the soldier as they neared it. Overhead, vultures were circling, and scores more could be seen on the ground scavenging.

They stopped the chariots some distance from the carnage so as not to upset the horses. Leaving both conveyances in charge of the drivers, the three leaders followed the foot soldier up through the dry rocky wastes.

They were expecting an even distribution of bodies, but it was not like that. To begin with, piles of corpses were scattered, in distinctly unique zones, as though whole groups had been slain together. The stench was horrific under the hot sun, and the dreadful birds flapped their annoyance at the newcomers. Further in the middle of the valley was a large concentration of dead, in parallel lines. It was hard to visualize how they had been killed.

Not a single Israelite body was found.

The soldier led them further up, passing a shallow depression with a dozen corpses, all with faces smashed in and blooded rocks nearby. Suddenly the format of death altered, and a line of militia were found with heads pointing up the gorge. It was as though they had been fleeing from something that had overtaken them one by one, slaying them in their tracks. Curiosity caught the men from Gaza, and they worked their way up to the end of the ravine.

A small group of bodies lay there. No doubt their final stand, thought the Mayor. One head was cloven through as with a blunt weapon, while a further two corpses lay as if pushed violently backwards, their chests opened up.

All sounds ceased. After the crunching through the sandy wadi and the rustling of their own clothing, there was nothing. An immense blankness hung. No sound, no life, no thought. The Mayor of Gaza was enveloped in the silence.

Is this multitude a casualty?

Achish broke the quiet as he noticed something and stooped to pick it up. At this the soldier jumped nervously. "That was his weapon!" he cried out.

All eyes swung to the bone Achish was holding. "This?" he uttered in astonishment. "Samson killed all these with only this?"

Even the Mayor was staggered. It was the final insult. After rousing all Philistia against him, the pride of our armed forces is called out, and a single man dispatches them with the closest thing at hand—the jawbone of an ass.

He, a man of destiny, had grappled with the nature of history to better the lot of his people. And now it was all under threat from a mere youth, not even a calculating killer. A loner who didn't even prepare himself when he faced an army.

His fury rose at the carelessness of the Israelite in contrast to his own studied planning. How dare he!

His son and bodyguard stiffened, hearing his rising anger in his forced nasal breathing. Unable to hold himself, he quietly cursed. "Damn you Samson, damn you!"

Elihu

Elihu thought through many events on the trip back from Lehi; the death of Abdon; no new judge emerging; Philistia's invasion; old Jacob; and this strong young man; this invincible Samson. One of their own. Had he been led astray by the Philistines in coming to capture him?

Was there a turn in the wind here? Was a change coming? He needed more time. Didn't have more time. When Philistia heard of this, what would they do?

It was a subdued journey home.

Before Elihu reported to the elders, he knew he had to take a side trip. While chatting with Samson, Elihu had learnt his home town village and parent's names. A background check would be good.

It didn't take him long to find out where Samson's family lived. Actually his mother and brothers, someone in Zorah kindly informed him. Manoah had died suddenly ten days ago. A rapid onset of an unknown cough. The local commented about the impulsive nature of his passing. It was so like Manoah.

Alone this time, he walked up the paths past the fields and trees where the lad must have grown up. A simple farmhouse came into view, and he made his way towards it. As he approached, a woman emerged. She stood still watching him. She was smiling. As though she knew something he didn't.

"Greetings." Her manner was polite, and careful about rituals of introduction. "Welcome to our home. Would you care for a drink?"

"Thank you, yes I would. Very much so in fact. Quite a warm day."

She fetched water, then invited him over to sit on the ground under one of the trees in the copse near the house.

Elihu opened their talk with felicitations about her husband. She thanked him for his concern, yet appeared serene as she did so. But it did not seem callous to Elihu. He felt she was able to embrace life with all its vagaries.

"I understand you have a son named Samson?"

She thrilled to the question. Be calm, she told herself, be calm. "Yes, I do."

"A strong lad from all accounts."

"Yes, he is." She could contain herself no longer. "What is it you wish to know?"

Her openness and composure were disarming. He was warming to her all the while. "I am an elder of Israel. I wish the best for our nation." He spread his hands wide. "What is it you can tell me?"

She liked his frankness too, and beamed back, asking only one question. "Shall I start from the beginning?"

"Yes, of course, please."

And she did. She told him nearly everything. Most of the words from the angel, memorized those many years ago. Bringing up the boy, and the growing power of the young man. But she halted just before the Timnah episode.

Surprised, he couldn't help himself. "There's more isn't there? I know some of it already."

She had easily surmised this, and so she laughed teasingly. "Oh yes, I am sure you do. But I have already spoken. You must tell me what you know now. For us to be even."

He took this with a grin, and decided not to hold back on the smaller incidents. Her eyes widened as she heard behind Samson's home silences. He moved on to how Philistia had come into Israel after him and his descent to Lehi.

This was the crux, and she felt it coming. He spoke direct to the facts. "We then delivered him, alone and bound with strong ropes, to the Philistines. To a battalion of more than a thousand soldiers."

"And?"

"Madam, your son slew one thousand and eleven armed Philistines. By himself."

Her face relaxed, and she looked away, down the valley. She remained silent for some time. Elihu knew to as well.

"How strange you used the word 'delivered' when you gave Samson to the Philistines. It is the very word the angel used about his life's work." She mused before facing him again. "I have a question for you now, sir. Does this latest act of my son not appear like he is beginning to deliver us from the Philistines?"

The five mayors

The Mayor did not speak much on their journey home from Lehi. Furtively they camped overnight in Israelite hill country far from the stinking reminder that their grip was crumbling. Hours in thought in the chariot had put the Mayor no further ahead. He knew he could not keep it a secret. He had to break this news to his colleagues.

Upon his arrival back in Gaza, messengers were sent to fetch the mayors of Philistia. For an important meeting in two day's time.

The four sat there while he outlined the status of the Samson affair. While they had heard of the Ekron incident, none of them could have predicted the magnitude of this latest tragedy. Indeed, were it not for the Mayor of Ekron's eye witness accounts of Samson's potential, they might have thought their colleague from Gaza had gone mad.

"Are you are telling us Israel has a giant protecting them?" the Mayor of Ashdod asked.

"No, not at all," replied the man from Gaza, realizing he hadn't given physical dimensions. "Samson is muscular, but actually no larger than, actually, no larger than Asaph. He is just unbelievably powerful. Incredibly. Words cannot express it."

Pauses were common during the discussion. Silent spaces.

Ashdod inquired again, "does he have children? I mean, are they developing a super race or something?"

"Good question. I don't believe so. Has anyone heard whether there are more of him?"

Shaken heads all round. "Let us hope he is alone. That might be one small consolation."

Back and forth it went until there was little more to relay. The Mayor of Gaza had to move forward. "Needless to say, there is not much point in sending out another garrison. We can ill afford a further such loss."

Everyone nodded.

He paused, alerting them to expect an idea. "There is one thought. About the way he works. He acts alone. He hasn't mustered a force because he doesn't need one. He does not appear to be a leader. In fact, after he commits an atrocity, he disappears into the wilderness."

They listened, waiting for his point.

He stood and paced around while he spoke. "Israel has been without a leader for some time. We rule them, we tax them, but not heavily. They enjoy prosperity under us. They even went to get Samson themselves. It may be he doesn't even aspire to leadership. He simply wanted revenge when you get down to it. He got hit. And he hit back. It just escalated, that is all."

He remained standing, gazing out the window. "Perhaps we need to pretend he doesn't exist. We could keep on ruling Israel even if he is alive. There is no need to bait a bear. Why bring trouble on yourself? Just leave him in his cave. Even drop some food at the entrance to keep him happy. You can still hunt on his mountain."

The others remained silent. For the first time in many years, they each felt uneasy. His ideas were usually brilliant. This didn't fit. Conversely, Samson was certainly unique. They were not up against anything ordinary here. It was difficult. And this visionary in front of them had always won through.

The thinker from Gaza glanced at his Ekron counterpart. He could already visualize him later on, spreading discontent among the others. So he leaned back to convey his own personal ease, poured himself a drink, and said nonchalantly, "of course, if anyone else has some other ideas, now is a good time to share them."

More silence, as the four lesser mortals waited on each other.

He drew his own conclusion. "We need unity here, gentlemen. Let's agree on this together. I will travel into Israel in the next few days to meet with the elders again. I will not be taking a large contingent. And I don't think we should all go either. If we all turn up, they will think this episode is bigger than we can handle."

Elihu

Elihu went straight from Zorah to summon the elders of Israel. Messengers were sent requesting an immediate council meeting. Within two days the elders had convened. All knew about Samson by now, and of Elihu's task to bring him in. They were uncertain as to what he would report, and it lent an air of suspense.

He started straightforwardly. "Gentlemen, thank you for coming. You are probably aware I am going to update you on the Samson issue."

"Get on with it Elihu," broke in Nahor from Judah. "Give us the bad news. We're sitting down."

Elihu was unfazed. "Actually, I honestly don't know whether it's good news or bad," he replied. "However, since you want it from the shoulder, here it is. Samson asked us to deliver him to the Philistine army alive. Bound with ropes. We did that. He then broke loose and killed one thousand and eleven soldiers. On his own."

They were stunned. And silent. Nahor finally spoke. "You saw this?"

"Yes, with my own eyes. As did the dozen who accompanied me. And who counted the corpses later."

"And Samson? What happened to him?" another inquired.

"He is very much alive. I mean, we think he is. He was last seen walking away from the battlefield."

He recalled his reticence to aid the blood caked warrior and decided on the truth. "I have to admit we were so shaken, that we didn't follow him. It was all so unreal. Taking out an army on his own."

Several questions of clarification were asked, until Elihu suggested it was time for a break outside. To remind them they lived in a mostly normal world. They broke into chattering groups, animatedly gesticulating to each other.

Elihu called them back in.

"Do the Philistines know about this?" asked Gershom from the tribe of Issachar.

"We must assume they do," stated Elihu. "It was impossible for Samson to kill everyone once the masses started scattering. We saw several soldiers fleeing."

Elihu's tone altered. "Gershom has raised the very issue we need to discuss. Philistia will find out, and they will not be silent. They rule Israel. They rule benevolently, not causing us stress, which is a new thing historically. But they have certain expectations."

"Perhaps their rule may not be so benevolent now," added Nahor.

A murmur moved through the room. Indeed. Perhaps not.

Elihu let the remark sink in before commenting, "Nahor may be right. But they might differ from that view. We know Samson has already caused havoc in Ekron and Ashkelon on his own, and escaped without being touched. Now he has slain over a thousand men, and he is still unharmed. Will Philistia throw another battalion at him again? To find out whether he can do it a fourth time?"

No, maybe not, murmured the elders as they considered this counter proposition. Silence ruled again for a period as they mulled over their thoughts.

Eventually the oldest, Kenaz from the remote reaches of Ephraim, spoke from his chair. "We are men of Israel here. For generations we have followed the Lord our God, albeit intermittently. I believe Elihu has some thoughts about this. He has met this young man who is turning our nation upside down. I would like to hear Elihu's opinions on these matters."

Mmm, they all murmured a third time. Yes, let Elihu speak.

Taking his time, he stood, starting slowly. "Some background to these events has emerged. Something you know nothing about happened twenty years ago in the hills behind Zorah. An angel visited a couple. And made a promise."

"Really, Elihu?" retorted Nahor, who had recovered some of his bluster. "We get reports of angels every month or so. Madmen in Israel claim they are led by angels and words of God to try anything. Remember that Eliphaz who got right into the center of Gaza and nearly killed the Mayor? He was led by God. Told the Philistines before he died."

He blathered on, seeing others were attentive. "And in any case, why would the Lord send anyone to save us? Nothing much to save us from. Trade has never been better, our businesses are booming, and crime is almost non-existent."

He was looking for support, but saw only wavering eyes.

In the break, Elihu spoke again. "You raise things I have often thought about, Nahor. Especially on my way back from Lehi. You are right. We have nothing to complain about. We're wealthy. We're worried about foreign exchange rises and trading terms, and interest rates. We all work hard and come home to think about the next deal. Life is faster than ever for us because we don't have time to raise our eyes above building our own secure nests. Sometimes I think, yes, we're rich. But we're not free. We are no longer worried about standing as a nation and facing the perils of the world. Instead we've happily given our decision making powers away so we can have holidays on the coast."

He was in his stride now. "If a Jephthah or a Gideon had arisen and tried to organize a rebellion, he would have been laughed out of town. There's not enough dissatisfaction around to hang an uprising on. Instead we get sent a single man. Youthful and violent perhaps, but one who on his own, his very own, has raised up the question of our sovereignty again.

"He alone is refusing to acknowledge Philistia as his overlord. And despite our long history of this type of leader, we tried to turn him over to them. And I was the guiltiest one. I recommended we did exactly that. I had him trussed up and delivered to their army like a goat for market. So, I want you to listen to the words of this angel, delivered many years ago. The whole story."

He had them on the edge of their seats, ears wide and hearts open to the fact they might be part of history in the making, and surprisingly, enthralled by the feeling.

Elihu told them about the angel's words, and how Samson's forays against Philistia began. Keeping nothing back, he relayed the facts as he had heard and seen them. When he finished he sat down. Silence ensued.

Soon, everyone could see old Kenaz had something more to say. They waited while he gathered his thoughts. Standing up, for he felt he should, he began. "This is an amazing tale, such as has never been heard before in Israel. I do not claim to have all the answers, but I would like to make mention of another episode in our history. We all heard the story of Gideon many times when we were young. And how he only needed an army of three hundred to defeat Zebah and Zalmunna's thousands.

"There is an often forgotten chapter to that account which I believe is pertinent. While Gideon was pursuing those kings of Midian, his small army grew famished. As they passed by the city of Succoth, he requested refreshments for his brigade. The elders of Succoth saw his miniature force and scoffed at him. 'Have you captured Zebah and Zalmunna yet? Why should we give you bread?'

"That angered Gideon. He replied, 'when I return with them, I will thrash you with whips made from desert thorns.'

"History tells us he asked the same question of the town of Peniel. And received the same answer. In similar vein, he promised restitution to them. Who knows whether these refusals gave Gideon the moral stamina to finish his task? But he did, and as we know, he captured both Zebah and Zalmunna. Alive.

"He returned to Succoth and extracted a list of names of the leading men of the city. Parading the captured kings of Midian in front of them, he had his men whip all seventy seven of those men of Succoth. By then his blood was up. He reached Peniel, and without any further explanation simply tore the central watchtower of the town down, and killed a goodly number of their menfolk too."

Kenaz stopped to let the story sink in. "Those two cities did not believe the Lord our God had rescued them using the hand of Gideon. And they paid the price. I feel there is great danger in attempting to impede the work of God. I am not telling you this young man has been sent from above, but I do not want to stand in his way if he has. My personal stance is this. If he has not been sent, all this will fizzle away. If he is as his mother suggests, we ought to heed what is going on."

A ripple of chatter arose as the old man sat down. Elihu watched them for some time, before signaling for silence. "There is much to discuss and decide here. So much. I feel we will have to do more than talk however. Philistia will make an approach to us in some form. The Mayor of Gaza is not a man to lie down easily. We need to decide, and plan. We cannot avoid doing so. To do nothing here will also be a decision."

International tactics

The Mayor took Achish and Asaph and a small squad with a few generals and leading merchants. He wanted the visit to appear friendly, but to suggest power. The meeting had been remarkably easy to arrange. A horseman had been sent directly to Elihu. The Israelite was quite amenable to such a gathering, almost eager, the messenger reported back.

They met outside the town of Hebron, on a grassy field. Several large tents had been pitched, and refreshments laid on. The Philistines felt surprised, but relaxed. Unexpectedly, the air was not tense. Perhaps this would go smoothly.

After some brief small talk, they reclined on the carpets provided.

Elihu sat at the front of the Israelite assembly, more formally a spokesman this time, the Mayor guessed. He encouraged the Mayor to speak, as the one from Gaza had called for this gathering.

The Mayor stood. "We have come today to renew our friendship with Israel. For many years now our nations have worked together for joint prosperity. Trade between us profits many of you." He paused, thinking to use humor. "Naturally it profits us as well, but is that not business?"

Normally the Israelites would have laughed. But this time they merely smiled, as though the Mayor was talking about the past, and yes, things once were like that. He was alarmed, but had the sense to move on. "And so, from time to time, it is good for us to come and share together our joint fortunes, and to think how we must sustain this into the future."

He talked on for a short while about some promising trading ventures in Greece. Meanwhile the Israelites sat patiently. It appeared like they were just being polite.

So he drew to a close. "I would like to call on our friends from Israel to speak now, to let us know their minds. Enough chatter from me. It is better to listen, is it not, than talk on."

And he sat down to a subdued applause.

There was no embarrassing delay this time while a leader was selected. Instead, after a respectable silence, Elihu stood. "Thank you for coming from Philistia to visit us. It is true there have been many years of . . . of economic union between us. That is true. These have been prosperous years. And we, like you, feel there is much goodwill between our nations."

He's prepared this, the Mayor told himself.

Elihu breathed in, giving himself strength. "Times and seasons change however. Epochs begin and end. This has been our own history, as it has been yours. Nothing remains forever, and yes, you are right again, we all need to look to our futures. All of us."

The band from Philistia started to catch his drift. Elihu saw it, and moved with them.

"We are glad you are here today," he said, directing his speech towards the Mayor. "We are glad you are here, because we want to outline some of our thoughts about the future. We are hoping you wish to hear our mind."

The Mayor knew he needed to respond, and without speaking he gestured openly with his hands, beckoning him on.

"We made a mistake a little while ago," Elihu stated, "and we have discussed this together in depth. Our nations heritage is deeply linked to the Lord our God. He guides and leads us. In bad times and in good. We need to follow His guidance now."

He drew his breath in again, signaling with his body language he was at the critical point. "God has given us a young man."

The Mayor knew immediately what was about to happen. A lesser man would have blanched. Not so the prime leader of Philistia. He sat impassively, unmoving, letting the scene unfold.

"We think you know who we mean," Elihu continued. "And we also feel we owe a full explanation of our decisions to Philistia, our nearest neighbor."

Nearest neighbor! Why, you patronizing little merchant!

The Mayor held himself in as he stared at the speaker.

Elihu's words came easier now he had voiced the main point. "Our decision is ultimately based on our relationship with the Lord our God. We do not expect you to understand necessarily, but we do need to state it clearly. Our God did not lead us out of the bondage of Egypt to become a vassal state. Our history clearly shows us this. From now on Israel will run its own affairs. We thank you for the years in which you have done this, but as you say, the future looms up."

Whispering broke out in the Philistine ranks. The Mayor turned slowly around, his gaze silencing the disturbance. Swiveling back, he nodded solemnly at Elihu.

The Israelite then went off on a tangent worthy of the Mayor himself. "Having said this, we see no need to dismantle any of the trading systems set up between us. Once more you are correct, those arrangements have been beneficial to us both. We have no interest in dissolving them. We may need to renegotiate interest rate terms and certain fees, but that is easily handled." Emulating the Mayor, he added, "in fact it is merely business, is it not?"

Elihu did not stop there. He went on smoothly talking about the potential for the two nations to work together into more enriching years ahead. He wandered into trade for a while, mentioning possibilities in Arabia. He knew nobody was listening. He was filling in, while the words sank into his recent rulers that the game had changed. It was so like the Mayor himself, that in the middle of the emotions tearing at him, he grudgingly respected the Israelite.

Elihu wound up. "We do not expect you to respond to us today. Much has been said here. There is a lot to consider. Please think on these things. Consider our position, and on your own future."

His arm swung round to indicate the refreshments behind him. "And please, stay with us for food and wine before your return journey. Share your thoughts with us over some of our finest reds. Mix with our people."

As he spoke, his hands still gesturing towards the pitched tents, the folds of one parted, and a powerful, well dressed figure stepped out. Everyone from Philistia knew immediately who he was, even though only two had seen him before.

The Mayor stared at him, mastering his hatred in order to take in as much as possible.

Samson's eyes swept over the group as they all stood. In a rehearsed move, the elders began mixing with those from Philistia to draw them into more talk over the wine. Elihu was clever, the Mayor admitted. Letting him emerge like that. A strong move.

Then Samson saw Achish. Their eyes locked. He walked forward, threading through the rows of elders, numbering his steps.

Achish was rooted to the spot, his adrenalin surging with the surprise encounter, knowing he could not retreat, the crowd parting as they divined Samson's intent.

The Mayor saw it instantly, his mind spinning. Asaph came in behind the golden youth. Samson drew nearer with deliberate carefulness, savoring each tread. He stopped in front of them.

"Achish."

The Mayor was transfixed, hearing his son's name emanate so directly, almost intimately.

"Samson." Achish spoke back clearly, fully exposed, feeling the deep, and immediate spike of hatred, like an arrow.

Samson's eyes held him for several seconds. He felt very good. No smart talk now. Lost for words, he briefly thought. Those were his weapons. He would not stoop to using them himself. Turning, he nodded at Asaph, conscious of the older of the trio following his every move. He walked back through the milling elders, and disappeared into the tent.

Elihu came up behind the Mayor. "Didn't realize your son knew Samson. Mind you, they do have the same physique."

The Mayor consciously restored calmness to his face.

Taking him by the arm, Elihu said quietly, "could we have a few words together?" Motioning with his head against the Philistine contingent, "alone?"

The Mayor waved his son and protector away and walked alongside Elihu towards a tent where a servant was conveniently stationed. The underling lifted the flap as they approached, dropping it behind them, and positioned himself firmly outside. The Mayor had no fear for himself, realizing Israel would not harm anyone today. They wanted peace, and they had a backup plan. Or a backup man, he conceded ruefully.

"Your worship," began Elihu.

Oh, very good, thought the Mayor. He's not about to provoke me by reminding me of my new status here. The new master respecting the old. Smart.

"We saw the battle at Lehi." Elihu waited a few seconds. "Can we speak man to man?"

This offer solicited a shrug.

Expecting such a non committal gesture, Elihu tried again. "Your worship, we will not meet often in such circumstances. We have the opportunity of covering valuable ground here, or remaining silent and paying in lives later. Neither you nor I want that." Another pause. "I ask you again, may we be direct with each other, as stewards of the people God has given each of us."

The Mayor of Gaza examined him again. A man of steel too, he thought. He rose to the moment. "Yes, indeed, let us speak. However, I retain the right to deny anything I might say in this tent."

Standing while speaking, and placing a finger to his lips, he moved to the entrance. Elihu knew what was coming. Quickly drawing back the folds the Mayor stepped outside. He saw a hubbub of drinking, eating and chattering as the Israelite and Philistine leaders mingled with each other. Walking briskly round the enclosure, he assured himself men had not been lying in wait listening. Slipping back inside, he instructed Elihu, "speak."

Elihu indicated the remaining chair in the tent, and proceeded to pour two goblets of wine. "Our discussion should not prevent us enjoying the reds I referred to," this gaining a slightly uplifted eyebrow from the Mayor.

Elihu spoke for some time, restraining himself mainly to a review of the numbers. Treating the exercise as though it were a game, he depersonalized success or failure so as not to arouse his counterpart. Dispassionately he informed the Mayor of the quantity of Philistine dead. He also reiterated no Israelites were lost.

". . . so it does appear to upset the military balance somewhat," Elihu finally summed up. "At least we think so. Within the walls of this tent, between us only, I need to ask whether you feel the same."

Elihu sipped some more before continuing. "I mean we could arrange another battle if required. Our gamble is not too high really. We throw in one warrior, you commit another thousand. Could be Samson can only do this once. On the other hand, we both know how he performed in Ashkelon and Ekron. At least I assume you were telling the truth when you informed us of his deeds."

The Mayor remained silent, holding what remained of his pride together. Finally he spoke, but as of others in history, in part to avoid facing himself just now. "Leaders do not often remain in power after a defeat. We also both know that. So, even when faced with certain destruction, they lead armies to battle, preferring to die with honor."

Tempted though he was to put a reply back to him, Elihu restrained himself. However, the Mayor answered for him. "Such leaders just take an extra few thousand lives with them, when they could have simply surrendered their own."

Presently Elihu commented, "that path does not pave the way for one's son. In fact the entire ruling family tends to get removed by their own people under those circumstances."

The Mayor nodded in assent. "However, giving way so soon, without a battle, can be interpreted as cowardice. Which also topples the leader."

They sat there, each with their own thoughts. Elihu felt it was going alright. The very fact he was able to talk with the Mayor was a major step forward. Dialogue would greatly assist in the making of a bloodless transition. Over the years of the Philistine occupation, he had learnt to admire this very characteristic of the man sitting with him now.

A war would not serve his business agenda. True, Israel was going to revise some trading terms heavily in their favor. But while holding the high ground, Elihu was arguing it was also in Philistia's interests to come around peacefully.

"Maybe there is a way out of this."

The Mayor glanced up at Elihu's comment.

The Israelite went on. "Rulers can survive when another cause is identified. Something outside their control. Perhaps an internal affair."

"Are you suggesting a scapegoat be found?" the Mayor asked him.

Elihu sat silently for some time, toying with his goblet before replying. "We think you are a very capable ruler, your worship. We hope you remain in power."

The Mayor gazed across the table at him, his face devoid of expression. It was like there were three of them in the room. He was both an observer and a participant. In one sense, he could barely contain his rage, but in another he admired his opponent. He was both seething with fury and yet also applauding the Israelite. Elihu's handling of the situation was impeccable. Very clever again, getting him talking like that.

He vowed two things. Firstly, he would survive the reversal. And secondly, they would meet again. They would meet again when Philistia's power had been restored. He was already longing for that day.

Family tactics

They did not remain long. After the Mayor emerged from the tent, he summoned his contingent, and they withdrew. Silence reigned in the Mayor's chariot. After a few miles, Achish could not restrain himself. "Father, I need to . . ."

The Mayor swung round, face coldly chiseled, his hand chopping the words off. "Later, Achish. In Gaza."

Asaph caught a murderous glance. He had never seen it before, but he knew the accounting would draw him into the circle too.

The Mayor was already on his thought trajectory. A mere youth was destroying his life's work. He could feel the pull of surrendering to his emotions, of festering in hatred. However, he knew that brief luxury would bring about his end at the hands of his own people. Elihu was right. His grip on Philistia was unsure. His past successes would not save him. He had to act quickly and decisively. And it would not be against Israel.

He remained silent for the entire return trip.

When the chariots entered Gaza, he directed the driver to pass by Asaph's residence. Looking at him strangely, the Mayor told him they would talk in the morning. There was much to cover. Would he come to the palace mid morning please. Driving home, he dropped his son at the gate. "Sleep soundly my son. And do not leave the palace tonight. I will see you shortly."

His instructions were clear, and the younger man went inside to a fitful rest. Several hours passed before his father returned. He was not sure whether to go out, or wait to be summoned. Feigning sleep seemed the best thing. He lay there, eyes closed, waiting for the knock on his door.

But it didn't come. After some time, Achish realized the palace lights were being extinguished.

He wasn't awoken early as he half expected. In fact he had to rise unsum-moned. Going down to the eating area, he found his father thoughtfully devouring a bowl of fruit. The Mayor had a resigned look on his face.

"Did you sleep?" his father inquired.

"Yes, thank you father," Achish lied.

"Good, good. I thought you might be asleep when I got back in late last night, so I didn't disturb you."

"Thank you, father."

"Try some of this fruit, it's delicious."

He doesn't know how to start, thought Achish. So he remained silent, willing his father on to the point.

The Mayor sensed it, and after he had finished an olive, he began.

"Achish, there are times when one must make public decisions. People need to understand incidents clearly, to have direction in their lives. Leaders must sometimes do things they may not want to, for two major reasons: to show they are still in control, and to bring out publicly the reasons behind events."

Achish had no idea what he was talking about, but remained quiet. The Mayor continued. "Something is about to happen. Something you will not like. I want you to remain silent during this episode. I want you to keep your mouth very much closed. Whatever happens. Do you follow me?"

Achish then knew he was about to be rescued. "Yes father, I under-stand you."

"If you are ever to rule Philistia, this is what you must do at this mo-ment. That is how important this is."

Alert to the obvious absence of others, Achish asked, "what are you talking about? What are you going to do?"

"You will see presently. And you will soon understand."

A servant appeared. "My lord, Asaph has arrived."

The Mayor acknowledged the interruption, and without smiling com-manded he be shown in. The calm, faithful, figure walked into the room. The Mayor stood, and Achish followed suit.

"Come," called the Mayor, beckoning the pair as he walked out of the meal area into a larger lounge room that had several doors leading out of it. They sat in easy chairs, pensively waiting on the Mayor. After a few seconds, he leaned forward, and clicked his fingers. Instantly six soldiers appeared through the various doors, swords already out, surrounding Asaph before he could move.

Achish was stunned. A protest rose in his throat, but the Mayor had already laid a restraining hand on his arm, and it died away.

His father began. "It grieves me to do this, to bring this upon one who has shown such service to Philistia. But you held secrets back from us when you should have known better. Many lives have been lost because of withheld information. It cannot go unpunished."

He rose from his chair. "For the sake of the many years we have been in each other's company, I ask you to go quietly. With dignity. Do this for me. We must all answer for our actions in life."

Achish was horror struck, his eyes flicking back and forth between the older two, somehow expecting Asaph would appeal to him, or that an outburst of denial would erupt from his lifelong mentor. But as their eyes met, he saw only resignation, as if the older strong man was playing out a role. Asaph was not even angry. It seemed like he grasped more fully than anyone exactly what was going down.

Rising from his seat slowly, he gave the armored guards measured time to fall in around him. They moved off without a word. The Mayor and his son could hear their echoing footsteps, then finally the opening and closing of the heavy doors at the front of the palace.

Silence fell again.

Achish exploded. "What the hell is going on?! That man is your personal protector, and you have just condemned him! What would lead you to do such a thing?!"

The Mayor let him rant away for a while before butting in. "Why did you not tell me about Samson?"

It was completely expected, and stopped him in his tracks. "I just didn't, and that's all there is to it."

The Mayor began his lesson on political reality. "Let me ask you another question. Do you think I could return from an international disaster where my own son was exposed as personally knowing public enemy number one—and do nothing?"

His own voice rose, timed with his questioning. "Do you think my life, and by implication yours, would be worth anything in two days time, if such contradictions found their way into the marketplace of Philistia?"

"Have you any idea how tenuous our grip on power is? We are expected to deliver the goods, to succeed and prosper. We are continually observed by our own people, let alone our peers like the Mayor of Ekron! They look for strength, but if they find weakness or confusion, it spreads like a grass fire. Philistia is under threat. Its citizens will be looking for an explanation. One way or another they will find it or invent it." He lowered his voice. "It is better we find it for them."

"But this is Asaph, surely the most loyal member of your servants. A hero who saved your own life, who does exactly what you tell him. My friend. And, I thought, your's too."

"All this might have been true, but both of you knew Samson. The connection with both of you was seen. We could have sent you where Asaph has now gone. As it is, we will spread a story of how you were misguided on this occasion. Your youth will be blamed. People can forgive a little if there are extenuating circumstances."

The young man was silenced. Sick to his stomach, he began forming a reply, but closed his mouth before voicing it. Standing and walking to the window, he stared out for some time, his hands behind his back, his fingers twining and intertwining repeatedly. Presently he walked back to his seat, eyes moist.

His father knew he was listening now. His tone grew kinder. "In a way Asaph has saved our lives, yours and mine. Samson has nearly ruined the credibility of the ruling class of Philistia. Now we have an internal explanation, a scapegoat if you will. If it hadn't worked out like this, you and I might have been displaced." There was only a slight pause as he delivered the clinching statement. "And Asaph would have gone anyway, believe me."

Achish avoided his father's eyes for a while.

Damn this Samson.

But it's more than Samson, boyo. Get honest. Youthful folly. Not much folly. It was just a riddle. But it's the way things are. It's just the way things are. Get past it. Somehow, get past it. Sometimes there are casualties. Keziah's family. Hypocrite.

Finally, the Mayor spoke again. "Asaph will not be killed. I couldn't do that. But he will be underground a long time. He has been sent to the grinders prison."

Words rose once more to say something, anything, then subsided. Achish stared at his father, and felt the unity of their common hatred.

Asaph

Asaph allowed himself to be led easily. As soon as the guards surrounded him, he grasped the plot. Even as it was being carried out, he knew the Mayor had to do it. To save himself and his son. There were no recriminations. In a way his lot had been cast right back at Timnah, at the very start. Events had tied him in, and he had gone along. It was his job to do so in the past, and it would now be his task to remain silent and take what was leveled at him.

When all was said and done, he had been fortunate to have any life at all. And he had had more than twenty good years when he should have been a dead galley slave. Strangely, he didn't feel angry, and even promised himself he would think about why he wasn't angry—if he got the opportunity.

It was also comforting to think his passing was not without effect. It would give Achish another chance at achieving his destiny. His own demise would clean the youth's slate.

As they walked out of the palace, he gazed at the puffy white clouds and the blue sky. No more would he walk beneath it, feeling his power as a man. He focused on the pavement and the houses as they trod down the lanes, absorbing their colors and textures, breathing in the odors of the street market, and the flower stall the breeze wafted to him.

In a way it was just, he thought to himself. Someone had once sacrificed themselves for him. They had given their life so he might escape. He realized his benefactor in the galley must have felt good on his last night. He had ended his existence with purpose, he had struck a blow which gave life to another. What better thing to do, he wondered as they reached the prison doors and began their descent.

Internal tactics

"Our day is not yet done, Achish," said the Mayor brusquely. "We still have work to do."

He called for the servants and ordered them to prepare food for two days and nights. Quickly. They were leaving within the hour.

Achish followed him around like a confused boy. Eventually his father stopped to explain. "Do you think I am going to lay myself open to a take-over by some ambitious generals? Have you never heard of a military coup?"

The youth stood wide eyed. "Military coup? Here in Gaza?"

"Think ahead, my son, think ahead." The older man paused, remembering history even at this moment. "Walk with me as we prepare. I'll tell you a story." Striding purposefully now, he began. "Jephthah was a hero right? Saved the nation of Israel?"

"Yes," stammered out his son, curiously.

"Anyway, shortly after his great victory, he returned home to rule Israel. He was offered the leadership by the elders of his tribal area, Gilead. In fact he made them promise it in one of their holy places to make it binding. No sooner was he back and hardly settled in, when another tribe of Israel, Ephraim, came calling. Ephraim had also been freed by Jephthah's magnificent victory. They should have been grateful. Wouldn't you? Your neighbor conquers your common enemy? You might thank him.

"Not the tribe of Ephraim. They complained they hadn't been invited to the fray in the first place. That they hadn't marched over the Jordan river and done their bit alongside Jephthah's crew. Strange logic if you ask me. Why get angry about the fact you didn't need to contribute lives to gain your freedom? I suspect there must have been earlier grievances unanswered, but that is not my point. My issue is, at the height of Jephthah's influence, right after his huge victory, he faced internal opposition."

He wheeled to face Achish. "And here you and I are, hardly returning from a great victory, are we? Do you really think we can come back after this devastating blow and expect to simply get away with it? By explaining a few things to people? Asaph's demise will help, and will be good public relations. But I assure you, we need to cover every base if our heads are to remain on our shoulders."

He started to walk on.

"What happened to Jephthah? You can't stop there."

"Oh, Jephthah. He set up a shrewd strategy. Firstly, he forced a scare fight with Ephraim. Those Ephraimite lads were suddenly surrounded by members of Gilead, Jephthah's home troops. Inevitably, they tried to escape. But he had thought his strategy out ahead of time too. Smart man, Jephthah, why do you think I make you learn history? He had already captured the fords of the Jordan river. They questioned everyone who came by. It so happens that the Ephraimite dialect gives some pronunciation problems.

"They can't use the 'sh' sound correctly. The armed militia at the fords simply asked everyone crossing the river to say the word 'shibboleth.' If they said 'sibboleth,' they slew them on the spot. 42,000 men of Ephraim fell. And Jephthah remained ruler of Israel."

He looked his son directly in the eye. "We need to head our own generals off at the river, if you can follow the metaphor. Keep silent on this trip and watch how we do it."

After depositing Asaph, the soldiers returned to the palace. The Mayor barked more demands, and they scurried away. Within the hour, the top three generals of Philistia had appeared at the gates, with chariots of their own and victuals for the journey. The Mayor only had one question for them. "Have your platoons received their orders?"

Yes. Understood.

The vehicles clattered out of the gates of Gaza shortly afterwards. After a while, the Mayor ordered a stop, and joined the first general in his chariot. He spent an hour with each one. Separately. Actually, all he did was talk about the massacre of Samson, and the thousand bodies in the wilderness.

On the second day they reached the battle site once more. Vultures were still picking away at the bodies. Ordinarily a flock could reduce a single body to bones in minutes. However, the sheer volume of corpses filled the bellies of every bird in the region. And there was more to eat yet.

As the contingent drew near, the generals witnessed the extent of the devastation. Every last set of remains wore the battle garb of Philistia. It was astonishing to Achish again, even on this second visit.

One man.

Just one man did this.

All three generals were stunned. While they had listened to the Mayor tell the story, the visual confirmation was still staggering. One of them recognized the clothing and insignia of his associate who had fallen.

"Here lies our colleague, General Sitterash," he pointed out. "If anyone could have handled this, he surely could have."

The other two nodded. "Even so, how could this happen?" they murmured, picking their way carefully amidst the decay and the stench. They wandered up the valley to the last stand of the group at the head of the ravine. Achish pointed out the asses jawbone to them.

"Is that all he used? Just that?" they queried in disbelief.

Mostly the Mayor remained silent, although he was careful to pick up on any conversation between them. But there was only wonderment. They walked back to the chariots. To avoid the scene and the smell and the vultures, they got back into the conveyances and drove some distance away. After finding a suitable spot in the shade of a cliff in the late afternoon, they built a camp for the night. Servants brought out the food and wine, and they settled down to discuss the day. The sun was setting, reddening the desert around them.

The Mayor started. "As you know, I appreciate your coming here today, and the arrival of your platoons tomorrow." His hand swept back behind him, cordially encompassing the dead as brothers. "These are fallen heroes of Philistia, and a decent burial for them in their homeland is not possible. However, we are a proud and responsible people. We will burn the dead in a full military funeral. This is why we asked the platoons along."

His face hardened. "We will not have Israel bringing crowds down here to gloat. All of us want to remove all trace. I know I can rely on you, my chief aides, to perform this task thoroughly.

"However, we cannot avoid the fact it was caused by one man. Only one man. He also massacred civilians and soldiers in both Ashkelon and Ekron. We are not talking about an ordinary person here. In fact, his appearance has upset the rules of war."

Allowing the point to settle in, he went on. "I know if I asked any of you to mount a campaign against this Samson, you would do it. Bravery is not in question here. But I will not ask you. I will not ask you, because it is asking you to do something completely new."

Suppressing their relief, they listened carefully.

"Such a man has never been seen before in the history of mankind," the Mayor explained. "I of all people ought to know, because I study history. Believe me. It hasn't happened. And furthermore, neither has anyone in the history of the world defeated such a man. By definition, since he is the first."

Again, the gap, to let this sink in. "So, I cannot ask you to fight him. Every attempt our good men have made has failed. This is not to say it can't be done. Not at all. I will welcome any strategy or solution you come up with in the days ahead. It will be music to my ears. But I will not penalize anyone either for not coming up with one. We just need patience. Time will restore all things to us."

In the morning, the Mayor and his son rose to leave. Once more, their leader bade the generals strength and fortitude in their cleanup task, apologizing again that it was not a pleasant one, but necessary for the glory of Philistia. They climbed into their chariot, and with Achish at the reigns, they left.

After an hour or so, the Mayor spoke. "I think we have crossed that hurdle. I believe we have."

Achish stared back, acutely aware of his steep learning curve.

"The generals needed to see with their own eyes," his father explained. "It is too unbelievable to swallow the story second hand. You have to actually see it, to fully take it in. We had to take the key military players there. Otherwise who knows what sort of discontent might arise back home amongst them."

Continuing, he outlined his ongoing strategy. "That also extends to the common man. Three or four days burning the dead by those platoons will spread the word amongst their peers in Philistia as well.

"There is a time for keeping things in the dark. There is a time for bringing things into the light. Guiding a nation through difficulty requires thinking. Once directions are set, they are hard to change, hard to control. A tragedy like losing Israel upsets the plans of many people. They might lash out. Against us. If we were unwise."

The chariot lurched, and his wit asserted itself. "Hopefully it's only a road bump. We'll get through it, if we cover the ground thoroughly."

Achish grinned, but there was yet more from his senior.

"Next move is placating our own peers, the mayors. We need to keep an eye on Ekron."

The five mayors

Affecting ease, but shuffling slightly, the lesser four leaders of Philistia looked on pensively. The prime man began by outlining the rise of Samson from mass murderer to protector of Israel. Defender of their faith. Israel was no longer under the dominion of Philistia. He spelled it out succinctly, immediately offering the overall leadership of Philistia to any mayor who wished to take it up. If they felt they could get rid of Samson, they should speak now.

He knew nobody would, and besides it was too soon in the discussion. But he was acquainted with the element of surprise and transparency in politics. The four regarded each other silently, then back to him without either speaking or nodding. It was sanction enough.

He broached the topic of Samson knowing his son. And Asaph. They had all heard of it naturally enough, and were curious as to how he handled it. Asaph received the blame. It was unforgivable. He should never have allowed any such contact to develop, let alone drag in the son of the Mayor. Asaph's chief error was in maintaining his silence and advising the young man to do so as well. Vital information could have been shared, and many lives saved.

The former weight lifter was a clumsy traitor. He had been instantly removed and would spend the rest of his days underground. In truth, the rest of eternity actually, the Mayor couldn't resist adding a macabre twist.

They did laugh in fact.

As for his son, the boy was young. He was misled. Who had not been as a youth? Who could pass those years without making a mistake? He outlined a few of his own and went on to say how the experience had taught him valuable lessons. So it was with Achish. Yes, the lad was his son, and again he reiterated, if it pleased the four mayors, he would resign. But now was the time to pull together, to find their way out of the problem they all faced.

And he carried them.

With his mixed potion of future focus, current answers, emotive intimacy and a warming offer to step aside. They were in a quandary anyway. Nobody had a proposal for getting rid of Samson.

Edred came in behind him. "I have seen with my own eyes what this Israelite is capable of. It seems unbelievable, but he is a one man army. Unfortunately there is almost nothing we can do at this point. I say almost nothing, because I agree with my colleague from Gaza."

He, too, was learning how to pause for effect. "There was a time when I doubted my friend here. I have to confess that. But we need to maintain a combined front. We need to display concord to our own people. Division is the last thing we need."

It was encouraging, hearing him of all people urge unity. The man from Gaza knew it helped swing the others into line.

Edred hadn't finished. "Let me go further. Misfortune feeds on itself. If our partner in Gaza falls, do you think the rest of us will be strengthened? I do not believe so. It would simply cause our own peoples to ask whether we too should be swept aside."

Good thinking, admired their leader.

Ekron summarized his support; "events have exposed Asaph's folly; we need to let our communities know; deceit has no place among us. I believe we will move forward now we have cleansed ourselves."

Word went out to all Philistia. Times had changed. Israel was no longer a vassal state. They had raised up a hero of mythical proportions. A misinformation plot had been uncovered at the highest level in Philistia itself, which aided the Israelite cause. That issue had been dealt with in Gaza, and the individual would never see the light of day.

However, punishing him did not turn the clock back. For the time being, Israel was no longer under their dominion. Philistia's leaders were attempting to maintain trading privileges, but a belt tightening period was expected. The five mayors were united in their efforts to restore the natural and prosperous state of affairs between the two nations. No stone would remain unturned.

Gossip from ordinary soldiers escaped into the public arena. It was true, Samson had killed one thousand men on his own. It was not long before everyone in Philistia knew someone who had personally been there while the bodies were gathered and burnt. And had not the Mayor of Gaza gone there himself to oversee a formal military funeral for the lost?

Dagon was patient. He was part history and part future. Bad times come along with the good. The ebb and flow of events. Various combinations of this message went forth from his temples across the nation, conveyed by earnest priests. Hard times are sent to forge us. Iron sharpens itself against iron.

We will emerge from this shadow stronger than ever.

The restoration

Israel revised the terms of trade in their favor. There was relief in the foreign exchange area and a lowering of interest rates. And of course, internal self rule was reinstated. All Philistine outposts were closed, their soldiers sent home, and the taxation revenue was abolished. Judicial personnel were appointed according to old statutes and performed their district rounds. The elders met periodically to discuss policy and significant legal issues. Samson was invited to everything.

Now and again Elihu visited Samson's mother. They found each other interesting. Her manner was lighter now. Content with the fulfilling of the angel's promises, she entered a time of public honor, a living mother of a hero.

One business which did falter was the shrines and goddesses. Israel promptly cleaned those out of every village. Pure worship was reinstated. This led to the demise of many large trading organisations in Israel itself, and it also impacted the manufacturing side in Philistia. Since the Mayor of Gaza had made a personal fortune over the years from this very trade, it was another personal sting to lose this income stream too.

For the meanwhile however, although many things rankled him, it was prudent to stick close to home, and mingle with his people. He knew the value of personal contact, of listening to complaints and issues, and building up his national support. He bided his time, letting normalcy descend.

But he would get him. He knew he would. It was taking its toll though. Endless days empathizing with people's downturns, and talking his way through their problems, making them feel better so he could survive. He was treading water, which did not befit a man of destiny.

The hero

Samson's life took on a vastly different perspective. He was now a hero. Accorded a place with the great ones of Israelite history, he was even made a judge himself, with high powers of decision making. In this he was guided by Elihu, whom he came to trust little by little.

Rumors about his ability spread everywhere, outstripping the truth by far. All this helped Israel as the same tales spilled over the border into Philistia and were wholeheartedly believed. They dissuaded any thoughts of military action. And, in a quirky way, were helpful in maintaining the Mayor's position of power. His own people agreed he could do nothing against such an opponent.

As Elihu had argued so strongly when he took Samson into the elders during those crucial days prior to the restoration, Philistia made no effort to attack them. They had been whipped by one young man. They were an intelligent race and highly unlikely to squander more men provoking him again. Especially if the Mayor of Gaza was in control. He was too smart to risk his own neck by repeated failure. It all balanced itself out.

Samson started to lead a life of relative ease. Adoring crowds followed him whenever he appeared. Local leaders sought him out. Young boys pleaded with him to perform, and he would catch a fox or tear a tree out.

And pretty girls smiled at him.

Everywhere.

This last scenario proved difficult for one whose veins were coursing with hormones. He didn't know how to talk about this with his mother, and indeed with the demise of the discos, and a stricter social life, the avenues for sexual release had dried up. Elihu wasn't much help, being more politically cautious, than aware of Samson's needs.

In an oblique talk one day, he mentioned how it was important for leaders to keep themselves pure sexually. It would do the nation no good to see eminent figures caught up in disgraceful acts. Samson understood him clearly. But his drives didn't go away. In fact with the decrease in fighting, his sexual energy seemed to rise further. At least while he was killing Philistines he had an outlet for his enormous powers. Now he had none.

News came to him about the decadence of Philistia. A trader from Benjamin had recently been exposed. Evidently, he had been traveling to Gaza on business for years and spending every night there in a brothel. After listening to the tale, and particularly the way in which the Benjamite maintained his secrecy, a seed was sown. Samson had tasted the feminine delights of Philistia once himself.

He decided Israel could do without him for a few days. He told Elihu he needed time to reflect in the wilderness like he did in his outlaw days. The older man was concerned at first, but Samson assured him he would be alright, smiling patronizingly as he said it. Elihu could hardly press a bodyguard on him, so he wished him a pleasant time.

The harlot

He walked to Gaza. It was not a revenge spree, so he saw no reason to hurry. Avoiding the towns of Timnah and Eltekeh was straightforward. He went up through the hill country. He could hear other men long before they sensed him. Security was not an issue, but neither did he want to be tracked.

On the last flat stretches to Gaza he acted nonchalantly, sometimes even greeting people. As yet, most living persons in Philistia did not know him by sight. The rumors depicted a much larger being. He joined up with a group heading into Gaza so he didn't have to walk into the city alone.

These villagers with occasionally straying goats and children, meandered into the town, and Samson appeared like one of the party at a casual glance. He had never seen such large iron gates, and he peered up at them, the bored guards lazily viewing him as a stolid country yokel. Briefly he wondered whether the gates could be broken, as he noticed their enormous locks.

The last of the youngsters were herded through, and he moved on again. It was absorbing, being in a large town without vengeance on his mind. The walled houses were high, and he was finally able to appreciate the wonderment of Elihu about his throwing a soldier up on such a roof.

The bleating goat herd trotted forward, and the crowds grew thicker and busier, as they headed into the city center, breaking through to the central square. By now he had forgotten his original intent, so amazed was he with the structures in this urban edifice. Separating himself from the villagers, he walked around the square passing all manners of life, from arguing merchants to beggars, from water carriers to fleet of foot messenger boys.

On the far side he halted beside a huge stone building. Wide steps led up to its vast doors, and his excitement mounted. He had never seen a stone stairway before, although he had heard of them many times from Lamech in his story telling. Marveling at their symmetry, he had to restrain himself from jumping up ten at a time.

The wide doors were open and he walked in unhindered. Inside he could see seating for thousands, and, as he surveyed the idol on the stage, he knew what the building was; Dagon's temple. Lamech had taught him about Dagon as a boy, and Elihu mentioned the idol as well.

Looking up he saw the clever design allowing more people to overflow onto the roof. Stairways inside the building wound up the walls, passing through a rain protected portico before disgorging up on top. A split level in the ceiling allowed those seated up there to look down on the stage.

It was fascinating, and he rapidly counted up the stairway leading on to the roof. Hearing his own steps as he numbered them, he ran up to gaze out at the auditorium. From center stage he could see every seat in the place, to the middle, to both sides, and up to the roof. It was especially designed so that the whole gathering could see whoever stood there.

Along the sides were special alcoves. It appeared like teams of important people could sit together. At the middle rear of the stage were two large stout columns. They rose up and supported the roof. His fingers reached out, feeling their solidness. It was a breathtaking experience, and he wondered whether you could ever number how many people would fit inside this temple.

And there was Dagon. Close enough to touch. This was their god. Made of stone. Again, he had never seen an image of either man or beast in stone, such were the commandments in Israel. He pondered briefly at the cleverness of those who fashioned him, but it didn't make sense. A nostalgia of children sitting around a fire at night, laughing and learning, swept through him unexpectedly.

He walked down from the stage and exited the building so he could look at it again from the outside. As he carefully stepped down to the square, he noticed a pair of colorfully dressed women sitting on the stone stairway with earrings and loose tousled hair streaming down their backs. One caught his eye and stood up with a wide grin. Without thinking he smiled back, the urge to see the exterior of the temple somehow receding. She seemed to be admiring his body as she asked, "did you enjoy your visit into Dagon's temple, big boy?"

Her eyes twinkled and she laughed delightfully. She was beautiful, and his response emerged in a sort of half truth. "Yes, I did. Could you explain what he is all about."

She giggled and took him by the arm, leading him down to the square. Her friend had vanished. "I would be delighted to. Are you a visitor to our city?"

"This is my first time here. It looks good so far."

Leading him towards a tavern, she suggested it might be better to relax over a drink while she explained Dagon to him. In the milling crowds of the marketplace and narrow streets only a few people gave Samson a second glance before hurrying on with their busy day. They entered a quiet bar, moving down into the cozy darkened interior.

"This should be comfortable," she assured him as he gazed around at the exotic carpets and wall hangings.

He knew he should ask what she preferred to drink. "Whatever you are having, beautiful," she replied, "whatever you are having."

He returned with two goblets of red wine. "Wonderful!" she cried, "my favorite. Now, where are you from?" she queried, appearing genuinely interested.

Samson was startled by the question, realizing his unpreparedness. He waved in a northerly direction. "Oh, up the coast. I travel a lot."

"Oh my, you must tell me all about where you've been, you must!"

And so it went on for an hour or so as she charmed him. Casually she began touching his hands as he spoke. Eventually her hand moved to his thigh. "My, you have such large muscles," she sighed.

Late in the afternoon she finally asked, "would you like to come home with me?"

This was exactly what he had come for. It was as easy as falling off a log. "Yes," he said. "I would."

She laughed, scooping up his hand. "Shall we walk through the evening together?"

As they went outside engrossed in each other, a soldier was sitting absentmindedly opposite the tavern. He nearly jumped.

Samson!

He couldn't believe it. He was one of the lucky few that got away from Lehi, creeping back into Gaza like the remaining survivors. His nemesis was strolling off with a whore.

The soldier had the good sense to follow at a judicious distance. The couple wound their way through a series of streets before turning into her rooms. Their tracker memorized the spot, then sprinted off. Gasping for breath, he arrived at his post.

"Samson is here," he spluttered out. "Here in Gaza!"

"What are you talking about, fool?" the captain retorted.

"I saw him with my own eyes. He picked up a harlot and went off with her."

His superior peered at him. "Are you sure about this? Like very, very, sure?"

"On my mother's grave. I was there at Lehi. You know that. It is Samson."

The troop leader fell back into his chair. "Wooo," he said. "Samson. Right here in Gaza. You know something," he told the soldier as he sat up again, thinking. "The man who kills Samson will be famous. And set up for life."

An idea dawned as he spoke. Yes, indeed, a man would be famous.

Samson was led into a small room which had a bedroom leading off it. Perfume laced the air, and the floor was covered in deep rich carpets. Cushions lay about and on the shelves were unlit candles. She made him sit on the carpets, gently pushing him back into the cushions as she drew her face close to his, and kissed him.

It had been so long, and his gorge immediately rose, his hands touching her arms and stroking her smooth skin.

"Oh, you are beautiful," she sighed, but drew back. "I want so much to make love with you all night, you wonderful, gentle, strong man," she explained. "But I have a debt to repay. A merchant I owe money to. If you were able to assist we could have a beautiful night together. I think a piece of silver would help."

He had prepared himself for this eventuality, and extracted the amount from his tunic. She gazed lovingly at him and secured it behind a shelf.

"Lean back, I will teach you everything." Her hands ran over his chest as he relaxed on the carpets and cushions. Slowly they slid inside his tunic, feeling the muscles of his arms and stomach. She leaned forward, her lips brushing against his. Her tongue moistened his lips, tentatively searching inside his mouth.

She lay back, knowing he urgently needed release, and there was time later for more gentle play. Her garments fell open as he parted them. The sight of her had him in a frenzy.

Samson's recuperative powers were amazing. It only seemed minutes before he was aroused again. He played with her body for hours, learning about his and her desires quickly. She told him where to stroke her, how to stimulate her, and then reciprocated in delightful ways to his pleasure.

He completely forgot about time in his sexual paradise. In fact he had to tell himself she was a prostitute, and it was only for one night. By the fourth time he had a grasp of what excited her, and took delight in bringing her to a climax. Exhausted, they lay in each other's arms, snuggling in for comfort and warmth.

He was drifting off when an unusual sound alerted him. A secretive noise, as of someone cramped, shifting their stance to relieve their muscles. He didn't move. Again he heard it, reminding him of a fox creeping off. He waited while it died away, as if it had gone around a corner.

Very nearly leaping out of bed to give chase, he realized he was naked. Laughing to himself, he calmed down again. He had nothing to worry about. Because now he knew something was out there. That was all the preparation he needed.

He slept for several hours, having warned himself to wake early. It was midnight when he came to. The whore was sleeping soundly, recovering from her exertions. He smiled down at her while he dressed. Yes, she was certainly worth the piece of silver.

Using the window for surveillance he peered obliquely through it from either side in turn. The street was safe. Looking up to the roofs on the opposite side, he could not see anything unusual. Next, the front door. Opening it a sliver, he peered out again in all directions. Up the street, down it, and the rooftops again. Still nothing.

Easing out, he crouched close to the wall. Glancing around, he could see all was clear there as well. Creeping down the street he started to ease up. Maybe the troops are somewhere else, he thought. He flicked a look around the corner into the larger street.

Deserted. Where were they? He raced through the possibilities. The next street. Could be. All the streets? Maybe. But he hadn't seen any yet. Whatever, better be prepared. It could be on any avenue. No, wait. Where do all the roads lead? To the gates.

Maintaining his caution, he slunk down the cobbles leading to the exit. Always checking up the road, down it, and the rooftops. Sidling up to the last corner, he allowed himself the briefest glimpse around it. There they were. In a flash he took it all in. Bows leaning against the wall, and soldiers standing around a brazier warming themselves.

They're planning to shoot me. But they're not in a pitch of readiness. They reckon I will come this way at dawn. And those gates are also chained and locked.

Suddenly his anger soared, his fury against Philistia. Why, you puny little band.

The impossible

The captain heard the noise first. He whirled up and around, his military senses screaming. Following his move, others leapt to their feet. Their commotion roused one or two of those prone in the gatehouse who sprang out of the room.

He was not even facing the soldiers. They had psyched themselves up earlier over the presumed speed of any attack. But he had his back to them. It appeared a deliberate posture, a disdain of some motley crew who tried to interrupt his departure.

Samson had finished striding up to the twelve foot high entrance. His hands reached out as it were to shake the bars impotently. Instead the hands fluidly grabbed the gates and began lifting them. Such was the magnificence of the act that the entire troop stood paralyzed, in the grip of what could not be done.

With a groan the huge heavy structure rose up. The ground on either side rumpled like tilled earth. Both reinforced doorposts were exhumed. The great iron hinges fastening wall to gates twisted, shrieking their protest before snapping off. Groans of metal against thick wooden planks intermingled with the pinging of rivets shooting off at angles from the edifice.

Not a man in the troop moved. The bows, many of them still strung, remained leaning on the wall. The swords lay in their scabbards. It was mesmerizing.

Suddenly the gates were free. He was holding them above his head like an ordinary man might carry an inside house door down the street. Briefly the captain feared he might turn and fling them at him, no longer was his thinking bounded by the normal possibilities of mankind.

But Samson didn't. Instead he tilted them so the whole structure fitted through the gap where they had formerly stood and walked out.

In so doing he passed from the captain's view, such that he was left looking at an enormously wrenched hole in the side of his city. Still in shock, he realized no more than a few seconds had passed since he first heard him. And now silence had returned.

Snapping out of his trance, he ran across to the gap, stopped and gazed down the moonlit road leading away from town. He could see Samson still held the gates above him, although they were partly resting on his shoulders. But he was a surprising distance away.

Because he was now running.

A day

Now there was a day when the angels came to present themselves before the Lord God, and the Tempter also came with them. The Lord God said to the Tempter, "from where do you come?"

The Tempter answered the Lord God, "from roaming through the earth and going back and forth in it."

Then the Lord God said to the Tempter, "have you considered my servant Samson, who has restored the hearts of my chosen people to me?"

The Tempter answered, "the man is puffed up with his own strength, and his heart follows harlots. Why must the Creator of all mankind require such a man of might to save his people? Are they helpless as babes? Does He seek children to follow him?"

The Lord God replied, "you know not the beginning from the end. Nevertheless, are not the rulers of men under your sway?"

Rage

The Mayor awoke unrested, his mind having worked its usual occupation. He dressed himself and went downstairs. To his surprise, one of his generals was waiting. The military man straightened up as he appeared. Walking past him, the Mayor poured himself a juice.

"Good morning, general," he said, attempting to be pleasant. "To what do we owe this honor?"

"Good morning my lord. I trust you slept soundly."

"If that is a condition to my hearing what you have to say, then yes, I most certainly did." He faced the man expectantly.

"My lord, there has been an incident."

"An incident. Do go on."

"Samson."

"Samson!"

Calm yourself man. Not in front of a subordinate.

"Samson," the Mayor repeated. "What has he done this time?"

"My lord, it is better if I show you rather than describe it."

Show me? Surely he hasn't been in Gaza under my nose?

"All right. Where do we go?"

"We can wait while you breakfast, my lord."

"Let's go man, let's get it over with."

They were in the waiting chariot in seconds. It drove off towards the gates. Neither spoke. As the vehicle turned the last corner, the Mayor's eyes went to the exit from the town. In place of the familiar, heavy, iron city gates was a gaping hole in the wall of his beloved metropolis. He was silent for some seconds as the chariot stopped. Dismounting, he walked over to the gap. Bystanders scattered. He inspected the remains of the hinges and the holes in the ground. Eventually he asked thickly, "who allowed this to happen?"

"A young captain my lord. He took it on himself to kill Samson."

"And where is this captain now?"

"After the gates were removed, he went down to a tavern and drank strong beverages for the night. He is now in our custody, awaiting your pleasure."

"My pleasure!" the Mayor yelled. He could not help himself. He loomed up to the general, inches away from his face. "Take me to him."

They drove through the city again. His temper rose beyond that which he considered himself capable of. Every descriptive epithet he knew passed through his brain. He was acting out of character, but for once, he didn't care. He wanted to give vent to it.

They stopped outside the barracks and climbed out of the chariot. Leading the way, the general moved down a flight of stairs to a room. A guard was posted outside. "Be gone, soldier," the Mayor grated.

He followed the general into the cell. In the corner, in a drink sodden state, sat the captain. He gazed up bleary eyed. "My lord," he slurred. "You wouldn't believe how strong that man is. Incredible. He stole our gates . . ."

The Mayor extended his hand to the general. Intuitively he handed him his sword. The Mayor turned back to the soldier and slashed him across the face and neck. It cut deeply into his cheek and mouth. In his drunken stupor, he feebly tried to protect himself against the furious blow. This further enraged the Mayor, and he leant himself to his task.

On the second swing he simply flailed the instrument at the mass of arms and shoulders. He felt the sword crack something as it crashed heavily through the captain's defenses and knew he had broken his right arm.

The soldier shrieked in pain, and instinctively his other hand clutched his shattered limb. This exposed his head and shoulders. As the next blow approached, the victim tried to duck so the blade bit deeply into his left shoulder as that was raised in a protective move.

Crashing the sword back against his head, he finally knocked the prisoner unconscious, and the body tilted over onto the floor. Blood was splattered about the cell, and onto the Mayor himself, but he was beyond recall. Horrified by this display, the general moved out of the room to ensure no-one else was in hearing range.

"You stupid idiot!" the Mayor screamed at the supine body, hacking away at its limbs, seemingly determined to cut the corpse into fragments. The head was severed from the body, and the Mayor kicked it into the corner.

The body was unmoving now.

The Mayor stood, trembling.

Slowly he slid down against a wall to sit on the floor of the cell. Silence reigned for some time, his head hanging forward, exhausted by the psychological and physical assault he had given himself over to. He was still quivering, and aware of it.

The blood. His emotive pathways were open now, and visions of his wife's redness on the floor came back to him, mingled with the desert baked odor of a thousand bodies.

You've killed now. You have shed blood too. You've killed a living being yourself in a blind rage. Yet another casualty. And you're shaking like a leaf. You are in danger. Don't fool yourself. This business has gone far enough.

Pull yourself together man. You're the leader of Philistia.

When the general came back, he handed the sword over. "Thank you general. He deserved that. Whatever he did or did not do, he most assuredly asked for that end. This has to stop," he vowed as the commander wiped the gore off his blade with a cloth hanging in the cell. "That Israelite must be stopped. I don't know how right now, but it must end!"

As he stared at the general his eyes were wild in a manner this subordinate had never seen before. Slowly, reason started to seep its way back until his normal shrewdness was apparent. "This captain was your man wasn't he?"

"Yes, my Lord, he was," replied the soldier, worrying what was coming next, while the Mayor worried how to handle his disastrous act.

"That's alright," the Mayor said finally. "It could have happened to anyone."

He took the general's arm and started walking out of the cell. "This incident doesn't need to go any further," he murmured coldly.

They drove back to the palace. He invited the general in for breakfast, a placating move thought the army man.

"Where did he leave the gates?" the Mayor finally asked.

"That is another strange part my lord. We cannot find them in the near vicinity."

"What! Did he carry them back to Israel!?"

Samson

Samson was not to know the gates weighed seven thousand pounds. It was easy carrying them while running. He was heading back to Israel anyway. And it was the middle of the night with a good moon. He paced along the main paths, not trying to avoid anyone, but nobody was out in this darkness. He felt he could keep his tempo up for hours.

And indeed he did. He ran all the way, carrying the gates on his broad shoulders like a totem, a symbol of Israelite freedom. The closer he got to home, the more significant his act appeared. So he headed towards Hebron, one of the holy cities. Reaching it just before dawn, he continued up a hill on the outskirts of the town and finally threw the gates to the ground, displaying his trophy for all Israel to see. He watched the sun rise in the east, spreading its glow over the land, acknowledging his gift.

Walking back to his lodgings, he climbed into bed around mid-morning, to dream of the whores embraces. When he awoke a few hours later, he went searching for Elihu to tell him personally.

"You did what?" the older man laughed when he heard about the gates. Samson left the harlotry out of it for the moment. "You left them at Hebron!"

Elihu couldn't resist, and got out a map. "You carried them thirty seven miles!" He burst out laughing. "I've got to see! Now! Let's go!"

Two horses were saddled and the pair rode across to Hebron. Already a gawking crowd had gathered at the top of the hill.

Elihu shouted out gleefully, "Samson stole them from Gaza!"

At this the Israelites burst into laughter, Elihu amongst the loudest. Samson was nonplussed at first, but started to see that, yes, it had an element of humor. He had removed the city gates of the main metropolis of Philistia, and transported them deep into Israel.

Yes, it was pretty funny.

The breakthrough

"Have you any idea what this latest outrage means?" the Mayor asked his generals. He answered without waiting. "It will make us a laughing stock.

We will be the butt of so many jokes, we won't know our backsides from our breakfast."

They hunkered down as he stormed around, hands waving. "If this gets through to Egypt, what will they think? I mean we have a serious issue of credibility here!"

Most present had never seen him in such a temper before. It was uncharacteristic of their normal jovial leader, always in control, even in a crisis.

Seeing nonplussed faces, he sensed he was getting worked up again. Having given vent once, it seemed to rise of its own accord faster.

Need to calm down, he told himself. Bad face to go on losing it like that. These men talk with each other.

He recovered quickly. "You know what I am saying. He is mocking us. All of us. I want you to go away and think about this Samson problem. We all want a solution. Many brains are better than one. Sometimes I don't have all the answers. We need to work together here like we have in the past. Teamwork."

Having soothed them a little, they stood to go. The Mayor nodded at the general who accompanied him to the cells. "We need a debrief," he whispered.

They went into an adjoining room. Achish was there, and rose when he saw the pair approaching. The Mayor waved him back down. "No, stay Achish, I want you to hear this. The background on the stealing of the gates."

The general related all he knew. Most of it he had gleaned from the archers when they returned to their barracks. Samson had come into town, picked up a whore, and spent the night with her. The captain thought he could shoot Samson. Using a group of archers from afar with the element of surprise.

Now that he heard it, it seemed a good plan mused the Mayor. Pity he hadn't informed me first.

But Samson appeared earlier than they thought. Given they had locked the gates, that was probably not a problem if he had been trapped inside. But the incredible display of a single person removing the gates shocked them into inaction. Simple as that.

They asked a few questions. "Who was the whore? Could she tell us anything else?"

"Yes," confirmed the general, quick to say, "we have already interviewed her of course. She didn't know he was an Israelite. Quite frightened to begin with, so I assured her nothing untoward would happen. She picked him up, she admitted that much. He was walking out of Dagon's temple. That was when she first saw him. They drank in a bar. The barman doesn't recall them. I gave her a few coins for her trouble."

He hesitated before adding, "it probably doesn't have much to do with anything, but she said he was a novice in the art of love. For what that is worth."

"I see," said the Mayor. "Any more questions from you, Achish?"

He shook his head. They dismissed the general and sat in silence for a while.

"Always a woman involved," muttered Achish.

"What do you mean by that?"

"Whenever Samson gets in a mess, it seems to have a female in the middle of it."

The Mayor stirred. "Go on. Explain yourself."

"I mean this whole incident started over a woman he was about to marry didn't it?"

"Yes, it did," breathed the Mayor. "Yes it did." He wheeled quickly to his son, his eyes alight. "Tell me again about your folly at Timnah."

"Look, we've gone over that before, there's no need to . . ."

"No, no, I'm not getting at you. You may have the seed of an idea here, that's all. Tell it to me again."

So Achish told his father about the gamble, and how he got Keziah to wheedle the answer out of Samson. "It took seven days, and a fair amount of persuasive talk, but we found out. Or she found out for us."

"She found out! The girl uncovered it!" The Mayor leapt up in his excitement. He whirled on his son. "Don't you see? He had a secret, one he wanted to keep! But he trusted a woman with the answer!"

It started to dawn on Achish. "Fair enough, but what do you mean by a secret in this case?"

"His strength. He is not a giant. He is the same size as you in fact. How can an ordinary man be transformed into what he becomes. What is his secret? Is it something he drinks? Or eats? Or exercises at? Or meditates about?"

His son caught it. "And who better to find out than a woman? Is that what you're thinking?"

"Yes, and further to that point, where do we find a woman who could find out? One who could gain his trust. One who wants to find out. A beautiful woman with ability and motive. Do we have such a female in Philistia?"

"There just might be."

"Who?"

"Delilah," Achish replied. "Samson killed her boyfriend."

Too late he realized what he had committed her to. But he couldn't retract. She was perfect for the job. Damn. She was ideal. And he was going to set up his enemy to make love with her.

The Mayor lay on his bed, working it over.

Has my mind gone completely, thinking a woman could extract a secret from him?

What else do we have? What else is on offer?

Think, man. Quantify. There are only two options. Firstly, you delay, hoping something else will emerge. And face the consequences. Or secondly you try the girl.

What happens if we wait? It will be interpreted as the ploy it really is. That I don't know what to do, and am stalling for time.

The second option. Get the woman in. What if she fails? I'm done for anyway.

What if he did get sent from his God?

Don't think like that. Keep your head together.

It is better to do something than nothing.

Achish

Achish made the trip to Ashkelon with only the chariot driver for company. After his own nights of tossing and turning, his mind was clear. It was a temporary expedient. It was the best chance they had. If it failed, their very lives were in jeopardy, let alone any future with Delilah. They had no choice.

He hadn't seen her since the evening of Michael's murder. Not long ago, but it seemed a lifetime with all the incidents. He wondered how he would be received. The truth, he decided. The plain facts are so bizarre, they couldn't be made up. And finally his request of her. It made sense, given Samson killed her boyfriend. The only doubt was, her relationship with Michael hadn't seemed that healthy. Perhaps it wasn't strong enough to exact revenge. Well, he had a trick up his sleeve.

Late in the afternoon his father's chariot pulled into Ashkelon, and he asked to be put down away from Delilah's house. Didn't want her second guessing anything from the fancy transport. It was only five minutes walk to her place through the narrow streets anyway.

She answered the door quickly, smiling immediately at him, with her arms around his neck before he knew it. So far so good. She pulled him into the room, laughing at seeing him again, her eyes crinkling with joy. Everything about her was beautiful. Her clothing was loose, and seductive in a low key way. Her tanned skin exuded nature. Her flowing black hair, with its natural curls falling over her forehead was irresistible.

Achish was in love with her again. She pressed her lips against his, and he grew dizzy with desire. She took his hand and led him confidently to the bedroom. They had hardly spoken a word before she was in his arms again, feeling so good, pressing against him.

He could feel her firm round breasts again, and the cheeks of her buttocks as his fingers strayed over her.

Oh, she is gorgeous. I want her so much.

They undressed each other lazily, taking their time, exploring and stroking as they did so. Even at this point he knew Samson could not turn her away. He was entranced with her again himself.

They made love twice that evening, lying in each other's arms afterwards. She prepared a meal, fending off the outside world for a while. He told her they had much to talk about, but it would wait until the morrow. This was their night of love.

Delilah

After the sun wakened them, he held her for a long time. He knew he had to be careful. They got up and ate before he broached the topic.

"Philistia needs you, Delilah." He began with a statement of national importance. "We have a problem we believe you can help us with."

"Me!" she exclaimed, shocked. "What could I do for Philistia?"

"Let's start at the beginning. You know by now of Samson, I am sure."

Her eyes flashed, a dawning apparent already. But she replied, "why yes, who doesn't?"

Glimpsing the look, he carried on nevertheless, telling her of all his exploits save one. He related the stories about the slaughters at Timnah, Eltekeh, and Ekron, the massacre at Lehi, then the loss of Israel as a vassal state. Her eyes widened as she listened. She had not heard such a complete story as yet. He ended by posing a question. "My love, there is one more tale I have not told you. Perhaps you can guess at it."

She didn't hesitate. "Samson carried out the killings in Ashkelon, didn't he?"

"Yes, he did."

"He slew Michael."

"Yes."

Her gaze strayed about the room awhile, coming back to Achish. "There is something I have to tell you, Achish." She spoke softly. "I didn't love Michael. He was beautiful to look at, that is true. But he was not kind. He did not deserve to die. But I did not love him. I mourned him. But I do not have revenge within me. It is not part of who I am."

Achish was prepared. "I did not expect you would. You are too beautiful a woman. But I needed to let you know the whole story. I have kept nothing from you."

She peered at him intently. "Then how can I help Philistia? What do I have to do with this Samson?"

"I am going to tell you now, my love, and I need you to listen carefully to the whole story. It may sound callous, but we believe you hold the key," he replied.

He told her an embellished version of the Timnite girl, and how she extracted a confession from Samson. Moving onto his attraction to a woman in Gaza, he wisely omitted the term whore. "We believe he has a secret. We are sure there is something behind his great powers. The right woman could uncover that secret."

He could see her feelings rise, that she knew he was going to ask her to make a play on Samson, to trick him, to lure him into a relationship. To lie with him. Before she could speak, he hurried on. "The mayors of Philistia are united in their quest. I speak for all of them today. They are willing to offer you eleven hundred pieces of silver. Each."

It worked.

"Eleven hundred pieces of silver each?! Why, that is a fortune!" She sat bolt upright. "A person would never have to work again with that sum of money. They could live surrounded by servants and ease."

Gazing around her humble abode again, she quietened down as she thought, eventually murmuring to herself. "Five thousand, five hundred pieces of silver."

The five mayors

"Eleven hundred pieces of silver each!" Edred had exploded two days earlier. "Why, that is a fortune!"

The Mayor of Gaza let him rattle on a bit. As he waited, he was mindful once more about timing in discussions. Don't break in too soon. Let him vomit awhile.

When he saw the initiator of the idea standing patiently, the one from Ekron subsided, realizing his senior had anticipated an outburst. "I suppose you have an explanation," he blustered.

Their leader held his silence pointedly before speaking. "I examined my cashflow. Turns out I have been down five hundred pieces of silver a month on my Asherah trade into Israel."

Pausing deliberately to let the figures settle in, he added, "two months and a few days restoration would see me recoup my eleven hundred pieces.

Which I fully intend to restart once Samson is out of the way. Are any of you in a similar spot?" he inquired pleasantly, beaming around the room, knowing full well the answer. "I forgot to say, sorry, the money is payable only on results. No Samson, no funds."

Once they started talking, he knew they would fall into line. It just took the matter of doing it.

Action. Plans. Implement. Keep your confidence high. You've done it before.

You'll get him.

Delilah

Obtaining the money and getting Delilah on board was only the start of the challenge. All sorts of logistics needed to be worked through. Now it had become a project, the Mayor buried himself in it. His whole manner lifted and he started to become confident and jovial again. Activity was always good for the soul. An action plan also bought him time, keeping the other mayors and the generals at bay.

Achish had a pivotal role for two reasons; he was the only person to guide a woman to obtain a secret from Samson; secondly, because of his relationship with Delilah. The Mayor warned him he must keep close to her through the entire episode in case she fell in love with Samson and spilled the beans. Asking one's lover to go to bed with the enemy was a risky strategy. Achish had to work at such logic even though it seemed to make sense.

Obviously the first hurdle was arranging a meeting between the pair in auspicious circumstances. Baiting the hook. Positioning Delilah outside Ashkelon had to happen of course. Samson could hardly be drawn into repeated visits to a Philistine city.

They chose a lovely valley called Sorek. It was close to the border, where Samson could come and go easily. It was also reasonably near Samson's home turf. On balance it was the best location.

Naturally the valley already had inhabitants, and the last thing this scenario needed was Philistine soldiers crawling all over it finding a house for Delilah. She got to choose one herself. The Mayor gave her a budget, nothing too outlandish. Only one instruction was attached besides obtaining a beautiful outlook. The house must have some sort of inner room which could be concealed. Certain personnel might need to be stationed there from time to time.

Delilah reveled in leading the real estate agents round the locality. Having never bought a residence of her own, she was going to enjoy every minute of this experience. In the end she even did the bargaining herself, a fact the Mayor commented on with approval. Showed she had a pecuniary nature.

As a final touch she let it out in the district she was moving there on the proceeds of a divorce case from a wealthy Egyptian. The Mayor wanted a bit of titillation and mystery surrounding her.

The bait

They had to send spies into Israel to track Samson's moves. Benhad's sons were taken on again, to feed information back. It wasn't difficult this time. Samson was a judge after all, and had public responsibilities. These entailed doing the rounds of specific areas. Elihu had seen to it they were peaceable localities without much crime. Didn't want the young man getting into anything out of his depth.

From time to time Elihu thought he should act as a protector for Samson and tried to dictate his movements. But the man of strength would just smile at him benignly. Without saying anything he conveyed his simple question. Do I need protecting?

His life was half organized and half free therefore. On one of his legal rounds he was called into an Israelite village to hear a small shop keeping case. Apparently a woman from Philistia had purchased a gift from a store. While the shopkeeper was tying a bow round it, the woman brushed against him causing the article to fall off the table and break. He maintained she should pay for it. She was adamant she wouldn't. Ordinarily such a case would get sorted out between the parties, but this woman raised a small ruckus in the community and accused the storekeeper of all sorts of malpractice. It turned the township upside down. A hearing was set.

Samson arrived and heard a few other cases before lunch. Court was adjourned for an hour while they ate a leisurely midday meal. Sitting at a pleasant table under the shade in the main street, Samson watched village life go on while chatting with the adoring village elders. Two women appeared across the street, and one of the elders noticed them.

"She's the one we see next," pointing to the older one.

Samson's eyes hardly touched her. He was riveted by her companion. He couldn't help asking, "who is the other one?"

The elder glanced across again, shaking his head. "Don't know."

When they settled in the small legal chambers, the two women were sitting primly at the front. The storekeeper presented his argument, explaining how the accused had broken his vase, insulted him and caused him social injury in the community.

The defendant was allowed her turn. She made as if to get up angrily, but her young friend laid a calming hand on her arm. The small gathering was intrigued by the delay as the pair whispered to each other in the front row. After a minute, the older one settled back reluctantly, while the younger one arose.

"My lord, may I approach the bench?" she asked Samson softly.

For a few seconds he was agog before finding his voice. "Yes, certainly, madam."

She drew closer to him as if to share confidential thoughts. "I have come with Elidia for her own good. I am so dreadfully sorry this incident occurred. We are fortunate you are here my lord, to hear it out."

Leaning yet further forward with a hushed voice, she told him, "she has such a temper." She glanced back at her companion, then at Samson again. Her soft curves were obvious, her dress brushing the floor as she moved.

"I see," he breathed, matching the whispering of her voice and raiment.

She bent toward him again. "Would you mind if I spoke with yourself and the storekeeper on your own? Elidia trusts me, and I would very much like to mend this problem so no-one ends up feeling hurt."

Samson glanced at the merchant, decided for both of them, and beamed back at her. "Indeed, madam, shall we move to the rear room?" Arising, he asked for a brief adjournment, and beckoned the shopkeeper.

She spoke for about ten minutes about her friend's troublesome upbringing, with a churlish father who often beat her. And how she took this out on people. It was all very unfortunate, and she frequently gazed into Samson's eyes as she talked. Eventually she asked, "would it help if I were to pay for this broken vase here and now? Myself." While asking, she retrieved her purse and held it to her.

Samson had the sense to turn to the aggrieved party first. The shopkeeper had thawed somewhat. "We can't have people running around abusing us merchants, you know."

"Oh, you are so right," she gushed. "Of course this sort of thing can't go on. I understand completely what you are saying. Believe me, I will be speaking with Elidia about this. She has learnt a lesson from this incident."

He had one small rebuff left. "There is the matter of my standing in the community, you know. My reputation has been tarnished."

Her eyes crinkled with concern as she quickly touched his arm. "Oh, you are so right. I'm so sorry, I just didn't think of that." Tears sprang from her eyes. "I tried to go through everything before I came too." She laughed briefly, dabbing her eyes. "I'm so sorry my lords, weeping in front of you."

The merchant was done for. But he managed to feign toughness. "I suppose we could leave it at that. If the young lady is counseling the accused, perhaps it won't happen again."

Samson summed up. "Thank you for coming with your friend today. This is a good outcome."

She blushed beautifully, sniffing away her tears and fussing with her purse, counting out the money. "Oh, not at all my lord, it has been so delightful talking with you both. You are most kind."

They returned to the courtroom, and the younger one herded the older out before she could speak. Other cases had to be heard, dragging Samson's day on for a further two hours, during which he slowly came back to earth.

In midafternoon, he emerged into the sunlight of the street. Looking round at daily life, he wondered what he would do that evening.

His heart leapt. She was browsing through some stores on the far side. Her friend was nowhere to be seen. As he stood staring at her, she caught his eyes. Breaking into a smile, she walked across the thoroughfare towards him. He was rooted to the spot.

"My lord, I just wanted to thank you for your kindness. I have sent Elidia on ahead. But I needed to see you," she exclaimed. "You were most thoughtful in your handling of her problem."

For a few seconds he stood there, then stammered, "madam, it was my pleasure."

She hesitated, as though waiting for something.

"May I get you some refreshments?" he finally risked.

Her radiance was beyond words. "Oh, my lord, what a lovely thought. It has been a tiring day hasn't it?"

They walked down the street to an inn and sat chatting for an hour or two. She told him all about her move to the valley of Sorek, and her new house.

Eventually she got up exclaiming she had to go. But she laughingly told him he must visit and see her house and garden. He would love it. Giving him clear directions, she brushed his arm briefly, turned, and went.

He could still feel her touch as she was walking gaily away. He ran after her.

"I am so sorry madam. I forgot to ask your name. I am Samson."

She giggled. "My name is Delilah."

Achish

"He will appear," Achish promised, as they lay in each other's arms that night. "In fact he may even come tomorrow. This must be our last night together for some time. You know what to do." He held her tight, stroking her gently. "I love you Delilah."

She snuggled into him, hoping he meant it.

Delilah

Achish was correct. Samson appeared only two days later. He had to return to Elihu and invent an excuse to postpone some of his circuit work. Strolling into Sorek, enjoying its beauty, his heart was higher than ever. He didn't need to ask directions, in fact he preferred not to, given his desire for anonymity.

The house did look cute, tucked in behind a line of trees. Flowers grew invitingly up the path, a creeper swathed over one side of the dwelling, and he thought he heard a bubbling brook further back.

Tentatively, he knocked on the door. Several seconds later Delilah answered. Her delight was obvious. "Samson! You've come to see me! How wonderful! Do come in. Come and see my lovely little home!"

She led him through, going into every room, pointing out the views from each area. She showed him the kitchen area, the bedroom and the washing bench. He wandered past a small door in the hallway. Out of curiosity he opened it. It was a small chamber without light.

"Storage space!" she cried happily. "One always needs that!" She bounced on her toes, holding her small hands together in front of her. "Oh, I am so happy to see you! Will you stay for supper?"

"Why, yes, thank you," he replied, immediately ruing his manners. "I wasn't expecting to stay for dinner, I have not brought anything or . . ."

"Don't you even think such a thing! There is plenty here." She broke in, laughing at his male awkwardness. "But first you must tell me what you have been doing. Sit down while I bring some bread and cheese. Talk to me while I am preparing."

He became obedient. He loved watching her move about the small kitchen, cutting the food while chatting or smiling back. She was a marvel.

They ate dinner as evening descended. She lit candles. They flickered off her face and made fanciful patterns between her rising breasts. His experience with the prostitute in Gaza seemed cheap in comparison.

The thought sobered him. She sensed it. "Is something wrong? What is it?"

He knew he must tell her, but held back until she pressed him. His heart racing, he asked, "Delilah, do you know who I am?"

The truth, the Mayor had told her. Whenever possible tell the truth. Because you don't need to memorize what you've said, and you won't get caught. Keep your lies to the very minimum. "Yes, I do," she murmured. "You are Samson, the liberator of Israel."

"And you belong to Philistia."

She didn't panic. "That is true. But we are also two people, talking with each other by candlelight."

His relief was obvious. "Yes, we are." And he laughed. "Yes, we certainly are two people, talking with each other by the light of candles." He didn't know he was capable of such lines, until he had spoken them.

She touched his arm. "That was lovely."

It was tantalizingly brief, and his mind was already on when he could touch her.

Now it was time for her white lie. "When you told me your name in the village, I knew. Who in Philistia does not know your name? If I had known before, I might not have gone with Elidia. I would have been too afraid."

His heart raced.

Don't blow it now boy. You're on to something here. Be the gentleman.

He stood suddenly, conscious of the night. "I must go. You have been most kind."

Instantly she knew he was trying to do the right thing. It touched her. She liked him then. Even though she felt she shouldn't. But there was Philistia. And the money. The huge amount of money. Jumping up, she exclaimed, "it's far too late to go home now. You must stay here. There is a couch here. You can go in the morning."

"No, I must go." He hesitated. "I should, really."

She heard the pause. Men are so straightforward, she thought. "Samson. The night is far gone. You will sleep on the couch." She glowered up at him, laughing.

He was done for, and he knew it and loved it.

She tucked him in, blew out the candles and went to her room. It felt very safe. She had expected the thrill of danger. But it wasn't there. Instead there was a shy young man, a decent, likeable person. She went to sleep, knowing he would not molest her.

Achish

Samson left soon after breakfast. She waved to him as he walked down the path, watching from her door. When he reached the road she was still there beaming at him. He felt very, very, good. He didn't say when he would be back. Neither had she asked.

She knew it was a game, but it felt like a love play. It was unexpectedly nice, getting to know his innocence. But it was also exciting, the cat and mouse nature of it. She felt she would be good at it, and at the same time enjoy it all. Her involvement with love and politics all at once, in her prime, gave her a sense of self worth.

The Mayor was careful on details, and Benhad's boys had a couple of skillful men unobtrusively take up residence nearby. They mimicked bird cries and followed prey. In a sense they were hunters because they kept an eye on Samson from afar, tracking him back into Israel. If he ever turned back one of them would have sped on to ensure Delilah was in place. It was a good plan. They had covered everything. It was up to the girl now.

She met Achish in a deserted dwelling in the hills. It was good to feel his arms around her again, comforting her, telling her he loved her. She wanted him, but not sexually this time. She wanted to be sure they were doing the right thing. Achish had been warned about this by his father.

There is a high chance she will fall for Samson, he had told him again. You need to be careful on this point. Stay in constant touch with her, because in a sense, it is important she does love him somewhat. It will make her advances genuine and he will be less suspicious. It is like telling the truth wherever you can, he said.

Achish withdrew and returned to Gaza. He wanted Delilah too. But soon she would give her body to this hated enemy who had stunted his own prospects. Now it was approaching, it made him cold.

His self-talk training helped a bit. This is a game, he told himself. There are rules to it. You want to run Philistia, then play by them. All the various elements from his upbringing came together to reinforce his determination. It's going to be a balancing act. There's no room for emotional judgments here.

Samson and Delilah

The sex didn't happen until the third visit. He was so polite, so naively eager to please and do the right thing. On the evening of this occasion, she simply walked across to him, and his arms folded around her naturally. Her lips expectantly rose to meet his, and they silently started undressing each other.

He marveled as her perfect body was revealed. She felt his firm frame, his iron arms and stomach, and his massive chest. Feeling her desire for him rise, she led him into her bedroom, still unspeaking. She drew him down on top of her, her legs parting quickly, wanting to receive him.

It was much gentler than she had imagined. She experienced no climax this time, but it was moving and fulfilling. They lay in each other's arms a long time, looking at the candles she had lit. Afterwards, they went outside and gazed up at the stars. His world was perfect. They made love again later, as the candles came to the end of themselves.

"They say you are the strongest man ever to live, Samson. There are many stories about you. Shall I believe them?" She leant on her chin above him as he lay on his back in a wheat field, the bread and wine nearby.

"Oh, yes. They are all true, every one," he smirked.

She struck him on the shoulder and laughed back. "Don't you tell me lies, you great big Israelite," she said, pulling him over and kissing him. He was hard even as he rolled onto her and she wanted him there and then. They made love endlessly.

He would return to Israel for three or four days. She asked him why he was going, and he always said legal work. He had to make a living, you know. And she would see Achish again.

It was wrenching to the young Philistine, visiting her, finding out how her relationship was evolving, exploring and even encouraging it. He lived two lives. One in love with her and supremely jealous of his worst rival, and a second guiding her seduction of him. He could feel her drifting each time, so he did his best to bring her back, although he wondered whether it was really for Philistia or himself.

"Remember this is just a game, Delilah. After it is played you will be one of the richest women in the land. And honored for your part in saving the nation. I know you will feel for him. Inevitable. But never forget your task."

It was good listening to Achish and hearing the truth. Samson was a mass murderer. He killed Michael. Five thousand, five hundred pieces of silver.

Don't blow it, he told himself. This is the greatest challenge of your life. *If this doesn't come off, I am lost. Get this dog. It's all that counts.*

Delilah

"What is the secret of your great strength?"

Samson glanced up at her, curiously. Sitting up, he thought about her question before answering.

"Bind me with seven strong cords of rope that have not been dried. I shall become weak. Like any other man."

He cocked his head quizzically at her.

"Oh," she replied.

But after he went she relayed his request to Achish anyway. "Yes, bring me seven cords of rope that have not been dried. If we bind him with those he will lose his powers."

Achish stared disbelievingly. "Are you serious?"

"Yes, I am! That's exactly what he told me! Do you think I spend my time thinking up pathetic answers?!" She leapt to her feet. "You warn me about what to do, I get an answer out of him, and you don't even listen to me!"

"Whoa now, hold on, I didn't say I didn't believe you. You want seven fresh cords, we will get them. Hey, I don't want to upset you darling. It just seemed, kind of weird, that's all. I thought his secret would be something really interesting, really deep, not seven fresh ropes."

"Anyway, that's what he told me. So there."

"I will bring the men, and the seven fresh ropes. Just as you say. Trust me."

You stupid idiot, he berated himself.

You should know better. Keep your brain on course. Every word, every opinion, counts.

He told his father. "I think he's having her on. Seven fresh ropes. He was bound tightly with ropes when the Israelites delivered him to us at Lehi. Fat lot of good that did."

The Mayor thought about this for a while. "It's not going to be straight-forward. We have to consider Delilah in this too. She is the key player. If we don't do what she suggests, she will lose faith in us. And stop trying."

He sat back, thinking around the issue, approaching it from different angles. Achish could see his brain was working, so he waited. As he returned from his tour, the Mayor had another insight. "You know, there is something else interesting here. Samson didn't deny there was a secret. It wasn't surprising to him someone asked. In other words, yes, we are on the right track. There is a key. And it is not in his interests to tell anyone. He is not a fool. It will only come out when she has his complete trust.

"This will be a war of attrition. We need to be patient. And we stay with the strategy. Take her the ropes, and set up the men in the inner room," he concluded.

Three young soldiers. All volunteers. All confident, and all arrogant. They had been warned intensively about Samson. If there was any doubt at all, even the slightest uncertainty he had not lost his powers, do not move an inch. Sit tight in the inner room. You will have a few water bottles and some bread, and even a basin to excrete in. Achish drummed the instructions into them savagely. Don't mess up, or you die. We won't need to kill you because we won't get the chance.

Eventually Samson went away for a few days circuit work again. In came the three young soldiers with their seven fresh ropes. Samson always came to the house via the road, so they didn't need to hide until he had been sighted by one of the spies with his bird imitation cries hiding across the field. Even before he arrived the suspense was growing. All this planning, and now some action.

They were hustled into the inner room, and their water bottles were full. A serious penny then dropped. They could hear everything going on in the small house. Including the lovemaking. In his growing confidence, Samson would draw her to him whenever he felt the need, enveloping her in his immense arms, expecting her to respond the same way.

In a curious way, she did always want him. The excitement of the whole affair, and its knife edge thrill was an aphrodisiac. The power of the situation stimulated her so much she was always ready for him. He would pick her up, carry her into the bedroom, and they would frantically take each other's tunics off, eager to couple repeatedly.

It was torture of an amusing sort to the soldiers, who could not even laugh about it. To save themselves from this untimely death, they all contemplated the floor or the ceiling, or feigned sleep. They heard the bed rocking, picking up momentum and reaching full pitch before one or both of the pair would climax. Then the quiet, followed by the washing, then more chat. Then dinner, then more talk, then more sex. And still they waited.

Finally, out came her ropes.

"I bought these at the local village my darling. I wanted to try them on you."

"Why not," he rejoined happily. "I will lose my powers."

She knew he wouldn't then. It maddened her, but her self control kicked in and she continued as if it were a game. "Let me bind you tight, my dearest boy." She tied the ropes as tight as she could.

While doing it, she started to second guess her first reaction. They were very strong ropes. No normal man could break these. Maybe he is telling the truth. "The Philistines are upon you Samson," she suddenly cried, half in jest, yet wanting to see the outcome.

It was amazing. The first time she saw it, it was absolutely astounding. There was no effort. No straining. He even grinned at her as he performed. His arms moved out as though there was no rope holding them at all; as though he were stretching in a yawn. A snapping sound crackled through the air as the cords broke in several places. Not just at one spot. The pieces sprang out as though thrown off him. And he stood there, free of them.

In their room, the three soldiers heard her taunt, and the breaking of the bonds in the next second. One of them lifted his finger to his lips, but there was no need for a warning. They had all handled the cords and knew their strength. Nobody was about to burst out of the room.

Achish and Delilah

Samson stayed with Delilah for a further two days, never leaving the house or garden. It was hot, the sun beating down on the abode and concentrating its power into the central airless room. The soldiers nearly expired, sparingly using their water bottles, and even saving their urine in case of dire emergency thirst. As the first of them was forced to excrete, they wordlessly realized the stench might alert Samson. Off came their tunics, and over the next two days, they rolled their dung into their clothes to keep the smell down.

None of them spoke during the three days incarceration. But when the coast was finally clear, they burst out of the room in only underclothing, clamoring for water and release from their fetid cell. One of them retched into the garden.

They exploded in rage. "What sort of stupid move was this, bringing these ridiculous ropes down so he could play games with you?!" yelled the leader. "Have you any idea what torture it is to sit in that room and endure this heat! And know your clothes have been used to roll up the shit from these two imbeciles?"

They then turned on each other, and several blows were traded before Achish arrived, having been warned by the birdman all was not going to plan. It was fortunate he did for Delilah's sake as well, who was beside herself weeping and wailing. She collapsed into his arms. "He told me he wanted fresh ropes! He told me and I trusted him. He is a beast doing that to me! Who does he think he is, Achish? Who does he think he is?"

He had the presence of mind to recognize she was just giving vent to her feelings, and hugged her, telling her everything was okay. Samson was a beast. He was worse than that. He was a murderer. You are going to find out what his secret is. You will be a heroine in Philistia. You will be richly rewarded for your efforts. He felt in control as he comforted her. She's mine. You lowlife, Samson, treating my woman like this. You will pay.

Some silent gestures to the soldiers to get into town and have a few drinks, and half an hour of soothing talk, and she gradually calmed down.

After dinner together, she had her house back in order, and felt a lot better. He asked her if she wanted to quit. It spurred her on. Her lips were pursed.

"I will get this secret from him if it is the last thing I do, Achish. He made me mad."

He reported this last interchange word for word to his father. The Mayor sat there, seeing the clash of personalities, and how it strengthened her resolve. In the midst of all the stress, he had felt himself wavering. It was good she was more determined, but it was still a gamble. Plenty could go wrong.

Fighting back to a positive conclusion, he reassured himself again. We have a plan. Any action is better than none. They were making progress.

This time Samson was away for a week. Delilah feared he had told an Israelite the story, and they had seen through her game. She didn't realize he couldn't tell anyone, a conclusion which had not escaped the Mayor. Elihu would never know what Samson was up to in Sorek. He would immediately have ordered the severing of the relationship. And Samson would have obeyed. So he didn't tell.

He simply loved her too much. In actual fact he had enjoyed the episode of the ropes. It enabled them to spar at each other, and added something to the love relationship he was convinced they had. So when she started asking questions about his strength again, he climbed into the fun.

"I was leading you on about the fresh ropes. I'm sorry. That wasn't fair. You need to try dried ropes. Seven dried ropes, but ones that haven't been used. New ropes, dried, are the strongest ropes you can get. Fresh ropes break easily because of the moisture."

She was taken aback with this new technical information.

"I shall become weak, like any other man."

It was like a challenge. She gazed quizzically at him as she finished packing their picnic. All the way to the riverside her mind was working. Her emotions told her Samson was fooling again. But her intuition prodded her to respond to the game play. Otherwise if she didn't come up with the ropes, he would simply tell her the same solution. Again and again. Until it was tried.

Word was sent back to Achish. He rolled his eyes when the document arrived. "Dried ropes," he told his father. "She wants dried ropes this time."

The Mayor felt despair hovering again. Samson was making a mockery of them.

He pulled himself together. It will work, he told himself. It has to work. They are a nation of children, what with their naive religion and customs.

Sure there may be some magic over there, like whatever this Samson has got. But no divine intelligence influencing events. I proved that already by taking them over.

"She gets dried ropes. What are you waiting for?"

The five mayors

Edred had called the meeting himself. He wanted a progress report. Citizens were asking questions.

"Of course we can't tell our own people what is going on!" the Mayor of Gaza thundered, betraying his stress, before reining himself in again, and lowering his voice. "If we do, word will get back to Israel as surely as the sun rises tomorrow. And then it's all over. Samson will immediately be warned, and we will never have the opportunity again."

His hearers sat back considering. Good point.

Edred spoke up again, attempting to show his meeting was not a waste of time. "Surely however, there is progress, some news you can tell those of us in this room. We are financial partners in this enterprise."

The senior mayor was back in control now. Smoothly he rose, agreeing as he did so.

"Indeed we are," he said warmly. "What do you wish to know?" spreading his hands as he was wont to. Before they had a chance, he shook his head, "no, that's not fair, let me tell it just as it is."

He walked around the room, this time like the leader of old, explaining all the details about the house Delilah had bought, and the manner in which she seduced Samson. Majoring on items like Samson's need to return back home to keep up his judge role, he intimated it would not be over in a few days.

"Has she asked him yet? What his secret is, I mean," queried Ekron, slightly irritated after twenty minutes of unrevealing information.

"Yes," said the Mayor, keeping to his own advice on honesty. "Yes, she has."

But his tone told them there was more. He waited a moment while they hung there. "She certainly has, and reports back to us on all such conversations."

He sat down this time, clasping his hands on the table top. "This is Samson's life secret. He will not share it until he is absolutely certain his trust will not be broken. The word trust is critical here. Confidence between people does not occur in a few days. It is built up over the years. Like the trust that exists between all of us here. That did not happen overnight. We have many years meeting together here. And within these four walls, we often share secrets. Knowledge that could prove perilous if it got into the wrong hands. So it is with Samson. It will take time."

It was also time to stretch out his window of opportunity. Looking up with empathy in his eyes, his fingers lifting and spreading apart, he said, almost as an admission. "I do not know how long it will take. I wish I knew the time frame. I would give my right arm to be able to say, in two weeks we will know. But I can't."

At that he stood, strongly and with purpose. "But this I can promise you. Every day the operation goes on, it gets closer to the goal. Samson keeps coming back to this girl. He is entranced by her. The more he gets enmeshed, the better our chances are." He paused again. "Everything has gone right so far, absolutely everything."

His open hand, palm up, rose to acknowledge Ekron. "Edred was wise calling this meeting. I believe we need regular updates like this. Keeps us all in touch with events. I suggest we get together again in a fortnight."

Achish

Achish nearly came unstuck with the muscular soldiers. They were definitely not keen to spend more time in the inner room. He had to raise their pay. And more importantly provide better conditions. When he was fitting out the room with containers and cloth lids so they could excrete in peace, he wondered what had become of his life. He was the son of the Mayor of Gaza, yet here he was assisting soldiers to move their bowels in comfort.

He hated Samson again. With more vengeance than ever. As he showed the men how to stuff rags on top of the excrement, he was nearly overcome by his revulsion of the man who would reduce him to such tasks. He became increasingly calculating, mentally toting up a score that he would repay.

Focus, young man, Asaph would have said. Ah, Asaph. Almost forgotten you. I'm sorry you had to take the blame. But there was no other way. I hope you understand.

He had not visited his former mentor once. It could not be done, said his father. No meeting could ever occur. You will have to play your part in this, the older man had said. Move on with your life.

Samson

The birdman whistled out his warning mid-afternoon. The lads hunkered down in the room.

Samson arrived.

Yet again they had to listen to the lovers chatter, the movements around the house, the preparations for the evening meal, and then finally to the bed. It was getting tiresome, all this noisy union and crying out in passion. He was insatiable. After several day's absence, he seemed determined to have sex with her three or four times before tiring. Each time longer than the previous. By the fourth time, he was lasting nearly an hour.

She got to the ropes. They had been told by Achish it might not do the trick either, but to bear with them all. Once more they heard her tying him up. He assisted her with instructions about knots, and asked her to tighten the thongs at certain points. She went right through the charade this time, knowing full well it wouldn't work. And so, as she stepped back, she commented cynically, "the Philistines are upon you Samson."

Snap went the ropes again, flying off him in pieces. She had to admit that part was equally impressive the second time she saw it too.

In their little prison the soldiers sat tight and shrugged at each other. But as Samson was picking up the pieces of rope, he opened the door and threw them into the dark interior without looking in. In the second the door was ajar, their hearts were in their mouths. But it shut again, and their pulses slowly went down.

And once more he left after a further two days. When they got out, they were tired and grumpy, but there was less tension. They wanted to get Samson now. They could follow the games he was playing and had more sympathy for the obstacles facing Delilah. An air of teamwork started to build. But it was hot, cramped work.

They talked to Achish about it. "Eventually Delilah will get the answer, we can appreciate that. But it's tormenting in the inner room. And in any case, he nearly burst in on us. Imagine if he saw us? We would all be dead, and the plot uncovered about Delilah. How could she explain storing soldiers in her house?"

Good point, thought Achish. Why didn't we see that to begin with? We've just been lucky. "Sure," he replied. "no more inner room duty until we have the real answer."

It took several hours to get this through to Delilah, who thought she was being abandoned. Achish reassured her, "no, we are in full support, but having the guards there is risky. Your life would be under threat. If Samson discovered them, do you think you would escape his fury at being spied upon by his lover?"

She wanted to succeed though. It was the money, but it was more than the money now. It was finishing what she had started. Achish could see her determination. In a way, withdrawing the men from the room added impetus to prove herself. It was a good move all round.

The soldiers had something else to tell Achish. They were sheepish though and didn't know how to broach it. Their leader was elected. He shuffled his feet nervously in front of Achish as they stood talking down the road away from the house. But Achish felt what was coming, quickly wondering whether the soldiers knew of the relationship between Delilah and himself. The real relationship. Or was it?

"It's about the sex," the military man stated suddenly, trying to get it over with.

Even though he had braced himself, Achish still blanched. In the same instant he knew why. It was the voicing of it, the verbalizing of the act he dwelt on in his own mind, but had not heard others actually speak about until now. Hearing it seemed to make the knowledge public. And, as his mind raced, he knew it could not be restrained from being spread. Could he, a future ruler of Philistia, have a relationship with the woman who bedded Samson?

"They certainly have a lot," the army man added. "And she seems to like it. In fact I would say, yes, she enjoys it. With him."

With him.

In addition to the sick feeling mounting in his stomach, this last comment stung. As though she didn't enjoy it with himself. Childish jealousy might arise, his father had warned, thinking through the dangers ahead of time. Be careful. But he couldn't help it. Inner rage rose.

He is in there having sex with my woman. She enjoys it. She has to enjoy it. To get the secret. He may be removing Delilah from me permanently, one way or another. You are debasing me Samson, and it will end in agony and horror for you. I will personally tear your manhood off you, I will make sure you never, ever, touch another woman for the remainder of your very short life.

Don't let your feelings show.

"Can't be helped," he grinned back at the soldier.

Samson

Samson came back. He was enjoying his double life. Elihu had no idea where he went on these regular trips, nor did he send any followers. The young man was his own protector, and he always came home safely. Even better, he came back refreshed, full of zest and life. Samson told him he went up into the hills. Fair enough. If the sojourns did this to him, it was only to the good.

He would do a few days judging in his districts, racing through the cases. Dining with the locals was pleasant enough, and he might snap a few planks for the small boys. Off he would go, telling only Elihu, or preferably, leaving a message for him.

He strode up to the front door, knocking on it. She opened it, smiling affectionately, but thoughtfully. In his maleness he could only tell himself she had been thinking about something. It didn't come out until the next day. Her moodiness had not gone away. Their lovemaking was not as passionate or long as before.

Finally he asked, "what is the matter, beautiful woman? You are always in thought."

She remained silent.

It took another couple of tries before she opened up. "You have deceived me Samson. Whenever I ask you about your great strength, you tell me a lie."

He was genuinely surprised. All along he had thought it was a game. Now it dawned on him she might be serious. "Oh, come on Delilah. We have a wonderful life together. We are young and in love. What more do we need?"

She could see a glimmering in his consciousness. He hasn't even taken me seriously so far. Part of her wanted to burst out at him. But another felt he was a boy at heart, enjoying this encounter of love and words. She still liked him, she couldn't deny that. Leaning over and kissing him, she murmured, "oh, Samson, my strong Samson, you are a mixture."

Confused by this statement, but delighted to hear her soft voice again, he allowed her to reach in and stroke his body, with its inevitable conclusion.

Two evenings later, she brought it up again. "Tell me then. What is the secret?"

She's still asking.

It hasn't gone away.

He thought for a moment. "You see my long hair, with its seven locks. If you weave the hair together so it is not freely flowing, I will become weak. Like an ordinary man."

She didn't believe him. And she didn't say anything this time. Just stared at him.

For the first time Samson saw she knew he was lying to her.

In a surprise move, given the exchange of looks, she came onto him in the bed. Their joining was powerful and passionate, she begging him to hold himself back. It became a marvelous endurance test for him as he brought her to climax several times before exploding inside her, crying out with his own release. It exhausted him, and she comforted him before he slept.

An hour later she climbed out of the bed and lit a small candle. He was deep in a satisfied slumber. Carefully she weaved the locks of his hair together. It took about forty minutes. When they were firmly in place, she leaned over, bringing him to life as she rubbed her body against his. She used her familiar phrase. "The Philistines are upon you Samson."

He came to, realizing his hair was knotted, and pulled out the pin. "You're right," he breathed back, "there is a Philistine upon me." Flipping her over, his sexuality sprang back to life. She lay there, receiving him quietly, rolling over to sleep when he was done. Awake now, he gazed across the bed at her, contemplating her strange behavior.

"How can you say you love me when you keep this secret from me? There should be no hidden things between us Samson. You are I are so close, we need to know everything about each other. Ask me anything," she went on, "and I tell you, don't I?"

This burst out before she realized her own contradiction. But he didn't know she was lying, she also grasped instantly. And she was right. He never challenged her back, never asked her probing questions. She resumed the offensive, "True love holds no secrets, darling."

Silently he got up and dressed. Her heart sank.

"I'm going for a walk," he said presently.

She watched him go down the path, not knowing what to say.

But he was only gone for an hour. He brought her some flowers back. That's a first, she thought with relief, hugging and thanking him. "Oh, they're lovely Samson, lovely. Where did you get them?"

His feet moved awkwardly back and forwards. "Just up on the hill."

In fact he had spied them high on a slope and obtained them at the cost of a rocky climb.

The rest of the day passed without mention. Over dinner, up it came again. She gazed into his eyes. "It's important to me, my dear. I don't know why. I just want to know so much about you, I love you so much."

"But why this thing Delilah? Why this? Ask me something else."

Immediately she knew she would find out. It was only a matter of time. He was starting to break. So, over the next few days she did not bring it up. Instead she went into a mood change. She became less animated, and talked with him a smaller amount. She still cooked for him, and walked in the fields. But her conversations were brief. She seemed distracted, and wanted to return home faster than usual. She would work in the garden on her own for a few hours.

At night, when he wanted sex, she sighed and lay there impassively. At first he tried to be sensitive and would leave her. But after a couple of days, his desire overcame him and he wanted her badly. She let him undress her, responding half heartedly. He lay her on the bed, and began stroking her, caressing her thighs and buttocks.

She responded to this slightly. She seemed gentle, but not connected intimately. After spending himself, he turned over and lay beside her, gazing at her, wondering what to do.

She finally spoke directly. "I want so much for us to be completely one, Samson. But I don't know whether we ever can be."

He was silent. She rose and went out to wash herself.

This time he didn't go back to Israel. He felt trapped. If he left without telling her, he knew he would not come back. He even started to think she might not be there when he returned.

As he drifted over these things, he realized he would tell her. It was not an earthshaking conclusion. It actually became a small decision. He didn't know how it became smaller. But it had. It simply shifted in his mind from telling her, to how he would tell her. He wanted the right mood.

And so it took place. She was silent over dinner, picking at her food. He was gazing into his plate, wanting her back, wanting those first carefree weeks of unfettered love.

"I will tell you now. You will then know everything there is about me."

He rose and walked over to the couch, her eyes on him. "My hair has never been cut. It is the sign of a Nazirite. A vow from my birth. If my long hair is cut off, I will become weak, like any other man. There. You know it."

Tears came to her as she went over to him. He had told her all that was in his heart. He was truly hers. He did love her. And she loved him more than any other man in that moment. He had bared his soul.

"Oh Samson, Samson." Her compassion was genuine. His openness swayed her, and she felt a union of spirit, a oneness she craved. She would not tell Achish. This was her secret. They would live together forever, holding each other, making love in her beautiful home. Let the world go away. This was her life.

Their lovemaking was exquisite that night, she wanting him desperately, lusting after the closeness and the security it gave. He went to sleep vanquished, but content, dozing far into the next morning.

He was late. He had to get back to Israel. But he would come to her as soon as he could. She held him close at the doorway. Walking down the pathway, she remained at the road until he had gone. Deliriously happy, she went back inside the house to clean and scrub it for his return.

Achish

"No word from Delilah for ten days now, Achish? It's a bit worrying." The Mayor's voice was edgy with his understatement.

"Yes, I must admit so." He had been sweating over it himself, willing the missive to arrive from Sorek, agonizing as he walked the city battlements each morning.

"I think something has occurred. Another request for ropes is one thing. Silence is another. It is always the worst sign. You better go down and see her. Be very careful. I know visiting her without request is not in the game plan. But we can't simply hope things are going well. We need to adapt to events."

He stopped, wondering whether he should share his final thought, and bare himself to his son. "I meet the mayors three days from now. Some news would be helpful. I've fended them off from the rope tales so far."

It finally came out. "She may have fallen for him. If she tells him the plan, you and I are finished."

It was the first time he had confessed it to Achish. The young man felt the pressure of the statement, even as he felt a newer connection with his father, a bond forged by their despair, bringing the strong man of Gaza to admit his fears like this.

But there was nothing to say in reply.

He traveled down in ragged clothing, with a cape like a priest. When he got near her house, he didn't use the roads however. He knew a back route over the hills. It would place him above her home at a distance. For a couple of hours he watched from the hilltop. She was busy, gardening, washing clothes, baking bread. Samson was nowhere to be seen, nor was there any apparent conversation back into the house from the yard.

It was clear. He went on down through the fields, still watching carefully. As a final caution he sneaked up to the dwelling and peered surreptitiously through a few windows. Scouting round the outside, he checked the bedroom. The bed was made and the room was tidy. Continuing his secretive circuit, he came to the front door and knocked.

It opened quickly, and her smile was ready. But it faded when she saw him. Bad sign, he told himself.

"Hello." She recovered quickly enough. "Come in. Where have you been?"

It was an inane question, but he was ready anyway. "Hey, it's such a nice day, and I thought I would like to take a nice girl out for a nice lunch. Somewhere nice."

She laughed at his words. First good sign. "Achish, Achish, my good friend." She brightened up. "Yes, let's. Let's do that. Let me pack some fresh bread. I've just baked."

"It smells wonderful," he replied gaily, lapsing into small talk.

Take it easy now boy, use your wits.

He took the basket and they walked off to a familiar spot near the river, under the shade of some trees. He deliberately talked about other things, getting to know her again. About Gaza, and the new garments coming in from Phoenicia, and a new eating place he must take her to. She was attentive, and yet distracted.

The conversation lapsed and they were quiet for a while, looking at the water flowing by.

"You know, don't you," he uttered, almost silently.

She didn't move. Then rolled slowly over, onto her back, looking up at the sky.

"Yes, I do."

He remained silent, some seconds elapsing before she sat up.

"He is so wonderful, Achish. You asked me to get to know a man, and I have ended up loving one. He trusts me so much."

Not knowing how to proceed, he let her talk.

"Samson is not evil, he is just a boy at heart. He told me why he slew those men in Ashkelon. He didn't realize it was Michael."

Damn it, thought Achish, the walls closing in.

She gazed directly at him. "That was cruel of you, playing that trick on his bride."

Always tell the truth.

He hung his head. "You know. You now know. Achish is not perfect. He has a skeleton in the cupboard. But do you think I had any idea he would go down there and kill thirty men? None of us knew about his strength!"

She maintained her gaze. "Yes, you did. He told you about the lion killing."

"But who would have believed him Delilah? Would you have swallowed a story like that straight up?"

No, probably not, she felt. But even so, "how would you feel if someone double crossed you, Achish? Tell me!" She sat up angrily.

He stared back, transparent. "I fouled it up Delilah. If you really want to know, I messed it up."

He is lovely too. He is vulnerable and beautiful too. Why do I have all these strong men with secrets in my life?

"Achish, I am so confused. It is too much. I can't go on like this. I can't tell you."

The sun dappled spot was beautiful, the water inviting.

"Let's go for a swim, Delilah," he suddenly exclaimed, jumping up, stripping off. "Come on!"

The surprise of his change caused her to laugh out loud. "You crazy boy, what's got into you!"

But she was up happily, removing her long flowing dress even as she spoke. He was goofing off near the waters edge, pretending to lose his balance, back and forth, his face showing mock alarm.

"Achish! You silly boy! You'll fall in!" It was intoxicating, moving from such deep talk to frivolity so fast. She ran over, her magnificent body gliding across the grass, wanting him again, not knowing why. When she reached him they fell splashing and laughing into the crystal pool. They came up for air, flicking water at each other like children.

She shrieked with delight, chasing him across into the shallows. He picked her up as she squealed, feeling her nestle into him, running back into a deeper spot, carrying both of them underwater again.

They emerged, faces close, quietening down. Impulsively she reached out and kissed him. She led him out of the brook by the hand, reaching down and spreading her dress wide. Quickly she pulled him into her, feeling the sudden glorious shock of him entering.

They had to leave. Samson would return any day, maybe today. Achish could not even risk returning to the house. He snatched kisses all the way back up through the wooded area, caressing her hands as he did so.

"I must go now." He was firm. "You know that."

She stopped. He knew she was deciding. He remained silent.

"Bring the money when you come."

Elation

He burst into the palace, running through to where his father sat pensively. "We've got it!" he shouted. "She knows!"

"She found out!" His lined face relaxed. "Oh, you genius, Achish!"

It had been so long. He had forgotten what the euphoria of success felt like. Flooding back, it reminded him the world was sane, and understandable. He bounded up and paced around, clapping his son on both arms and beaming at him. The breakthrough. At last. He couldn't wait to face the other mayors again, and walk round the table leading the discussions once more. How sweet it would be to get off his back foot.

As it welled up inside him, he could also feel the horror recede, and physically turned slightly, facing the window as if to banish the nightmare.

Returning from his brief trance, he asked the obvious. "So? Don't keep me in suspense."

"I knew you would ask. But I don't actually know."

"What do you mean, you don't know!"

"She didn't tell me the secret, she just told me she knew."

An explanation was in order. "She fell in love with him, as you suggested. It was a close thing, me seeing her like that. But it was the only way. She wasn't going to tell us. And that is how I know she really knows," Achish stated with finality.

Now clear of negatives, his father took in this logic, processing it quickly. "Yes, I see your point."

He brightened up again. "Right. the next move?"

"She wants the money. Up front."

"Clever girl. Are you sure she knows?"

"Positive. Absolutely."

"Achish."

"Yes?"

"Bring him back alive."

"Alive!"

"Yes, Philistia needs to see him, broken, at first hand. Besides, if he is weakened, you can easily do that."

Achish thought for a while. "What if the weakening is temporary? What if he regains his strength?"

"There are ways of incapacitating a man permanently."

The Mayor faced his son. "And here is some advice for you alone. I know you want the girl yourself. But she has done her piece. For you, for me, for Philistia. You might lose her. That is not the end of the world. Men of strength move forward. There are always other women."

Achish took only the three young soldiers with him even though they also carried all the silver. They were bodyguards enough. And if Samson was reduced to an ordinary man, the three could easily bring him back.

"Yo guys, the final trip. No more inner room bladder control," he said, trying to be the old happy Achish.

They were polite and stared back at him, but he could see their minds were not in a fun mood. He spoke more directly. "Our instructions are to bring him back alive."

They gazed at him, then away, still without comment.

"Didn't you hear me? I said alive."

"We heard you. You said alive. Your father already briefed us."

Think, Achish. He had to tell the soldiers. He's just trying to cover all the bases. Don't make meaning of the fact he didn't assume you would tell them. That's backup for you.

The leader of the trio added, "however, he did not say, bring him back in one piece."

They all laughed together. "Don't you worry boyo, we know what we're doing. We've got some shit to repay."

And they burst out again.

You can laugh, Achish gritted to himself. *I've got a mountain more than you to unload, and I can't even joke about it. I won't even get to slug him in the face.*

But he couldn't resist getting the last word in. "Wow, you don't know how lucky you really are. You get to walk him all the way back to Gaza by yourselves. Make sure there are enough pieces left for him to face some music when you arrive."

Delilah

Any inner room strategy was uncalled for now. If the man was weakened, they would see it when he came outside. They were warriors, used to assessing a man's abilities on sight alone.

The birdman made his calls to let Delilah know everyone was in place in nearby fields. She prepared dinner for Samson, and chatted in a reserved manner to him. He still looked wonderful, although awkward in her presence again after the knowledge they now shared. She took him to bed for the final time, wrestling and grappling with his body. He felt like she wanted him, but that something had changed. Nevertheless it was good lovemaking, and satisfying after a weeks abstinence. She didn't talk much, and he pulled the blankets up and slept deeply.

An hour later she emerged from the house. Achish was waiting near the gate. She stole down the path.

"Do you have the razor?"

He nodded wordlessly, still not knowing what she wanted to do.

"You must cut all his hair off. He is a Nazirite. They take a vow from birth."

It still didn't seem magic enough to Achish, but he had heard of the Nazirites during his history lessons. Yes, come to think of it, they did take vows to maintain their locks. And Samson surely had a solid mane of hair. Wow. That simple.

A thought occurred to him, but she saw it coming. "He won't wake. I've knotted his hair before while he was asleep."

He followed her back on tip toes. Samson was slumbering soundly. Gently she held his head in her familiar hands. He used the sharp razor with untrembling fingers. Slice by slice the locks fell away to the floor. It only took two minutes to remove the bulk of it. His head was lain down again, and Achish walked backwards out of the room.

When he was out of the house, he ran back up to the fields, quickly telling the three what he had done. "I don't want him dead. You know the deal."

"He won't be killed," the leader repeated coldly.

Achish threw his arm up to give the signal to the birdman. Out rang the call.

Delilah heard it clearly, and ran to the bed. She shook him. "The Philistines are upon you Samson!"

This time there was a different urgency in her voice. His head felt different, and his hand swept back through his hair. Gone. On the floor.

He sat on the bed, understanding, yet not believing.

"Out there," she pointed. "Philistines."

She sounded desperate, as though she was doing something she didn't want to do, but had to finish.

His hair. On the floor. Cut off.

He went out. Nobody was there, just strong lamps burning, throwing light on him. Figures emerged from the bush. Men with sneers on their faces.

One of the three ran at him. Strangely he was not moving slowly. He was fast. As the gap narrowed, he swung a fist at Samson. It was terribly quick, swifter than any he had ever seen. He was struck and smashed backwards.

It had never happened before. He couldn't believe it. Someone hit me. His anger grew, as he stood up and charged. *Come on boy, there are only three of them.* And again the unexpected fist, this time from another one. Harsh laughter rang out. "Samson, the strong man of Israel. Come and get us, you can do it!"

But they couldn't wait any longer. All three leapt at him, smashing blows into him. He was knocked to the ground. They pounded him harder, he feeling their fury. Vaguely he wondered why they were so angry, because he had never seen any of them before. Two of them pinioned his arms to the ground, while the third stared at him. "Remember me hero, it's the last thing you'll see."

He pulled a sharp bone out of his jerkin, as his fellows held Samson's head firm. Horror-struck, he realized what the man was doing, and the end was stabbed into his right eye, then twisted down the side of his forehead.

A terrible suction noise occurred as his eye was gouged out. He gave vent to the first scream in his life.

This can't be happening, his mind was shrieking. As the bone was stabbing into his second eye, other voices rang out, Delilah screaming and weeping as she tried to pull them off. It was the last thing he saw as the dreadful pain from the front of his face set in.

Another voice assisted Delilah. "Get off him, you animals! Get off him!"

He knew it. It was Achish. It didn't make sense. It sounded like he was trying to rescue him, even though the tone of voice was wrong.

"He must be left alive! You know that!"

Suddenly in his complete darkness and pain now, Samson felt the soldiers release him. "He's not dead," one snorted. "We promised. Have a look."

At this pun the guards burst into more laughter, kicking Samson as they did so. Not knowing where the blows would come from, he huddled into his arms. "Oh, doesn't he look sweet now, like a baby," said another before Achish finally silenced them.

Samson could hear Delilah weeping in the background. "You didn't tell me you would do this to him, you beast!" she shrieked.

Her voice changed, as though it were being muffled by someone holding her tight. The thought of another man doing that unstopped Samson's mouth.

"Delilah! Delilah!"

But there was no answer. Just footsteps moving back into the house.

Achish pulled her away, holding her as she beat at him with her small fists, crying hysterically. He buried her face into his shoulder to stifle the noise as he moved both of them back towards the house.

Oh, that felt good, seeing those boys do that. I only wish I had the chance to smash him one myself. It's disgusting, I know it's positively evil, me enjoying it, but he nearly ruined my life.

I don't know whether I'll get Delilah back after this. We might be finished. But it was worth it.

He couldn't win. Not against me.

Samson

Rough hands grabbed Samson, and pulled him to his feet. He lashed out, not knowing what he would hit. Immediately he was struck on the side of his head. The blow sent him to the ground again. Hard booted kicks came from both sides into his torso. He huddled to protect himself.

The kicking stopped. He could hear breathing. Someone spoke. "Samson, my boy, we want you to come quietly. We are going to take you somewhere. If you argue back, this is what will happen. Every time you try and hit us, we're going to kick you to pieces."

The speaker paused. He guessed it was one of the soldiers. "I'm going to help you stand again. This time, just get up without doing anything stupid."

Again a pause, before an instruction was issued. "I'm going to tap you now on your shoulder. You will feel it."

The commands had a calming effect. His shoulder was touched, then he was helped to his feet. The soldiers started to think through the elements of leading a blind man. They began directing his moves. Turn right. Watch this step. Silently he obeyed.

Sometimes they would not warn him, and he would stumble over a rock, or walk into a tree. Immediately they would laugh, then make apologies. But their revenge had been satisfied mostly, so they treated him more carefully.

He was led down the road some distance before the soldiers bedded down. His hands were tied securely behind his back, and the rope looped around a large tree.

He managed to fall asleep, from sheer exhaustion. Although he didn't know it, his mind was in shock at the complete change of circumstances, and needed rest of its own. The shift from victor of Israel in love with a beautiful woman, to defeated blind man, was not yielded to lightly by his brain.

So it was at dawn, he woke up, and opened his eyes, but couldn't see. It flooded back once more. A respite of sleep had not repaired anything.

Samson had to walk to Gaza, led by a rope around his hands. The soldiers followed orders strictly now. Make sure he is fed and given water.

Frequently falling and cutting himself, he had many hours to think through his life. Gradually the gravity of his betrayal sank in, and the fact that yes, he had lost his powers along with his hair.

From time to time, his bitterness rose and he cursed inwardly. He cursed Philistia, and he cursed Achish, who was undoubtedly behind the plot. He abused himself for his stupidity and waste. But mostly he was in pain, and he was tired. The effort of walking in darkness and attempting to be careful displaced his rage.

Blaming Delilah never entered his mind. Convinced she was misled somehow, it was impossible to think she had deliberately done this. Her beauty floated before him.

In the mornings he would awaken in pain, his reflexes still opening his eyes, only to recall they were no longer there. Another endless day of walking in darkness and heat lay ahead, to the sounds of rough men jeering, and strange objects to crash into.

Eventually they reached Gaza. He heard many voices clamoring, and there were blows from all sides as he was dragged through the streets. He was tripped repeatedly, to fresh laughter every time. Voices petered off as he hit stone stairs, falling heavily onto their edges, and feeling the rope pulling him upward. He recalled these steps, and how many he had to climb. On all fours, he scrabbled up, mercifully free from the crowd striking him. The rope went slack as they reached the top. He sank down, lying on the paved stone, breathing heavily, hoping to die somewhere.

The Mayor looked down at the bedraggled body. He looks small, but that is probably psychological. A dead lion doesn't look that big either. It was difficult to imagine this pathetic creature dispatching a thousand troops. It didn't bring happiness, seeing him like this. Just a sense of completion. We are through it.

Samson heard a different voice. Already his sense of hearing was growing, informing him about people. This one had authority. He had heard it before but couldn't recall where.

"So ends this saga," it rang out. Samson realized he must be talking to a crowd. They would be below, at the foot of the steps. "We have finally triumphed, as we knew we would. Here is Samson, dreaded defender of Israel. Sightless, with the strength of an ordinary man—if he is lucky!"

The crowd cheered wildly. Samson's mind flew. He was listening to the real voice behind everything. He knew who it was. The Mayor of Gaza, the strong man of Philistia according to Elihu. Father of Achish. Drowning in despair at more evidence of his downfall, he nearly sobbed.

But he held back. He was still a man. There was no need to give them that as well.

The Mayor's speech droned on, but Samson wasn't listening anymore, lost in his own world. Until finally the words, softer now, "take him away."

The rope jerked, pulling him to the edge of the stairs. Knowing what was coming, he laid himself flat, feeling the edges of the hard steps rushing at him, still reeling their number off, even as he bounced down to the amusement of the crowd again.

A cart waited at the bottom. The Mayor had thought of a victory lap around the square. Samson was pushed up onto the vehicle and tied to the edge so he could not lie down. It jolted away, moving and clattering along the street. It was better than before, because at least people couldn't hit him. And he didn't need to walk or bang into things.

After several circuits, the driver changed direction, veering off down a different street. The noise of the crowd died away. He sat, half propped up against the side of the cart, rolling with its movement, waiting for his destiny. It was not long.

The vehicle pulled to a halt without warning, causing him to lurch forward, twisting against the ropes. He heard the gate at the rear of the conveyance being unlatched, then the rustle of the bonds being untied.

"Come on boy," said someone, strangely in a not unfriendly tone.

They walked across a pavement, the voice telling him, "there are steps downward here. Feel along the wall."

He could not sense the change from light into darkness, but was aware of echoes as they moved slowly downwards. A level corridor replaced the stairs. It was cooler down here. We are underground, he surmised. Groaning, shuffling noises drew nearer as they walked along. Suddenly they were louder as he heard a door being thrown open.

"You can earn your keep, my lad," stated the not unfriendly one. The captive felt the heat of a lantern as it was raised up beside him.

"Samson!" a voice breathed. He had heard it before. But his memory finally failed him.

The groaning noise ceased. He was tied to a wooden bar. Instructions followed. "You just push here, my boy. Turns the wheels. Welcome to grinders haven."

Elihu

"There is someone to see you m'lord," the servant said.

"Does he have an appointment?"

"It is a Philistine soldier m'lord."

"What does he want?"

"He has a package for you."

The curiosity was too much. Elihu stood up from his desk and went outside. Standing casually under a tree in the yard was the Philistine. He saw Elihu appear, and calmly walked over to him.

"My lord, his worship the Mayor of Gaza has sent you a request." He handed over the package, stepped back and waited. Elihu understood he should open it in the soldier's presence.

Inside were two objects. The larger was a bundle of long hair, knotted and tied together. There was something familiar about it. Elihu picked out the second piece, a slip of paper with a message written on it.

He was horror stricken. It simply read 'We have Samson. Meet me in Eltekeh three days from now.' Several seconds passed before he looked up at the soldier. Elihu asked him, "did you know what was in this package, or was it sealed before you received it?"

The soldier nodded. "I knew what was in it. I have seen him myself."

Aware of his mission, he didn't say he had personally torn the man's eyes out. It seemed judicious to keep it at the third party level. But it was enjoyable delivering the message, and he had jumped at the opportunity.

"Where is he now?"

"He is safe. He is alive and safe. And he has lost his powers."

"What is this?" Elihu inquired after composing himself, holding up the bolt of hair.

"It is his hair."

"Why are you bringing me his hair, for goodness sake?!"

The soldier appeared genuinely surprised and remained silent for a few seconds. "Do you not know?" he finally asked, even as he himself understood why Elihu did not.

The wife of Manoah

After dismissing the envoy, Elihu raced to find his horse. He was quickly up and away, heading to Zorah. His heart pounded for the entire journey. It could not be true, it could not be true. He was only here five days ago. He galloped through the startled village, swinging onto the hill path. He had never ridden up there before, but it didn't matter now. He knew she would be there. Seeing him before he saw her.

And as the horse came into the clearing, she was there. Looking straight at him, already worried. He leapt off, clutching the parcel, and ran towards her. Without speaking he pulled the hair from it and thrust it at her, urgently inquiring with his eyes.

For the first and only time, he saw her shattered. Her cries rent the air in a desperate keening. She clutched the hair, smelling it, confirming it, sobbing into it, rocking back and forth, wracked with grief.

He held her for some time, gently stroking her locks. She buried herself into his shoulder. The angel promised, she told herself. The angel promised.

Then she started to accuse herself. What did I do wrong?

He felt her shift and guessed what she might be thinking.

"No, you did nothing incorrect," he broke in. They were his first words to her. It seemed fitting. Samson always thought actions were more important than words. "You did everything a mother in Israel could do. You took him to hear the stories of our past. You brought him up with belief in himself. And his mission. There is nothing more you could have done."

Tears sprang to his eyes as he said it. He wiped them away in an embarrassed manner but she saw it, and it warmed him to her.

She sat up, her eyes also full. "I am in a state, aren't I?"

They both laughed, and it helped. Grief. And mirth. How incongruous, he thought.

Elihu stayed on the farm for several hours, busying himself building a fire and heating water for a broth. She had told his brothers, and like sturdy young men, they stood about awkwardly, trying to help out where they could.

The meal would help the grieving. She was ready to talk now, and she told him about the Nazirite vow, something she had never done before.

Elihu couldn't help himself. "Why did you not warn me?"

"I always worried about the risk of people knowing. He was brought up strictly not to tell anyone. In fact he was in his teens before we told him." She glanced away, over to the copse of trees and the track to his rock. "And now it turns out he has told somebody himself. A Philistine."

She was thinking, even in the midst of her grief, he could see that. "Perhaps you are right. I should have told you. I don't know. I don't know anymore."

Slowly he picked himself up and prepared to go. She came to him, and his arms went around her, comforting her again. "Will you be alright?"

She sniffled, sensing his care. "Yes, yes, the boys are here with me. Let me know when you find out. Please."

Meeting Elihu

Revenge is always sweeter to think about than participate in, concluded the Mayor of Gaza as he watched the hunched Elihu climb down from his mount.

In truth, he gave me dignity when it was his turn. I will do the same.

They sat at the table silently for some time toying with their goblets of wine. The Mayor spoke decisively. "Do not take this hard, my friend, we do not intend punishing Israel now."

Elihu was slightly startled, before settling back into his chair again. He hadn't thought about possible recriminations against Israel, as his mind was so full of them against himself. "How did you do it?" he got out.

Be direct. Don't boast, just be straight.

"A woman. Tactics. Perseverance," the Mayor shrugged. "The usual. It just took time."

The usual. Even if he didn't intend to sound patronizing, it was, re-flected Elihu. As though Israel was not capable of such things.

Okay, perhaps we aren't. And then again, maybe that is not such a bad thing.

He gathered his thoughts. "We have to be businesslike, you know. I will need to visit him in order to verify your claims."

The Mayor paused, grudgingly admiring his counterpart again for do-ing his job thoroughly.

"I understand you asking this. I would have done the same." His hands parted and shoulders lifted, as though Elihu was asking for something he was powerless to deliver. "It places me in an awkward spot. For example what if there was a magic elixir that reversed Samson's weakness? An elixir an Israelite was able to slip to him. I am not suggesting there is, but I too, have to think of security measures.

"And as for proof, you could always just wait for him to return to you. Perhaps I am lying. Perhaps he is even now walking into your house seeking you. And what about Samson himself? Think of him. Think of what it would be like to be put on display to you as a trophy."

Each gap between his statements was precise, and he could see the Israelite heard him.

"Let me be frank," he concluded. "He feels very bad about his circum-stances now. Your visit might be catastrophic to him."

Good points, thought Elihu again. He is clever, this Mayor of Gaza. Formidable, one might even say.

There was a silence, until the Mayor spoke again. "You asked me once if we could speak man to man. Directly. I am asking you if we can do that now. A second time.

"History, or fate, or destiny, favored you temporarily. Now she has withdrawn her blessing. We have no desire to rub defeat in Israel's face. We only seek to live peacefully beside you, and work together for mutual profit." Once more, his hands spread. "What can be wrong with that? You didn't want violence. Neither do we. I have only one question to ask. Can we live together in peace?

"Now you know there is only one answer. But you also know I need to demonstrate to Israel we are in charge again. That means stationing a few troops here and there. It means juggling the trading terms.

"And of course, freedom of religion. Philistia has never forbidden Isra-elites from following their own beliefs. We happen to think it should be up to the individual. Introducing other systems merely gives choice.

"Again, is this harmful?" He stopped there, waiting for the Israelite to respond.

Elihu took his time. He was being outwitted by the best there was. Israel's position was hopeless if Philistia was breeding men like this. Not even Samson could last against him. What hope do we have as a nation?

Asaph

Asaph watched the wreck beside him in the guttering light from the brands on the wall. They shuffled endlessly around, pushing the groaning wheels. It was not difficult after a while, and its meaninglessness allowed one's mind to wander. After two days he could see Samson was starting to get over the pain from the dreadful hollows in the front of his face. He was getting used to the rhythm. But he was thinking, Asaph could see him thinking all the time. And grieving.

Regrets, undoubtedly. Every man here suffers many. Our life will cease in dark and sweat and cursing. Every dream has been torn asunder.

He had seen it all before, and escaped once. But it had only been an intermission. He was back now, perhaps where the gods wanted him all along.

"Samson."

"Samson." Again, with gentle persistence.

It was the familiar voice again. But it did not sound unkind. And maybe it was time to talk with someone. Anyone. "Yes, it is me."

"I know."

"I remember your voice. Who are you?"

"Asaph. The one time protector of Achish."

"Asaph. Yes, I remember. At the bridal feast. And later on." Samson thought again. "The one time protector of Achish? Are you a guard here now?"

Asaph chuckled quietly as he trudged. Of course, he could not see anything. "No, I am bound to the same arm of the wheel that you are. I walk beside you every hour."

"Oh," replied Samson, not curious enough to ask why.

Later in the day Asaph spoke again, knowing this man could have not been captured by surprise, but by some trick of shrewdness. "Who did this to you?"

At the question, Samson's head hung down while he walked. Asaph recalled him as a striving, but insecure young man, full of dreams. Now all gone. No way back. He could feel the awful dawning which must be registering in his mind. All his potential lost. Forever.

"Can you not guess?" Samson finally replied.

Achish.

There weren't many options, Asaph appreciated that. Samson knew not the Mayor of Gaza. The blame for everything would lie at Achish's feet. Asaph thought back to that initial contact in Timnah. How Samson had appeared uneasy in their company.

Once Asaph thought it through, it was straightforward. Samson had been forged in the rustic villages of Israel. Who born such would not feel uncomfortable in the presence of youthful confidence as Achish had been raised to possess?

Is this the source of our plight? A rugged farming son games with the clever city youth—and fails. With revenge in his arms, he begins iniquities which lead to the rise and fall of many, myself among them.

Marveling at how a small emotional tangle could have such great consequences, Asaph could also feel the outcomes. Achish had won, but at what cost to his soul? Samson had lost, and now behold the price. And of the two, who would turn now to examine himself? To that there was a simple answer.

I am drawn to learn more. And I shall not be required elsewhere. For some time.

"How was it done unto you?" Asaph asked the next day. He had thought long about how to put the question, and decided on directness, based on the few conversations he had heard Samson in. He was not a man of words.

For a while there was no answer, and he thought he had chosen the wrong approach. But he looked again, and he could see his body shift as he grappled with his answer. Asaph remained silent, trudging around in their dark circle.

"They tricked me," Samson eventually said, knowing it was inadequate even as he said it. But he wanted to respond for some reason. Asaph did not sound cruel. And it appeared he might have been double crossed too. Perhaps some sort of bond existed. A brief grin appeared on Samson's face at the word bond, and its dual meaning in this existence.

Asaph caught it but couldn't make sense of it.

Samson spoke again, brighter now. "And you, were you tricked as well?"

It took Asaph by surprise. He too, would be asked deep questions. It was not a one way conversation. Two men with deceit common in their backgrounds brought together at an underground wheel.

Intuitively Samson this time felt Asaph was thinking and taking his time before answering, so he now remained silent. Asaph saw how the tables had been turned, and burst out laughing.

"Your question is fair. It hit me like an arrow!"

Samson laughed with him, and it made it easier to continue.

So it began. Gradually over the days they began to communicate with each other. Long periods of silence intervened as Asaph let the natural processing work. Samson's words would cease, and Asaph would stop talking to him. He would leave him for several days before taking up the conversation again.

Occasionally Asaph wondered why he was doing it. He stood to gain nothing. Why, his thoughts should be on escape rather than communing with this young ruin. But the desire to flee had gone. After his years of good fortune, Asaph had a contentedness within him that he could not fathom at times. He had had a life. A far better one than he originally envisaged. If it was his destiny to end his days like this, so be it.

Sooner or later, Samson would begin again, and he would respond. He couldn't help it. It was compelling to be involved, to see the changes. He knew Samson was healing. Inside at least. And he wanted to be there, to be part of it.

Asaph answered everything. He had nothing to hide any more, and it felt cleansing. It even gave a meaning to his existence. Watching this so called mass murderer confronting himself in the bowels of the earth. In turn he drew out from Samson the story of his love and his betrayal. It was all new to him. And fascinating to hear it from Samson's side. Asaph was able to reconstruct all the Mayor's moves. In one sense it was a marvelous ploy. A credit to the intelligence of the man, and his son.

After listening to it all, he withdrew for a few days. He tried to tell himself Samson was a murderer, and sympathy did not belong to such. Even though he was now broken, his wickedness, and the slaughter of so many, could not be excused.

However, his thinking started to widen. Had not the Mayor spoken about history and the wider context? Did he not say the acts of men carried significance for all?

The questions started slowly again. Samson talked about his upbringing, his impulsive father and unusually sensitive mother. He even spoke of the visit his mother had received from an angel before he was born.

He knew it off by heart. He told Asaph every single thing, including the secret of his hair. It was only the second time he had done it. In fact, as Samson found in common with Asaph, it was cleansing to talk it out. He remembered those many intimate conversations he had with Delilah, and how alive he had felt.

Asaph for his turn drew sustenance from this new relationship. It was a fourth episode for him. He was now the older man, tied beside a younger. He had been the older walking alongside another younger. Before that he had learned from the wiliest man in the region as he built his empire. In the earliest chapter, he had been the younger, and the seat they sat on swayed to the rhythm of the ocean. He marveled at life and its many circles, its sequences and purposes.

Samson woke to another rhythm. Although he could not tell day from night, it did not mean his body was not in timing with the daily cycle. He woke shortly before everyone else, becoming alert quickly. In his dreams he had been running again. Running down the road to Ashkelon, flying through the air, knocking the arch out of the gate, then racing to Timnah. And finally back to Delilah. Delilah, always Delilah.

Don't be a fool boy.

The admission was hard and long in the coming. She had betrayed him. He felt it as he stumbled out into the yard from her bed, but couldn't face it. He had clung to her love all that long staggering path to Gaza and in the first weeks in prison. It was an illusion, a useful deception, enabling him to blame someone else.

In truth, he had let himself be taken, he had fallen for a bait. His failure reared up at him now, heaving inside him. Conscious he was bound to a wheel with other men, he could barely muffle his sobs. He had failed everyone. He had failed Elihu. He had failed his wonderful mother. He had failed God.

Asaph watched quietly, painfully, fully acquainted now with his journey, ruefully conceding he had bonded with the worst criminal Philistia had ever known, grieving for him, as he divined now that he also did for the young man he had helped raise, and his father, indeed for a world that had brought them all to this.

Life as it should be

The Mayor arose refreshed every morning. His sleep was back to normal, and the city was buzzing with anticipation of better times. The gates had long been replaced, and merchants were bustling around again. He was firmly in charge of Philistia again, the hero who had brought them through the rough times of Samson. His son had shot to a fame of his own for his role in the affair. The blemish of Achish's early encounter with Samson was long forgotten.

Delilah refused to see Achish. She remained in her lovely house in Sorek.

"I understand your feelings," said the Mayor to his son. "But we had to do it. You know that."

He's correct, thought Achish. We did the right thing. Sometimes there are casualties. Look ahead. Your future is bright again.

Plans were made in a number of areas. Troops were sent into Israel again. However, there would be no violence if it could be avoided. Asherah factories were restarted. Lessons learned would not be forgotten. The Mayor loved the thinking and planning phases. He also delighted in having his son alongside him, growing into the role he envisioned long ago.

All was as it should be.

Samson and Asaph

"Has an angel likewise visited you, Samson?"

"No, not me." He laughed to himself, but felt he needed to explain. "I am not worthy to receive such a visit. Not me." He finished, "and definitely not now." His tone dropped away.

After some time, Asaph came back. "Is it that your parents were more worthy than you, that an angel came?"

Samson cocked his head to one side as they trudged around. "Mmm. My mother was. Perhaps. That is a good point, Asaph, that's a good point."

"What point is good?"

"Angels don't visit righteous people. That's not their job."

"What entails their task?"

"To deliver messages. Tell people important things."

"What manner of importance?"

Samson kept walking round, his hands on the pole, but his mind elsewhere.

"Messages from God."

Asaph was about to ask another question when he noticed something. Samson's hair was growing again.

"It is written in your books that he who you worship is all powerful. Tell me about this your God," Asaph asked the next day.

Samson had to think a while. Time did not matter. Asaph would wait days for an answer if necessary. When it came, his answer was brief, and summed up in a two word query.

"My God?"

Asaph didn't answer, sensing more was coming.

"I never thought of him as being my God. He is Israel's God. He leads and guides the nation."

More silence.

"I should have been part of God's purposes. But I messed up."

Asaph changed direction. "In truth, the Mayor believes your God is merely of your people's minds. That he does not exist, except in their imaginings."

"Is that so? God doesn't exist?"

"So the Mayor speaks and teaches," Asaph added. "This man fulfills his own desires. That which he wants, he obtains. It was he who conquered Israel once." He felt he needed to complete the sentence. "By your capture he has done it a second time."

"How did I get the strength I had? No normal man had that."

Asaph paused before answering. "I know not. Truly I know not."

Tarry yet, the older man said to himself. Your thoughts have brought you far. Does a guiding hand steer our fates. What is a guiding hand if it is not divine?

My God?

Samson retreated to his mind.

What a strange thing to ask. The only sure thing is, I've fouled up God's plan. I do know that. I'm not sure I know much about God.

Although I have learnt about someone else. I've started to find out things about Samson, the one time hero of Israel, I could tell you a bit about him. But the more I look at him, the worse I feel. All that potential, gone forever. The strongest man in the world, throwing it away, trusting a foreign woman. It would be better for me to leave this wretched life, this nonexistence down here. I have nothing left.

Would that God might take my life, and give me rest.

Focus, Asaph pondered.

My staff since my youth. I tire of focus. Let my mind drift, let it go where it will. I, Asaph, a strong man brought down, like my companion here. Were I to live again, I would take life and people as they came to me.

To live without secrets. The hidden things of men have brought me high and low.

The guard's shout brought them all to their feet. Angry at being caught out, Samson sprang up, grabbed the pole and started pushing. Unbelievably it started moving although the others were not yet in position. He stopped quickly in surprise.

The five mayors

"We need to get Dagon back on track," declared the Mayor of Gaza at the monthly meeting. "We started this religion for a purpose. It needs sprucing up. We put Dagon in place to provide vision for the nation."

His hearers nodded approval at the return of his confident eloquence.

"He got knocked around temporarily, but now he has been proven. We outplayed Samson. And we will attribute success to Dagon. Our people will believe it. Not only that, but I think the Israelites will also start to believe it. I want Achish to outline information we learnt throughout the Samson project."

Achish now attended council meetings. He rose to speak. "It is necessary to understand certain basics of the Israelite religion in order to grasp the Samson phenomenon."

The four lesser mayors sat back, impressed already by his language. He sounded more like his father every time they heard him.

"The first thing is their belief in angels. These beings appear to them in the form of men. This is the first misconception that foreigners to Israel, including ourselves, might have. We think their so called angels fly around with wings. That picture comes from some early brass work Israel did, hundreds of years ago. Under Moses, they built a holy device called the Ark of the Covenant. It has angels with wings on top of it. It still exists in Israel today.

"When angels visit, they look like men. In fact, many Israelites don't even know they are talking with an angel until later. By their own admission." He paused. "We don't know whether these visits are made up, or are engineered by their own priests, or are even psychological events due to stress. That is not important. What is crucial, is if something is attributed to an angel, it carries immense meaning and power.

"Samson's parents were visited by an angel. Or so they claimed. However, to our knowledge, they didn't tell anyone else. They didn't want to because of the secret of his hair. Doesn't take much to work that out. If the secret had got out, anyone might have got him while he was sleeping. As we in fact did.

"But they did tell Samson of course. His mother drummed the angel visit into him from his infancy. Once he attained a reasonable age, she told him about the sacredness of his hair.

"It became the key to his strength. He was so persuaded by her talk, that he believed he had great powers. She herself had no doubt. She was not telling him things she hoped were true. She told him things she knew were true. Her unshaken belief in the message turned him into the person we feared.

"And once his hair was gone, his belief in his own strength went with it."

He sat down to the murmur of the admiring mayors.

"Are you saying Samson was strong merely because he thought he was? I mean, I could try that tomorrow. I could persuade myself to lift a chariot. But I don't think I'd get it off the ground," mused the Mayor of Ashdod.

"Exactly," said the Mayor of Gaza, assuming his renowned mentor pose. "You have said it your very self. In one breath, any of us might say 'I think I can lift that chariot,' but underneath that thought is another telling us 'I don't think I can.' Guess which wins? The deepest one, the one with conviction. And we don't lift the chariot."

A glimmer of understanding emerged. They sat and thought awhile.

Edred from Ekron spoke up. "Can we learn from this? I mean, could we train our youth to do this sort of thing?"

"Brilliant, my old friend," complimented the senior Mayor, genuinely meaning it now. "That is what we should be doing. Now, we don't have all the answers on how to raise youngsters like this, but we do know it is centered around religious beliefs. Our aim in creating Dagon is the start of that journey."

He deferred to Achish again. "Tell them about Samson's mission."

"Yes," replied his son, "important point. The message from the angel to Samson's mother, was this. 'He will begin to deliver Israel from the Philistines.'"

This stung them.

"Will he really!! I bet he's having second thoughts now!" exploded the Mayor of Ashkelon, who had never gotten over the loss of his arched gate.

"Let him rot in that prison cell for the rest of his life! Death is too good for him!" added the Mayor of Gath, usually the quietest attendee.

The man from Gaza stood up from the table, hands out, calming them down. "We understand how you feel. But that was their message. We will just reverse that a little. Achish had a suggestion he wanted to put to you."

His son jumped up. "I think we should celebrate Samson's demise. In the temple of Dagon. Lay on amusements, a feast for everyone. We will show our people the prisoner. Sitting at the feet of Dagon. Then whose god will be greatest?"

It was unanimous.

Invitations went out all over Philistia. This was the event of the year. Dancing troupes were contracted, and celebrity singers arranged. Achish worked on the script with an event management consultant, and it became the talk of the town.

Everyone gossiped about it. Street chatter maintained the Mayor would announce the future plan strategy during the grand gathering. This rumor spread, soon arriving back into the palace. The Mayor laughed and dropped hints to feed it.

As the day drew nigh, visitors poured into Gaza. All five mayors and their families had seats conspicuously in the premiere booths. There was no question of demonstrating who ran Philistia. Military representation was compulsory, and all the merchants indicated their desire to be there.

The Mayor wanted spaces for the man on the street as well. "No sense just having the leaders," he counseled Achish. "The common man has to see this too."

Subsequently, they also sold tickets to the rooftop seats. Three thousand extra could be fitted up there, besides the large crowd inside.

The day arrived. Every inn or boarding room in Gaza was packed out. Billeting of overflow visitors had been arranged. During the day festivals were held in the squares, restaurants were brimming, and taverns literally overflowing.

The doors to Dagon's temple were opened at seven in the evening. In flooded the rejoicing throngs, many already inebriated. It took a whole hour of steady movement in and up the roof stairs before the place was filled.

Right on time, the first acts started. Out came the scantily clad dancers, leading the crowd to start on the wine they had all privately brought in on their own persons.

Accomplished singers were next, with various breaks by clowns and acrobats. It was superbly orchestrated, and Achish languished in praise from the mayors.

After an hour or so, at a pitch of excitement, someone on the roof started a chant. "Samson! Samson! We want Samson!"

The entire rooftop picked it up. Downstairs in the main boxes, the mayors roared with laughter.

"This is perfect!" Gaza's mayor was ecstatic. "Perfect! The crowd want him here. It has become their idea! They want the Dagon showdown too!"

He stood up conspicuously to further cheering and clapping, motioning for silence.

"Why not?!" he cried to his audience, and immediately to a nearby general. "Bring him!"

The crowd erupted.

Thousands

The chariot swung up to the door of the grinders prison, two of the guards alighting before it stopped. With the Mayor's handwritten orders in their grasp, they marched down, thrusting them at the warden.

"Sounds like a good idea," he said after he read them. Rising and reaching for the key he added, in his kindly tone, "wait here."

He walked down alone, opening the door to the familiar pacing and groaning. "Time for a break lads," he shouted. Gratefully they stopped as he walked over to unlock Samson. "You're going acting tonight. For the Mayor. In Dagon's temple."

Thoughts swirled in Asaph's head as he watched them work with the chains. Suddenly it came to him. He couldn't help himself. It was full of contradictions, it was ridiculous, it was probably revenge, and it might turn out to be a joke. But above all it may be destiny. One of the Mayor's favorite words.

"Let me wish my friend well," he asked.

The warden hesitated, knowing a little of the bond that had developed. It would do no harm.

"Sure," he replied. "Be quick." He stepped back.

Asaph used his feet to draw Samson closer. Samson understood and shuffled nearer, feeling his friend for the first time. He reached up to hug him, for the human contact, he strangely and fleetingly felt. Asaph whispered in his ear, "your hair grows again Samson. Did you not move the wheel on your own?"

Prisoners hugging each other, thought the warden. What next?

"Let's go!" he called and paced forward catching Samson's arms.

Still in a daze, the blind man pulled away, trying to grasp what was going on. It was all so fast. Firstly a surprise visit to the temple, the very one he had walked in. And now Asaph telling him his strength was returning.

Guards led him up the stairs, and he was herded into the waiting chariot. They dispensed with bonds for this blind weakling. What harm could he do?

He felt the breeze as the vehicle picked up. Involuntarily he drew his hand up. Asaph was right. The locks were growing. But more than that, the temple, the temple, there was something about the temple. What was it?

It didn't take long. Actually, it came to him quite easily, almost impulsively, like his other ventures had. He straightened up in the chariot. After a few minutes he even started to smile. The vehicle sped on, as his mind raced through his life; the first love of Keziah; the killing of the lion and how it amazed him; all his mother's stories, her face floating before him; and finally

Delilah, whom he loved, and who betrayed him. Her soft skin and voice, her hair curling, eyes crinkling, laughing.

The chariot stopped. He was pulled down. The noise of the crowd was evident, even outside the building. A rope was tied around his waist. Obediently, he lifted his arms. Up the correct number of stairs they went, allowing him to feel his way since he was on good behavior. It became flat and he knew he was on the level of the door entry.

"Gatich here will lead you, Samson. He knows his way around the temple doesn't he, Gatich?"

Samson realized they were talking to a young boy. He walked forward, guided by the rope. The Mayor had set this up while they fetched him. It would look good, a lion being led around by a mere boy.

Suddenly the crowd noise exploded into cheers and catcalling. Knowing he had passed through the wide doors and could now be seen, he played the part. Tilting his head upward as though he could see through the hollows that had been his sight, he feigned looking around the temple.

Seeing their humiliated foe, in the middle of their drunken spree, drove the masses into a frenzy. In their box, halfway up the center, the mayors gloated, silently luxuriating at the cacophony of the masses.

"Lead me onto the center stage, Gatich," Samson said to the boy. "They will see me clearer there."

They walked up the zigzag staircase, he recalling the stone banisters. Coming out onto the level area, he stood straighter, turning around in the direction of the noise. Casually, he listened. Those nearest could see his grin, and wondered.

"Take me over to the pillars so I can rest between them, Gatich."

Obediently the rope took up the slack and he followed it. Ten steps later it went loose again. He reached out and found one. The lad guided his other hand onto the second.

He stood between them, resting up against their stone massiveness, peering sightlessly still. He could feel it all, his anger, the orchestrated hatred of the mob, and his body, muscles rippling again. For the second time in his life he prayed. It was part challenge, and part vengeance. It was an admission of failure, and a hope he might have one more page to turn.

"O Lord God, please remember me and please strengthen me just this one time, O God, that I may be avenged of the Philistines for my two eyes." Grasping the pillars he added, "let me die with the Philistines!"

His body bowed as the arms started to push out.

The Mayor of Gaza was watching closely.

And then he saw it. It was amazing how fast.

He knew he was about to die. He was the first to grasp it, his quick brain seeing and understanding everything.

"No!" He leapt up, startling the others who followed his gaze to the front.

As the seconds ticked off the Mayor took in Samson's growing hair, cursing himself for not thinking of this, so simple to remember, but he had missed it. In his rage, he knew he had purposely gathered the entire ruling class of Philistia inside this huge heavy stone building resting on two columns. Two pillars that God himself could not budge. The horror of his nightmare flew up at him, robbing him of every idea and principle he had ever believed in, stripping him in seconds of truth, insight, power, his planned succession, and his stature in history. In those dying seconds he knew he would be remembered only for making Philistia a casualty.

Achish saw it too, his adrenalin rushing up, his brain screaming, feeling the hatred surge for the last time, watching helplessly, knowing he would never achieve his potential, and never rule Philistia. He knew he was the best, the most likeable, just forced by circumstances to pull every ploy he could. And now, as if to nail home some personal reckoning, he himself had arranged Samson to play the final act.

The crowd saw the columns move, and the building started shaking. Some were mesmerized, as if this was a dream. The catcalls of others became shrieks.

His arms pushed on outwards until the physics of imbalance took over. Samson felt the massive pressure change give way to collapse. For a second he could also hear the tumbling huge blocks. Although he could not see it, the entire rear of the building pitched forward once the cantilever was gone. The masonry started falling on the gathered aristocrats and ruling class seated below, while the wailing crowd on the roof was thrown into the opening they had been laughing at Samson through.

In turn the front of the edifice started to fall back, huge blocks raining down on the masses pouring into the temple, already mixed with the falling stone and the bodies of those below. It was as if the very structure had been designed to kill everyone inside when it collapsed.

In the last seconds of his life Achish looked across at his father again. He was shrieking and shaking both fists. But not at Samson.

He was railing against the heavens.

Again a day

Again there was a day when the angels came to present themselves before the Lord God, and the Tempter also came with them to present himself before the Lord God. The Lord God said to the Tempter, "where have you come from?"

Then the Tempter answered the Lord God and said, "from roaming through the earth and going back and forth in it."

Then the Lord God said to the Tempter, "have you considered my servant Samson, a man who humbled himself before me, and gave his life to deliver my people although you reduced him to darkness and sorrow?"

Then the Tempter asked, "how can the Creator of all mankind countenance the loss of innocent life such as this stone building fell upon? Are the foes of your people mere dross to be discarded?"

The Lord God replied, "did you not incite me to allow temptation? Behold, the sons of men may yet learn that power turns upon those who desire it. Moreover, did I myself not bring up Israel from the land of Egypt, and the Philistines from Caphtor? Among those who know me I mention Rahab and Babylon; Philistia too, and Tyre, with Ethiopia. Do I not record as I register the peoples, 'This one was born there?'"

The Tempter answered, "this is not the end of the matter."

"That is true."

"It will discredit even you, the God of all the earth."

The Lord God replied to the Tempter, "do you always tell me things I already know? Am I not aware that the enmity between these two peoples will arise again after many days? Do I not know that the eyes of the whole earth will be upon them in the latter times? But neither you nor the sons of men know the beginning from the end. It is beyond understanding."

Freedom

Something was different. For more than two days now. The guards appeared occasionally, and some food and water were brought. But Asaph knew events were afoot. Samson had not reappeared. He must either be dead, or he had been moved elsewhere.

Over the past days he had pondered why he told Samson about his returning strength. Watching his sightless companion confront himself, Asaph knew he wanted a door out. He could not have escaped. Blind men don't leave town. But it gave him a chance to go down fighting.

On the third day the kindly keeper came in bearing a torch. "You are all free to go," he said, starting to unlock their chains.

They stood there, not comprehending. Many had been there for decades. Several could not even hear the warden's words, so absurd were they. But he went on undoing shackles and slipping bonds free, eventually coming to Asaph. Shrugging, he released him too. "What does it matter anymore," the keeper muttered.

"It matters what?" queried Asaph. "How say you?"

The warden stood back now they were all done. "Up the stairs you go, don't worry, there's nobody waiting to harm you." He added, "there's nobody left,"

As the newer prisoners began moving, the long termers shook off their paralysis and also shuffled to the exit.

"By the heavens man, what passes?" Asaph inquired again.

Gazing oddly at him, the kindly keeper conceded, "no, there is no way you could know is there?" But he just pointed. "Go up and find out. Philistia has been destroyed."

Asaph came out into the sunlight for the first time in months, shielding himself against its blinding rays. Even walking was difficult. He was so accustomed to chains. Focus, he told himself. Hasten over this. You have aged, but your body is as an ox.

Not knowing what to do, he moved away from the prison a distance, sitting on a low wall to think. As he watched, he observed the attitudes of passersby. They all seemed in a daze, wandering without purpose, without orders.

Standing and berating himself for forgetting the obvious, he began walking. It took some time to wend his way through the city. He practiced strolling normally and getting a stride to his pace. By the time he reached the central square he was balanced again.

Before he could see the temple, the stench hit him. A reminiscent smell. As he rounded the corner and the devastation of Dagon's sanctuary became apparent, he remembered. Lehi. The reek of decaying soldiers. Amidst this rubble must lie human dead. Many.

A dozen low ranked soldiers stood nearby. He walked over, aware of his bearded face, soiled garb and fetid body. They watched him, again with glazed expressions, saying nothing. His filthy appearance had no impact.

"I come from afar," he started. "A hazardous and long journey from Egypt. What takes place here?"

They glanced around their group, then to one of their number, perhaps a more conversational one, Asaph felt. "Temple fell down," he said.

Asaph knew he would need to be patient. He stood and thought for a while. "Who rules here?" he finally asked.

Once more their eyes flicked around at each other. His question seemed to spark something. Asaph waited while the words sunk in.

Eventually the first speaker answered, but not to Asaph; to his fellows. "You know, that's the key question isn't it? We haven't been asked that yet. Not by anyone. But it's what this is all about."

Facing Asaph, he declared, "there's nobody in charge here. They're all dead."

"All?"

"Yes, so far as we can figure, all," he explained. "Everyone who was anyone went into that temple a few evenings back. Every army commander, every politician, merchant and ruler, every priest in the land. And the mayors. All five with their wives and families."

Suddenly it dawned on him why the denizens of Gaza were walking around in a daze. They were leaderless. Authority had been destroyed. Philistia was rudderless. It's entire ruling class had been wiped out, in a single blow; all the nerve centers of law, religion, and commerce, were gone. Ships sails would not unfurl, money owed would remain so, laborers would sit, waiting for their lords to arrive, law would not be read. At least not for a while. A long while perhaps.

He went to go, but stopped. Wait. "What caused the temple to fall?"

The young soldier with the voice replied, "nobody knows. It just came down. Quite quickly according to some people standing outside. Screaming was heard, but before anyone could move, it was falling. Everyone inside or on the roof was killed. Every single one. Nobody came out."

His heart racing, Asaph asked his final question. "Why would they venture in there? Was there a feast of importance?"

"There was a feast," came the answer, warming now to speaking with someone displaying an air of authority. "We were celebrating the capture of Samson, the Israelite outlaw," he elaborated, thinking a visitor from Egypt may not have heard of him. "Matter of fact, they had just taken him inside."

Asaph stood impassively at the confirmation. Samson had not struck out in the chariot at the nearest soldier. On his way to the temple, he must have cold bloodedly worked out his most effective strategy.

A glimmer came into the soldier's eyes. Quizzically he cocked his head sideways. "You look familiar. Have you been here before?"

Slowly Asaph returned his gaze, then shifted it back to the remains of the temple. "That may seem so. A brother moved here in years past. I seek to know him. His paths may lead elsewhere now," he concluded.

After wandering amongst the aimless in Gaza for a few hours, he came to his decision. In some respects it was a strange one. And in some ways not. He was now free, freer than he had ever been. Unencumbered by ties to either slave galleys or ruling families or even a country, he was able to go where he pleased.

Walking to the Mayor's palace, he found it unattended. Asaph expected as much because the Mayor would have seen all his servants had seats in the temple that night.

He strode in and found his way to the bedroom of Achish. Although it brought mixed pangs, he was focused enough to find clean clothing. Knowing it would fit him, he moved down to the bathing room. A few cisterns of water waited there. He cleaned off his filth, discarding his prison rags.

His new garb aroused old emotions, but at least felt good to wear. The cooking area was next. Sure enough bowls of grain, and a cupboard containing bread, wine and cheese was found. It was the best meal he had had for months. Filling a bag for his journey, he tidied up the remains.

He decided not to take a weapon. Start again, he thought. Without bloodshed. Yes, he caught himself before the thought disappeared. Start again.

It was then he saw the central dilemma of his life. A core part of him had been steeled not to give himself completely to people. But he had failed at that, trusting and believing in the Mayor and his son. The deeper part of his soul rejoiced in human contact, in observing and connecting with others, whatever their state. It could not be repressed by the safety of aloofness. His failure in trusting others was not defeat. It was the door to a new life.

The breakthrough was uplifting. What is my heart's calling? Life had been kinder than it seemed, and more chapters might yet unfold.

Would that I could do the things I have learnt to love—to listen, and occasionally to guide. Perhaps even find love itself.

And now that I have begun, I desire to learn more. To read. And write. The Mayor was correct. Perhaps I should have been a poet.

The mother of Samson

He walked along the wide avenue leading to the city gates. Their portals still shone with newness. The mark of Samson is everywhere, he noted.

It was not a long journey, and with the directions he had gathered from the many conversations in prison, it almost seemed familiar. Deliberately he walked through both Eltekeh and Timnah. Evidence of reconstruction was still apparent. New boardings had been erected in the marketplace, and patches of plaster were apparent on several buildings.

He slept outside in the fields, dining on his bread and cheese. Looking up at the stars, he thought how insignificant he was. His sleep was sound, and he awoke with no regrets, taking to the road again in the cool mist of the dawn.

As he approached Zorah, the sights started to blend with the descriptions given by the blind Israelite. How strange he had never realized a sightless man can turn much more to speech. For one who spoke little during his lifetime, Samson had learned to accurately describe sights.

As with all villages, he was noticed as he walked through, but he was not questioned. Let the stranger make the first move. The path to the homestead became obvious, winding its way up through the wooded copse.

She is always there, Samson had told him fondly. Whenever I return, she is always there. The real woman of my life, he confessed once. The one I used to hear, and should have stayed listening to. And, as Asaph came around the bend, she was indeed. Not sitting. Not working. But not idle either. His first thought was she had been doing something, and paused as she sensed someone approaching.

Berating himself, he recalled he had not prepared anything to say. The Mayor wouldn't have made such a mistake. He started very directly, even clumsily, he thought later. "I was alongside Samson in prison. Within Gaza."

She looked at him, confused. Then he knew she had not heard about the destruction of the temple. It was up to him to inform her. He paused. "I perceive this is not known to you. Shall we sit?"

Flustered by his directness and her forgetfulness, she fussed over him, apologizing for her lack of manners. Running inside, she poured water and cut some cold meat and bread while he sat outside admiring the view her son had told him about.

They sat eating together for a while. It had given him time to put together a few words. Finally he spoke. "Madam," he began. It was only the second time someone had addressed her like that. "Your son brought destruction upon Philistia several days ago."

Her heart leapt.

He felt it, but knew to continue. "The temple of Dagon was brought down by him on the heads of those who govern Philistia. Onto all the mayors and the generals and the judges and the merchants—indeed upon anyone who wielded power. They were slain by the falling stone."

He hesitated, and she knew why he did. "Your son also passed away. No being could live through that." As if to give credence, he added, "not even one such as Samson."

It was enough. Let her react.

She gazed at him, then away, her face serene. Presently she asked him something.

"I would very much like you to stay here and dine with our family to-night. My sons are at the river, and they are sure to return with some catch. There is bedding in the outer shed. I am sorry it is not noble, but it is dry."

She stood, smoothing her long dress. "Would you stay? I want to hear more. But I need to walk awhile and let my thoughts come together. I need to be alone. Afterwards I want to ask questions. Many questions."

She said it one more time. "Please stay."

He broke into his reluctant smile, nodding as he did. "Of course. I love fish."

She laughed with him, then excused herself and wandered up the path further into the woods.

After the fish, and around the inside fire lighting their faces, Asaph told everything he knew about Samson. The eldest of the sons had been sent to fetch Elihu, but it was late, and he could not arrive until the morning.

The simplicity of their life relaxed him so much, he slept soundly, waking only when the horses arrived. He lay in the outer shed, hearing her greet him. Excited, Elihu could hardly restrain himself. "Is he awake? Is he awake?"

Smiling, he stretched and walked outside. Elihu spun round, his eyes widening. "You!" he exclaimed. "You were with Achish! At the council!"

Asaph remained silent. It was bound to happen sooner or later. She was concerned and confused. At this he stepped forward. "Yes, it is true. Did you not know the outcome?"

Elihu looked back and forth seeking clarification.

"A scapegoat was necessary," Asaph explained. "For the Mayor and his son to prevail. So it was I ended up in prison."

Elihu's mind flew. A scapegoat. My idea to the Mayor.

He could see the indecision, so Asaph spoke again. "Many words are yet to be said, even as I have much to ask. Where do we make a beginning?"

They both stood agog.

What would the Mayor have said, thought Asaph. "In truth, breakfast may assist."

She stood there for a full five seconds, then began to laugh. Loudly, and long. It caught onto the two men. In a short while the boys emerged from the house to find the three of them doubled up with paroxysms of mirth.

"Yes, it is what I suggest," Asaph told them. "No one reigns in Gaza. All who once did are no more. To walk in and gather his body from the ruins is but a small task."

"But what if someone stops us?" burst out one of the boys.

Elihu turned to him gently. "Asaph is telling us there is no-one to stop us."

Samson's mother gazed across at Asaph, already with fondness.

He is so open, so measured, so straight.

Then his brothers and his father's whole family went down to get him. They brought him back and buried him between Zorah and Eshtaol in the tomb of Manoah his father. Judges 16:31

Elihu

Without a ruling class, Philistia was adrift for many years. Israel was left to its own devices. Unfettered by foreign domination, they ruled themselves poorly and chaotically for a while. But at least they were free.

One of them had one last thing he wanted to say, to answer a question he had not as yet.

He walked up the familiar trail, wondering if she would be where she usually was. He was not disappointed. An unusual and sensitive woman. He saw her as she was already looking at him. There was no need for an introduction as much had already been said and done in completeness. Silently she made a warm drink, and they both sat outside looking down where Asaph was talking with the boys. They were in the very fields a young Samson used to chase foxes in.

Elihu finally spoke. "You were right. From the very start. He did begin to deliver us from the Philistines."

Psalm 83: A psalm of Asaph

O God, do not keep silent; be not quiet, O God, be not still.

See how your enemies are astir, how your foes rear their heads.

With cunning they conspire against your people; they plot against those you cherish.

"Come," they say, "let us destroy them as a nation, that the name of Israel be remembered no more."

With one mind they plot together; they form an alliance against you—

the tents of Edom and the Ishmaelites, of Moab and the Hagrites,

Gebal, Ammon and Amalek, Philistia, with the people of Tyre.

Even Assyria has joined them to lend strength to the descendants of Lot. Selah

Do to them as you did to Midian, as you did to Sisera and Jabin at the
river Kishon, who perished at Endor and became like refuse on the
ground.

Make their nobles like Oreb and Zeeb, all their princes like Zebah and
Zalmunna, who said, "Let us take possession of the pasturelands of
God"

Make them like tumbleweed, O my God, like chaff before the wind.

As fire consumes the forest or a flame sets the mountains ablaze,

so pursue them with your tempest and terrify them with your storm.

Cover their faces with shame so that men will seek your name, O LORD.

May they ever be ashamed and dismayed; may they perish in disgrace.

Let them know that you, whose name is the LORD—

that you alone are the Most High over all the earth.